ICE

by

Barbara M. Hodges
&
Randolph Tower

Coastal Dunes Publishing
187 Alyssum Circle
Nipomo, CA 93444

Acknowledgements

Barbara Hodges

Ice's setting is on the central coast of California for the most part, but fictional hotels and night clubs were added as needed.

A big acknowledgement to my co-writer, Randolph Tower, his book would have never happened without him. Thank you so much for the special touches only you could provide. And to Kimberly Graham, I don't know what your correct title is now, Chief, Director, or whatever, so good friend will have to do, thank you so much for answering my questions about Santa Maria Police Department. Any changes from the normal SMPD procedures to suit Ice's storyline are mine and Randolph's alone.

My local writers group, The Word Wizards, again provided much needed and appreciated feedback on Ice. The story is better because of all of you.

And to the two people who mean so much to me in my life. My mom, Jean Stites, who bestowed upon me a love for words and stories as a child, and my husband Jeff, who puts up with everything that comes along with being married to an author. Thanks so much to the both of you.

Randolph Tower

This story could never have been told without the diligence, skill, and persistence of my writing partner Barbara M. Hodges, nor without the patience of my loving wife Beverly who gives a lot every day, living with a writer. I want to thank our writing group The Word Wizards of Santa Maria who are a great collection of writers. We have taken some liberties with Santa Maria's streets but have tried to stay true to the feel of the Central Coast of California.

Books by Barbara M. Hodges

The Blue Flame
The Emerald Dagger
The Silver Angel
Return of the Ancients
Aftermath
A Spiral of Echoes with Maggie Pucillo
Shadow Worlds with Darrell Bain
One Last Sin with Randolph Tower

Anthologies

Scattered Hearts
Felons, Flames and Ambulance Rides

Books by Randolph Tower

The Last Dawn of Reckoning
One Last Sin with Barbara M. Hodges

Anthologies

Scattered Hearts

Chapter One
Sherice Solomon

Beyond the etched glass doors of the hotel's lobby I watched Manhattan's traffic inch by. I tapped my foot against the marbled floor, echoing the Hunger's nip of impatience inside me.

"Soon, soon," I promised.

"Ma'am, your cab's here."

The Hunger leapt at the doorman's words. I stood, smoothed my satin tank top and made my way outside. A wave of blaring horns, car exhaust and sultry air surged over me, all the pleasures of New York City in August. He held open the door to the cab. "Thank you," I said as I pressed a bill into his hand.

"Where you go, Lady," the cabbie asked as he pulled down his meter flag.

"I'm new in town. Take me to the hottest jazz club around."

His gaze found mine in the rearview mirror. "That be Beau's in Queens."

"Then Queens it is."

"Very good Lady, but maybe $75.00. Nobody come back. I can't…"

"I'll cover it. Will $200.00 do?"

"Okay, very good. You got money?"

I opened my clutch purse and held up a $100.00 bill in each hand.

"Hot jazz comin' up."

The cab surged forward. It shot through a yellow light, slowed for man in a cross walk and then rocketed by. "So, you new to Manhattan. Have you…?"

"Stop," I said. "There's another twenty for you if you don't say one more word."

With his eyes again on mine in the mirror, he grinned, showing ragged dentistry through his straggle of beard.

I settled back in the seat and watched the people hurry along, all lost in their petty concerns.

The Hunger nipped again, growing more insistent with each second that passed. I pressed my hand against my stomach. It had been that way since early afternoon. It would have to be a swift hunt tonight so I'd dressed for the occasion; short black skirt, satin tank top, no bra, and my favorite *Christian Louboutin* silver, sling-backs. A small leather clutch with money, fake I.D. and the two room keycards completed my ensemble.

We passed beneath a street light and in the momentary brightness my fingernails glistened. I'd painted them special for this evening, Dead Red.

"What's your name?" I said.

The cabbie shook his head.

I laughed. "You may answer any questions I ask without losing your extra twenty."

"Dawud, David in American."

"Are you Arabic? My husband and I spent some time in Iraq. His name was David."

He nodded. "Yes, I be here three years now."

"I've been back in the states three years now myself. This is my first visit to Manhattan though. I don't know why I waited so long. It's perfect."

"Yes. Yes. The city that never sleeps." He eyes found mine in the mirror. "You like your hotel? My cousin, he…"

"I love my hotel. It has everything I need. I checked it out thoroughly on the Internet."

"If you change…"

"I won't. I never do. Now, no more talking please. I want to enjoy the view."

People scurried along the crowded streets, eyes straight forward, most with cell phones pressed to their ears, all concerned with their neat little worlds, unaware that any one of them could be my next kill. I looked away from the window. "How much further?"

The cabbie glanced at me in the rearview mirror. "We there, almost. You want I wait? You already pay for trip back."

"No, I'm meeting someone."

He frowned."You not know you come here."

I smiled. "Oh, I am meeting someone; they just don't know it yet." He started to speak and I held up my hand. "Not another word, that last comment almost cost you your extra twenty."

We finished the ride in silence.

The cabbie pulled to the curb.

From a squat building's dim window, red neon blinked Beau's. A sign advertising, *Smokin' Hot,* and showing three smiling men, almost blocked the narrow doorway.

Before the cabbie could exit, I climbed out and handed him the two $100.00 bills.

As I turned toward the jazz club's entrance he said. "Can be very bad in there. Be careful."

"Thank you for your concern, David. I'll be fine." I smiled as I walked away.

Inside the doorway of the club, I stopped and let my eyes adjust to the dim lights. A visible haze of cigarette smoke, perfume and sweat hovered over the room. The murmur of voices made my thighs quiver and the Hunger twisted inside my stomach in response.

There were as many women in the club as men. The dress code stretched from blue jeans and tennis shoes to silk shoulders draped with fur. My prey was among them. I felt it.

On an upraised stage in the back, three men stood, smoking and drinking, obviously they were *Smokin' Hot.* Must be break time. There were a few empty tables, but I sashayed toward the bar.

I love bars. Love the way my skirt hikes up when I climb upon the stool; love the feel of the polished wood beneath my hand. This bar had a soft patina, like worn leather.

Behind the bar bottles of liquor lined the wall on both sides of a huge mirror. Mirrors were always a plus for I could scan the room without anyone being the wiser. I examined my reflection. I'd chosen the shoulder-skimming blonde wig tonight, with the ends that dipped downward, like fingers pointing to my cleavage. No jewelry. From my chin to my breasts you saw only skin. My eyes were pale blue, translucent. I'd played the color up with sapphire eye shadow, black eye liner and mounds of mascara. My lips matched my fingernails, Dead Red.

Shifting my gaze to the crowd behind me I spotted interested appraisals by three men and two women. The bartender worked his way toward me. "What can I get you, miss?"

"Gin and tonic."

"I'm buying that for you."

I met the man's eyes in the mirror. He was one of the three I'd spotted. He looked middle-aged, carried a few extra pounds, but he had a full head of silver hair. His eyes were nice, the warm brown of cooking sherry.

"I don't think so," I said. "My mama always warned acceptin' drinks from strangers is how a good girl becomes less than pure."

"Well, your mama sounds like one smart lady. The name's Bradley Williams."

He settled on the bar stool next to me. I swiveled to face him, crossed my legs. It achieved the desired result. I watched his eyes widen. "Mister Williams, are you always so pushy?"

His smile displayed white, even teeth. "It works for me."

The bartender came back with my drink. I took it from him. "Yes, I can see it does."

The man dropped a ten dollar bill onto the bar.

The bartender nodded at me as he turned away.

"I didn't get your name," Bradley Williams said.

I sipped from the glass as I looked at him over the rim. "Rita."

"Well, Rita, am I catching a tinge of Texas in your voice?"

"Damn. Is it still there? I've been workin' hard to be rid of it."

"You an actress?"

I let my lips form a pout. "I will be. Right now I wait tables at a steak house in Manhattan."

The jazz trio started again. They swung into *Taurus* by Aaron Goldberg and I felt a tug at my heart. It had been one of mine and My David's favorites. I downed the last of my gin and tonic.

Bradley Williams motioned toward the bartender. "Rita will have another one, a seven and seven for me."

The number ended and the trio flowed into *Sweet Georgia Brown* and he swore softly.

"What?" I said.

"I'm beginning to hate that song. They play it at least once a damn night."

The bartender set my gin and tonic in front of me and handed the bourbon to Bradley Williams. I took a long drink and placed the glass on the bar.

The man on the stool to the other side of me rose, he brushed against my back and I used the excuse to slip forward and into dear Bradley. My knees forced his legs apart and he was almost straddling me as he caught me by my bare arms. I made a show of wiggling back up on the bar stool. "Sorry."

He reached into his shirt pocket, brought out a pack of cigarettes. His fingers trembled as he took one out, held the pack toward me.

I shook my head. "I don't smoke."

He lit up. Inhaled. Blew smoke into the air. "I shouldn't either. The doctor bitches at me to quit, but shit, it's my life. The big C's not getting me. The devil would kick me out of hell anyway."

"Nothing wrong with having a few vices."

I watched his face and could almost hear him shuffle through scenarios in his head. The entire encounter had happened fast, but still the Hunger twisted, rose up and demanded a speedier end.

I leaned toward him, gave him a good look down my blouse. "It's hot in here. Don't you think?" I settled back, downed the rest of my drink. "It's been nice Mister Williams, but I'm calling it a night."

"What? Hell no. You're not leaving." He placed his hand on my arm. "The night's young."

I stared at his hand until he removed it from my arm. "Look Bradley. I like you. I think we've got a lot in common, so I'm gonna be up front with you. What I want this place doesn't have."

He nodded. "I know exactly what you need."

I held his gaze with mine. "Do you think you're the man to give it to me?" I stood, walked two steps and turned. "I could use a ride home."

"My car's outside," he said.

I nodded and moved toward the door.

*****

We were two blocks from my hotel. "In there," I said and pointed to a parking garage. "My hotel uses valets."

He pulled into a dark corner.

I reached into my clutch purse and brought out a keycard. "My spare. It's room 512. I'll go up first. Give me five minutes and then you follow."

Bradley Williams pulled me against him, crushed my lips with his. "We could do it right here." His hands fondled my breasts.

I faked a moan, placed my hand on the bulge in his pants. "If you want, but I've got something in my room that'll make his night truly remarkable."

He grinned. "I'll be right behind you."

I climbed from his car. "Wait five minutes. I want to get ready for you."

He licked his lips and nodded.

I walked to the hotel door, glanced inside. The front desk was vacant. Just like the past two nights at one A.M.. I hurried to the elevator, stepped inside and pushed the button for the fifth floor.

Inside the room I stripped off my clothes and waited.

11

*****

I watched Bradley Williams' eyes as I rolled the second joint. Ten minutes had passed since I'd slipped the GHB into his seven and seven. He should arrive in fantasy land any time now. We were both naked and in the hotel room's four-poster bed. I preferred them that way when the drug took hold. It made things easier.

His hand rose to cup my breast. Dear Bradley was becoming more insistent. I wondered if screwing would be required. I didn't want to, but sometimes shit happens.

His hand dropped onto the sheet. I put the rolling-paper and marijuana into the baggie and glanced across at him. His head had fallen back on the pillow. I pinched his pale, naked thigh. He didn't even flinch.

From the nightstand I pulled the surgical gloves from beneath the length of coiled rope and slipped them on.

Twenty minutes later dear Bradley lay trussed like a luau pig, his hands and feet tied to each of the four posts.

Smiling down at him, I tore a piece of tape from the roll and slapped it against his mouth.

I moved to my suitcase, pulled out a flower-print nightgown. Rolled inside the gown was a sky-blue, silk sash, and wrapped inside the sash, the knife. My David said it was called a shafra. The blade's name was Arahni. My David brought her home one night from Baghdad's Sunni district. He won her in a poker game; drew into an ace high flush, an incredible bout of luck, he said.

I believe Arahni made it happen, for when he laid the shafra on the table I felt in my heart her call. That night she came to me in a dream, a tall woman of mature years, with ivory skin, pale blue eyes and an aristocratic bearing.

I am Arahni, Queen of the Greek Isles. She told me. I have chosen you. Together we will draw those into our web, and drain them. I thought it an interesting dream—until my first kill.

My David had taken me to Bangkok, Thailand for a long weekend.

Alone in the open air market, I'd seen him and for a heart- stopping moment I thought it was my father.

The man bellowed at a shop-keeper and I could see his joy as the shop-keeper cringed.

It will bring us much pleasure to kill him. Arahni whispered to me.

The Hunger bit and I gasped at the pain in my stomach. The Hunger had been a part of me, as it had with my father, for as long as I could remember. My father assured me it was normal for our bloodline. It made us invincible in our business dealings, and yes, I fed it by being as ruthless and merciless in business as he, yet it was never fully appeased, but with Arahni's words it became clear. This is what the Hunger craved, to kill this man who was so much like my father.

"Yes, but how?"

If you permit, for this first I will guide you.

I walked up to him. "You're American, aren't you?"

He turned, looked me over as if I was another bauble he might buy. I saw my father give others the same look many times.

Inside of me the Hunger writhed in expectation.

"And who might you be?" He took a step toward me and I stepped back, an automatic reflex. I felt my shoulders rise in defense for the expected bombardment of mental abuse. My reaction angered me. It made me feel weak and I felt nothing but contempt for weakness. "Sherice," I answered. "I'm here with my husband."

"Where's your husband now? A pretty little thing like you shouldn't be wandering around by yourself."

"He works a lot."

I watched him scan the crowd, no doubt looking for any who paid us attention.

He grabbed my arm. "Let's you and I go somewhere quiet where we can get better acquainted."

"I don't think so." I tried to pull back.

His fingers dug into my skin. "I insist."

"Let go of me."

"Or what?"

I could see the shop-keeper start to come from his doorway. I shook my head at him, and with a shrug, he stepped back.

The man pulled me into a dark alley.

The Hunger leapt in joy and inside my head Arahni whispered. *You did well. I will guide your hand. Our pleasure will be great.*

It was.

Five minutes later I walked from the dark ally, alone. The shop-keeper spoke to me as I passed.

"You okay Miss?"

"I'm fine."

"And the bully pig?"

I smiled. "He won't be a problem anymore, to anyone."

He glanced into the ally, then at me, and we both turned away.

Two weeks later My David was dead and I returned to America. The following week the Hunger demanded again. I knew what it craved, and Arahni and I first hunted in my homeland.

In the days that followed I researched and found no mention of a Greek queen named Arahni, but I did discover that arahni is Greek for spider. To me it was another sign we were meant to be as one. I've always had an affinity for spiders. I find their webs fascinating. As a child I rescued many from my father's stomping foot, until he discovered me doing so. He then forced me to stomp them myself. I cried the first time and for once my mother tried to interfere. He sent her fleeing with one look and I sent the spider to its death as my father watched and nodded his approval.

Last month one of my kills called me a black widow. Raved about how I lured him into my web. I'd leaned close and softly corrected him. "A black widow kills her mate. You insult me by calling me yours." Then I sliced his throat.

I picked up Arahni and twisted her back and forth. She felt natural in my hand now, an extension of me. I carried her into the lamplight. Light glinted along the seven-inch blade. I admired the gleam of the sapphires in the hilt. Sapphires were my birth stone, another sign our destinies intertwined.

Arahni took time to master, but she had whispered her encouragements to me as I sliced open melon after melon, worked to gain strength in my wrist and arm. At first I used a two-handed stroke, but it proved to be awkward and messy. With time and practice I perfected the one quick slice, just enough pressure to get the job done. I learned so from My David, to exert only the force required to accomplish my task.

I heard a moan and moved toward the bed. Mister Bradley Williams had come back from la-la-land. Arahni held at my side, I looked into his face, waited and watched as he became more aware by the second. His eyes widened. He jerked at his bound arms, kicked his legs and arced his body off the bed. Muffled whimpers came from behind the tape and a shiver went through me. I almost wished I didn't have to tape their mouths. I would like to hear their questions turn to pleas and begging, before they became screams.

I smiled as I lifted Arahni. A hoarse gurgle came from him and he jerked against his restraints.

The Hunger rose like a starved tiger. I leaned forward, kissed his cheek. "Good night, Mister Bradley Williams," I whispered, and swiped Arahni across his throat. Warm blood spurted into my face, down my cheeks and breasts. As the life pumped from him, the Hunger lapped the blood with greed. I laid Arahni next to Bradley's still twitching body and cupped my blood-drenched breasts. My nipples hardened and I shuddered with an intense release.

It is good. It is good. You have become quite adept. Arahni praised.

The Hunger, purred, receded.

Mister Bradley Williams' head listed to the side. He was nothing but a shell now, an empty cup.

I picked up Arahni and walked from the blood-soaked bed and to the bathroom. I turned the sink faucet on, let the water heat, then with light caresses sluiced the blood from the shafra. Holding her before me with two hands, I walked to my suitcase, then wrapped her again in the sky-blue sash of silk. I picked up the sash, kissed Arahni's hilt through the silk, then placed her inside.

Hot water from the shower head poured over me. Still wearing the surgical gloves I lathered with lilac-perfumed soap and watched in fascination as the pale, red stream disappeared down the drain. I turned the shower control to cold and let the water sting my skin.

My shower completed, I stepped out. Naked, except for the towel wrapped around my hair, I walked back toward the bed. On the round table in front of the window I'd laid out a red, white and blue jogging set. I picked up the notebook that lay next to the outfit and double-checked my notes, the dark wig and brown contacts. I knew I'd set out the right ones, but it never hurt to be sure.

I removed the towel from my hair, folded it and added it to my discarded clothing. I hummed as I dressed.

With suitcase in hand, I dialed up the air conditioner. It wasn't a warm night, but no sense taking any chances with escaped odors.

I stopped for a moment and smiled down at the bed. "Sweet dreams, Mister Bradley Williams."

I looked around the room. Other than the doorknobs, what had I touched bare-handed? I played the scene over in my mind.

Nothing.

I moved to the door and looked out. The hall was empty. I wiped both knobs clean with a scarf and switched off the light. In the hallway I hung the, 'Do Not Disturb'," sign on the door. I stripped the surgical gloves from my hands, tucked both them and the scarf into my purse and walked away.

*****

Bright sunlight flooded the hotel bathroom. It seemed the weatherman had gotten it right this time. There wouldn't be anything slowing my early flight to San Francisco. I looked around. Nothing of Sherice Solomon remained, not even a strip of dental floss. I picked up my suitcase, swung my purse over my shoulder and sauntered from the room.

Chapter Two
Morgan Garrett

With a groan I rolled to my side, flung my hand out. It landed in something warm and slimy. What the...? I pushed myself to a sitting position and stared at the yellow mess that coated my hand. My head felt like a kettle drum someone was going to town on and my mouth tasted like socks worn two weeks too long. Not that I've ever had a pair of them in my mouth, or have I? Yeah, I think I have.

I sat up, rubbed at the back of my head with my clean hand. Where the hell was I? Last I remembered I'd been down on Broadway, across from the Santa Maria Inn. Some idiot gave me a twenty, like I was a broken bum. I glanced down at my stained, sweat-soaked golf shirt. Maybe right now I do look like one. Through blurred vision, I could see I lay next to a big dumpster. With its help I pulled myself to my feet. The world seemed to tilt around me and gut-wrenching, dry heaves doubled me over. I spit out green bile.

A broken mirror lay by my right foot. Great, all I need is seven more years of bad luck.

The reflection in the mirror needed a haircut. I stared, frowned at the amount of gray in my sideburns. When had that

happened? My dark eyes looked sunken and bloodshot. Deep wrinkles surrounded them. "CIA Operative, Morgan Garret. Damn-it-too-hell, just look at you."

What am I doing to myself? How long can I keep this up?

A wave of dizziness washed over me. I grabbed the top edge of the dumpster and felt my fingers dug into something soft and cold. What the hell? Leaning closer, I froze at the sight of a red-coated hand. I blinked, followed the arm across to a body slumped in a bloody pile. My heart pounded as I looked down at my own hand. It was covered with blood. Oh God. That wasn't good. Not good at all. I scrubbed it against my pant leg, stumbled back and retched. My hands shook. God, I needed a drink. "Get a grip, Garrett. God knows it's not the first body you've seen." What the hell had happened? I should call 911. As I reached for my cell phone I became aware of a siren's wail.

It abruptly cut off.

I heard car doors open.

"Hands in the air where I can see them," a voice commanded.

Shit, just shit.

*****

"We're recording," the police officer droned in a monotone. "You have been read your rights is that correct, Sir?"

"Yes." They'd taken my clothes as evidence and gave me a blue jump suit to wear. I was more sober now and my guts were on fire. They'd offered me food, but I could only eat some crackers and wash them down with water.

"State your name."

"Morgan Garrett."

"Address, or do you live in a flop house somewhere?"

A smirk I wanted to wipe off of his lips followed the question.

"I have a God damn home."

"All right, state your address."

"I don't think I'm going to say anymore without a lawyer. Am I being charged with something?"

"We arrested you with a dead body, so, yeah buddy, you're being charged, with public intoxication if nothing else."

Some of the fog had left my head, but I still didn't recall any fight or argument. Sure, I woke up in that alley. There were some blank spots, that wasn't the first time for them, but murder? The guy in the dumpster had been opened ear to ear with a knife. I couldn't do that. Well, yeah, I could, but I hadn't. In Iraq I shot some. That was my job, but, then there was that kid....

"Hey, Harry, the bum wants a lawyer. Wha-da-ya think?" The officer spoke in a loud voice, obviously to someone not in the small room.

From the speaker in the corner over my head a scratchy response come back. "From the way he looks I'd say he can't afford one on his own. Get him that new one with the long legs; she ain't won a case yet but we can enjoy looking at her."

I stared at the officer and his grin faded. "Are we through here? I need some sleep."

"Yeah, we're through. Harry, get someone to take this piece of shit to the substation."

*****

I had the cell to myself. The two shades of gray on the walls, light and dark, did nothing to cheer the place, but again it wasn't supposed to be a four star resort.

I stretched out on a bench that had been repainted so many times it looked like it had been slapped on with a scraper. Tired as I was I drifted off to sleep.

Twelve hours later I still hadn't moved from the same damn bench. Well, except for some unsteady trips to the commode in the back of the cell. After the third visit to the toilet, I'd asked a passing officer why I still hadn't had my day in court. He told me there was a shortage of judges today to hear cases.

They offered food again. I accepted and washed down a dry, turkey sandwich with a bottle of water.

The food helped, but my guts still felt on fire. God, I needed a drink. They'd taken my tennis shoes and socks with my clothes. I frowned down at my bare feet. After my last trip

to the toilet bowl, I'd wrapped them with a blanket from one of the cots, but the chill rising from the cement floor still seeped into them. I'd slept for about three of the twelve hours. It surprised me I'd slept at all with this shit going on. The remaining nine had given me a lot of time to think. Could I have killed that guy?

Hell no.

That annoying voice in my head popped up again. How do you know, smart guy? There's that little memory thing.

Where'd I get the knife? I argued back. That guy had been cut and where's the knife now?

"Garrett, got some company for you."

An officer opened the cell door and ushered two other guys inside. One had to be in his eighties, the other about twenty. The young one looked scared shitless. He glanced at me and almost ran to the far side of the cell.

The older gent sauntered in like this was his home away from home. "Good evening, young fella."

"When's my arraignment?" I said to the officer. "And I still haven't heard from my lawyer."

"It'll happen. It'll happen. Now you all play nice in there."

The older guy moved over to stand next to the young kid. "My mom's monkeys both died," he said.

His mom? She'd have to be close to a hundred.

The kid just looked at him for a long moment before saying. "Both of them? That's too bad."

The old guy nodded. "Yeah, but she's going hav'em fixed."

The kid looked like he could care less, but he replied. "You mean mounted?"

"That's what the taxidermist asked. But she said naw, just ta have 'em holding hands would be fine."

When the kid didn't respond to his joke, the old guy cackled a laugh and patted his arm. "You're going to be okay." Then he moved to a far bunk, laid down and curled into a fetal position.

A couple of minutes later I heard him snoring. The young guy just sat there and stared at his feet.

The officer came back. "Garrett, you got your wish. It's arraignment time."

Five minutes later they shoved me into the back of a squad car and slammed the door. Ten minutes after that we were at the Santa Maria courthouse, a white, sprawling generic, county building. My lawyer waited for me in the courtroom. His name was Charles Milkin. I'd picked his name out of the phone book. He took one look at me and I could tell by the expression on his face he wasn't impressed. He walked to one of the wooden benches and sat down.

I followed.

I'd sobered up some more, but it all still seemed a crazy dream. Soon I'd wake up in bed with another roaring hangover, but three fingers of scotch would fix that. Shudders ran through me and my hands shook. God, I needed a drink.

When my turn came we stood. The judge looked straight at me, frowned, then turned to the Junior Assistant District Attorney and snapped. "This man smells. Is he even sober?"

The ADA looked flustered, "We've had him in locked up for over twelve hours, Sir. He must be sober."

"What's he charged with?"

Before the ADA could answer, the back door opened and a clerk hurried in. The ADA frowned. "One minute, Sir."

He quick-stepped it to the clerk. They had a whispered discussion and then the ADA approached the judge again. He took a deep breath before saying. "We're dismissing the charges against Mister Garrett. Paddy O'Grady has given Mister Garrett an alibi?

"Fine. Get him out of my court room. Next Case."

Twenty minutes later I was a free man. I couldn't help but smirk as I passed the two who had booked me. If looks could kill I'd have been dead on the spot.

Chapter Three
Darcie Devonshire

I stared at the name typed into the report. Morgan Garrett. "Bloody hell," I murmured and then glanced around to see if anyone had heard me. I'd grown tired of the ribbing about my English heritage two years ago. I tried to play it down, but my accent was here to stay, even though I'd lived in the states since I was twelve.

I read the name again, not wanting to believe. Morgan Garrett. It could be a different Morgan Garrett. In the whole world there had to be more than one. "Right, Darcie Elizabeth," Grandmother Devonshire's voice scolded inside my head. "And tomorrow the Arabs and Jews will be having a pork barbeque."

Had Morgan come to Santa Maria because of me? My heartbeat went into overdrive at the thought and it twisted my knickers. I didn't care about my ex-partner anymore. We hadn't spoken in the six years I'd been out of the CIA. The last Christmas card I'd sent to some PO Box in Saint Louis, Missouri, had been returned.

I scanned the page.

His interview said he'd come to in an alley and didn't remember how he'd gotten there. So he was still drinking. Well that was a bit of a bother, but it didn't surprise me. I wondered how he'd remained alive for so long.

There was no identification on the dead body found with Morgan; in fact there hadn't been anything on the body. The man had been naked as a newborn.

Next to Morgan's name were two words, suspect and witness. A question mark followed each. I shook my head. It would be neither. If it was one of his bad drunks, where he'd fallen too deep into the hole to climb out, he would have been so messed up he wouldn't remember much of anything.

The paper in my hands shook. Bloody bastard, no! It's not going to happen. I'm not getting back on that roller coaster.

He'd been arrested and booked so there had to be a picture. I flipped to the last page of the report. Morgan scowled at me from the black and white photo. He looked older, more lines in his face, with some gray hair now, and he was too thin. The scowl didn't surprise me. Morgan hated having his picture taken, said he always looked like a dork.

I thought of the only photo I had of the two of us. We were in between assignments and I'd brought him to Santa Maria to meet my folks. We were at Lake Cachuma. A man had seen me with my camera and offered to snap one of the both of us.

In the picture I'm molded against Morgan's side, the lake in the background. With the sun straight overhead, it made the auburn hair I had inherited from an Irish great-uncle look like it was on fire. His little Spitfire, that's what Morgan called me from the first time we had worked out together and I'd flipped him over my shoulder.

The memory of the last day I'd seen him pushed to the front of my brain. I didn't want it, I never did, but I knew I'd have to let it play out, before I could bury it once more.

We were still in Iraq on the Collins assignment. I'd gone back to our apartment. It was past noon and Morgan still lay in bed, snoring. He missed the briefing and I had to lie for him again. This time they did not believe me. I could see it in their eyes.

I walked to the bed and shook his shoulder. "Morgan, wake up."

He muttered, pushed my hand away.

I shook him harder. "Get your bloody arse up.

He opened his bloodshot eyes. "Wha' is it?"

"You missed Grogan's briefing, again. He's not buying the flu story."

"Flu? You used that last week. Shit, of course he's not buying it. Couldn't you be more creative?" He kicked the sheet aside, sat up and then groaned. "Oh God, my head."

I stood, walked to the stove and poured a cup of coffee. "Here." I handed it to him.

He took a sip, grimaced. "What time is it?"

"One forty-five."

I watched him lick his lips. "Do we have any beer in the fridge?"

"Morgan, this can't go on."

He moaned and pressed at the base of his skull. "Keep your damn voice down." He stood and lurched his way to the bathroom.

My vision blurred with tears, I stared at the bathroom door. I couldn't take it anymore. I didn't know what was worse, Morgan coming back to the apartment shit-faced, or me watching him take chance after chance with his life. Fate was going to win sooner or later, and I couldn't be here to watch him die.

As he vomited into the toilet, I walked to the satchel I'd packed last night while I'd waited in vain for him to come in. Inside, on the top, was the letter I'd written, splotched with tears. I placed in on the table, picked up the satchel and walked out.

We had not seen or spoken to each other since. My vision blurred and I blinked my eyes hard. "Damn you, Morgan. Damn you. Why didn't you choose me?"

Had they already taken him to the substation? I flipped to the third page. They had.

"Detective Devonshire."

I looked up. A young female officer stood in front of my desk. "Yes?"

"You asked for the rest of the information on the John Doe." She held a file toward me.

"Thank you," I said taking it from her. "The crime scene report here?"

"Yes. Top page."

I opened the file. There were two close photos of the man's sliced throat. I looked closer. It was there, the two distinct cuts, right to left, and the top one shallower than the bottom. It was Ice's signature. The serial killer was in Santa Maria. Ice had been killing all over the country for the past three years. Nineteen homicides had been attributed to him, twenty counting this one. Last year some officer had given him the name Ice. He had to have a chunk of it for a heart, and ice water in his veins to do what he did to his victims. I'd been following the hullabaloo in the papers and on television. Ice had killed two more in San Francisco only a couple of days ago. I stared across the room. Why would Ice dispose of the body in the dumpster? Why change his M.O.? The other nineteen had been in the hotels where the butchering took place.

"Will you need anything else?"

I jerked my head up. I'd forgotten the girl was there. "That will be all."

She turned to leave.

"Good job, Officer," I added. "Thank you."

"You're welcome, Detective."

I spread the pages and photos out on my desk, frowned. The Commissioner would be screaming it wasn't Ice. The body was in a dumpster, not in a hotel. Different M.O. equaled different guy. I couldn't blame him. Who wants a serial killer setting up shop in your town, but it was him. I knew it. I felt it. It was like when I'd worked a terrorist case. I knew in my bones when I was right, and even Morgan had come to trust my intuition.

I looked at the photos again. There could only be one answer. The bloke had been moved, but from where, and why? The Santa Maria Inn was across the street from the alley, no, that wouldn't be Ice's choice. No rooms with four-poster beds, the Santa Maria Inn was one of the first hotels I'd checked out, in fact I hadn't found any hotels or motels with four-poster beds in the area, at least not yet. I glanced down at my left hand and could see I was twisting my Oxford class ring again. I forced my fingers to stop. As nervous habits go, I could do worse, but it drove my mum crazy. A thought hit me. No hotels with four-poster beds, but.... did I remember correctly? There was only one way to be sure. I reached for the phone.

It was answered on the first ring. "Detective Wes Smith."

Wes and I had been together for two years. I had fought like crazy not to have a partner. I'd had that with Morgan, and look how it had turned out. But the Captain hadn't listened and it was okay, Wes and I were a good match.

"You finished eating?" I said. "Feel like taking a ride?"

"What's up, English?" He was the only one I let get away with the nickname. "This got to do with the John Doe? I saw the pictures. You thinking Ice?"

"It's him."

"Uh huh, well they haven't issued us a new car since you totaled the last one, so we'll take my truck."

That was Wes' way of saying he planned to do the driving.

"Fine," I said.

On my way out I stopped in front of Captain Drake's office. He was on the phone. The Captain hung up. His whole body screamed tension. I started to back from his door, but he glanced my way. "Devonshire." He waved me forward.

"Yes, Sir?"

"That was the Commissioner. He wants that John Doe from the dumpster this morning I.D.'d yesterday."

"Understandable, Sir."

He looked into my face. "What do you know about it?"

"What I read in the file." I hesitated.

"And?"

"Captain?"

"Detective, your profiling of Ice is a well-known secret, even to the Commissioner.

I took a deep breath. "It's his kill."

"Damn. The body was in the dumpster. We all know Ice leaves his victims in the beds where it happens."

"Have you seen the crime scene photos, sir?"

The captain frowned. "What about them?"

"The cut, two trails, one shallow, one deep. It's the same."

"The Commissioner likes this guy Morgan Garrett for the murder."

I shook my head. "He's not the one. Morgan Garrett's left-handed. Ice is right-handed. It says so in all of the coroner reports."

"You know this Garrett's a leftie for sure?" The captain's eyes narrowed.

"I do. Morgan Garrett is ex CIA. We worked together for five years."

"Well, shit. That stirs the pot." His telephone rang. "You wait," he said as he picked it up. "Captain Drake."

I watched his face as he listened. It became even less joyous.

"You positive? Okay." He hung up the phone and faced me. "Garrett's been cleared. A Paddy O'Grady heard about him being picked up and called. Seems like Garrett closed the bar with him, then they had a couple more beers together. Garrett didn't leave O'Grady's until after three. They found the body at nine A.M. and the coroner said the guy had been dead at least eight hours, so Garrett was with O'Grady. Garrett's been released." He turned, looked toward the phone and sighed. "I've got to tell the Commissioner."

I was glad to know Morgan had been released, but I had something else on my mind. "Captain, I want the alley homicide. I deserve it."

A frown drew his eyebrows together. "I'm sure you do, but don't you and Smith have your hands full with the gang-bangers?"

"We can do both."

"I don't know."

"Captain, Wes and I've been lead on a number of cases the past two years. We can apprehend this fellow."

"You so damn sure?"

"I am."

He turned, looked out the window. While I waited I formulated more of my argument. Ice was meant for me to bring down. I knew it. As sure as I knew Christmas would happen on December 25th.

The captain faced me. "Okay, the John Doe is yours." He leaned forward. "And Devonshire, we're not saying it's Ice. Understand? Not until we know for sure."

"Understood. Thank you. Wes and I are on the way to check something out now. Give us about an hour before you call the Commissioner. If I'm right there'll be some answers about our John Doe."

"I guess I can wait that long." The captain tried for nonchalant, but I heard the relief in his voice.

"I'll call it in as soon as we have something." I turned and walked out the office door.

Wes waited in his black 250 Ford pick-up. I climbed in, nodded as I buckled the seat belt.

"Where too?"

"South McClelland Street."

He glanced at me as he pulled out into the traffic. "What are you thinking?"

"Following a memory."

He nodded; then, like always, he changed the subject. Wes said it helped him clear his head, made his brain fresh for when we arrived on the scene. "So, how's Becky doing?"

I smiled. Becky or Rebecca of Sunny Brook Farm, was my year-old tri-colored basset hound. "Working out fine. She's a smart little thing. Spending the day at doggie day care."

"Jackie's asking for a dog."

"How old is your daughter now?"

"Eight, on the twenty-first. Janey and I aren't sure about it. They're piling the hours on her, and you know who always gets stuck with caring for the pets."

Wes turned left on Broadway. "I had my first dog when I was seven," I offered, "a beagle named Snoopy."

He glanced at me. "You've got to be kidding. Even in England they know about Peanuts and Charles Schultz?"

"Don't be a Yank ass. Of course they do."

Wes grinned. "Well don't get your knickers in a wad. You take care of the dog yourself?"

"I did. That was the deal. The first time I let them down Snoopy had to go." I smiled out the window. "That goofy dog lived to be almost eighteen. God, I loved him."

"You brought him to the states with you?"

"I bloody well wouldn't leave him behind." We crossed the railroad tracks. "Left up there onto South McClelland

Street." I watched the houses we passed. It was an older neighborhood, mostly 50's bungalows; all set back from the street with manicured front yards. Two or three Spanish haciendas had sprouted among the bungalows, but if I remembered correctly one house was different than the others.

"Where are we going, Devonshire," Wes asked as he made the turn.

"I'm looking for a bedroom."

"I'm flattered, but I don't think Janey would approve."

"Bite me," I said and knew without looking that he was grinning again. "This kill is Ice's. And he uses bedrooms with four-poster beds, so we need one close to that alley. Slow down. We should be coming up on it." We were, and I'd remembered rightly. "Stop."

"Grapevine Bed and Breakfast?"

I admired the two story blue and white house. It had a white picket fence, a wrap-around veranda, with four slat chairs and a swing. I loved B&B's. I'd seen photos of this one on the Internet. One of the bedrooms, I couldn't remember which, had a four-poster bed. "Come on," I said opening the car door.

I walked to the gate, unlatched it and headed up the cobblestone sidewalk. At the front door I pushed the doorbell and heard the strains of A Bicycle Built for Two. Wes arrived behind me as the door opened. A middle aged woman stood there. She wore jeans, a yellow t-shirt and a flour-coated apron. A splotch of white decorated one plump cheek. The woman smiled and behind black-framed glasses her skin crinkled around blue eyes.

"Yes?"

I held up my badge. "I'm Detective Devonshire. This is Detective Smith. Are you aware of... '

"Is this about that poor man they found in the dumpster?"

"Yes, it is Miss...?

"Mrs. Heather Thatch. My sister and I are the Innkeepers of Grape Vine Bread and Breakfast." She wiped her hands on her apron. "I'm making the bread right now."

"Sorry to interrupt you, Mrs. Thatch," I said.

"Please, call me Heather. And it's okay I just set the bread to rise. Come in." She stepped back.

Wes and I walked in.

We stood in a foyer. A dark wood hat rack sat on my left. The walls were painted a pale green. Someone had stenciled a border of spring flowers and vines across the top. Light oak hardwood covered the floor.

"Let's talk in the kitchen."

She led the way and we followed.

In the kitchen were more pale green walls, but the stencil work this time vines with green leaves and mounds of purple grapes. A bay-windowed alcove held a round table. Blue and white checked gingham valances topped the windows. At the table's back was a window-seat padded with the same blue and white checks, and in the front were three white, wooden chairs. The scent of apples and cinnamon filled the air. I heard my stomach rumble in response and Heather Thatch laughed.

"Just cooled some apple scones. Would you like one?"

"I'd love one," Wes said before I could answer.

We settled at the table with still warm scones and coffee.

"I'm afraid I'm not going to be much help," Heather said. "I wasn't here last night. Scott, that's my sister's husband, was looking out for everything while Viola and I caught a movie."

"Oh," I said. "Maybe we could speak with Scott?"

"He and Viola took off at daybreak this morning, for the rest of the week, a second honeymoon. Scott just sprang it on her. Viola called and woke me up to tell me. She was giddy with happiness."

Wes and I exchanged a look.

"Did they leave a number where you could contact them," Wes asked.

Heather smiled and shook her head. "No they didn't. Scott wouldn't let Viola. He didn't want anything to interfere with their seclusion. He even made her leave her cell phone. It's all so romantic."

Wes took out his notebook from his shirt pocket. "What's Scott's last name?"

"Stevens. Oh, Detective, you're not going to interrupt their second honeymoon are you? Viola's been wanting one for years."

"I'm sorry Mrs. Thatch, but we really need to talk to your brother-in-law about last night," I said.

"Oh, Scott's not going to like that. Wait a minute. Consuela was here. She and her mother live in the cottage out back. Maybe they saw something. She's upstairs now. You can talk to her. " She stood, walked to the living room door. "Consuela, please come down to the kitchen for a moment."

"Si, Senora." I heard called back.

A small Latino woman came into the kitchen. She froze in place at seeing us. I watched her dark eyes quickly glance around the room. She looked ready to bolt. I stepped forward and held out my hand. "Consuela, I'm Detective Devonshire, this is Detective Smith." I watched the blood leave her face and she swayed.

"Consuela, what's wrong?" Mrs. Thatch's distressed voice demanded.

I grabbed the young woman by her shoulders. "Let me help you to a seat." I guided her to the kitchen table. At the same time Wes moved to block the only exit.

Consuela looked one last time at the doorway, before she collapsed into a chair. "I didn't want to do it, Senora," she wailed. "Senor Scott made me."

"Made you do what? I don't understand," Mrs. Thatch said.

"He knew I had no papers, but he hired me anyway." Consuela reached to grab Mrs. Thatch's hand. "I can't be sent back. My mami has cancer. I'm the only one who can care for her."

Mrs. Thatch wordlessly shook her head as she handed the other woman a box of tissue.

"I don't care about your papers," I said. "Tell me what happened last night."

"If I tell, you won't make me leave? I can stay?"

I glanced at Heather Thatch. "That's not my call. But we won't be reporting anything about your immigration status. Will we Wes?"

He didn't reply and I gave him a beseeching look. Maybe it was wrong, hell it was, but it was Ice I wanted and if this played out the way I thought it would her being an illegal wouldn't be half of her problem. "Wes?"

He finally nodded, looked away from her face as he said, "I'll give you two weeks to get things sorted out."

"I will. I will. I promise," Consuela said and then dabbed at her eyes with a tissue.

"Okay, tell me about last night," I said.

"I was in the kitchen making mami some tea. She couldn't sleep last night." She glanced at Mrs. Thatch. "You said it was okay to sometimes use the teas."

"Yes. Yes. I know. Go on, Consuela."

"I had finished. When Senor Scott screamed." Consuela crossed herself. "He sounded mucho loco. I went to the bottom of the stairs and looked up. He came running from the hallway, saw me. I asked him if he was alright and he said, 'Get your ass up here.' I did." Consuela swallowed. I saw her look down at her hands. "Senor Holt lay on the bed. Much blood covered the pillow, had soaked the quilt. Senor Holt...he was dead."

Mrs. Thatch gasped.

"Why didn't you call 911?" Wes said.

Consuela sniffed. "I wanted to. Senor Scott would not let me. He did not want bad things to be talked of, Senor Holt could not be helped, he said."

"Oh dear," Mrs. Thatch said. "Things have been a little lean, but it isn't that bad."

I shook my head.

"What's Holt's first name?" Wes said.

"Jake," Mrs. Thatch answered. "From Lincoln Nebraska. He was here on business. He's been our guest before. I have his information on the computer. Would you like me to retrieve it?"

"In a minute." Wes looked at Consuela. "Then what did you do?"

"Senor Scott sent me to get cleaning supplies, much bleach."

I heard Wes softly swear.

Consuela looked fearfully at him.

"Go on," I said.

"When I come back. Senor Holt was gone. Senor Scott told me to wash the sheets with much bleach and then put them out with the trash.

It was my turn to swear. "And did you?"

"They are in the dryer now. They were too nice to..."

I interrupted her. "I'd like to see the room."

She glanced at Mrs. Thatch for permission.

"Of course. Of course," Heather Thatch said.

She led us from the kitchen and up a flight of stairs. A hall stretched to the left. She stopped at the second door on the right. "The Cabernet Room."

Wes opened the door. It was a beautiful room, all burgundy and gold, with a large four-poster bed of dark wood that gleamed from fresh polish. The room smelled like vanilla, with bleach undertones. Bloody hell, but there was a chance forensics could find something. They hadn't before, but....

I walked to the bed, stared down at its burgundy comforter. With a sigh, I gloved up then pulled the coverings aside. Fresh sheets of a pale gold color lay beneath it. "New pillows?"

"Si. The old ones were gone. Senor Scott must have taken them."

"Consuela, where's Grandma's hooked rug," Heather Thatch demanded.

The Latino women looked down at the floor. "I did not notice it was gone."

"Scuff marks here on the bed posts. Must have been from the rope," Wes said. He flipped open his cell phone. "I'm calling it in."

I nodded as I stripped the sheets from the bed. There should have been blood stains, but the mattress was as clean and pure as my Gram's heart.

I looked at Mrs. Thatch who was scowling at Consuela. "The memory foam and pillow-top?" she said.

"I don't know. Senor Scott must have taken them."

And most likely dumped them somewhere between here and wherever they were going to have their second honeymoon.

"You will need to come to the station with us," I said to Consuela.

"Yes. Oh, yes. I can do that."

I turned to Mrs. Thatch. "Anything else missing?"

She looked around the room. "A bottle of wine. Two glasses and." She moved to the dresser. "The guest journal. It's always right here."

I nodded, walked to the free-standing wardrobe. A suit hung inside, some shirts and a pair of dress shoes. I looked around the room. Behind the door I could see a pair of tan slacks, a yellow golf shirt and a plaid pair of boxer underwear. Stevens must have kicked them there when he was removing the body. I turned to Wes. "I'm calling the Captain." I knew who had killed our no longer John Doe, and how he'd ended up in the dumpster. Ice. I did wonder why a B&B, and not a hotel room. I added the mental question to the list of others I planned to ask Scott Stevens, right after I cuffed the bastard.

Chapter Four
Sherice Solomon

I remained in my seat as people stood, opened overhead bins and gathered carry-on bags and computers. The trip from New York had been tedious. We'd spent an extra fifteen minutes circling San Francisco because of a back up of flights and thick fog. I'd amused myself by discussing with Arahni how different people on the flight would die. The guy in seat twelve would probably scream like a baby we decided. The woman next to me who smelled like violets would care less, maybe even welcome death, judging by her on-running monologue since we'd cruised over the Rockies. She stood now, entered the queue with the rest of the cattle.

I sat, waited. Debbie, the tall brunette flight attendant stopped beside my seat. We'd become friendly during the trip. I'd asked her if Madeline's was still open in San Francisco. She'd laughed, said she couldn't tell me since she was into C&W.

"Enjoy your vacation, Miss Solomon." She smiled down at me. "If you change your mind and want to visit a good honky-tonk, try Willy's on Seventh Avenue."

"I may do that, Debbie. Thank you."

Except for a few stragglers the plane was empty now. I stood, picked up my tote bag.

In the terminal I made my way toward baggage claim.

Shoulder-to-shoulder with the crowd I waited. With each bag that dropped onto the carousel my heartbeat quickened. I felt sweat form on my palms. You checked in early. It will be one of the last to come off. I had nightmares about losing my luggage, but what was a girl to do? I couldn't very well carry Arahni with me through security. I saw my first black suitcase with the blue piece of yarn I'd tied around its handle come into view and I pushed myself to the front of the crowd.

*****

The Hertz rental agent looked up and smiled as I stopped in front of the counter. "Good afternoon. How may I help you?"

I handed her my membership card.

"Oh, yes, Miss Solomon. It took some scrambling but we were able to get your requested automobile."

I don't know why they always had to give me the spiel. I rent the same type of car, a Ford Mustang convertible, each time. The only thing that changes is the color and the year. I nodded without smiling.

"Your car is waiting for you."

I did manage to say, "Thank you."

The Mustang this time was dark blue with wide, white racing stripes and black leather interior. I stowed my bag, slid into the seat and turned the key. The engine purred to life. I backed from the parking spot and headed toward the freeway.

At a Chevron station, I parked in back by the bathrooms, grabbed my bag and went inside. Ten minutes into my identity change someone pounded on the door and a shrill female voice hollered. "You gonna be in there all day?"

"Stomach issues," I answered. "Use the men's."

"Well, God damn-it-to hell."

I heard the door to the men's room open and then slam.

Ten minutes later I emerged with shoulder-length white hair styled in a page boy, green eyes and wearing a two-piece purple, polyester pantsuit. Mrs. Amanda Rail was ready to check in. I'd already made the reservations at Golden Gate Suites. An internet search while in New York had shown me their Garden Suite, featuring a four-poster bed with Cloud Soft mattress. Their Bridge Suite had the same. I'd reserved both suites, one for Amanda Rail and the other for Benny Scott, a Platt and Platt senior VP.

Inside the Mustang, I opened a folder and removed the itineraries I'd printed for both. I had to make sure I used the right credit card for each reservation. Twyla Clark, Mr. Scott's assistant, had made the reservation and would be picking up their room keycards. The hotel would just need to see the credit card, to have a copy on file for any charges during their stay.

It still surprised me how easy it had been to make contact with the young man who supplied me my fake ID's, credit cards, credentials and anything else I desired. Isaiah had been an associate of My David's. It wasn't until My David died I discovered just what Isaiah had supplied for him. I'd emailed Isaiah, told him who I was, and that was all it had taken. A computer whiz, he provided anything I asked and with no questions

*****

I paced the room in my hotel waiting for the dark to come. After checking in as Amanda Rail, I'd changed my appearance, checked in again and picked up the room key as Tanya Clark. I'd planned my check-in to coincide with their busiest time. They had been so harassed I could have told them my name was Marilyn Monroe and they still would have smiled and said thank you as they pushed the key toward me.

I walked to the table and picked up the other room key. The Bridge Suite was two floors below mine. I'd already visited. Inside there was the twin to the four-poster bed in my room. I'd trembled as I'd walked to it and ran my fingers across the dark wood.

I'd asked the front desk clerk about Madeline's and found out the jazz club had gone bankrupt. I'd had my heart set on Madeline's and on hearing that I'd hoped I could wait until tomorrow night to hunt, but a sharp jolt from the Hunger told me differently.

At my request room service had sent up a bottle of champagne before my arrival. I poured a glass and sipped as I went over my options. The yellow pages had shown me there were other jazz clubs in San Francisco, but none seemed right.

I thought of the flight attendant's words. I flipped to the W's. There it was. Willy's I picked up the phone. "This is Mrs. Rail in room 1210. I'd like a cab at 9:30 please. Oh, and a 6:30 wake-up call."

*****

The Ford Mustang's top was down and the sun warmed my head, while the cool notes of a jazz saxophonist blasted from the stereo and heated my heart. Laughing into the wind, I shifted down to take a hairpin turn. To my right the cliff dropped off into the bright blue of the Pacific Ocean. I breathed in the briny smell of kelp and sea. Taking California Highway 1 to reach Santa Maria took longer, but the gorgeous expanse of white-capped water made it worthwhile. My plan was to lunch in Carmel and maybe stop and see the elephant seals just south of San Simeon.

My David and I had loved the central coast; Cayucos and Cambria were our favorite towns. I planned to overnight in Santa Maria though, since I didn't know if my heart could handle Cambria or Cayucos yet. I had been back in the good old U.S. of A for three years, in California twice, but I'd been avoiding those two beloved cities. I feared they wouldn't have the same magic without My David.

I would pull into the parking lot of the first nice Santa Maria motel I saw that had a sign flashing vacancy. Any room would do since I didn't plan on leaving it for the rest of the night.

*****

I looked around the dim bar, fingers caressing the tote bag with Arahni and the coil of rope inside, as I sipped from a glass of Chardonnay. My room at the motel and had grown smaller by the minute. Going out for one glass of wine couldn't hurt. I'd dressed as Miss Mousy, drab enough to blend into the fake leather booth I sat in, well except for my shoes. I couldn't resist slipping in to my metallic, Manolo Blahnik pumps.

There were twelve bodies in the bar, all men, and most of them wore plaid shirts and jeans. One did stand out in his tan cords and yellow golf shirt. Tourist. Our eyes met and I looked away. No. Don't come over here. Not tonight. What about Miss Mousy could even attract a man?

In memory of last night in San Francisco I'd put money in the jukebox and punched in some rock-a-billy tunes. Travis Tritt spelled out Trouble as I glanced at the man again. I'd turned sideways in the booth, crossed my legs. I saw that he watched my foot swinging in time with the music. I stopped, uncrossed my legs. Our eyes met again and he smiled before I could look away.

My fingers moved over the tote bag and I shifted in the booth. I should get out of here. I finished the last of my wine and placed the glass on the table.

"May I buy you another?"

I looked up. Of course he stood there at the edge of the booth. I pulled my tote bag closer toward me. It could still be okay, the Hunger did not rouse at his mild words."Why not?"

One drink led to two. The man was a witty, flatterer, but I was still shocked when the waitress came to our table and said, "Last call." Where had the time gone?

He leaned toward me. "I'll walk you to your car."

Outside the bar he whispered into my ear." Your place or mine?"

"Excuse me."

"I'm thinking we should continue our little party."

The Hunger stirred.

Say no. Get in the Mustang and go back to your hotel room. "Yours."

He stopped in front of a dark blue Buick. "Okay. It's not far. Go get your car.

I'd parked my Mustang next to his. I walked to it. "This is mine."

We exchanged a long look.

"Karma?" he said.

"I don't believe in such nonsense."

I followed him into a housing development and for a moment I wondered if I had been wrong, that he wasn't a tourist, but he'd never mentioned living in Santa Maria. Then he stopped in front of a blue and white two story house. The sign above the front porch read, Grapevine Bed and Breakfast. I pulled to the curb and sat with the Mustang idling. Maybe I should rethink this? What if someone saw us?

No. He is a gift. We want him.

"We are not hunting. We did last night."

Then why did you bring me and the rope?

"I couldn't leave you in the room. What if...?"

In the middle of the night? Arahni's voice held amusement.

"There may not be the right bed. We can't kill without the right bed. Everything must be perfect."

I heard a tap on the driver's side window. He stood there. I pushed the button and lowered the glass. "A B&B?" I said.

"I've stayed here before. The breakfast is to die for."

I frowned.

He grinned. "I get it. You live here. Discretion and all that. Don't worry. They're always in bed by nine." He glanced at his watch. "And that was hours ago. I have a key."

I still hesitated.

"You changing your mind Melissa?"

"What is your name?" I said.

"Jake Holt. I wondered if you'd ever get around to asking."

I reached for the car door handle. "I haven't changed my mind." I looked at the tote bag. I could leave it in the car. No, I couldn't take a chance on someone stealing it. I picked the tote up and draped it over my shoulder.

Jake led the way to the front door. I followed and stood to the side as he fit the key into the lock.

A Tiffany-style lamp cast a dim light across the hallway. To the right stairs led upward.

"Second door on the left."

I nodded and began to climb, careful not to touch the banister with my bare hand.

Arahni laughed. *We do not hunt. Yet the precautions you take are the same.*

Halfway up the stairs, I heard a door open below me and then footsteps.

"Mister Holt," a man's voice said. "I thought your wife couldn't make it?"

The words were innocent, but if I turned I knew there would be a smirk on the speaker's face.

"A business associate. We ran into each other at a bar."

I kept my back to them.

"Another one? Funny how that always happens. Want me to fire up the hot tub for you and Miss…?"

"Melissa," I said.

"Tempting," Jake Holt said. "But we'll pass on it."

Was the man going to be in the house all night? He seemed the type to listen at the door.

"The Middle's didn't show," the man said. "I'm heading home. You've got the place to yourself, except for the maid, but she's way out back in the cottage, so you can make all the noise you want." He laughed.

I felt my face heat and almost turned and invited him to join us, but then we weren't hunting tonight, there wouldn't be a kill.

"I'll sit the hot tub on a timer, just in case," the man added.

"Might take you up on using it. You have a goodnight now," Jake Holt said.

I stood where I was, until I heard the front door open and then close.

"Don't mind him. He's an ass."

I felt a hand touch the middle of my back, give a little push and I continued up the stairs.

At the door to the room I stopped.

He unlocked it, turned to smile at me. "The Cabernet room. I hope you like red." Jake opened the door.

The room's walls were burgundy, not red, but it was the four-poster bed in the center that captured my gaze. Inside me I felt the Hunger surge to life. I stood, frozen at the entrance. The tote bag slid from my shoulder, nudged my side.

He will bring us much pleasure.

"Pour us a glass of wine," Jake ordered.

I walked into the room. There was a floral-print journal laying on the nightstand. "I bet you won't be writing about this night."

"Yeah, maybe we'll write in it together. It'll make for some great reading."

Not in this lifetime, I thought.

He suddenly frowned, reached into his pocket, pulled out a cell phone and flipped it open. "Damn, woman. I've got to take this."

He turned his back to me. I heard him say. "Hello, Samantha." He listened for a few minutes. "No, you were right to call. What did Rory's pediatrician say?"

I wandered around the room. Stopped in front of the bed, trailed a fingernail along the glossy, dark wood of one post. The Hunger bit savagely. I moved to the side table and poured two glasses of wine. Reached into the tote bag and pulled out the small vial. Jake's voice went on behind me as I added the drops.

"Good bye," he said.

I turned to face him, holding his wine in my right hand. He came to me and I held out the glass.

He took a long drink. "My ex-wife. Our son has the flu. Her new husband's out of town so of course she calls me."He finished the wine, sat the glass aside. "Would you like to freshen up?"

The Hunger purred, while in my head Arahni laughed in exulted expectation. "No," I said. I placed my glass next to his and began to unbutton my blouse.

*****

I woke to sunlight streaming through a crack in the drapes of my motel room. I slowly stretched, sighed, if I was a cat I'd be purring.

Arahni laughed softly.

I played over the events of last night in my head. It was all a little impulsive for me, but it had been a rare, unplanned, treat.

I decided I would visit Cambria. It was time. I couldn't let a ghost keep me from enjoying the eclectic town. I felt an urge to nest, settle down for a bit. The traveling was becoming a chore instead of a treat and there were plenty of towns within 100 miles where I could hunt, from Paso Robles to Santa Barbara. A cabin in the woods, nestled beneath pine trees, sounded sublime.

I glanced at my watch. Eleven o'clock. Too late for breakfast here. I would check out and get on the road.

*****

"Yes. It's perfect," I said to the young man hovering at my side. In Cambria I'd stopped at the first real estate office I'd seen and inquired about a vacation rental, preferably a cabin in the woods. The man I spoke with said they had just the thing. They all said that, but this time he was right. The couple who owned the cabin lived in Arizona. They normally used it during the summer months and rented it out for the rest of the year, but the man had developed heart issues and the cabin was available.

The red painted, log cabin was in the middle of thirty acres of oak and pine trees. It was two miles to the nearest neighbor, but only five miles out of Cambria. The light and airy interior had one bedroom, a modern bathroom and a kitchen with everything I'd need to whip up a gourmet meal when the notion struck me.

I loved the rock fireplace in the living room. A pile of wood lie next to it, as well as kindling and newspaper. The realtor showed me more stacked wood in a lean-to off the back door. He seemed particularly proud as he pointed out the small satellite dish. It was high definition and acquired all of the premium channels. I listened and nodded. I didn't watch much television.

Back in his office I signed all of the required paperwork to rent the cabin for the remaining five months of the year. By New Years day I'd decide if I would stay any longer. He told me about an art exhibit and wine tasting event happening that weekend in Cambria. I smiled and thanked him as I left. I wondered if he would bother to check the information I'd supplied. It was all lies, but would come back as complete truth, thanks to Isaiah.

I strolled along the city streets. There seemed to be a flyer advertising an upcoming Christmas Boutique in each window. Christmas shopping in August? What next? Halloween in July? I didn't care for the reminder of the upcoming holiday season. When My David was alive we'd observed all of the Jewish ones, but I was Jewish by marriage only and hadn't kept

up since his death. My David and I were both only children. His well-to-do-parents were his only living relatives and they had been killed in a boating accident the third month of our marriage. My parents were still alive somewhere, but I hadn't seen them since I'd married David. My father had threatened to wipe me from his memory and life, if I married a Jew-boy, so of course that meant Mom had to do so also. I guess it had happened since I'd heard nothing from them for five years. In truth I'd never bothered to let them know that David had died.

I settled into the Mustang's seat and started the engine.

Back at the cottage it didn't take me too long to unpack. I frowned at my meager clothing in the closet. My shoes and hairpieces filled up most of it. I'd learned to live out of three suitcases, but I was settling for awhile. I needed some new outfits to go with my new life. I'd heard San Luis Obispo had some cute boutiques. I'd donate everything old, except my shoes and hairpieces of course, to a local women's shelter. There had to be one close by.

I unwrapped the blue scarf from around Arahni and lifted her into the light. "What do you think?"

It is nice, but we will not remain here long.

"Awhile. I'm tired of traveling."

We will still hunt? Our pleasure not forsaken?

"Of course."

I do not…

"The choice is made. We stay."

Arahni's voice went still.

I carried the shafra to the nightstand by the bed. In the top drawer was a bible. With a smile I slid the bible to the side and placed the blade beside it. Last night I had used up my last length of rope. I'd have to purchase more, but not locally. Perhaps in Paso Robles.

My stomach rumbled, reminding me I hadn't eaten. I glanced at the small alarm clock. Three in the afternoon. On my return trip to the cabin I'd stopped at a market and bought needed supplies. Now the thought of a smoked turkey and Swiss cheese sandwich made my mouth water.

Taking a bite of the sandwich I read the front page of the Santa Maria Times newspaper the realtor had given me. The bold headlines screamed of a body found in a dumpster. I didn't pay much attention until six words jumped out at me, across from the Santa Maria Inn. I remembered us driving by the hotel, but it couldn't be. I read the story. It was a man, unidentified. Halfway into the account they mentioned the two cuts on his neck. It was Jake Holt. How had he ended up in a dumpster three blocks from the bed and breakfast? I felt insulted, violated. How dare someone move him. Jake Holt was mine. My hunts were a scenario of purity and it had been bastardized, defiled.

My breath came fast and I felt a wave of dizziness. The bite of sandwich in my throat seemed to swell. I coughed, gagged, and spit it onto the table. With shaking hands I picked up the newspaper page and shredded it.

I pushed the sandwich away, the joy in it gone, shoved the chair back and stood.

On trembling legs I walked to the living room and straight to the red, lacquered, ornate chest I'd placed on an end-table next to the sofa. I'd bought the chest at an estate sale in Kansas City, Missouri. From my purse I took out its tiny key. My hands shook so that it took three times to fit the key into the lock of the chest. I opened it, sighed as I stared at stationary, pens, and even one ash tray. Each had the name of a hotel printed or embossed upon it; one souvenir from every room where I had completed my hunt.

Choosing a pale-blue envelope, I read the name, closed my eyes and let the memories flow over me. It was the couple from San Francisco. I'd let them pick me up at the cowboy bar. Agreed to a threesome, but demanded it be at my hotel. I'd ordered champagne, watched them make love, them brought them full glasses.

The man had come to first. I had tied them with him lying on top of her, his head at her feet, her face buried in his crotch. My body grew tense as I again smelled his cologne, tasted his fear, felt my fingers tighten around Arahni as I reached between them.

Pleasure flooded my body and I shuddered.

With a smile I opened my eyes.

My gaze moved to the tote bag. I stood, walked to it and removed the floral journal. The brownish stains upon it made my stomach quiver. Jake Holt's blood. I carried the journal to the chest and carefully placed it inside, closed the lid, and locked it

I stood, paced the length of the room. The Hunger slept, sated, but I could not sit still. I walked to the window, looked out. The setting sun was a fiery backdrop for the gnarled oaks and sentry-straight pines. I opened the door. A warm breeze bathed my face. A drive, that's what I needed.

In the Mustang, the top down and the wind kissing my face, I made my way to Highway 1. I passed a college campus, a prison and minutes later I was in San Luis Obispo, SLO town, I remembered My David calling it. I found a parking spot, climbed from the car. Meandering along the streets, I turned left and then right. I didn't care where I went, I simply walked.

In front of a tattoo parlor, Republic of Ink, I stopped. The photos of the artist's work captivated me. I'd never thought of getting inked, but the more I considered, the more it appealed to me. I knew just what I desired, and where on my body it would be.

I walked inside. The four walls were covered with framed designs. A long counter was the only furnishing. A young man stood behind it. He had long blonde hair, wore a tank top and jeans. I moved toward him. When closer I could see tattoos of dragons, angels, and fairies, covered his arms.

"May I help you," he asked.

"I'd like a tattoo."

"See anything you like?" He pointed to a book on the counter. "My best custom work is in there, or did you have something in mind?"

"I know what I want, a black widow spider."

"A widow huh? Do you know what a black widow signifies?"

"Tell me."

"A widow tattoo symbolizes independence. They've also been called a symbol of dark, twisted love."

I smiled. "Interesting, but I'm getting one to celebrate my one year anniversary of being a widow. My late husband and I always talked about getting matching tattoos."

"My guy and I do." He pulled up his shirt and showed me a spiral that started at the top of his groin circled inward and ended at his navel.

"Nice."

"Where do you want yours?"

"Do you want me to show you right here?"

"Just tell me. You can do the showing in the back room."

"I want it on my left ass cheek."

"Want to keep it private, huh?"

When I didn't answer he flipped through his design book. What about this?"

The photo of a young woman showed a black window on her shoulder blade, but the spider looked as I'd imagined it, petite, somehow both feminine and deadly. "It's perfect."

"Daniella," he called toward the back of the shop. "Take over the front I've got a pretty woman to ink."

A tall woman, with skin the color of milk-laced coffee, came from a doorway. She wore a bikini top and low slung jeans, every inch of skin from her chin downward showed tattoos. "Got it, Shane."

"This way." Shane led me toward the same door.

*****

I dreamed. I knew I did. My David and I lay side by side. On the nightstand an envelope and letter rested. He'd read the words to me at least three times. His construction company had bid on and won a large contract. "Should we go? It's such a long way and so different. You'll come with me of course, won't you? I'll say you are in charge of pay roll."

I felt a wave of anger. I hated his indecisive blathering. What had happened to the strong man I'd married. The man who told me I was to be his wife, the man I'd stood up to my father to be with? It wasn't up to me to make the decision! I turned toward him.

David stared beyond me. "Of course we're going. And you're going with me. I'll take care of everything tomorrow. We'll leave in two weeks. Make sure you're ready."

My David was back. I leaned forward, kissed him. He placed his hands on my shoulders, pushed me onto my back and, pain shot through me.

I jerked awake, but the pain remained. It radiated from my ass. Then I remembered the tattoo. I rolled onto my stomach, thought about the dream.

It had been some time since I'd dreamed about My David and I traveling to Iraq. I didn't like to think about his choice. If we hadn't gone, would things be different? Of course they would. David would still be alive.

I kicked the coverings aside and stood. A tube of antibiotic with pain killer lay on the night stand. I opened it, rubbed some onto my ass cheek and then picked up a hand mirror and admired my tattoo, still a touch red and puffy, but seeing it made a tingle start in my toes. The tattoo guy had said it would only be bad for a day. I moved to the closet, pulled out a loose shift and slipped it on.

Over coffee and toast, I looked at yesterday's paper. On a whim I flipped to the classifieds. I sometimes wondered what I'd be doing if I hadn't married My David. He'd insisted I didn't work outside the home. In fact I hadn't worked inside our home either, that's what the help was for. I'd kept busy with charities, tennis lessons at the club, beauty treatments, and shopping.

I scanned the help wanted ads. Clinical psychologist. Humm, and the name of the place, Pacific Winds, sounded peaceful. I'd worked as an advertising executive for a month and once on whim, even as an exotic dancer. I smiled. Maybe I should have gotten a tattoo of a chameleon instead? No, the black widow was perfect.

Doctor Sherice Solomon. I liked the sound of it. I wonder what credentials I'd need to land me the position. A degree of some sort for sure. A search on the internet would tell me, and Isaiah could easily insert them into a background check. Clinical psychologist. Why not?

*****

"Doctor Solomon, Mister Granger will see you now," the young receptionist called.

I turned from the window with its sweeping view of the ocean. "Thank you."

"Through the door on your right," she added.

In the office large windows framed a view of the sea. On the far wall I could see what looked like original, abstract oil paintings, quite attractive against the cream colored wall. Mister Granger wasn't so eye attracting. Brown hair combed sideways to cover a bald spot, florid skin, and a weak chin. I walked to him, held out my hand. "Mister Granger. I'm Doctor Sherice Solomon. Doctor Malachi has told me much about you and the fine work you are doing here at Pacific Winds." Doctor Malachi didn't exist as far as I had been able to discover, but he didn't need to know that.

Mister Granger grasped my hand. "That is kind of him."

I gave his a shake, then released it and stepped back. "My late father-in-law was an alcoholic. It's devastating to the family as well as the addict." I smiled at him. "I've researched your treatment protocol. It's up to date and achieving an eighty-two percent success rate, good, but I can raise it to one-hundred percent."

"You can?"

"Alcoholism is a mental disease as well as physical." I smiled again. "I'm sure you all ready know that."

His chest seemed to swell. "Pacific Winds hires only the best." He glanced down at my resume.

Thanks to Isaiah, on paper I was the best. "That's why I chose your facility."

"Doctor Solomon, your background in clinical psychology is impressive. Why did you leave Johns Hopkins?"

I moved to the chair in front of his desk and settled into it, making sure to let my skirt rise to an acceptable level. Not too high to be slutty, but high enough to attract his attention.

"My late husband and I loved Cambria." I glanced down at my hands. "And I needed a change of scenery, you know."

"Sorry for you loss, but it looks to be a gain for Pacific Winds."

I looked up, feigned surprise. "You're hiring me? Don't you want time to check out my references?"

"Oh I will. I will. But what I see here, and in front of me tells me what I need to know." He made a show of straightening he papers in front of him. "Can you start today? It's unusual, but I'm a man who goes with his intuition."

"Today? Well, okay."

"Good. Good. There's a client, a Mister Morgan Garrett, admitted two days ago. Mister Garrett has issues with alcohol. He's detoxified, so is ready for therapy. The cause seems to be a past trauma, but then that will be your call.

"You are an astute man, Mister Granger. I'll take your judgment to heart."

His face flooded with red. He reached for a manila file. "Here is his information. He is in room 219."

"I'll settle in and then see him right away."

He pushed back his chair and stood. "Let me show you to your office."

Chapter Five
Morgan Garrett

Outside the door of the police station I called a cab and had it give me a lift to O'Grady's Bar on Main Street where I hoped I'd left my truck. I thought about going in, but discarded that idea right away. "If Mrs. Garrett's little boy is going to get off the booze he has to start now."

There she set, my old F-150, covered with dust. I should clean her up. The black finish still looked good when washed and waxed. I needed to clean up my own act too. First I needed some sleep. I headed north on Broadway, toward my apartment on Donavan.

I pulled into the parking lot of the apartment building. Not the swankiest in Santa Maria, but most definitely not a flop house.

I unlocked the door and flipped on the light. The place smelled musty and needed aired out. When had I been here last? I couldn't remember.

Opening all the windows, I noticed how bare the walls were. The place came with a drab brown sofa, chair and end

tables. The television moved in with me, and that was it. I knew my kitchen and bedroom weren't any homier.

I frowned as I looked around. Except for my clothes and day-to-day living stuff, there wasn't one personal thing in the whole damn apartment. Not a photo, book, or even a magazine. This place doesn't look like anyone even lives here. I raked a hand through my hair. Well, hell. I haven't been living. I've been existing.

After showering, I stretched out on the bed in my shorts and stared at the white walls, the white blinds. It needs some kind of curtains, and a comforter with some pizzazz. Despite the new awareness of my stark living accommodations, the blessed quiet after the jail cell soothed. I dropped into sleep, and into the dream.

The boy ran toward me arms outstretched. I couldn't tear my gaze from the bomb strapped to his chest. The M-16 jumped in my hands as I fired. Its roar filled my head…I jerked awake, lunged upright, my hoarse scream still echoing in my ears. My next door neighbor was pounding on the wall.

"Shut the fuck up, whacko. I'm trying to work in here," she yelled.

"Lord, please. Make it go away." I dropped my head into my hands. "How long? How long?" I begged and like a thousand times before, no answer came. Maybe there never would be one.

Sunlight still streamed through the window. The damn dream had ended any hope of sleep. I might as well get up and wash the pick-up. At least that was something I had control of.

I turned left out of the carwash.

My refrigerator held only some clabbered milk and moldy cheese. I'd stop at Vons and pick up a few things, then maybe email some contacts. It was past time I got back to work. Not the Company, but an oil conglomerate had made me a nice offer.

Paddy had been urging me to take some kind of step. O'Grady's was on my way to Vons, I'd drop in and let him know I'd finally listened to him.

The pub was dim and empty except for two guys shooting pool in the far back. Hank Williams' *I'm So Lonesome I Could Cry,* played from the juke box. Paddy didn't buy into Happy Hour. If you wanted food at his place, you paid for it. That meant that most of his patrons didn't show up until they stuffed their bellies at other establishments. Paddy didn't give a shit. He knew they'd roll in and be here until closing time.

I started toward the bar. One beer wouldn't hurt. It wouldn't be polite to take up space and not order something.

Yeah, it's real crowded in here.

I ignored the voice in my head as I settled onto my bar stool. "Draw me a frosty one."

"Morg me boy-o, they spring you?" Paddy stood all of five feet four. He was willow thin, with white hair sheered close to his skull. His skin had the florid look of a drinker, but I knew for a fact his limit was two beers when he did partake.

"Only because you gave me an alibi, thanks for that."

He shrugged. "Only told the truth." He turned away to draw my beer. One thing I liked about Paddy, he never tried to police any ones drinking. His answer to overdoing was to take your keys and call a cab. If that didn't work for you, then you walked. He placed the frosted-mug in front of me on a plain white napkin. The cool beer was like a balm to my foul soul, and after two more I switched to Scotch and water.

*****

My stomach roiled. I gagged, spit, looked around with blurry vision. What the hell? Still in the truck. How and where...? The last thing...heading toward the bathroom at O'Grady's. Why had Paddy let me leave? I must have walked out while he wasn't watching.

My stomach rolled again. Oh God I'm gonna' puke. I fumbled with the door handle. Open damn you. Open. It swung wide and I more fell, than climbed out. On my knees, in the dirt, I vomited what seemed to be my guts out. When I could catch my breath, I crawled a few feet from the stinking pile.

I pushed myself onto my knees and turned to look at my truck. The front wheels were in a ditch. A tree was next to me. Using it for support I stood on shaking legs.

I stumbled around my 150. "Shit. The whole damn front end's caved in." I had to have hit the bank, and at high speed. I rubbed at the back of my pounding head. How far out of town was I? I looked up and down the road. Not another damned car in sight.

Having to hoof it home was good therapy. At first I was pissed at Paddy. Why had he let me leave? By the time I hit Donavan Road I was sober enough to feel the usual regrets. Big deal smart guy, you're sorry. Whoop-de-do. You're always sorry. I waited for my head to start offering excuses, but it didn't happen. What filled me was disgust and fear. I could've killed somebody. This has got to stop. In the morning you're calling Johnny Scott. He'll know what to do.

I awoke slowly. Even with eyes still closed I knew I'd fallen into bed still dressed. Memories of last night washed over me like a giant wave. "You dumb asshole. You need help. Driving shit-faced. You could have killed yourself, or worse yet somebody else." Saying it aloud made it even more real.

Johnny Scott and I went way back. Doctor of medicine, friend, and drinking buddy before he, 'Heard the angels' wings.' As he always put it. The way Johnny tells it, he awoke one day just like this, desperate and at the end of his rope. He went to a clinic and dried out. He lived in Pasadena now. We talked about once a month, but I'd never had told him I moved to Santa Maria. With a shaking finger I punched in his phone number.

"Hello."

"Johnny, it's Morgan."

"Hey big guy, what's up?"

"I need help? I'm fucked up with booze and have to shake it."

"Where are you buddy?"

I loved that about him. No unnecessary questions, 'just the facts ma'am'. "I'm in Santa Maria."

"California? When did you get to California?"

"Been here awhile; my last assignment in Iraq was a bad scene. Left the Company, well actually they asked me to retire. Drinking you know."

"What's the address? I'll be there before noon. You stay put."

I gave him my address and ended with, "I'm not going anywhere." And wasn't that the God damn truth.

I had three hours to stew while I waited for Johnny. Twice I picked up the phone to call and say I'd changed my mind, but I didn't have his cell phone number. I even went out the door, heading for my truck so I wouldn't be home when he got here, but it was still where I'd left it. I'd looked down the street, thought about walking. Wasn't there a corner bar five blocks from here?

The woman next door came out her apartment, glanced at me with disgust, before she got into her car and drove away.

I looked down at myself. I hadn't showered or changed. My knees and tennis shoes were still crusted with God-knows-what. I'd rubbed at the stumble on my chin, caught a whiff of myself.

Grimacing, I'd walked back into my apartment, started some coffee and headed toward the bathroom.

Within minutes of his arrival, Johnny was making phone calls. There was a room at Pacific Winds. It was a good place, he'd assured me. He used it himself last year when he'd fallen off the wagon. I'd looked at him in surprise when he said that. He'd shrugged, said, sometimes it happens. We'd check in today.

"I'll drive you up, Morgan and you can call me anytime, but you have to do this yourself." He stared off into space for a moment. "Take it from someone who's been there, the next couple of days are going to be hell. You get beyond them and you'll make it."

He sounded so damn grim. How hard could kicking the booze be? I'd spent weeks in Iraq, up to my ass in scouring sand and blistering sun. It couldn't be any worse than that, could it?

Pacific Winds was near Cambria and located on a hill overlooking the ocean. The check in procedure was simple. As soon as I was settled, Johnny patted my arm, wished me luck and then left for his long drive back to Pasadena.

Uncertainty had gripped me as I'd watched him walk away, but then I'd mentally shaken my head. You can do this. You're the only one who can.

My room was one step above a hospital's. The one thing I noticed at once was there wasn't any way to lock the door from my side. I wasn't sure how I felt about that. They'd added some blue, gauzy curtains and a darker blue quilt. The bed did have a wood headboard. It was some kind of dark red color. There was an end table and a chest-of-drawers that matched.

I was located on the second floor, a few doors from the lounge. On the other end of the hall was a workout room with several treadmills and a couple of, unknown to me, torture devices.

As I hung up my last golf shirt in the closest, someone knocked on the door. "Come in."

A man entered. He was tall, stout, with a florid complexion. Looked like a sneaky drinker to me. He held out his hand. "Mister Garrett. I am Walter Granger, the executive director of Pacific Winds. I always greet our new arrivals."

I gave his hand a quick shake.

"Did they explain the detoxify procedure to you?"

"Sounds like I'm going to be sweating the booze out," I answered.

He smiled. "Pretty much. A nurse will be on duty to aid you, keep you hydrated, but the hard work will be yours. Don't expect to do much for the next couple of days. You are going to feel like hell. It's true, we don't prevent you from leaving, after the detoxifying, but you will not be allowed to leave during the process."

"Wait a minute, I don't like the idea of being a prisoner."

"That's why I'm being upfront with you now, Mister Garrett. You can be a harm to yourself if we let you leave before the process is complete. There will be stomach pain, which we can help with, most likely hallucinations, nightmares. You'll be too weak to walk far. After you have the alcohol from your system we will provide you with therapy so you can discover why you are an alcoholic."

"I get it." I didn't like the word alcoholic, but the rest I understood.

"So I have to ask, sir. Do you want to go forward with the treatment?"

I looked down at my shaking hands. "Yeah, I do."

*****

I stood and walked on still shaky legs to the bathroom. Walter Granger had been right on, what little I could remember of the previous two days had been hell. One time I'd yanked an IV from my arm, and I dimly remembered banging on the locked door of my room. I did recall the shaking and thinking I had to fall apart, no way could a body shake like that and stay together, but it did.

I made it to the toilet. On my way back to the bed, I changed my mind and flopped into the chair instead. My legs weren't quivering too bad. Maybe I could go down to the dining room today?

Someone knocked on the door. "Go away," I snapped.

The door opened and a kid walked in.

"Did you hear what I said? I don't want cheering up. Go earn your damn high school credit somewhere else."

She walked toward me. "Thanks for the compliment, but I'm definitely not a kid," she said and held out her hand. "Doctor Sherice Solomon." She was short, with a cap of red hair and the greenest eyes I'd ever seen, but up close she looked about twenty-five, still a fucking kid. "You're the shrink. Well, I don't give a rat's ass. Now get the hell out of here."

"Mister Garrett, you know this is a part of your path to healing. Pacific..."

"Lady, I'll heal when I'm damn good and ready. This is my room right?"

"Of course, but..."

"Then get out."

I watched her frown. "I'll come back in an hour."

"Knock first and I might let you in."

She nodded curtly and walked away.

As soon as the door closed behind her, I felt like a stupid asshole. It wasn't her fault I felt like shit. Johnny had told me talking with a shrink would help.

I stood and walked to the window. Not much to see. It overlooked the parking lot, but it made me feel less penned in. I still felt weak in the knees, but my mind felt clearer than it had in years. With the clarity came the sure fact that if I didn't share my demons with someone, it wouldn't be long before they chased me back to the booze.

I turned and looked at the closed door. The doc said she'd be back in an hour. Well, if she did come back, and I wouldn't blame her if she didn't, I'd talk. I'd take it slow, but I would talk.

True to her word, I heard a knock on my door sixty minutes later. "Come in."

"Well Mister Garrett, you in a better mood now?"

I felt my face heat. "Sorry about earlier, but I think I'd do better with someone closer to my own age. No offense, but what the hell could you know about life?"

She closed the door behind her and walked toward me. "For your information, I'm only three years younger than your own 45. So, yes I do know a little about life. Now, how are you feeling, besides irritable?"

My newly found niceness vanished and I glared at her in silence.

She backed up and perched on the end of my bed. "You might as well answer. You're my one and only patient and I've got all day. I'm not leaving until we've had our preliminary talk."

"Like I've been hit by a truck, but better," I said grudgingly.

She nodded. "See that wasn't so hard." She opened the folder she carried and looked down at it. "When you checked in you mentioned a death that bothered you? Do you feel it's the cause of your problem with alcohol?"

Whoa. She didn't waste any time. I knew she was talking about the body in the alley. I'd told them about that when they'd asked why I was here. God knew, that wasn't the reason I drank, and maybe I'd tell her the truth and maybe I wouldn't. I shrugged.

"You don't have to talk about it. I thought you might want to."

"Found a guy's body in a dumpster. His throat was cut."

She stiffened for a moment and that surprised me. Wasn't she a little sensitive for a shrink? They must hear worst stuff.

She went on. "The man in Santa Maria? I saw it in the paper. What happened when you found the body?"

"The police arrested me and then let me go."

"Why did they let you go?"

"Is that important for you to know? They did."

"Just want to make sure you're safe and not some kind of killer." She smiled after saying that.

I found myself grinning back. Doctor Sherice Solomon was okay. "I'm left handed and someone vouched for my whereabouts when the killing went down."

"I see." She wrote something on one of the papers in the folder.

"The killer is right handed," I added. "A man who kills like that shows which hand he uses."

"From your background information you would be a good judge of that. I'm afraid I know little about killing." She leaned toward me. "You're looking a trifle green."

"My gut's still killing me."

She stood. "Alcohol abuse tends to do that. I'll send a nurse with something to help." She turned away.

"Huh, Doctor Solomon, again I'm sorry about being such a jerk before."

"That's okay Mister Garrett, I can be a bitch myself. You're just seeing me on a good day."

I really liked her. "So, will I be seeing you again?"

She smiled at me. "Starting tomorrow, we have at appointment at 10 in the morning. Please don't be late."

Chapter Six
Darcie Devonshire

Wes, the coward, opted to let me report to the captain while he got the ball rolling to locate Scott Stevens. The captain was happy to know we identified the body, but that didn't stop him from shouting at me to find the damn idiot who moved Jake Holt.

"Sir, we have a BOLO out on them. As soon as we know where they are, Mister Scott Stevens will be apprehended."

The captain grunted. "Well, keep me informed. The Commissioner's ordered me to have him on speed dial, so that goes the same for you.

"Yes, Sir. Understood."

He pushed back from his desk. "It's been a long day. I'm glad to see it come to an end."

That was my clue to say goodbye and head for my own desk where I grabbed my jacket and headed toward the parking lot. Halfway there Wes caught up with me. "Coward," I said by way of greeting.

"Hey, I had to check in with my buddy with county."

"Any news?"

"Not yet." We stopped in front of my car. As I reached for the door handle he said. "English, why the hell do you drive this abortion?"

"Abortion? Abortion? You ignorant, un-mechanical arse. This is a BMW. Look at the speedometer. The top speed is 150. How many of your Yank cars can do that?"

"Yeah, and where except on the autobahn will you ever be able to drive that damn fast?"

I grinned at him. "A girl has to have her secrets."

He snorted. "Well, they must pay you a lot more than they do me."

"Not hardly. I bought it at a drug sale. Gale Crain tipped me off about it; you remember Gail, the FBI agent from the Doliver case. I put in a bid and it was the highest."

"You're in America now. You should buy American."

"Is that right? I believe Janey's car is a Toyota Prius."

"She wanted a hybrid. Not my idea." Shaking his head, Wes turned and walked to his truck.

Entering Highway 101, I pressed down on the gas pedal. It was a tad bit hard on petrel use, but I loved the feel of the Beamer at high speed. It seemed to suck down tighter to the road the faster I went. My excuse today was I had to pick up Becky at Gloria's Doggy Day Care, and they closed in ten minutes. I knew they wouldn't lock me out, but any excuse was good enough. I'd driven my first BMW while on holiday from Oxford University. A gal-pal and I had spent seven days in Germany. I'd promised myself then that someday I'd have one, that and a basset hound. Now both were mine. Well, at least the Beamer was. In Becky's mind, I'm pretty sure I belong to her, rather than vice-versa.

Becky greeted me with a mixture of joy and displeasure, as usual. Her grumbling into my ear didn't stop until we were halfway home. My turning into our driveway set her to jumping back and forth. "Settle down, Sweetie. We're almost home."

*****

My cell phone rang as I scooped food into Becky's bowl.

"English, it's Wes."

"What's up?"

"My buddy just called. The Solvang sheriff's substation has located Scott Stevens. They want to know if we'll come down and make the collar."

"You bet your sweet bippy we will. I'm leaving now. I'll pick you up in ten minutes.

"English, don't you think I should…?"

I hung up. I had to finish with Becky. No time for chit chat. Besides, it was my turn to drive.

It took longer than ten minutes to get to Wes's house; but not much. Wes climbed into the car and made a big show of fastening his seat belt. He even went so far as to pull on it after he snapped in to test the security.

I ignored his mother hen act and said. "Where's Stevens staying?"

"He and his wife are in the Danish Days Inn. It's right on the highway."

*****

I pulled to the right to pass a road-hog in the left lane, and then accelerated back to cruising speed.

"God damn, English, you're doing ninety. Slow this thing down."

"Bitch, bitch." I switched to the so-called fast lane. "You know this jack-a-nape isn't going to help us much. His screwing with our crime scene is a bloody bother, but he really doesn't know anything we haven't already figured out."

"True," Wes said with a shaky voice. "I want him anyway. What the hell are you doing? You can't pass both of those trucks."

"Of course I can."

The Danish Days Inn looked more like your standard motel; not very Danish. I spotted the deputy as soon as I drove under the portico. We got out of the Beamer, Wes a tad faster than me.

"Is Stevens still in his room?" I said to the deputy.

"Yeah. 309. He's waiting for you. We could'a nabbed him for you and saved you a trip down here."

"He mucked with our crime scene. You understand how it is."

The deputy nodded.

"Let's do it Wes."

The hall was empty, with no sign of the maids. Wes flattened against the wall to the right of the door. I knocked. Hard.

"Santa Maria Police, open up."

Not a sound came from the other side.

I knocked again, harder. "I said police. Do we need to take care of the bloody door ourselves?"

It opened a crack, large enough for me to see two, frightened, blue-gray eyes. "Yes." The voice was a woman's. She had to be Viola Stevens.

"Open the door, Mrs. Stevens."

The door closed. I heard a chain rattle before it swung open to show a tall thin man, wearing dark-framed glasses. He stood just behind a much shorter and much plumper woman.

I started my mandatory Miranda speech. "Scott Stevens, you are under arrest, you have a right..."

Wes pushed by me and had Stevens in handcuffs before I made it halfway through. "You, sit on the bed," he ordered as Viola looked at him with confusion and a little fear on her face. He turned on Stevens. "And you, dumb ass, tell us about moving Jake Holt's body into a dumpster."

"What do you mean?"

"Oh Scott, just tell them what happened. You didn't kill anybody." Viola Stevens started to cry.

"Look." I leaned toward him. "We know what happened. Tell us where you dumped the bloody bedding?"

"I didn't kill him," he blurted.

"Yes, I know. Just tell us where you dumped the bedding."

"Well, uh, Consuela took the sheets. The rest were covered with blood. I threw them away."

"Where the hell did you throw it away? Quit stalling," Wes demanded.

"Nojoqui Falls. You know, that little state park over in the Santa Ynez Valley I stuffed them in the dumpster in the picnic area."

"You sure got a thing for dumpsters," Wes murmured. He jerked his head toward Viola. "What about her? Do we take her in too?"

"Do you think it's necessary? We know where to find her if we need her."

Wes shrugged. "Fine with me."

Driving into the park we spotted the picnic area right away. The dumpster sat just as Stevens described. We moved to it. Wes lifted the lid and immediately jerked back. The sweet, rotting odor rising from it made me want to upchuck. Holding my breath, I leaned in, looked down. The comforter was soaked in blood. The hooked rug, pillows, memory foam and pillow-top coverings weren't much better. Jake Holt had completely bled out, just like the others. I swallowed hard. This sure the hell wasn't the best part of police work. "I'll call the county sheriff."

Jeff Macon, the Santa Barbara County sheriff arrived within five minutes. He must have been waiting for our call and not that far away either. Another deputy, this one much younger than the sheriff, followed a few minutes later. It became his job to extract the bedding from the dumpster.

Wes and I stood back and watched it happen. It was a nasty job, but I wasn't about to leave until we'd seen everything bagged and labeled. When we caught this asshole, I didn't want him slipping through any loopholes.

When the last bag was loaded, the sheriff turned to Wes and I. "That's it. We'll get it to the lab and get the report to you ASAP."

"Thanks so much, Jeff."

He shook his head. "Whoever did this is a real sicko. We've got to catch them fast."

"I plan to do so."

Wes turned to me. "Let's go pick up Stevens."

We'd stashed Scott Steven's at the Sheriff's Sub-Station. He started complaining before I could put the Beamer in gear, yammering how this had all been just a mistake."

"You were trying to save your own ass," Wes said. "How about just plugging your pie hole? God Damn, English, do you have to go this fast? Someday you're going to kill us both."

"Jeez, I'm only doing eighty. That's like low cruise." I did let up a bit on the accelerator.

"What's our next step?" Wes said.

"We see what else we can find out about our killer." I was careful not to him Ice. At least not yet.

"Yeah," Wes said.

*****

Scott Stevens had finally shut up. Wes stared out the windshield in silence. I almost wished Stevens had kept yammering. The quiet gave me too much time to think. There's no way around it. I had to talk to Morgan. What's the big deal? What is there to be afraid of? It's over, had been for years. I'm being stupid. The decision was made. Morgan was my next move.

Chapter Seven
Sherice Solomon

Over a vanilla latte I re-read the file on Morgan Garrett. Retired CIA, never married, no children, age forty-five. No job at this time, his physical health good, considering what he'd done to his body for the past six years.

There had been a brief consultation with another doctor before admittance. I frowned as I read the notes. He hadn't revealed much about his emotional wounds. I would change that. True things hadn't started well, with him refusing to speak with me and ordering me from his room.

I sat back in my chair, thought about the electrical charge that had went through me when he'd looked into my eyes. Had the chemistry been noticed only by me? Had I imagined it? I hadn't felt that spark for a man since My David. Morgan Garrett intrigued me. The telephone on my desk rang. "Hello."

"Doctor Solomon?"

"Yes."

"Walter Granger here."

"Yes, Mister Granger, I recognized your voice."

"I wanted to inform you I checked out your references."

"And," I prompted when he did not go on. Had Isaiah slipped up?

"Johns Hopkins hated to see you go and recommend you highly."

I laughed to myself.

"Doctor Solomon. Are you still there?"

"Sorry Mister Granger. I was just speechless for a moment."

"You can call me Walt if you like. We're pretty informal here at Pacific Winds, like to keep a family atmosphere."

"Of course, Walt."

I heard him clear his throat. "Well, now that it's official, please feel free to personalize your office."

I scanned the room. It was a blank canvas, white walls, beige carpet. It did offer a large picture window with a view of the ocean.

"I know the desk is a relic," Walt Granger went on.

"It's fine," I said. I loved the light-oak banker's desk. It had been gently used and I wondered about its history. "I will add some art."

"Uh..." I heard him hesitate. "About our budget...."

"I understand, Mister Granger. Any personal touches will be just that, things added by me and at my own expense."

"Thank you for understanding. Uh, do you have plans for this evening? I thought maybe you would like to go for a drink. I could tell you about the area."

"Don't you have to get home to Mrs. Granger?"

"She's back east visiting her mother."

Some company and a drink, was that all my new boss wanted from me? "Thank you for the invitation, Walt," I said. "But I'm still settling in. Maybe some other time?"

"I'll hold you to that."

Was Mister Walter Granger going to be a problem? "Good night, Walt. I'll see you in the morning." I hung up the phone without waiting for his answer.

I stared out the window. The fog had crept in over the bay. My David and I loved the fog. I felt an itch to drive to the beach, kick off my shoes, feel the cool sand between my toes and the chill mist upon my face.

I pushed back my chair, stood, and surveyed my office again. I liked the sound of that...my office. I'd seen an antique mall in Cayucos when I'd driven through. Saturday I'd pay it a visit. Some Middle Eastern, framed prints, ceramic elephants, their trunks raised high of course for good luck and maybe a Turkish carpet in red and gold, would liven up this white space.

A camel saddle, I thought. Right there in front of the window, a perfect spot to place the chest with my souvenirs. I smiled. I'd even put Arahni inside the chest. It would be good to have her close to me.

I put Morgan Garrett's file into my briefcase and zipped it closed. I'd look it over again at home, maybe with a glass or two of white wine.

Maybe we hunt? Arahni whispered and the Hunger stirred at her words.

"No, we need rope and I don't feel like a drive. Perhaps we'll hunt Saturday when I go to Paso Robles for the rope."

Our pleasure...

"I said no. We'll look through the chest, but that is it."

I felt her sullen withdrawal and frowned. That was twice within days Arahni had challenged me. It had to be nipped in the bud. There could be no doubt who was the master between the two of us.

*****

I dreamed I stood at the entrance to an alley. Someone groaned. I followed the sound. Deeper inside the alley, shadows lined the walls, flowed toward its center. The smell of dank water, garbage and urine flooded my senses. Why was I here? The sound of misery came again. It called to my heart. I knew what such pain felt like, for I'd inflicted it.

In a wash of golden sunlight a man stood beside a dumpster. Even with his back to me I knew him. Morgan Garrett. I walked closer. His fingers rested on a hand. I looked into the dumpster, recognized the bloody face of Jason Holt. I felt my heart race again. Rage flooded through me. Who had moved my kill?

I placed my hand over Morgan Garrett's. He turned, looked into my eyes. His were shadowed with pain. I grew moist between my legs. I took his hand, pulled him away from the dumpster. "Come, it is not right for you to see him like this," I whispered. "He has been defiled. The purity stolen." I felt an urge to share with him the moment when death claimed my kills. The thought of our bodies joining at that exact second made my knees tremble.

I shuddered and gasped...my eyes flew open as the orgasm ripped through me. I lay there enjoying the pleasure it wringed from me. When I could move I turned on the bedside lamp and reached for the glass of water I'd placed there earlier. Sipping, I stared at the wall. I'd never even thought of sharing my kills with any but Arahni, but when Morgan's and my gazes had connected, I felt another wave of pleasure. It was like nothing I had ever felt before, not even with my beloved David. Was Morgan my soul mate? Had this path I'd chosen been only to bring us together at last, and my David only a tool to bring Arahni into my life. No. I'd loved My David. If not it wouldn't have hurt me so, his death.

Morgan Garrett. I closed my eyes, felt again his warm skin beneath my fingers. A moan escaped from between my lips and I felt my nipples harden. I glanced at the bedside clock. Midnight, the witching hour. I had my first session with him today.

I kicked the covers aside and a stood. My blood raced. Naked, I wandered around the front room, went even so far as to turn on the television. With the remote I flipped through a hundred channels. Nothing caught my interest. With disgust I turned it off, stood. I couldn't sit still.

I walked to the window. Stared into the dark, moonless night. I liked my solitude, except for when the Hunger commanded, but tonight I needed someone besides myself and Arahni. I threw on jeans, a sweater and red stilettos.

Twenty minutes later I sat in my idling Mustang in the parking lot of Pacific Winds. All of the windows were dark. What had I been thinking? How could I arrive at his room in the middle of the night? What would I say, I was in the neighborhood?

Which window was his? I tried to picture in my mind Pacific Winds' layout. Second floor. Nineteenth room. Right about there. As I stared a light came on. Before I realized it my hand was on the door handle. I had a key. If someone saw me I could say I'd forgotten something in my office. That wouldn't explain my being on the second floor. I took my hand from the door handle. This compulsion was madness.

I put the Mustang in reverse and backed from the parking spot. Entering the highway, I turned right, toward SLO town. I felt on fire. With a loud laugh I rolled all of the windows down, let the chilled air flow over me.

I drove by Cal Poly. Minutes later, I didn't know how many, I saw the lights of the airport. I remembered David and I coming out this way. There was a nightclub, down a street. Yes. I remembered where.

Even at close to 1:00 in the morning the parking lot was packed. I walked to the front door, paid the cover charge and strolled inside.

Young flesh packed the place. They leaned against the bar, smiled and flirted. On the large dance floor bodies writhed. A couple stood, walked away and I filled their spot at the bar. A young male bartender leaned forward. He wore a blue plaid western shirt, open to his navel. In his nest of chest hair a silver star of David rested. He smiled as his gaze swept over me. "What can I get you?"

I needed something to counteract the fire inside me. "Straight shot of tequila, and hold the salt and lime."

He grinned. "A lady after my heart."

As he turned and walked away I admired his ass in the tight jeans. When he placed the tequila in front of me I reached out and touched his hand. "Stay right there." I downed the drink in one smooth move. "I'll have another."

"Yes, Ma'am."

When he brought the second drink I handed him a twenty dollar bill. "Keep the change."

"Thanks. Is there anything else you need?"

Our gazes held.

I sipped more tequila. "What time do you get off?"

He glanced at his watch. "In ten minutes."

"I'll wait."

*****

I led the way out the front door. "How far is your place?"

He grinned. "Close. It's a motor home 'round back."

I raised an eyebrow. "What is your name?"

70

"Jason."

"Well, tonight it's Morgan."

He shrugged. "Whatever. What's your name?"

"Anything you want it to be."

In a far dim corner of the parking lot I saw the white motor home parked beneath an oak tree. I felt a flare of excitement. Fantasy games were always fun, especially when I scripted the plot.

Jason stopped at the motor home's side door, opened it, and then stepped back.

I entered. Inside was compact, but neat and clean.

"Would you like a drink," he asked.

I shook my head, reached for him.

*****

I rolled away from Jason and stood. He'd been good...very good and creative. As we'd romped I'd called him Morgan and he'd called me Rachel. I did wonder who Rachel was, but he didn't ask about Morgan so I ignored my curiosity.

I swept a gaze over his naked body. Not an ounce of fat on him, uniformly tan except for where brief swim trunks had been.

His eyes opened and for a second he looked annoyed at seeing me, before he put on his game face. I didn't mind. I used him as much as he'd used me.

Jason grinned. "Sorry about that. I usually don't fall asleep afterward."

"That's okay, lover. I won't deduct anything for your little nap."

His cheeks colored, but he didn't try to play coy. We both knew how things stood. "You know what I first noticed about you?" he said.

"What?"

"Your red stilettos. Those are fuck me shoes if I've ever seen them."

I glanced down at my shoes. He'd asked me not to take them off.

"I have a thing for shoes," I said. "But leaving them on while gettin' it on was a first."

He winked at me. "I'm glad I could be your first."

I crossed to a chair where I'd laid my clothes. "You were very good."

"There's a bathroom if you..."

"I'm fine." I felt him watch as I pulled on panties and fastened my bra.

"I don't think I've ever watched a woman get dressed...you know afterward. It's a turn on."

I glanced at him as I picked up my jeans. "Sorry. Don't have the time, the inclination, or the money."

To his credit he didn't get riled. "Might do it just for fun, just to get another look at that sexy tattoo on your ass."

What the hell. He deserved it. I turned my back to him and pulled down my panties.

"Damn, that's hot. A black widow. It's fresh isn't it?"

"Yes." I pulled my panties back into place, turned to face him. From the tent rising from the sheet above his groin he wasn't lying about being aroused. Maybe? I looked at my watch. I had to be to work in four hours. Then I'd see the real Morgan. I felt heat blossom between my legs. "I'm tempted, but I don't have the time." I reached into the pocket of my jeans, pulled out two fifties and laid them on the small table. "Thanks. You were great."

"This was only a one night shot for me," Jason said.

"What?"

"The bartending gig, I filled in for a friend. My band's playing in Avila Beach tomorrow night. Maybe...?"

"Maybe," I said, pulling on my sweater. I knew Jason and I would never cross paths again. I walked to him, leaned, kissed his lips. "You have a good life. And if I was you, I'd be more careful about who I invite into this motor home."

He still stared in confusion as I closed the door behind me.

*****

I drummed my fingers on the desk and looked at the clock. 10:30. I checked my appointment book again. Morgan's session with me was to begin at 10:00. Where was he? Over coffee and toast this morning I'd chided myself about my insane

72

reaction to the man. By the light of day it seemed ludicrous. How could I obsess over someone I spent all of ten minutes with? The dream had been the cause...the dream and my loneliness. I missed My David. Arahni was always a part of me, but I needed someone to touch and who could touch me.

Unable to sleep, I'd arrived early at my office and did some decorating from things I already owned. The chest sat beneath the window, Arahni inside. On the walls I'd hung some photos I'd taken, enlarged and framed. They were of bazaars and Middle Eastern buildings that appealed to me. The floor was still too bare, but I would take care of that this weekend.

It was 10:45.

Enough.

I pushed back my chair, stood, and walked out the door.

My breath come fast as I pushed the elevator button for the second floor. As the doors closed I realized my hands were clenched into fists and I opened them, rested them against my thighs. I'm only upset because of the slight. I assured myself. You don't miss an appointment and not even bother to call and cancel. It has nothing to do with the man personally. I ignored the logic that I could have simply called Morgan Garrett's room.

In front of his door, I lifted my hand to knock, hesitated. A wave of emotion forced me to lean against the wall for support, if I went in my life would change, forever. I felt it in every nerve. I shook my head, turned away, a scream, full of anguish and pain came from inside. My Morgan needs me. I shoved the door open and rushed in.

Chapter Eight
Morgan Garrett

I wanted out of the damned dream. I had to wake up before the kid happened, but the dream wouldn't release its grip.

The driver stopped the Hummer.

"This is the corner," Darcie said. "He's supposed to be waiting."

Something was wrong I felt it all the way down to my toes. The seat between my shoulder blades seemed to have become a sheet of ice. I looked out the narrow opening of the windscreen. "We can't wait. What's that kid doing," I asked and then he was running toward us. "Eddie, get us the hell out of here."

Two men appeared on the roof of the house to our left. The sound of automatic fire filled the air. The windscreen splintered in front of my face. I watched the kid. He held a satchel bag. He pulled a wire from the back and swung the satchel. I pushed my M16 out the shattered window and fired a short blast, followed with another.

The kid went down in the dirty street and immediately exploded. His blood and body parts splattered all over the front of our Hummer.

I screamed. "Dear God, I shot a kid." I screamed again—couldn't stop.

74

I rolled. My legs were bound in a blanket. How did...? I tried to turn. Someone had their arms around me. It had to be Darcie. "Darcie, Darcie I just shot a kid. I just shot a kid."

"It's all right, Mister Garrett. You're okay."

I opened my eyes, came back to this time and place. A woman sat on the bed next to me. She had her arm around my shoulders

"Who? Where's Darcie?" Then I remembered. The bender. The truck. The tree. Pacific Winds. "You're the shrink from yesterday."

The doctor took her arm from around my shoulders. It surprised me that I missed it as soon as it was gone. "Doctor Sherice Solomon." She stood. "You were having a bad dream. Are you okay now?"

"Yeah, yeah. I'm fine." I kicked the coverings aside.

"No. Don't get up yet. Just stay comfortable. Who's Darcie? Do you want to tell me about it?"

I stared at her in silence for a long moment. "Darcie is, or was, my partner. We had a thing, but she's long gone."

"You were calling for her. It didn't sound as if she was long gone."

Was that a thread of jealousy I heard in her voice? It couldn't have been. We barely knew each other.

Doctor Solomon moved to the one chair I had in the room. An ugly green thing, it didn't match the other stuff, so it must have been added for just this purpose.

"I had a bad experience in Iraq. The dream was about that."

"It was more than a bad dream, Mister Garrett. That was a full-blown nightmare."

I shrugged. "Yeah, okay, nightmare."

"Would you tell me about it?"

Hell no. How could I talk about it? Just thinking about it tied my stomach in knots, but isn't that why I was here? I rubbed at the back of my neck. Shit. Let her do the talking. She had a nice voice, a husky quality. My throat felt raw. How long had I been screaming?

Doctor Solomon stood and crossed to the nightstand. I liked the way she moved, a determined, no nonsense stride, yet sexy as hell.

She poured water from a pitcher into a glass. Who had brought that in? It wasn't there before. I didn't like the thought of someone coming into the room while I slept, but the damn door didn't have a lock on my side.

She walked to me, held out the glass. Our fingertips touched. Hers were warm.

"Okay, I'll talk. We were sent out to pick up an Iraqi who had been giving us information on the Al-Quida. Darcie was with me. The Iraqi had called, said he thought they were getting suspicious and he wanted to come in. When we arrived at the rendezvous he was a no-show. Instead we walked into a trap. A kid, maybe ten or eleven, started walking toward us carrying a satchel. That didn't feel right...then they fired down on us from the roof tops. They had us in a crossfire." I stopped talking and stared at the wall. I felt a warm hand on mine. I looked up, stared into her green eyes.

"I know it hurts, but you should go on. You are over the hard part. You've started."

"They fired at us from the roof. The kid kept on coming. I knew something was wrong. He pulled a wire in the pack and started swinging it...to throw." I looked away from her. "I shot him and he exploded right there." Suddenly I wanted her to understand that I'd had no choice. There were five of us in the Hummer, but I was the only one who saw what was happening. I had to shoot. I had no choice, but all I could say to her was, "I had to shoot."

"I take it the body you found in Santa Maria is not the death that really bothered you than, is it?" Doctor Solomon had a strange expression on her face. A chill went up the back of my neck, but before I could respond she went on. "I think you need a sedative. I'll send the nurse in with something. Get some rest."

She stood and moved toward the door. "Doctor Solomon, why were you here?"

"We had an appointment, remember. You missed it. I came to see what the problem may be, and found you in the throes of a nightmare."

I watched the doctor walk out of the room. I felt better than I had in a long while. I still felt the urge to blot everything out with Scotch, but not so bad this time. Was it just finally talking about the kid and that day?

I rubbed at the back of my head. Darcie? I'd called out to Darcie. Damn, can you believe that? Well, boy. Darcie blew you off a long time ago. All she ever wanted was to love you, and afterward all you wanted was the booze.

Darcie and I had made a good match. We'd worked well together. It was inevitable we found we liked having each other's company. After I shot the kid everything changed. Back at the green zone Darcie had been sympathetic and tried to help me. She'd even tried to take me to bed that night but I was totally unable to respond. That pissed me off and embarrassed me at the same time. I didn't stop loving her; I was just incapable of loving anyone.

Then the drinking started. Darcie tried to play at first, but she could see it was hopeless. "I'm not going to try and nag you out of this," she'd said one night when I came in from a drinking spree. "Your drinking is going to get you killed. You know this job is dangerous enough without this. I'm taking the transfer back to the states. You better get your ass out of Iraq before you die here." She left six days later.

The truth was I didn't give a shit and had it been left to me I would have done nothing, but the powers that be posted me to the embassy in Rome. That took me out of the combat zone and gave me too much time, too many places to drink.

I lasted six months before the embassy had me transferred to Langley with a marginal rating and a recommendation I get help. The help amounted to a stiff lecture and a warning. Six months after I was encouraged, no forced, to retire.

*****

Even striding as fast as I could on the treadmill I was losing ground. "Can we slow this thing down?"

Ernie, the therapist smiled and turned his back. I kept going, barely hanging on. If sweating was getting more alcohol out of my system then I was doing a bang-up job.

"Damn it, Ernie. How far do I have to go?"

"A lot further then you've gone so far. Keep walking and don't bitch so much. You're wasting wind."

I glanced up and saw Doctor Solomon standing in the door. It looked as if she had been there watching for a while. Maybe I was her special project. I tried smiling through the sweat.

"Are you feeling better?" She stepped into the room, came and stood by my torture machine. I liked the little bit of a smile she gave me.

"I'm okay."

"How often do you have that dream?"

"Well, you know, once in a while."

"I am a doctor Mister Garrett. No bullshit please."

"Okay, alot."

She nodded. "I've rescheduled our appointment for two o'clock tomorrow. Don't keep me waiting." She walked out leaving me with Ernie the Masochist.

Chapter Nine
Darcie Devonshire

Captain Drake did not believe in using the intercom system they had installed last year at great expense to the tax payers. "Devonshire." His bellow could be heard all the way over at the new public library.

I strolled down to his office. "Morning Sir, what's up?"

My casual attitude seemed to increase his ire by a factor of ten. "The commissioner wants to know when we are ending the gang violence over on Newlove," he snapped. "That's what's up."

"Wes has a lead. We're working it."

"Yeah, when? When you get a break from Ice? You've got to quit obsessing over him."

When I didn't reply he went on.

"The fed's are taking over Ice. He's crossed state lines. We've got enough on our plate with the damn gangbangers. Get on it. And I want yours and Smith's reports delivered personally. I don't want any miscommunications. Got it? We had another drive-by last night. A nine year old kid got caught in the crossfire. She's dead. The Commissioner is shittin' bricks. I've got to give him something, and fast."

Our gazes locked as I slowly counted to five. "Captain…

"Forget Ice. Get me some gang-bangers."

"Captain..."

"Not another word Detective Devonshire." He pointed at the door.

I turned and marched from the office. I'd liked to have stomped, but I wasn't ten anymore. Where the hell was Wes? Why wasn't he in here with me? Some partner. Turning down the hall I spotted him in the break room with a donut in each hand. "Hey partner, didn't you hear the captain's bellow?"

"Wasn't my name."

I looked him in the eyes and his face reddened.

"Sorry, English. I should have been in there with you, even if the captain wasn't screaming for me."

"Bloody right, you should have been. I don't know what partner means around here, but from where I came from it meant one and one equals one."

Wes' color deepened even more. "I hear you. It won't happen again."

"Well, at least get rid of the damn donuts. I refuse to be a worn out cliché, cops with donuts. Don't you have any pride?"

He dropped the donuts onto the counter. "Yeah, well good morning to you too."

"What's so good about it? Captain wants some gang-bangers. What have you got on that guy Flores? Can we pick him up?"

"Come on English. We talked about that." Wes turned and walked toward our desk. "There's enough for an arrest, but if we pick him up, there'll be another tomorrow. Until they start deporting these gang members it's mostly a waste of time."

"Maybe so, but the commissioner wants action, especially since there have been two killings over there this week."

"Yeah and we're elected," Wes said as he picked up and then jangled a set of car keys. "They gave us another car. I had to promise you wouldn't be driving though."

I glared and he grinned. "That wasn't my fault. That damn fool ran the red light."

He shrugged. "Whatever, I'm driving."

The Newlove neighborhood looked quiet this time of morning, but I knew that was deceptive. The housing project had little grass growing. Its gray paint had seen better days and even then it couldn't have been very jolly.

Wes pulled the car to the curb. "Apartment's upstairs in the center unit."

I nodded as I climbed out.

With stairs at each end of the apartment building we parted and I went to the far side. Wes waited until I reached the steps before he started up.

The quiet rattled my nerves; I saw a curtain flutter as I walked by the window next to the unit we believed Flores occupied. Backing against the wall I watched the door as Wes pounded on the wood.

"Police, open up." The sound of scuffling came from inside. Wes leaned back and then kicked the door just above the knob.

He went through the door first. I was right on his heels. Inside, I darted to the left as he went to the right. We both had our guns in hand. In the middle of the room a petite, naked Hispanic girl tried to put on a pair of shoes. From the next room I heard a loud crash.

The girl screamed at us. "You have no right to come in here. Get the hell out."

Ignoring her I started toward the next room. Wes grabbed my arm and walked around me.

I couldn't believe it. What the hell did he think he was doing? I wasn't some little lady who needed to be protected. Seething, I followed him into the room which turned out to be a small kitchen. We found a short, thin, Hispanic man standing on the table, trying to get his nerve up to go out the second floor window. I grabbed his pant leg while Wes yanked his arm and pulled him down to the floor.

"Flores, get your ass down here," Wes said.

"Hey, hey, hey. I got rights. Let me go."

"Shut up," I said, as Wes turned him over, jerked his arms behind him and cuffed him. Before I could read Flores his Miranda rights, the women charged into the kitchen and started beating on Wes with her fists.

"Get your hands off of him," she screamed.

81

I caught a handful of her hair and jerked her away from Wes, then leaned in close to her contorted face. "You're about a second away from going in with this scumbag. If I hear anything more from you I'll cuff you and haul your naked ass to jail. Now sit down and shut up."

"You have no right. I watch CSI. When my…"

"What part of shut-up don't you understand?" I turned to Flores, "You have the right to remain silent. Anything you say…." I continued to recite the Miranda litany as Wes dragged Flores over the broken chair and toward the smashed front door.

*****

Tomas Flores had been booked and now cooled his heels in a cell. Wes and I had decided to give him overnight to stew things over. Now it was time for me and my partner to have a little chat. What was he thinking in Flores' apartment? I wasn't some wuss to be pushed aside at the first sign of danger. I found him in the break room, eating another damn donut.

"Wes, what the bloody-hell was that all about at Flores' place. I'm your partner, not your wife."

"Southern upbringing, English," he muttered. "It kicked in. I'm sorry, but you're the first female partner I've ever had."

"We've been partners for over two years. It's never happened before and it better not happen again

He shrugged. "I can't make any promises. I don't know what else to say."

I turned and walked away, not trusting myself to respond. I was so glad this day was over. As I passed the captain's office, he came out.

"Devonshire."

"Yes, Sir?"

"Nice work on Newlove, but remember what I said. Ice isn't our problem. Got it?"

"Yes, Sir." I watched him walk away.

I fumed as I climbed into my Beamer. I'd never let a case slide, and I wasn't starting now. Just because the feds were after Ice too changed nothing for me. "I don't care even if it's Gail Crane. Sure she's a damn good agent, but Ice killed in my town." I slammed the Beamer into reverse and backed out of my parking slot. Someone leaned on a horn. "Bloody hell?" There hadn't been anyone in the way, I'd looked.

Two parking places over Wes sat in his Ford 250. He motioned toward me. I thought of ignoring him, then sighed as ingrained politeness won out over pettiness. I pulled up next to him and rolled down the window.

"Wanta go grab a beer?" Wes said.

I shook my head. "Got to get home to Becky."

His face flushed. "Janey and I decided to give pet ownership a try.

"I bet that made Jackie happy. What did you get?"

"A golden retriever. Female. Three years old. We adopted her from animal control. Janey insisted we go there first. I couldn't believe my eyes when I saw her. Jackie fell in love at first sight.

I felt myself thaw a little. "That's great. I'll drop by sometime and you can introduce us."

"How about Saturday night? Janey's making lasagna. You can even bring Becky. I don't think Miracle has been socialized much."

Socialized? That was Janey talking. I grinned. "Miracle?"

"Jackie named her. Said it was a miracle we'd all found each other."

"Can't wait to meet her, but Saturday won't work. I promised to visit with Mum and Da."

Wes shrugged. "Well, drop by anytime. The doors always open."

I felt a surge of remorse. "Hey, why don't you come to my place instead? I'll barbeque. You bring the lasagna, Janey, Jackie and Miracle. I'll invite Mum and Da too. We'll make it a party."

Wes' face brightened. "Sounds great, but I have to check with the boss first. I'll give you a call later."

"I'll be there." I smiled as I eased down the accelerator. It made no sense to take out my frustration on Wes. I turned on McClelland. Maybe the captain had it right. We were short handed. The feds had more money and time. I mulled it over all the way down Main Street. "Hell, no." I shook my head as I accelerated onto Highway 101 north. "I'll just have to keep things on the quiet side."

I switched to the left lane and sped by a red corvette dawdling along at eighty. I saw the Tefft Street exit sign and switched to the inside lane. A glance at the clock told me it was 5:50. Late again. Her Highness would be pissed.

*****

I heard Becky's bark of demand as I closed the door behind me. "I'm coming, baby." I un-buckled my shoulder harness and placed my holster and gun on the kitchen counter. I loosened the laces of my shoes, kicked them off and then walked to the master bedroom.

"Hey, there girl," I said as I opened the door. She charged out, warbled a greeting, then turned her back on me and walked to her food dish. "I'm not that late. Head outside and make the backyard safe for America."

She snorted at me, and then went out her doggie door.

As I unbuttoned my blouse I watched her start her backyard patrol.

Smiling, I finished undressing and pulled on sweats. Da had offered to adopt a dog for me for my birthday. He was involved with Labrador rescue and the humane society called him whenever a lab came in. I knew that's what Da had in mind. A nice Labrador retriever for his cop daughter, preferably male, with big teeth, but he knew what I really wanted, and when the puppy came in, he called me at once. One look at the black, brown and white basset puppy and I was in love.

Becky came back through her doggie door and stared at me. "Okay. I'm ready." I stretched out on the bed. Becky used the stairs Da had built for her to join me. We began our together time, and my transition from cop to woman.

Ten minutes later I stood. "How about dinner?"

Becky didn't need to be asked twice. She beat me to the kitchen.

My dinner was a Lean Cuisine and a glass of chardonnay.

Settled on the leather sofa, Becky beside me, I pulled up the television programs I'd recorded and read down the list until

I found Survivor. "Let's see who back stabs who first." I regretted the word stabbed as soon as it left my mouth. My brain grabbed it and held on, stab led to knife, knife led to Ice.

I made it a rule, to drop any thoughts of cases, along with removing my shoulder harness. Most times it came easy, but not this time. I couldn't seem to let it go.

The telephone rang. I let the answering machine get it.

"Cupcake, it's your ol' Da. You home?"

I scrambled from the couch and hurried to the phone. "Hey, Da."

"You still coming over Saturday?"

An innocent question, but alarm bells went off inside of me. "Why?"

"Your Mum wants to know. She..."

"She hasn't done another fix-up. Has she?"

"You need to ask her that." I knew a dodge when I heard one.

"Da..."

"You seeing anyone?"

I frowned. "Work keeps me busy." Two could play the dodging game.

"Cupcake, work's been keeping you busy for six years." Da was ready for some tough love. I heard it in his voice.

"Don't go there. This has nothing to do with Morgan."

"How many guys have you been out with since him?" he demanded.

"You know the answer to that." I felt resentment rise and knew it came through in my voice.

Yes. Six. One for each year since Iraq. And all of them your Mum orchestrated."

"And all disasters."

"What happened with Morgan wasn't your fault. You gave him chance after chance. Bloody hell, girl. The man's probably dead by now."

I don't know why I didn't tell him I knew Morgan lived and had been in the area only three days ago. I knew he'd been released. I even knew his address. I still planned on dropping by, but I'd been a tad busy. "Da, why don't you and Mum come here on Saturday? I'll barbeque. Wes, Janey and Jackie can come over. They have a new dog, a golden retriever they adopted from animal control. Her name's Miracle."

"That so? At least some one chose a real dog."

I laughed. He always teased about Becky, but I knew he adored her almost as much as I did. "So what do you think?"

"Let me check. Samantha, Darcie wants us to come over Saturday for a barbeque?"

I heard Mum say something.

Da replied. "I don't know. I'll ask her." Da spoke to me again. "Your Mum wants to know if she can bring a guest, Maynard Gerardi?"

"Maynard? Are you serious?" An Italian vision of Maynard G. Krebs popped into my head. In the eighties I'd watched a lot of The Many Loves of Dobie Gillis on Nick at Night. If this guy screeched, "work," one time I would be so out of there.

Da's words interrupted my thoughts. "Now don't let preconceived notions close your mind. Maynard's a nice guy. He's the nephew of a lady that you Mum plays Bridge with. He just moved here from San Francisco," Da said. "Has all his teeth and everything."

I couldn't help laughing. "Okay. I give in. But I'm making no promises."

"What time Saturday?"

"Let's say noonish."

"We'll see you then. Love you Cupcake."

"Love you too, Da."

He hung up and I stood for a moment smiling at the phone. Becky whined and I looked down at her. "They're at it again. This one better not be a cat person like the last one." The guy before had cringed when Becky had gotten a little drool on him. "How about a treat?" I'd just opened the cupboard when the phone rang again. My, my, I was popular tonight.

"Darcie, it's Wes. We've got a bad one."

I grabbed the phone. "Where?"

"1012 Newlove. Two dead. Gang-bangers."

"I'll meet you there."

*****

Not a person walked the street or stood in their yards as I screeched to a halt on Newlove next to Wes' pickup. He stood behind the front fender, his weapon aimed at a small, gray and white house. Two gangbangers lie in the front yard on yellowing grass. There was a Santa Maria Police Department cruiser in the driveway. A uniformed officer sprawled beside it.

Damn. Damn. Damn.

From inside my Beamer I could hear the pop-pop-pop of gun fire. We needed to get this whole area blocked off first thing and fast. I knew from my radio that four more units were on the way.

I exited the Beamer and staying low and using Wes's truck as a shield I hurried to him. "There are at least two of them still in the apartment," I said.

"Yeah, and dispatch says there's no back door." He pointed to the downed man. "The officer called that in before they took him down. We got 'em trapped."

I wondered just who was more trapped, them or us.

I could hear the sirens of our back-up, but they were still minutes away.

Wes stood and started shooting over the hood of his truck at the nearest window.

"What the hell are you doing?"

"I'm gonna drive them away from the window before they hurt someone else."

"Get down you fool. We'll have back-up in a minute."

"No time. They're coming out," he yelled.

I looked and could see both gunmen running from the front door. Wes fired and dropped the first man while I took aim at the smaller man in the rear.

"Halt right there," I screamed as loud as I could. "Hands in the air."

The man stopped, looking like a deer caught in the headlights.

"Drop the gun," Wes shouted.

The man slumped, bent slightly.

Had he been hit?

"I said drop the gun asshole." Wes straightened.

The man swung his gun up and I fired mine.

We both ran forward as the man slumped to the ground. Wes landed on top of him. I grabbed the gun out of the man's hand. I'd hit the gangbanger above the belt and he was pumping out blood. "He needs an ambulance."

"Let the fucker bleed." Wes said, but he yelled it over his shoulder as he was sprinting back toward his pickup to radio for EMS.

*****

The sirens were silent as the ambulance drove away. Could be very bad or very good. I hadn't been able to get an update on the condition on the fallen officer; I'd been busy fielding questions from a reporter.

My stomach knotted. Damn I hoped he would make it. I didn't know Georges well, but I knew he had a wife and two little boys at home.

The gangbanger I shot still waited on the ground. The second ambulance hadn't arrived yet. He'd been patched up, but from the way he moaned it didn't look like his pain meds had kicked in.

I turned my back.

The sheriff's department had sent over the county coroner. He'd legally pronounced the three other gangbangers dead. From what we found out from the few locals who would even talk to us, it looked to be a drug deal gone bad.

I frowned, shook my head. The dead were kids, couldn't be more than seventeen each. Bloody hell! I wanted to punch something. Gangs. Drugs. Bodies. It was becoming a weekly thing. Santa Maria wasn't some big city. This had to be stopped It pained me to even think it, but the commissioner had it right. No more messing with Ice, Devonshire. Let the feds handle it. The voice in my head tried to feed me arguments and I smashed it down. "Clean up my own backyard first," I muttered.

"Damn straight," Wes said from behind me. "It won't be easy, but yeah."

I turned to face him. "Okay partner, what's next? How do we find these assholes who are killing our kids."

Ice

Chapter Ten
Sherice Solomon

Below my office window the sun glittered off the blue expanse of sea. I loved the ocean, but today it received only a glance from me. I turned checked my watch again. 1:50, five minutes later than the last time. Why was I anticipating my two o'clock with Morgan with such nervous jitters? He was just another guy, mentally wounded, but not weak, I'd seen his strength. He was a take charge kind of person who would let nothing stand in his way, nothing or nobody. Much like me, and he already knew how to hunt. What would it be like to have another with Arahni and myself during a kill? We could shower together; wash the blood from each other's bodies. My face grew hot.

I do not wish for another. Arahni's voice interrupted, sounded sulky.

"He would make it better. More pleasure..."

For you. Not me.

"You would feel through me. His hands, his mouth..."

I have never desired men.

Arahni's words shocked me. I hadn't known her preferences.

Of course you did. She accused. *Were the women we hunted your choices?*

I frowned. "Of course they were. They were all my choices."

Arahni did not respond, but I felt her smugness. I thought about the women we had killed. I had enjoyed watching the blood flow from them, but it had not given me the orgasmic pleasure that killing the men did. Arahni wanted me to linger over them, and for her I had. I felt a pang of unease knowing Arahni had played a bigger part in their deaths than I had thought.

A knock on the door made me jump.

I tugged at the hem of my white blouse. Professional. Keep it remote. "Come in."

Morgan Garrett opened the door. He grinned at me. "Hey, it's two and I'm on time."

"Yes you are. Sit down, please." I motioned toward the chair sitting across the desk from me.

"Sleep was good last night. No nightmares."

"Yes that's one very important step, but only a step. We have a long way to go Morgan. It's okay if I call you Morgan?"

"Sure, sure, why not."

Why not indeed, My Morgan. Across from me, he fidgeted in his chair, looked around the office. His eyes stopped their search when he reached the chest.

"Now Morgan, we should talk about the body you found in Santa Maria."

"The one in the dumpster?"

I smiled. "Have you found more than one lately?"

"Not lately."

I looked at him, thinking he meant the words as a joke, but his face told me differently. I went on. "Yes the defi...yes that one. How did it make you feel?"

"Well, I was pretty hung over and just trying to stand up when I grabbed his hand. Hell, Doc, I only told you about it because I didn't want to talk about Iraq. You asked about a body and..."

"Tell me what you saw." I want to know. I have to know. Someone defiled my kill. Steady, steady. I stood and moved to the chest below the widow. My fingertips grazed its surface. "Go on. Tell me about the body. It will help you to talk about it."

91

"I knew right off the guy had been put in the dumpster. He wasn't killed in that alley. The cops came, saw me, took me in, and that's about it."

I turned to face him. "You touched the body." We'd both touched the body. My Morgan and I.

"Well, yeah, but just for a moment."

"When you killed the boy in Iraq; how did you feel?" For a few seconds he did not answer and his suddenly remote expression told me he'd left me, gone somewhere back in time. "There is a reason for my asking."

He blinked, came back to me. "Like shit, hell he was a kid. Yeah, he had a bomb strapped to him, but he was a kid. It was all wrong, all wrong."

"Had you killed before?"

He frowned. "It was part of my job. I wasn't an assassin, but yeah I'd been in some firefights."

"The death of the child was what started the drinking?"

"Yes. Why are we talking about this?"

I turned back to the window. Clouds had formed along the horizon. It looked like it could rain. "Morgan, we must get it all out. Purge the poison."

"The killing was bad but I could deal with that. They were soldiers and knew what they were in for; they shot at me I shot at them. I was a better shot and here I am."

I looked at Morgan again. He still sat in the chair shoulders straight, head held up. He isn't ashamed of his killings...all except the child. "Have you used a knife when you killed?"

He stared straight at me for a long moment and then shook his head, but I knew he lied. He had killed with a knife. Why didn't he want to tell me? Had he enjoyed it? Watching the

blood spurt. Feeling its warmth on naked skin. A fierce joy went through me and my knees quivered. "You..."

"I don't see why that's important. Can we talk about something else? Don't you want to know if I hated my mother?" He smiled and my heart fluttered.

"Maybe. Tell me about yourself. Where did you grow up?"

The next forty-five minutes passed quickly. I made notes, but mostly I watched his face, listened to his voice. When he stopped to take a breath, I smiled. "That's all for today. You're scheduled for 2:00 tomorrow and we'll talk about the drinking."

"You know, it's funny but I'm doing okay with that."

That is due to the structured environment here. We'll talk tomorrow."

He stood, walked to the door and then out it.

Watching My Morgan go I knew I had to have him. He would love me and he would share my life.

A sudden ache to hold Arahni swept through me. I walked to the chest, lifted the gold chain from inside the neckline of my shirt. A small key dangled at the end of it. Images of Morgan and myself, together, over our first kill filled my head. It would be like no other that had come before. I felt heat build in my lower stomach. A knock sounded on the door. Without waiting for my response, Walter Granger barged in. The walls of my office seem to pale with his presence. I dropped the chain and key back inside my blouse. Hot anger flowed and my gaze went to his soft, white throat.

"So, how is our doctor doing?" He smiled showing lots of white teeth. "You're finding everything you need?"

Our doctor? Never in your lifetime, little man. "Everything is going fine. The staff has been very helpful."

"So maybe we could have that dinner and talk it over. There's a nice place just up the coast."

Struggling to stifle the rage I felt in my stomach, I glanced from him, to the chest and back. The stumbling, interfering, buffoon. Seeing his blood spout, watching his eyes glaze over, no, one didn't play where one worked. "Sorry. I have another commitment tonight."

His smile faded. "You're a busy little bee, aren't you?"

When I remained silent, color flooded his face.

He shrugged. "Well, some other..."

"Yes, we must...all three of us...when your wife returns."

His comment was a grunt as he backed from the doorway.

I walked to the door and closed it. Like every room in Pacific Winds there wasn't a lock. That would have to change. There were no other appointments for me today. I moved to the chest, picked it up.

You should not have brought the chest. Arahni said.

"I see that now."

He clouds your judgment.

"Stop. I will not hear it!"

I turned off the lights as I left my office.

The graying lady at the receptionist's desk looked up. "Early day, Doctor?" Her tone sounded accusatory.

I nodded, without slowing my pace.

"Nice box," she said. "I saw one like it at *Big Lots.*"

"It's a memory chest from the eighteenth dynasty," I snapped, having no idea if my words were true, but she aroused an urge within me to slap her down.

"Oh. Well, it looks the same." She began pushing papers from one side of her desk, to the other.

"An unlocked office provides no protection for it," I added.

She jerked her head back up. "We don't steal at Pacific Winds."

I smiled. "Who said you did, but why tempt fate?"

Her eyes narrowed as color flooded her face. The phone rang saving me from her, no doubt, viperous reply. With another smile, I turned and walked away.

*****

Inside the cottage, my briefcase joined a pair of jogging shoes. I carried the chest to the coffee table. I lifted the chain from the neck of my blouse and opened the chest with the key.

Arahni lay in the nest of souvenirs, the jewels from her hilt winking at me. I picked the shafra up, sighed as she settled into my hand.

"Practice. We must practice," I said. "It's been too long."

Holding Arahni before me, we flowed into a series of Ti' Chi moves. Twenty minutes later my right arm trembled and sweat streaked my face. Not good. Before it had been at least fifty minutes before I felt any strain. More practice was needed. I thought of Walter Granger's soft white throat and felt the Hunger respond. I shuddered. "To pretend I want him. Even I'm not that good of an actress."

The Hunger bit, insisted.

"No. I have decided. My Morgan must be with us."

My stomach cramped and I pressed the side of the Arahni against it. "It will be worth the wait." I walked to the chest, found the blood-splattered journal from the bed and breakfast in Santa Maria. "Look. Remember." With closed eyes I relived the instant the wine had touched Jake Holt's lips, how we'd kissed, stumbled toward the bed.

The Hunger purred.

A breeze blew across my sweat-soaked body and a shiver climbed from my toes. A breeze? My head jerked toward the door. It stood open. Stupid. Stupid. Stupid. What if someone had seen me with Arahni, or my souvenirs? I padded to the door, slammed it shut and twisted the deadbolt.

Inside my head Arahni laughed softly and another shiver moved through me. A shower and a glass of wine would take care of the chill.

Wrapped in my bathrobe, a glass of cabernet in my hands, I sat at the kitchen table, looking down at Morgan Garrett's admittance form. Pacific Wind's phone number teased me. "A call to My Morgan would be okay. A doctor checking on a patient." The clock behind me chimed. Six-thirty. He would be back from the evening meal. My Morgan wasn't the hang out and chat in the lounge kind of man. "He'll be bored. Thinking of our session. Could he have a bottle stashed in his room. We can't let him start drinking again." I picked up the phone. Dialed.

"Pacific Winds." A female voice answered.

"Room 219."

"One moment."

The phone rang and rang. After the eighth time the woman came on line. "They aren't answering."

Oh really, you dumb cow. I hung up without replying.

I pushed my chair from the table, stood, paced the length of the kitchen. Where was Morgan? It was seven o'clock. Who did he talk to? "Damn him." I picked up my half-full glass of wine and threw it against the wall. It flowed like bloody tears down the white paint. Now look what you made me do. I'll have to replace the glass.

Beyond the backdoor was a mop and dustpan. With a sigh I went to get them. Who was My Morgan with? Who would not bore him to tears? The brunette with the big boobs? The few words we'd shared hadn't branded her an Einstein, but men would overlook a lack of brains when their third leg took control of their heads. No it couldn't be her. My Morgan wasn't so shallow.

I moved to the trash can and poured the pieces of glass inside

My eyes returned to the wine-stained wall. The rivulets did look like tears of blood; they had even dried to a rusty brown. But, they lacked something. I walked to the bottle of wine, poured some onto a dish cloth and drew two large eyes, one to each side of the dried wine.

"Beautiful."

I took another glass from the cupboard, filled it with wine.

Standing beside my bed I took a sip and then dialed Pacific Winds' number again.

"Pacific Winds," the same female voice answered.

"Room 219, please."

"One moment."

The phone rang.

Morgan picked it up on the second ring. "Hello."

I hung up. He was back in his room, but where had he been? Pacing the room provided no answers. There was only one way to solve the problem. I had to see My Morgan.

Chapter Eleven
Morgan Garrett

The phone rang. "Hello." There was breathing, but nothing else. "Who the hell is this?" The call disconnected with a soft click.

I felt the hair on the back of my neck rise. Who could it be? I made some enemies in my time with the CIA. I'd like to think they couldn't track me down, but that kind of fantasy could get me killed. I stood, paced the room. Tonight it felt the size of a postage stamp. I didn't do well in confinement. Three years ago some Pakistani extremists had captured me. They'd left me in a cell for three days with just water. It hadn't been the lack of food that almost broke me; it had been the walls that had seemed to steadily creep closer. My heart pounded. Get hold of yourself, sport. You're not locked in. You can walk out of here anytime you want. Back to what? The apartment? The booze?

My throat felt parched. I walked to the nightstand and poured myself a glass of water, gulped it down, but it didn't do a damn bit of good. My hands trembled. I knew what I thirsted for and all the water in the world wouldn't quench the need. The doc had warned me this could happen. It's psychological...the need. Knowing didn't help.

Fuck it. I had to get out of this room. I put on my shoes, laced them up. Go where? The downstairs lounge didn't excite me. I'd end up fending off another assault from Miss Big-Boobs or worse yet struggling through another mind-numbing board game with good old Norm. A walk on the beach? Yeah, that'd do it. Some fresh air would clear my head.

My hand was on the doorknob when the telephone rang again. Let it ring. No, it might be Johnny. Shit. "Hello."

There was soft breathing. Ready to slap the phone back into its cradle, a voice stopped me. "Morgan, what's wrong?"

"Sherice?" I felt like a drowning man who had just been thrown a lifesaver. "I mean Doctor Solomon."

"We're not in session you may call me Sherice if you'd like."

"I'd like."

"Now tell me what's wrong?"

"The room's feeling small tonight." I tried to laugh after the words, but it came out almost a groan.

"You're wanting a drink?"

"No. Of course not." Silence from the phone. "Well okay, but I'm not having one, okay?" My voice sounded surly and my face heated. "Why did you call me?"

"I thought you needed...that you were in trouble."

"You what? Are you some kind of psychic?"

She laughed. "Of course not. Sometimes it happens...the connection with a patient."

There was that chill again along the back of my neck. "Well, no offense Doc, but I don't want to talk tonight. I've had enough of that for the day."

"What do you want?"

Good question. "I need to get the hell out of this room, no, away from this whole damn place."

"Can you wait for another couple of minutes?"

"What? I didn't mean...I'm not asking...."

"Willing volunteer here."

"Can we do that? Is it permitted?"

"I'm in the parking lot now, Morgan. Do you want me to come up, or will you come down?"

"I'll come down."

Halfway down the stairs it hit me. Why was Doctor Solomon in the parking lot at this time of night? She must have needed something from her office. It was the only reason that made sense. I thought of my earlier words, maybe she was psychic. I smiled, shook my head. I didn't much care. Her showing up tonight was a lifesaver for me.

No one manned the receptionist desk and I sailed right by and out the front door.

A blue Ford Mustang idled next to the front entrance. The driver's side window came down. Smooth jazz flowed out along with Sherice's words. "Hop in. Or would you rather drive?"

"No, you drive." I slid into the leather seat and fastened the seat belt.

"There's a nice stretch of beach up the way."

I watched as she guided the convertible with ease along the dark highway. The full moon provided enough light for me to see she looked good in some tight jeans and a green tee-shirt. As if she could read my thoughts, she turned and smiled. Whoa, is she interested in me? I wasn't sure how I felt about that. There had been women since Darcie, one night stands, others like myself needing a body to help get them through the night, but I hadn't let any get too close. I frowned into the dark. Had any of them even wanted to get close?

She slowed, turned into the parking lot of an overlook.

The ocean beyond was one dark mass, but the pounding roar of the waves filled my ears.

Sherice parked the Mustang and without looking at me climbed from the car. I watched her walk to the rail. "There's a flashlight in the glove compartment."

"Okay." I fished out the light, then sat there with it in my hand. What now? I wanted out of that damn room, but did I want this? I exited the car, walked to her. Still not looking at me, she took my hand and we started down the dim path to the beach.

"I'm carrying the light," I said. "Let me take the lead."

She nodded.

The path was steep in some spots and we both tripped several times.

Near the bottom I turned to ask which way she wanted to go. Before I could say a word Sherice stumbled. I caught her with my free hand. Our bodies molded together and it seemed natural to lower my mouth to hers. The kiss, soft at first, erupted into fire. I pulled her closer still. Sherice moaned against my lips. I took a step back, stumbled and almost pulled us both the rest of the way down the path. We broke apart. I heard her laugh shakily.

"Come on," I said.

She pulled back. "No. I've changed my mind. The beach isn't going to work."

"Sherice uh, I..."

"Back to the car."

I thought of the bucket seats of the Mustang. I couldn't see how they would work either.

At the side of the car I pulled her into my arms again. She came willingly, but some of the heat had disappeared from her lips.

"What is it?" I said.

"I'm not sure you want to do this."

I took her hand and pressed it against my erection. "Does that answer your question?"

She smiled as she removed her hand from me. "I'm your doctor. You're vulnerable."

I cupped her firm butt. "You don't feel like my shrink tonight."

She grabbed my hands, took them from her. "No Morgan. I have to know it's really me you want."

I stepped back from her, walked to the railing. Staring across the dark mass of water I took deep breaths and let my body calm. She could be right. I'd shared more with her than I had with any woman except Darcie.

"Morgan," she called. "I'm sorry if I led you on. I thought...."

"Don't Sherice. You're right. We need to take this slow. We've only known each other a few days." I turned walked back to where she stood. "I do want to get to know you better."

"You will, Morgan. When we make love you it will be after you've left Pacific Winds."

I pulled her close, kissed her again. "I'm going to hold you to that."

Sherice stepped back from me. "How about some coffee and a piece of pie? I know a great place between here and Pacific Winds."

"Sounds good. And this time I think I will drive."

*****

I stretched, opened my eyes. Sun filtered through a crack in the blinds. I lay for a minute taking stock. Something felt odd, and then it hit me. I was sober, completely so, and without a headache. It felt damn good.

Last night with Sherice. I wasn't sure how I felt about it this morning. Sure she'd felt good pressed against me. I'd enjoyed the hell out of kissing her, but she was my doctor. How much of my emotions had to do with that? She'd been right to put the brakes on. I had enough to cope with, getting out of here, back to the shambles of the life I'd fled from in Santa Maria. I needed to straighten everything out, or at least get a good start. I might even try and find out where Darcie lived now. Begin my own twelve-step program. I needed a job. Johnny had suggested I get a private detective's license. It wasn't a bad idea. God knows I'd spent more than a little time ferreting out secrets.

I got up, dressed, and headed down to breakfast.

I took the chair next to Big-Boobs and let her flirt away.

"Morgan, how come you're not married?" She leaned way over, giving me a good view of her treasures as she asked the question.

"Marriage is a great institution. I recommend it for married people." I watched the blank look on her face. She gave me an inane smile and then turned to poor old Norm. I halfheartedly listened to their sexual repartee as I gulped down my breakfast.

I pushed back my chair, stood. "Later all."

As I opened the door of my room, the phone rang. It could be Sherice. Did I want to talk to her? I hesitated a moment before picking up the receiver. "Garrett."

"Morgan, howzit going boy?"

"Johnny, good to hear from you."

"I'm in San Francisco and thought I'd stop and see you this afternoon on way back. I need your help."

"Man you need my help you're in real trouble. Just say the word, I'm yours"

"I don't want to go over it on the phone. We'll talk when I get there."

Johnny needing my help was a big deal...I owed the guy way more than I could ever repay. "You got it pal. I have a appointment with the shrink at two. After that I'm yours."

"That'll work. I won't get there until about three."

I hung up the phone, stood and walked to the window. I thought of my apartment in Santa Maria. I hadn't stopped the paper, mail or anything.

I moved to the wall, looked at the calendar. August 11th. I'd only been here five days, but it seemed like three weeks. In here I remained pretty safe from the lure of booze. I'd bet they didn't even use cooking sherry, but how would things be on the outside? Norm and Big-Boobs had each been here a month. I'd seen Big-Boobs' room the night she'd tried to lure me inside. She had plants, pictures and woven rugs, all very homey. It looked as if she planned to stay for some time. I could see why, safe, no threats. Pacific Winds didn't care how long you stayed. I shook my head. Not for me.

Johnny had made it clear when I checked in, I could check myself out anytime I chose and today was that day. I'd have my meeting with Doctor Solomon, then adios to Pacific Winds.

So, now it's no longer Sherice?

An annoying little voice piped up in my head. I ignored it. I'd let her know my plans. Johnny and I could have our talk on the drive to Santa Maria.

The decision made, I grabbed my suitcase from the closet and began tossing my clothes inside. I couldn't wait for 2:00 to get here.

I knocked on the door to her office.

"Come in."

I took a deep breath and opened the door. Sherice sat behind her desk in a wash of sunlight. Her short, red hair seemed to be on fire. She wore a green, low-cut, sweater that matched her eyes, but on her it looked classy, not trashy like Miss Big-Boobs. A gold chain rested against her pale skin. "Good morning, Morgan." She smiled.

"Good morning to you, Doctor Solomon."

I could see her eyebrow go up.

"Please shut the door and take a seat," she said.

I did and walked to the chair across the desk from her. I felt her gaze as I settled into the chair.

"You seem tense today, Morgan. Is something bothering you?"

I looked into her eyes. "Feeling a trifle unsure of my footing..."

"Because of last night?" She interrupted and then nodded her head. "I was afraid this would happen."

"Last night was great." I hurried to say. "I was going crazy. If you hadn't showed up I'm afraid I would have ended up in a bar somewhere."

She stood, came around the desk and placed her hand on my shoulder. Her fingers burned through my tee shirt. "Perhaps, but I don't think so."

"Is that your personal or your professional opinion, Doctor?"

She leaned close, whispered her answer into my ear. "Both."

Her warm breath made me think of other hot parts of her and I felt my body react. I shifted in the chair to find a more comfortable position.

Sherice laughed, then returned to her side of the desk. "I know how you feel. It's the same for me. If I had a lock on that door...." She sighed. "I don't."

God. This woman. What would it be like to take her to bed? She'll be wild, uninhibited. Green-eyed women were like that. Real spitfires. I sucked in a deep breath, sat back in my chair as I looked into Sherice's eyes. Green eyes, red hair. Like Darcie. I frowned. Why hadn't I made the connection before? I stood and walked to the window.

"Morgan. What is it?"

"I'm checking myself out of here today. I can't thank you enough for your help."

"Are you sure?" Sherice said. "You're strong enough?"

I faced her. "Yes and yes."

She smiled. "I think so too. You've put the past behind. You're a purified vessel waiting to be filled."

I shook my head, laughed. "I don't know about that, but for the first time in six years I think my head is on straight."

Sherice stood, came to stand in front of me. She reached to touch my cheek. Her fingers were soft against my skin. "

You've went through the fire, came out tempered like fine steel."

I felt hard as steel. And she'd be a soft sheathe to bury myself in. I remembered her breasts last night, pressed against my chest and the feel of her firm ass.

"Remember what I said last night?" she said and trailed her fingers along my chest.

"Uh...."

"After you leave here, you're no longer my patient." Her fingers stopped at the top of the zipper on my suddenly too tight jeans.

"Right. I recall something like that being said."

Sherice stepped back from me. "I get off at four. I'd be happy to give you a ride back to your apartment."

I raked my fingers through my hair. "Thanks. I already have a ride."

I could see her body stiffen. "You do?"

"Yeah, the guy who brought me here, my friend Johnny, he's coming to pick me up."

"Morgan, you didn't need to call him. I would have..."

"I didn't call him. He called me. He's on his way back from San Francisco, planned to stop for a visit anyway. It just worked out that way." Why was I explaining myself? I needed to get some distance from Sherice Solomon. She made my head crazy. I had to un-complicate my life, before I added anymore complications.

"I see."

She sounded hurt and I felt a pang of guilt.

"Give me your business card and I'll call you when I get resettled." The words sounded lame. I knew it, but they were all I wanted to offer at this time.

"Of course you will." She reached into her desk and pulled out a pen. "I don't have any business cards yet." She

wrote on a prescription pad, ripped the paper free and held it toward me. "If you need anything, you call. The first days back are the worst."

I glanced at my watch. 2:15. Close enough. "Well thank you Doctor Solomon. You made this whole experience life-changing," I said as I walked to the door.

"You're welcome, Mister Garrett. Please close the door as you leave."

I hesitated, looked into her face. She smiled, all the irritation I felt earlier from her gone. Sherice Solomon was a chameleon, a fascinating puzzle, but did I want to put the pieces together? I walked through the door and closed it behind me.

True to his word, Johnny showed up at three, and twenty minutes later I was checked out and belted in to his Mercedes sedan. As he backed the car from the parking spot, I looked toward Sherice's office window. She stood there. She must have been watching for me. She lifted her hand and waved as Johnny and I accelerated away.

Chapter Twelve
Darcie Devonshire

It was Friday afternoon and everyone in the station seemed to be running around trying to tie up the whole weeks loose-ends. No different than everyone else, I scoured the area for Wes who had wandered off and left me to type up the report on Flores.

"Detective Wesley Irvin Smith, where the hell are you? I'm not doing this paper work alone. Not again," I shouted.

"Uh oh, Wes boy. Your momma's using all three names," a voice said.

Hennessey's head popped over the partition. "Cool it Devonshire, he's right here."

On the other side Wes and several others poured over a chart of the upcoming Forty-Niner's game. These Yanks knew nothing about real futbal.

"Wes..."

"Okay, okay. Put me down for five." He walked back to our desk, sat across from me. "So what do you need from me?"

I pushed the report at him. "Sign the bloody thing."

Wes grinned as he did so. "I owe you."

"Whatever. We need to get to Flores in the interview room. Let's see if a night in a cell has made him a tad more cooperative."

The small, oblong and gray interview room held one metal table and two chairs. It wasn't designed to bring happy thoughts and it didn't. It didn't bother me, but Flores looked to be all nerves. He jumped from his chair as we entered the room.

"Sit down," Wes commanded.

Flores did, but his eyes drifted toward the door.

Something had this boy scared.

Wes started. "You know you're in trouble…"

"Where is she?" Flores interrupted.

"Who?" I said.

"Tisa, she was there when you grabbed me."

"We didn't arrest anyone but you, Chico," Wes said.

The man's face flushed at the racial slur just as Wes intended. "They'll get her, she don't know what to do. They'll get her."

We had moved into our good cop, bad cop routine. I was playing good cop this time.

"You want to tell us something?" I watched Flores' effort to pull back and calm himself. Not what we wanted.

Wes got right down in Flores' face. "Chico here don't want to talk, he's a tough guy. He wants to go away for a long time and be some guy called Osso's girlfriend."

"No, uh, I can make a deal."

"We don't need a deal out of you. What do you have to offer?" Wes moved back to the opposite side of the table.

Flores fidgeted and squirmed.

"All right," I said after a long pause to let him wiggle on the hook. "Give us a name. Who brings the stuff in?"

"No, no. You gotta get Tisa. You gotta, you know protect her. You gotta give me…like a promise. You know on paper."

"Who do you think you're dealing with?" Wes was on his feet. He came around the table again. "We're not the feds, and we don't run some big elaborate witness protection program. You cooperate and we can help you. That's all we'll give you."

Flores' gaze went to the door and then with a sigh he blurted, "Her name's Theresa Marie Scarsdale. I call her Tisa. I'll give you the names I got, but you gotta get her out of there. Francisco can't protect her."

"Who's Francisco?" I said.

"Friend. He lives on the end apartment, by the steps. Juan Carlos, he's the guy who we meet on Thursdays. He brings the shit, we pay him for last week's sales that's all. We don't deal with nobody else. Just Juan Carlos."

"Where do you get with him? Exactly." I knew this was a critical point.

"We go to Santa Barbara."

"Careful, Flores, don't lie…"

"You lie to us you piece of shit and you'll never see your little naked Tisa again," Wes interrupted.

"She's a good girl. You protect her. Juan will go after her when I am gone."

"Gone?" Wes grinned. "Oh, you're talking witness protection again. I believe we all ready covered that subject. Why would we help your sorry ass?"

"Now Wes, of course we'll help," I said, as gently as I could force myself to do. "Mister Flores, what have you to offer?"

"Start with where you meet the other scumbag," Wes snapped.

Flores' lips tightened and for a second I thought we had pushed too hard, then he went on.

"At the rest stop, south of the Gaviota tunnel. He's got a red Ford F-250 crew cab pick-up. He'll come about eight at night. We make the transfer, and we come home."

"Okay." I stood. "Wes, let's go get the girl."

"Let her rot."

"No. No. You promise." Flores sprung from his chair.

"Sit your ass down," Wes ordered.

"Now Wes, we made a deal. If we don't stick to our deals, our word isn't much better than…" I looked at Flores. "We'll take care of your Tisa."

"What you do with her?"

"That's none of your damn business," Wes said.

"You send Tisa home, back to Santa Barbara. Her parents 'ill be happy."

"I don't give a shit about her parents. Maybe we'll arrest her ass too. She has to know something about your…"

"She know nothing. I make sure."

"Mister Flores, we'll take care of Tisa. I promise. We'll talk some more later." I stood and Wes followed me from the room.

He closed the door.

"Nice bad cop," I said. "Mind if I use some of it next time?"

He grinned down at me. "What's mine is yours, partner."

*****

The apartment looked the same, same dirt, same graffiti. Wes took the near stairs and I went to the other end.

The door had been fixed. I hoped Wes wouldn't have to kick it in again. I knocked, hard, it opened immediately.

"Where is he? What have you done with him?" The girl demanded.

On closer inspection I could see she had to be about seventeen.

"Steady there," Wes said as he pushed into the small, dim room. "You alone?"

"We arrested Flores, Tisa, and he's going to be busy for a while. You need to pack a bag. You're going home. How old are you? Is your face on the side of a milk carton?" I watched as she built the lie.

"Twenty, I'm twenty and I'm not going anywhere. Do you know who I am?"

Wes walked back in from the kitchen. "Honey, we don't care."

"I am Theresa Scarsdale. My father is Lyndon R. Scarsdale, the next Senator from California.

"The Lyndon R. Scarsdale?" I put awe into my voice.

Miss Scarsdale's shoulders went back and she lifted her chin. "Yes."

"Never heard of him," I said, and then smiled.

Her face filled with color. "My father is an important man. He'll have both of your badges."

"Oh," I said. "What's a senator-to-be's daughter doing hanging out with a two-bit gang-banger?"

Theresa's face grew sullen. "I love him."

"You a druggie?" Wes said. "You using? Flores your supplier? You supply him with sex and he..."

"I don't do drugs," the girl screamed. "Tomas and I have plans. One more big score and we would have been out of here and living like royalty in Mexico."

"Well little Princess, your regime's been overthrown," I said. "We're calling daddy. I bet he wastes no time coming to fetch his darling daughter.

She flounced to a chair and plopped into it. "Fine. Send me home. I'll be out of there by the next day."

I walked to her, kneeled so our eyes were on the same level. "I'd re-think that if I were you. Your boyfriend's supplier may have other plans if he gets his hands on you."

Theresa's face paled. "I don't know anything about that. Tomas kept it all away from me."

Wes laughed. "I'm sure Juan Carlos believes that.

"It won't make a difference if he does. Girl, you're a loose end. Guys like Carlos don't like loose ends," I said

Theresa Scarsdale stood. "Fine. Call my father. I have a cell phone in my purse." She pointed to a red-leather number sitting on a scarred coffee table.

As I turned to walk to it, my cell phone went off. "Detective Devonshire."

"Detective are you are at the Palms Apartments. " The dispatcher asked.

"Yes."

"We've received a complaint about a rotten smell coming from one of the units. The Captain wants you to check it out."

"Which unit?" I said, but my tensing stomach already I knew.

"Nine. It's..."

"The end unit, by the steps. " I finished for her.

"Yes, that's correct."

"Bloody hell."

Wes came to stand beside me. "What is it?"

"We'll check it out," I said to the dispatcher and flipped the cell phone closed. "Rotten smell coming from an apartment." Wes and I exchanged a look.

He motioned to the girl with his head. "What about her?"

"She'll be fine. Miss Scarsdale knows the score. "I looked at her. "Right?"

She picked up her purse. "I'll take care of calling Daddy."

Wes and I walked to the still open door.

The end apartment seemed quiet as we approached. Two feet away the smell greeted us. At the unit we stopped. I pressed my ear to the door and heard nothing but silence.

The next unit's door opened a crack.

"Hello," a raspy voice called. "Are you the police?"

I held out my badge. "Detective Darcie Devonshire."

"Well that was damn fast." A querulous voice from inside the apartment called. "Never been here sooner than sixty minutes before."

"We were nearby," I said. "Are you who called it in?"

The door opened wider. An elderly man and woman stood there.

"We did," the man said. He held out his hand. "Ralph Rienholt. This is my wife Imogene."

I shook his hand. "This is my partner, Detective Smith."

Wes already had his notebook out. "Spell your last name, please."

Mister Rienholt did.

"When did you first notice the odor?" I said.

"This morning when I took our dog Cakie for her walk. It was foul. I didn't know where it came from, but Cakie pulled me right to it."

"This door," Wes said and pointed.

"Yes, a young Hispanic lives there," Mrs. Rienholt said.

"A gang-banger," her husband added.

Mrs. Rienholt nodded. "Suspicious activity. Lots of coming and goings. Here and that other apartment."

Wes wrote in his notebook again. "And lately...anything else? Loud voices, gunshots?"

Mrs. Rienholt shook her head.

Her husband snorted. "Imogene wouldn't hear anything like that unless she stood in front of the door."

His wife's face colored. "I don't hear as well as I used to."

"And she won't get a hearing aide."

"I'll get a hearing aide when you start wearing glasses," she snapped. "He can't see anything clear more than twelve inches away."

They glared at each other.

"Have long have the two of you lived here?" I said.

"Twenty years come January," Mister Rienholt answered.

"That's a long time," Wes murmured.

Mr. Rienholt grunted. "Things have changed what with all of the gang activity."

"Why don't you move," Wes asked.

"Humph. Now you sound like our kids," Mister Rienholt snapped. "This is our home. We're not letting anybody run us off."

His wife patted his arm. "That's why we formed the neighborhood watch. "Things are better now. We're the captains."

I looked at the two of them. She couldn't hear all that well and he had poor eyesight. How much help where they to the neighbors? I kept my thoughts to myself, but Mrs. Rienholt must have read them on my face.

She touched my arm. "Ralph has fantastic hearing and my visions 20/20. Together we make a healthy person. So don't you worry about us. I figure we'll have our streets back in less than six months."

"Less," Mister Rienholt said. "If you guys pay us a little more attention."

"I'll see what can do about that," I said. "Thanks for your help. Now the two of you better go back inside. You're not going to want to see this."

"Oh. Okay." They stepped back into their apartment and closed the door.

I pounded on the other units door. "Police open up." There was no response so I tried the knob. "Locked."

"I'm taking it down." Wes leaned against the porch rail for leverage.

"Wait," I held out my hand. "I'm calling for back-up."

Before I could dig out my phone Wes and his size-twelve's had smashed the flimsy door off its latch. The dead body smell assailed our senses, strong enough to drive us back.

"Geez," I said placing my hand over my nose and mouth.

I stepped through the door with Wes on my heels.

The place was a mess. The furniture totaled, clothes and papers scattered. In the middle of the room, on top of a mound of kitchen garbage, laid a slight Hispanic man with his neck broken. Multiple burn scars and shallow cuts covered his body. The buff colored walls were splattered with blood.

"Wonder if they got out of him what they wanted?" I backed out of the room. "I'm calling it in. Let the captain decide what comes next." At the door I glanced back. These guys played rough. No wonder Flores was worried about the girl—bloody hell, the girl. "We'd better get back to little Tisa."

We ran down the railing, found the door to Flores' apartment standing wide open. The girl was gone and a panel in the ceiling over the closet had been ripped down and left lying on the floor. "Shit I bet they had money hid up there," I said.

"Damn-it-to-hell," Wes said, charging toward the stairs.

I knew we were too late.

He came back three minutes later. "Some kid saw her get into a blue car. Late model Toyota. Civic maybe."

"Plate number?"

"Are you kidding?"

I wanted to scream. "How could we be so stupid? One of us should have stayed with her."

Wes frowned into the air, but didn't say anything.

"The captain's going to chew us a new one," I said.

"Hey, she wasn't under arrest. We weren't here to baby-sit," Wes replied.

I glanced at him. "How much do you think Flores will give us now that his lady-friend's in the wind?

"Maybe we don't tell him for awhile?"

It tempted me. "No. We level. On second thought he'll probably be even more cooperative when we tell him about his buddy."

Wes smiled. "Yeah, he's going to want his little Tisa to be found right soon."

I reached for my phone. "May as well call this mess in and get the brass on duty."

*****

I closed my phone and leaned my head against the window in Flores' kitchen. All in all the captain had let us off lightly. Wes came through the door.

"They ID'd the body. Francisco Ruiz."

"Flores' Francisco?"

"Has to be. Right apartment. Right name."

I flipped open my phone again. "Maybe she did call daddy. Let's see what he has to say." I got the number from information and punched it into my cell.

They answered on the third ring. "Scarsdale residence. Jerry Waldren speaking."

"I'm Detective Devonshire of the Santa Maria police. I'd like to speak to Mr. Lyndon Scarsdale."

"I'm sorry, but Mr. Scarsdale is a very busy man. If this concerns the campaign you should call the office."

"I said I am a police detective. This concerns his daughter. Not put him on the phone."

"One moment please." I could hear movement in the background and in quick time a voice said.

"This is Lyndon Scarsdale."

"Mr. Scarsdale I am with the Santa Maria police. About an hour ago your daughter said she would call you. Did she call?"

"No. I've been looking for her for months. Is she okay? How did she look...?"

"She was okay. How old is your daughter?

A voice in the background could be heard asking if Theresa was all right.

"She's seventeen. Can we come and get her?"

"We didn't arrest her, we were helping her to return home but she ran. We were hoping she'd called you."

"She didn't. She hasn't talked to us since she ran off with that Flores punk.

"Mr. Scarsdale, your daughter is involved in some nasty business. If she calls or contacts you call us at this number. I gave him the station number and hung up.

"Wes, my loyal partner, that was a waste of time. They don't know anything. Let's get out of here."

*****

I crumpled paper, stuffed it inside the charcoal chimney. Saturday had started off foggy, but the sun had won the battle and now bathed the back yard. The steaks were seasoned, the pasta-salad chilling, and two bottles of cabernet breathing. I twisted the last piece of newspaper, coated it with olive oil, added it to the chimney and then lit it. I waited until the flames died down, then turned and walked toward the kitchen. My guests were due for arrival any minute.

As if on cue Becky let out a bark and charged toward the front door. Passing the hall mirror I took a minute to glance at myself. Red hair in a braid. Check. Green eyes, with dark circles somewhat disguised. Check. Face too pale, but when did I have time to get in any sunbathing, besides I burned like crazy. I smoothed my tee shirt and looked to make sure I hadn't wiped my hands on my jeans...yet. I looked clean and neat. Mum would approve.

"Becky, sit," I said. She looked at me like I'd lost my mind, but she did stop barking.

I opened the door. Wes, Janey and Jackie stood there. Janey held a huge casserole dish. "Where's Miracle?"

"In the car. I thought we'd bring her in through the back gate," Wes said as Jackie kneeled to pay homage to Becky.

"Lasagna." Janey held out the dish. "Needs to be reheated."

"We'll get it in the oven right now. Come on in." I took the dish and stepped back. "You've lost weight."

"Twenty whole pounds. Doing it with Weight

Watchers."

"You look great."

I led the way to the backyard.

Wes zoned in on the Weber Kettle. "What can we do to help?"

I could see it in his face. Me male. Me cook over open fire. I almost expected him to start beating his chest with his fists. He walked to the Weber, glanced into the charcoal chimney. "The coals look about right."

"I'll get this in the oven and bring out the streaks. Jackie, why don't you get Miracle? Make sure you don't let Becky out."

"I'll be careful, Aunt Darcie."

A pang of pleasure made me smile as the young girl walked toward the fence gate with Becky at her heels. Would I ever have my own daughter? Times like this my biological clock ticked loud in my head.

As Jackie closed the gate almost into Becky's nose I heard her call. "Your mom and dad are here. Hey, who's the guy? He's hot."

Hot? I smoothed my hair.

"Jackie, lower your voice," Janey said, but she smoothed her hair too.

"Your folks get you another date?" Wes smirked.

"Didn't I mention Mum was bringing a guest?" I threw a glare at him. "You'd better be on the up and up."

"He will be," Janey said, a threat in her tone.

Wes lifted his hands in surrender. "Hey. Hey. I'll be good."

"They're coming around this way," Jackie called again.

Taking a deep breath, I jogged toward the gate. "Got to grab Becky." I reached it the same time my folks did and hooked my fingers beneath Becky's collar as the gate opened. "Come in and close the gate."

"Nice to see you to, Cupcake, "Da said. Then he grinned and added. "Oops. I forgot no family nicknames in front of strangers.

My face heated

"Don't be silly, Brady," Mum gushed. "Mayo isn't a stranger."

"Mayo Gerardi." said the man, holding out his hand.

I gave it a brief shake. Mayo. He fit him much better than Maynard. "He's a stranger to me," I muttered, looking down at Becky.

Da closed the gate. "You can let her go."

I looked dubiously at the tall, God's-gift-to-women, standing next to Mum. Dark hair, blue eyes, and damn did he fill out those jeans and t-shirt. What the hell was wrong with him that he needed someone to fix him up with a blind date. "Becky's rambunctious."

"I love basset hounds," Mayo said.

His voice flowed over me. Good God. He sounded like Sam Elliot. "Oh? How many do you have?" The question was bitchy of me, but I didn't like my reaction to this guy. Mum threw me a sharp look.

Mayo smiled.

Dimples. He has dimples.

"I was owned by one when I was a kid. With my schedule it wouldn't be fair to have one yet, but when things starting running more smoothly I will start looking."

"I could give you the name of a reputable breeder..."

"No. I'll adopt. Your dad's keeping an eye out for a basset hound at the Humane Society."

"If not I'm sure you can check things out with basset hound rescue," Da added. He sounded very pleased with himself.

"Sure," I said and released Becky. She walked over to Mayo and sat down in front of him. He reached to scratch behind her ears and her tail thumped the grass.

"Darcie dear, you need to chill this fruit salad," Mum said.

I'll take it," Janey said stepping forward. "Mrs. Devonshire, it's nice to see you again."

Becky let out a bark and ran toward the gate.

"Miracle. Down," Jackie's voice commanded.

"That's the newest addition to the family, Miracle," Janey added.

The next few minutes were spent watching the two dogs greet each other. Then the two, along with Jackie, set off to explore the backyard.

"Becky's got an unused tennis ball in that basket to your left," I called. "You can even take it with you when you leave."

"Becky doesn't fetch?" Mum said.

I laughed as I shook my head.

Mayo glanced at me. "When you toss it she gives you the, you threw it away, you go get it, look. Correct?"

This guy really did know basset hounds. "What would everyone like to drink?" I said.

*****

The steaks were a memory as well as the two bottles of wine. I listened as Wes and Mayo argued over who had been the best Forty-Niner quarterback, Joe Montana or Steve Young. Joe Montana, I thought. No one had been better than Sweet Little Sixteen as far as I was concerned.

I stood, picked up the empty casserole dish and walked into the kitchen. This was what the central coast was all about. Not bodies lying in parking lots of apartment buildings. I hated the thought as soon as I had it. No thinking about work. It was understood.

"Would you go out with me?"

The question came from behind me and I whipped around. Mayo stood there "Bloody hell. Don't sneak up on someone," I snapped.

"I walked, I didn't sneak."

I frowned. "Is there something you need?"

"Would you go out with me?"

"Why?"

"I like you. I think it would be fun…and your mother would love it," he added with a grin.

"Yes, she would." We looked into each other's faces for a moment. Why the hell not? "When?"

"How about tomorrow night? Dinner at Steamers in Pismo Beach."

"Sounds good."

He smiled at me, and then turned and went out the patio doors.

A date? Well, here we go again. At least on a Sunday night I could plead an early return home, work the next morning, if things didn't pan out.

I followed him into the back yard

Mum and Janey were still exchanging recipes. It seemed both of them were on Weight Watchers. Becky, Miracle and Jackie were all napping on a blanket in the shade. On the table, next to the patio door, my cell phone went off. Seconds later I heard Wes' unmistakable ring tone. Oh no, I thought as my phone went off. Wes and I exchanged glances as I headed to it.

"Devonshire," I said.

"You wanted to know if anyone spotted the Scarsdale girl," dispatch said.

"Yes."

"Officer called it in. She's at Vista Rio Verde Mobilehome park, space number two-twelve."

"Thanks." I walked to Wes.

He flipped his cell phone closed. "That was Thorne. Our little Tisa's been spotted."

"Vista Rio Verde MobilehomePark," I said. "Let's go." I motioned to Da. "We've got to leave. Hold down the fort for us."

"For how long," Mum asked. Disapproval in her tone.

"As long as it takes," I answered.

"You go Cup...I mean Darcie," Da said. "We'll take care of everything here."

"Thanks, Da." I turned to Wes. "I'll grab my gun and badge and meet you at the car."

"You're blocked in, so I guess that means I'll be driving," he said

I sighed. "Fine, but let's get there before sunrise."

Chapter Thirteen
Sherice Solomon

I stood in the window and watched the car drive away with My Morgan inside. I still stared long after he vanished from sight. My mind played over our last session, his withdrawal. It hurt, after the night we'd spent at the beach. My Morgan seemed to need time and he would have it, but how much longer could I wait?

As if in response to my inward question, the Hunger squirmed inside my stomach. I pressed my hand against it. "Not now. I'm not in the mood to deal with you."

"Excuse me." Came from the doorway.

I whipped around. Walter Granger hovered in the doorway. Hadn't Morgan closed the door? Yes he had. I remembered the final-sounding click, and there'd been no

knock. I felt my face flush. "Oh, not you. Just wool-gathering." I walked to my desk and sat behind it. "Was there something you needed?"

He sauntered forward without an invitation. "We need to discuss your new patients now that you've settled in and Morgan Garrett has left us."

I dug my fingers into my thighs. "Who did you have in mind?"

"Alyssa Crane."

It took me a few seconds to know whom he spoke of, oh yes, Miss Big Boobs.

Walter Granger droned on. "She seems to have a problem with promiscuity. Low self esteem leads to the abuse of alcohol, which then leads to...well, you know. Talking with another woman should help...you know, girl talk."

Of course I knew. I was a much revered clinical psychologist, wasn't I? The framed pieces of paper hanging on the wall said as much. Miss Big-Boobs? I took a deep breath and mentally shrugged. It really made no difference I didn't plan a return to this office. There would be no more time for this masquerade. My Morgan needed me. "How about ten tomorrow morning?"

"That will be fine. I'll drop by her room and let her know."

Drop by her room? Was he and Miss Big-Boobs an item? The snake. "Walt, I'm free tonight. How would you like to have dinner with me? We can come back here afterward and tell Miss Crane together." Dismay clouded his face and inside I laughed.

"Can I get back to you? There's something..."

"A previous commitment?" I forced a sigh. "We can't seem to get our schedules to meet. We'll have to keep trying." I gave him a wide smile.

"What about later? We could have a drink. Perhaps at my place?"

The eagerness in his voice turned my stomach. First Miss Big-Boobs, then me for desert. You greedy little bastard. I could take Arahni with me. He lived out of town on ten acres. No neighbors...his screams could go on for hours. "Sorry, I'm not a night owl. I like to get to bed early."

His eyes narrowed. "It will be only the sweeter for the wait."

Oh God. Did this schmuck deserve to die or what. "I really have to make a phone call now...a consultation with Johns Hopkins. I promised to be available to for special cases. You know how it is."

"Of course, their loss is my gain." He backed from the office.

"Close the door please. I hate people who just barge in." My barbed comment was lost on him.

"Can't have that, can we," he said. "You know, you need a lock on this door. Yes, that would be great, and one for my office too."

I smiled and imagined his slit throat pumping blood across the pristine shirt that no doubt his cuckolded wife had a hand in keeping so white.

He closed the door. I released a deep breath as my gaze went to the place the chest had stood. It was as if it had known I would leave Pacific Winds soon. Karma played such interesting games, so many twists and turns.

I scooped up My Morgan's case file, stood, grabbed my briefcase and walked toward the door. It was only three thirty. I knew Mrs. Iron-drawers at the receptionist desk would glare.

She did and looked pointedly at the ornate clock on the wall.

"Yes, a little early," I gushed. "But Walter...." I giggled. "I mean Mister Granger told me to take of early." I batted my eyelashes. "He's going to show me his favorite restaurant. He says it just reeks of ambiance. Can't wait. Cambria for all of its natural beauty does lack men." I winked at her. "And a lady does need companionship."

Her face flushed as she sought words to condemn me. Before she could find them I sailed by with a wiggle of my fingers in her direction.

*****

I stared at My Morgan's apartment. The complex's architecture mimicked southwest style, tan stucco, with orange tile trim, too common, too tacky for My Morgan. The GPS in

the Mustang had brought me here with ease. It had been hard to wait at my cottage until dark, but for this first visit it was best to go unnoticed. I'd had to slap the Hunger down twice. The trophies in the chest were losing their power to charm. A hunt would be required soon. I frowned. Not without My Morgan. .

We may hunt without the man.

It was the first time Arahni had spoken to me today and I could tell the words came grudgingly. I'd felt her in my head, sullen and pouting, but she'd been stubbornly silent, waiting for me to coax words from her. I hadn't. "I want him with us."

Why? Will I cut any less sharp without him? Will the kill's blood be any more hot upon your body?

"Of course not, but our pleasure will be more with him beside us."

Yours will be more.

"Fine. Mine. I want it...I want him."

You need not please him. The man is not your father.

"You go too far." I pushed her away from me.

A light went off in one room of Morgan's apartment, went on in another.

I focused binoculars on that window. There was still much to learn about My Morgan. How could I be sure he could withstand temptation out here in the big, bad world?

His door opened and he came out. I leaned forward in the seat. My Morgan. My Morgan. He wore jeans and a dark green windbreaker. He didn't glance in my direction as he walked with a fast stride toward a black pickup with a bashed in right-side fender. My heart beat quickened. I hadn't planned to speak with him tonight, but Morgan knew my Mustang. When he saw me, he would stop.

I sat the binoculars aside, fluffed my hair and checked my face in the mirror. I knew what I could say, he should have copies of our sessions together and I had brought them. What luck it was that I still had his file on the seat beside me. Karma again?

His pick-up went by without slowing.

My fingers tightened on the steering wheel. He did not see my Mustang. He couldn't have, or he would have stopped. What had My Morgan so pre-occupied he would drive by me without stopping? I started my car and followed.

He drove by a mall, turned down an alley and then parked behind a squat building. O'Grady's Pub, the sign read. "No. No. No." I pounded my fist against the steering wheel.

"You will not do this. Not to me and not to you." I opened the Mustang's door and scrambled from my seat.

Chapter Fourteen
Morgan Garrett

Paddy had a line-up at the bar so I took the one empty stool left and filled the time by re-hashing the day in my mind.

Driving back to Santa Maria from Cambria, Johnny and I didn't talk much, but it was clear he had something to say and was waiting for the right moment. The silence worked for me too since Sherice was in my head. She'd seemed so intense and I couldn't figure why. Our relationship hadn't amounted to much. Not that it couldn't. The door was open. She'd made that clear. Did I want to walk through it? Damn, why was I even hesitating? She was good to look at, even better to touch. Hell, it'd been such a long time since I'd been in any kind of relationship, not since Darcie, and look how that turned out. I don't think I knew how to be a we, instead of an I.

I felt my guts tighten and I'd learned to trust them. Some time was needed. Who knows with some space I'd forget all about Sherice Solomon, and her me.

We'd turned onto my street. Everything looked the same. Somehow I thought it would be different.
"Your truck is in your garage. Got the front end aligned and replaced the tire. You'll have to take care of the body work," Johnny said as we parked in front of my apartment.

"Hey, you didn't need to do that."

"I figured you'd need transportation. It was no biggie."

"Thanks Johnny. You've been a pal."

He glanced at me for a moment, then reached and slapped me on the shoulder. "I owe you more than I can ever pay. You know that. Let's get inside."

Leaning against the small counter in my kitchen Johnny cleared his throat. "So, you need something to do and I need some help. Are you up to it?"

"Sure for you. Who do you want me to kill?"

He laughed. "Nothing like that, and it's really not for me, so feel free to say no if you don't want to do this."

"You're dancing around Johnny. Lay it all out."

"A golf-buddy of mine is running for the U.S. Senate. His daughter took off with some gangbanger and he wants me to find someone to locate her. He called me in San Francisco and soon as he told me I thought of you. It's your line, and I figured you'd need something to occupy your time. She's here in Santa Maria."

"Sounds good. I'll talk to him, but no promises."

"I'll call and see if we can see him today."

"He's more than a golfing buddy, isn't he?"

"A friend too."

"Are you campaigning for him Johnny-boy?

"No, but I'll vote for him. He's honest and unless Washington corrupts him, he'll do us all some good."

*****

The drive to Santa Barbara had been traffic-free, well traffic-free for the 101, that is. On the way down Johnny had given me some background on Lyndon R. Scarsdale.

The senator-wanta-be was forty-five. Had learned politicking at his daddy's knee. Scarsdale was married, had the one daughter. Anything else Johnny said I needed to see for myself. He knew I worked better that way.

Around two, Johnny drove us up a wide circular drive that ended at a huge double door guarded by white columns.

A man opened up as soon as we rang the bell. Scarsdale I assumed. He was in his forties, tall and trim. Money was obvious, not from the house, but all the antique furnishings inside it.

"Johnny, good to see you. Is this the detective?"
Scarsdale had a well-cultured voice with a little southern twang.

"I'm not a private detective Mr. Scarsdale, but I can find your daughter."

"Good, good. Come in; we can talk in the library."

"This is Morgan Garrett, Lyndon. He's CIA trained and as good as they come."

"What can you tell me Sir to get me started?" I said.

"You don't waste time. I like that," Scarsdale answered. "Theresa Marie lives with a punk in Santa Maria; you can shoot him if you'd like. I want her back. Ramona is never going to have any peace of mind until she is."

Question by question I learned his daughter lived with a gang member named Tomas Flores. He was the grandson of the gardener. Scarsdale didn't know the address, but he knew the area.

"Lyndon, is this the man who will find our Theresa?"

The question came from behind me. I turned. A short, matronly looking Hispanic lady of strong Indian descent stood in the doorway.

"My wife, Ramona."

She walked to me. "I want my baby. Can you find her and bring her home?"

"Yes, ma'am I can. Do you have a recent photo?"

"You can have this one," she said as she turned and removed a picture from a frame on the table behind her. The face in the picture was pretty, although a little thin, her Hispanic heritage evident.

"She is my daughter from my previous marriage." Ramona Scarsdale spoke with a defiant tone. No doubt she and the senator had taken some heat over her first marriage.

Scarsdale moved to his wife, put his arm around her shoulders. "Yes, but she is like my own. Please get her back."

"I'll do my best."

We left right after that.

Johnny dropped me in front of my apartment and headed home. I felt a moment of panic as the door closed behind him. My hands started to shake. I stumbled to a chair and plopped into it. "I can do this. I'm the only one who can." A couple of deep breaths and I'd reduced the feeling of doom to manageable.

I stood, walked to the counter and made myself a cup of coffee. What now? How do I begin? Who did I know? Before it would have been easy to make a few calls, but I hadn't left the Company with many bridges still open. Darcie entered my mind. I wondered how she was. Did she find the right guy, one who could love her more than a bottle of booze?

Then it hit me. Paddy O'Grady would know the happenings in Santa Maria. He could update me on the gang situation, but, a bar and so soon? Maybe I could call him and we could meet somewhere else. The thought galled me. I'd always faced things straight on, until I let alcohol screw me up. It was time to make the acquaintance of the old Morgan Garrett.

Someone bumped my shoulder and jerked me from my thoughts.

"Sorry," a man mumbled, then continued his swaying gait toward the back. He stumbled into two more chairs on the way.

A couple days ago that would have been me, a part of me still wished it was.

I twisted on the bar stool and looked around. I'd never noticed O'Grady's furnishings before. The place looked like a genuine Irish pub. Dark wood, beer signs with pool tables and a taint of cigarette smoke, even though no one would dare light up in here now. The state of California said, no smoking, so you didn't smoke in O'Grady's.

Paddy drew a beer for the last customer and then came to me and smiled. "Morgan me boyo. Where yah been?" He reached for a mug.

"Nothing for me, Paddy. I've been up the coast in a dry out clinic trying to save my life."

He nodded. "Then cola it is?"

"Make it coffee, black."

Paddy turned to the coffee pot.

"I've got myself a case. Need some information. I thought of you."

"A case huh? When'd you become a private dick?"

"I'm not really. Just doing a favor for a friend."

He placed a napkin in front of me and sat the cup of coffee down. "What makes you think I'd be a knowing anything?"

"You keep your ears open and you've lived here for twenty years."

"Twenty-two years, Morgan, me lad. Ten of them behind this bar."

"What do you know about the gangs here in Santa Maria?"

Paddy shrugged. "We have them. And they're growing. I wish to hell they'd remained down south, but that's progress for ye. Keep their violence among their own mostly, but now and then they branch out."

"Looking for a guy named Flores. Tomas Flores. You ever hear of him?"

"Can't say I have. Wait a minute; a cop I know arrested a guy named Flores. The cop's name is Wes Smith. He mentioned it because this Flores had some colleen he was really concerned about, rare in those punks.

"Morgan. What are you doing? This is crazy." The words came from behind me and I turned.

Sherice stood there.

"Sherice? Wha...?

"You can't drink. You know that?"

"Morgan, do you know this lady?" Paddy moved from behind the bar.

"Yeah, Paddy. Look Sherice I...

"No excuses. We're getting out of here now."

"Look Miss, you can't come in here and...." Sherice turned her eyes to Paddy. I'd seen him take on drunks three times his size, but at Sherice's glare he stepped back in silence.

She turned to me, touched my arm. "You can't ruin everything by drinking. You can't."

I held my coffee cup out toward her. "Does this look like booze?" I said. Who the hell did she think she was? Ordering me around? I didn't answer to her.

She looked from the cup and then back to me. Her face filled with color. "You must think I'm some kind of fool, but I went to your apartment...you drove by me like you didn't even see me. I couldn't believe it when I saw you come in here. After everything we'd talked about...your nightmares. The thought of you sliding back into that hole." Her eyes filled with tears.

My embarrassment and anger fled. "Sherice, don't cry. I can see why you thought..." I looked at Paddy for help. Weepy women left me speechless.

Paddy picked up a napkin and handed it to her. She took it and dabbed at her eyes.

"I feel so stupid." She held out an envelope to me. "I thought you'd like to have your files from…." She glanced at Paddy.

"He knows." I took the envelope.

"I'll be going then." She turned away.

"Sherice. Wait. Let's sit down." I pointed to a booth. "Would you like something to drink?"

"A glass of water would be great."

Paddy nodded.

The booth was an old wooden table with high backed seats on each side. The wood stain was old and faded, marked by years of use and abuse.

I waited for Sherice to choose a side and then slid into the other. She still held the napkin and I watched her shred it into little pieces as she stared down at the table in silence. Oh God. She wasn't going to start crying again. That was one thing about Darcie, she didn't cry. I don't think I'd ever seen her cry. In a panic, I looked toward the bar.

"You can relax, Morgan. I'm not usually a weeper."

"You didn't need to drive all the way here to bring me those papers."

"I know I didn't. My place seemed lonely tonight. I thought...after last night...maybe I was wrong. Would you like me to leave?"

Paddy came with her water. "Sherice this is Paddy O'Grady. He owns the place. We've been friends since I arrived in town."

She held out her hand. "I'm very glad to meet you, Mister O'Grady. I'm Doctor Sherice Solomon."

Paddy clasped her hand. "Morgan's friends are always welcome. Sorry about how things..."

"My fault. I shouldn't have jumped to conclusions."

"You're a wee, pretty thing aren't you?" Paddy lifted Sherice's hand to his lips and kissed it.

"And you're full of blarney," Sherice said.

"I promise ye little one. The boyo won't be a gettin' any alcohol from the likes of me."

I groaned. "Hey, no ganging up on me."

Paddy walked away chuckling.

"It seems you've got another conquest," I said.

Sherice looked into my eyes. "Another?"

I didn't know how to respond to that.

She saved me by sighing and shaking her head. "Good God. How stupid did that sound. The next you thing you know I'll be batting my eyes at you."

"Hey, it wasn't...that bad."

"Yes Morgan, it was. I don't know what you've done to me. I keep making a fool of myself. I'm not a sixteen year old with a crush."

I couldn't help smiling. I bet she was real heart-breaker at sixteen. Sherice took the smile wrong.

"Don't you dare laugh at me. This is your fault. I'm a doctor for goodness sake. Not some trembling little virgin. God Morgan. You're stirring up emotions I haven't felt since David was killed."

"David?" I said.

"He was my husband. He died three years ago in Iraq."

It hit me again, how little I knew about this woman. "I'm sorry about that."

"David died doing what he loved. I just wish I hadn't been the one to find his body." She looked away from me.

"Good God," I said. "You found his body? And you're not having your own nightmares?"

Sherice looked at me. "Another doctor helped. A shrink's shrink." She smiled.

I reached across the table, laid my hand over hers. "Aren't we a pair?"

"Yeah, just made for each other." She turned her hand beneath mind, twined our fingers together. "It's scaring me, Morgan. These feelings. I don't want them again." She released my hand and sat back. "Sex was always just fine."

"What?"

"Since David's death I've picked up men, or let them pick me up. I like sex, but it was just a physical release. Not a one touched me here." She pointed at her heart.

"Sherice..."

"No. Don't say anything. It's all too new. We've only known each other a few days. Things are moving too fast." She scooted to the end of the booth and then stood.

"Where are you going?" I said.

"Home. I need time to think." She turned from me.

"Sherice, wait. I'm feeling things too."

"So, what do we do Morgan?"

I stood, reached for her hands. "We could start by having us an old fashioned date. Where I pick you up, take you to dinner and we find out more about each other."

Her fingers curled around mine. "I'd like that. When?"

"How about tomorrow night? Seven?"

She smiled. "You don't know where I live."

"Well then, I suggest you tell me."

"My address is in the envelope along with your files."

I watched her blush.

"Forward of me, wasn't it?"

"I'll walk you to your car. Then just so you know, I'm coming back in here. I've got to talk some more to Paddy."

"I understand, Morgan."

With our fingers linked we walked toward the door.

Chapter Fifteen
Darcie Devonshire

The Vista Rio Verde Mobile Estates lay nine miles from any river and that one dry and the riverbed full of trees. There were two gates. Wes and I went in the back one. He drove slowly as we looked for space number two twelve.

We were on the third role of units when a woman ran out in front of us waving her arms.

Wes jammed on the brakes.

The women leaned in Wes' window. "You're the Cops right?" She spoke loud enough to be heard even over at that dry riverbed. The smell of booze wafting from her was 150 proof. She wore a blue house coat and had big pink curlers on one side of her head. The other side hung wet and limp.

"Yeah lady, we're the police. Now get out of my window and tell me what's the problem?" Wes said.

"Damn punks are coming around here. We don't need no punks. I saw her and she'll have the whole pack of them in here again if she stays. Get 'em out of here."

"Who did you see?" I said.

"That little skinny-ass hussy. The one that hangs out with Flores."

"You know Tomas Flores?"

"Yeah, yeah. The punk was hanging around my granddaughter before Bud run him off. They go visit the slut in number two-twelve."

"All right lady, you go back in your house. We'll take care of this." Wes turned forward.

I called out, "What's your name?"

"Jane Smith," she said and then smiled smugly at the bald lie.

"Let's go." As we drove down the street I looked in my rearview mirror. "Our Jane Smith lives in unit one-o-nine."

"Got it," Wes said.

We approached number two ten and continued past.

"Wes, stop here and let's walk over."

He pulled the car into a parking slot that told us in black letters it was for guest only.

Wes unfastened his seat belt. "I'll cut between and see what's in back."

Unit two twelve held a older-model motorhome. Everything looked calm, still I walked with care. I'd been fooled before. As I reached to knock, Wes moved out from behind a storage shed.

"Nothing back there and this is the only entrance."

I rapped hard enough to shake the flimsy screen door. "Police, open up."

No one responded.

Wes reached over and banged on the side of the motorhome. "Police, open the door."

The door opened a crack. "What'd you want?"

"Open up," I said.

"I ain't done nothing."

I flashed my badge. "We're looking for Tisa Scarsdale, Theresa. Is she here?

"She don't stay. She left."

"Open the door," Wes ordered.

"She ain't here." The door opened wide enough for us to see it was a girl who stood there.

Wes shoved into the room.

"Hey, you can't do that."

"We'd received a tip that you're harboring a runaway," I said.

Wes hustled to the back of the motorhome while I watched the girl. He raised his hands palm up as he came back. "Nothing."

"Where did she go? We know she was here. Where is she?" I said.

"She left. I give her a ten and she left. That's all I know."

The girl looked to be about eighteen, going on fifty. She was dressed in a tight, red bodysuit, with black thigh-high boots.

I handed her a card. "If she calls, you call me."

"Yeah, right."

I took a step closer. "You call. Us having to return here would be a bit of a bother. Understand?"

Her lips formed a pout. "Yeah I get it. Tisa calls...I call you." She tucked the card in her low neckline.

"Let's get out of here," I said.

Wes looked back at the motorhome as we walked away. "Maybe we ought to arrest her on general principals."

"If I thought it would do any good I would. It wasn't a total waste of time though." I held up a coaster from the Metro Club.

"Where did you get that?"

"It was under this note." I read it to him. "Here's one for your collection. Love Tisa. "

"I know the place. It's over on the west side. You want to check it out?"

"Wes, we left some people in my back yard, remember? Barbeque."

He looked at his watch. "Shit. It's after 4:00. You think they're still waiting?"

"I'll call Da."

"And I'll call Janey." He walked a few steps from me.

Da answered on the second ring. "Hey, Cupcake. Everything alright."

"I'm sorry about having to take off. You still at my place?"

"No, we had a piece of cake, and then cleaned up and left. Becky was a trifle miffed at having the gate closed in her face."

"I bet she was. We'll do it again soon."

"You going home now?"

"There something else I need to look at, now that the barbeque is over."

"Yes. Yes, I'll tell her." I heard Da say. "You mum wants you to call her in the morning.

"Will do, Da. Later." I ended the call.

Wes walked to me.

"Everything okay with Janey?" I said.

He nodded. "She's a cop's wife. We stopping by the Metro Club?

"Let's go by the station first. Give our face-face to the captain if he's there."

"Face-to-face. When did that happen?"

"Yesterday morning. Maybe if you'd been…"

"Okay, English. I get you."

I opened the door to the car and got in.

*****

A white manila folder lay in the middle of my desk. Paper-clipped to the front of the folder was a note. You asked for any information about murders with Ice's signature, the note said. It was signed by Dale Hurt from Dallas Texas Police Department. I'd forgotten I'd even called him. The Captain was in his office, but he could wait one minute longer. I flipped open the file. The crime photos glared up at me, the man tied to a four poster bed, blood everywhere and in a close up, the two distinct cuts. Ice's kill. No doubt. I looked at the date. April 1, a little over four months ago.

I opened my desk, pulled out a map and opened it. There were eighteen large, black dots on it and beside each a date. I found the state of Texas. Made a dot next to Dallas and wrote the date and then added the two in San Francisco and the one for Santa Maria. Twenty-one kills in three years. What had set him off? I sometimes wondered if he'd been killing before, maybe in Mexico or Canada. You don't just wake up some morning and decide to start killing people. The dots were all over the place. It seemed Ice showed up on a whim, killed, and moved on

My phone rang. I picked it up. "Devonshire."

"I saw you come in. What news about the gang-bangers?" the captain demanded.

"Wes is in the bathroom. We'll be right there. Then we're on the way to checkout a lead."

"Lead huh? Forget my office. Get the hell out of here." He hung up the phone.

I folded the map, placed it in the desk and closed the door.

There was s sign taped in the middle of the Metro Club's window. Closed because of a death in the family.

"Well damn-it-to-hell," Wes said. "There isn't even a date when the place will be open."

He leaned and peered in through the window. "We could find out who owns the place and track them down."

"Probably not the person we want to speak to though," I said.

Wes frowned. "Then I guess we wait 'til tomorrow and try again."

"Tomorrow's Sunday. I have plans."

Wes suddenly grinned a me. Yeah, me too. Jackie's spending the night at her grandparents place." He sounded delighted. "Janey's got something special planned. And now I can get to it, and her, an hour earlier."

I felt a pang of jealousy. I had my date with Mayo, but I didn't think it would lead to the look of relished anticipation that Wes' face showed.

"Woo-whee," Wes said. "Wally wants some and now he's gotta get some even sooner."

"Wally?" I said, and then it hit me just who Wally was. "Good grief. How crass can you be? And Janey puts up with this?"

Wes laughed. "She's the one who named the big fellow."

I groaned. "Braggin'. Braggin'. Braggin'."

"How about you? Where's mister tall, dark, and Italian,

taking you?"

"Steamers in Pismo Beach."

"Make sure you get a booth by the window. It's much more romantic."

My face heated. "Romance? I'll settle for some good \seafood."

Wes reached and grabbed my hand. "English, folks like us never settle. We deserve only the best.

I squeezed his hand and turned back to the car. "Come on. Let's call it a day. Can't keep your Wally waiting."

*****

I stared at myself in the mirror and then tugged the neckline of the dress higher. I still wasn't sure it was the right choice. You can never go wrong with a little black dress, I heard Mum's voice in my head. It was the same line she'd used when she'd bullied me into buying it. And simple it waS—A long black, stretchy tube with spaghetti straps. I looked down at my exposed legs. And it could have been a couple of inches longer tube. I turned and checked out my back view. It was nice, but I wasn't sure I wanted to share so much nice with a guy I barely knew. My first inclination had been a simple pair of black jeans and a simpler black-silk turtleneck.

It's a sit down dinner, Darcie, not a picnic. Again I'd heard Mum's voice in my head. So I'd opted for the black sheathe. The tube had a built-in bra, so the only thing between me and it were some control-top pantyhose.

I looked with longing at my tennis shoes as I slipped my feet into two-inch, black, patent sandals. Silver and turquoise earrings, a squash blossom necklace to match, add the turquoise and black patterned shawl draped across the back of the sofa, and I was ready as I ever would be.

I frowned at my reflection. I was dreading this evening more by the minute. Why had I agreed to this date? Dating and I didn't mix. It was like blending chocolate with vinegar.

Becky bounded down the steps from the bed and raced toward the front door in full voice. A moment later the doorbell pealed. With a grimace I turned from the mirror.

At the front door I stood for a couple of seconds calming my jitters. "Becky, quiet." She settled, her brown gaze glued on me in expectation. I smoothed my dress, fluffed my hair and opened the door.

The gorgeous man who stood in the pool of white light made my breath catch. Mayo wore black too, form-fitting trousers and a glistening silk shirt. He looked sexy as hell and a trifle dangerous.

He swept a quick glance over me and his white teeth flashed. "We match."

Becky woofed for acknowledgment and he kneeled and scratched behind her ears. "Bella, Becky. Bella."

Her tail beat a staccato welcome against the foyer tile.

"Give her a good scratch and she's yours for eternity," I said.

Mayo stood. "I understand. There's this place between my shoulder blades...."

I laughed. "Would you like to come in?"

"Perhaps later. I hate being tardy for a reservation."

"One minute then. I'll put her highness up." I turned away.

"Come Becky." I thought for a moment she would refuse, but with one last adoring look at Mayo, she walked ahead of me and toward the bedroom. Inside, I gave her a pat, a cookie, and then returned to Mayo.

He'd moved into the living room and stood before a wall of photos holding my shawl. I'd invited him in, but I still felt a stab of irritation at the invasion. "I'm ready."

He faced me. "Will you be warm enough with only this?"

"I run a little hot," I said and then wanted the words back.

He smiled, his dark gaze moving over me again. "Yes, you are."

My heart beat quickened as he moved toward me. A flicker of disappointment followed when he picked up my wrap and draped it across my almost bare shoulders.

In the kitchen the telephone rang and I tensed, waited. Part of me wanted it to be a call out, but Mum's voice came on.

"Darcie, have a nice evening, dear. Call me tomorrow and let me know how things progressed."

With burning cheeks, and. avoiding Mayo's eyes, I turned toward the door. "Let's go. I hate to be tardy also."

The dinner was superb. Grilled salmon with capers and three glasses of chilled Sauvignon Blanc. We'd both passed on dessert.

Now setting beside Mayo in his MGB, my heart started its thumping again. "How fast will she go," I asked, and then hated my breathless tone.

"Speed isn't her thing, but throw her some curves and she responds like a tigress." He glanced at me. "Much like you, I suspect."

I laughed. "I do like a tad bit of speed."

"But Darcie sometimes slow is better. To savor the moment, a suspension in time."

My stomach did a little dip and I licked my lips . "Yes, sometimes taking your time is super too."

"Let me show you," Mayo said and then added, "please."

"What?" I looked at his profile in the moonlight. I'd seen a painting of Michael, the fallen angel, and that is who Mayo looked like. Beautiful and dangerous. I felt a flash of heat.

"Let's go for a ride. The way to Lake Cachuma offers interesting curves."

Before I could respond, he pulled to the side of the road. I watched in bemusement as he put the MGB in neutral, set the hand brake and climbed from the car. In seconds Mayo was sliding the rag top into a compartment behind us.

"You think it's warm enough night for this?" I said.

He slid into the driver's seat. "I'll keep you warm." With a grin he reached and turned on the heater. "Let me know when you are hot enough."

I could only nod.

The little car zipped along south Highway 101. The stars were like diamonds in a black case, the moon huge and white suspended among them. The wind bathed my face and lifting my hair. I wanted to whoop my joy to the world.

The turn off arrived and Mayo shifted down. The MGB growled her acceptance as he took the exit with speed and control. Then we were climbing. With skill, he coasted around curves. The man and car seemed in tune. We didn't talk and I loved the lack of words.

He slowed, pulled to the side of the road. "Would you like to drive?"

"Me? You'd let me drive her?" I was stunned.

He smiled. "I would."

A wave of emotion swamped me. "Not this time," I managed to say. "But thanks."

He looked satisfied at my response. "Yes, there will be other times."

I reached to dial the heat back and saw that my fingers trembled.

"You are feeling just right?"

I hadn't felt so just right for a long time. I nodded.

He reached across and laid his hand across mine. "Would you like to see my home?"

I knew what he was asking. I twined my fingers with his. "I'd love to see your place." I didn't resist as he pulled me toward him. His lips were warm and soft against mine and then grew hotter and harder as the kiss went on. Our mouths seemed to melt into each others. I heard myself moan. With a soft gasp, I broke the kiss, settled back in the seat. Not another word was spoken as Mayo turned the MGB around and pulled out onto the blacktop.

*****

I stretched, savoring the exhausted pleasure coursing through me. Mayo's naked form pressed against my back. I'd be sore for a week, but damn he was worth it.

The bedside clock read three AM. I needed to get home. Becky would be throwing a fit. I worried my bottom lip with my teeth. I was out of practice. What was the proper after-coitus protocol? Emily Post didn't have a Chapter on that. Did I wake Mayo up...ask for a ride...call a cab? Behind me he stirred, pressed against me. I smiled into the darkness. It seemed Mayo was already up. Damn the man had marvelous re-cooping

141

power—m ore than my sore body could handle at the moment. I pushed the sheet aside and stood.

"Stay the night with me," he said.

"Can't," I replied. "You know...Becky." I began gathering my clothes. The pantyhose were a washout...a victim of impatience. "I'll call a cab."

"Take the MG."

"How will you get around?" He looked damned good, his muscled chest bare above the tousled sheet.

"I have a motorcycle, an Indian."

A thought floated to the front of my mind, along with a stab of pain. Morgan and I had planned to buy two of the bikes, restore them and explore from coast to coast. It hadn't happened.

"Darcie? What is it?"

"Nothing." I stepped into my tube of a dress and pulled it up my naked body.

Mayo's groan in response was ego building. "You sure you can't stay, just a little longer. I'll make it worth your time."

I looked at him again, felt a flicker of lust. "No, I can't."

"Then take the MG. You can bring it back tomorrow. I'll fix dinner for you, Italian, my grandmother's spaghetti Bolognaise."

"Sounds great. Then you can show me the rest of you place."

Mayo grinned. "You were impatient to see only the bedroom."

My face grew warm. "Seems the impatience was double-sided."

"Next time it will not be so. I can be a very patient man." His dark gaze moved over me, almost like a touch, and his next words made my knees quiver. "I will be so patient it will drive you mad."

I took a deep breath. "I can be plenty patient myself."

Mayo smiled. "Then we will see who drives whom over the edge first."

I didn't have an answer so I stood in silence and looked into his eyes.

He leaned over the edge of the bed; the sheet dropped and gave me a great view of his ass. When he straightened he held a set of keys in his hand. "Catch."

He tossed and I caught. "Thanks. I'll take good care of her."

"I know you will Darcie Devonshire."

I turned and walked away.

Chapter Sixteen
Sherice Solomon

My Morgan was coming. I had to look perfect. What should I wear? A dress? Yes, a dress. I didn't want to look like a field hand. I'd taken a long bath, shaved my legs and smoothed Warm Vanilla scent over my skin. Wrapped in a bath-sheet I walked to the closet. I'd been told my ass was perfect and suddenly knew just the right dress. I took the ice-blue, silk, slip-dress from its hanger and let it slide over my skin. The dress's high, almost nun-like neckline, looked demure, until I turned. The back was almost non-existent, dipping low to stop at my waistline. The dress' hemline ended right above my knees.

My reflection in the mirror made me smile. The silk hugged my curves like a second skin. Of course no bra, and no panties equaled no panty lines. It needed the perfect shoes. Open toed with at least three-inch heels to show off my legs. I decided on the white, Camilla Skovgaard, peep toe booties. They always drove men wild.

Make up next, not too much, a little gold eye shadow, peach blush and a splash of color with Rum Raisin lipstick. One thing about short hair, it was a cinch to style. I added some extra-volume gel and combed my fingers through it.

144

This morning I had called Pacific Winds, told the receptionist I had the flu and would call when I was feeling better. I heard her outraged sniff as I'd hung up the phone.

The door bell pealed as I misted my body with more Warm Vanilla scent. I drew in a deep breath. My Morgan. With one last appreciative look in the mirror I went to the door.

"Morgan, come in." I stepped forward stretched up and kissed his cheek. "Would you like a drink?" I needed to know his response. His answer wasn't the one I wanted.

"Yeah we have time for a drink. I made our reservation for eight."

"You're going to have a drink?"

"Well, yeah, I expected you to give me cola, or iced tea, or something."

"Morgan, let's just go. I wasn't thinking…It's normal to think you can have just one, to think you're under control, but…"

"It's not giving me that much trouble." He sounded on edge.

I must have looked unsure, because he added. "I'm serious. Now don't worry. You have whatever you want at the restaurant. I'll be okay."

"Oh Morgan, it's like the drunk said, 'I don't drink anymore, but I don't drink any less either.'"

He laughed, but it sounded forced "I said I was okay. Enough about the booze. Did I tell you how good you look?"

I leaned toward him. He opened his arms, enfolded me, his mouth lowered to mine. It was a long, deep, and beautiful kiss. I felt my knees wobble as I pulled away. "If we're going to eat we should leave. Now."

"Somehow I'm not as hungry as I was." Morgan said.

I laughed. "Get in the car and drive." My Morgan, My Morgan.

The garden décor of the restaurant in Cambria was nice enough, not Boston or Chicago, but My Morgan made it enchanting. His palm heated the middle of my naked back as we followed the hostess.

As I settled into the chair across from him, he lifted the large flower arrangement of Stargazer lilies in the center of the table and handed it to her.

"I prefer to look at the beauty I'm with, so place these somewhere else, please."

"Yes Sir. Of course." The woman removed the flowers.

"I love lilies, but not when they block the whole table." I watched My Morgan.

"Tell me what you do like Sherice."

I felt a shiver down my back as he said my name. "I like looking at you."

"And I like looking at you. In fact I'd like to see a lot more of you."

My cheeks heated. "Well of course we'll go out again."

"That's not what I meant." He grinned.

"Oh, Morgan you will see all of me." I'd decided earlier to play coy, so I lowered my gaze.

"I want you right now."

I lifted my foot and ran it up the front of his leg. "Dessert," I whispered.

Morgan smiled. "Heard it said you should have dessert first, in case you're taken before you finish dinner."

"Oh, you will be taken, Morgan, many times." I heard his quick intake of breath.

Two tables away from us someone's cell phone rang. A man answered and began a not so hushed conversation. "I hate that," I said. "Don't you? I keep mine on buzz in situations like this." I looked at him. "Morgan, do you have a cell phone?"

Before he could answer the waiter arrived at our table and begin his reciting of the night's dinner specials. Morgan stopped him halfway through.

"I want a small sirloin, medium rare, and...."

I watched his lips as he ordered, fantasized about them on my breasts, my stomach.

"And the beautiful lady will have," the waiter asked.

"The same, but make my steak rare. And water with lemon."

"Black coffee," Morgan added.

146

He leaned toward me as the waiter walked away. "So, do you want to tell me about David, or would you rather not talk about him?"

"David was the purist thing in my life, but I would rather talk about you. What did you do before Iraq?"

"My assignments were all over, but mostly in the Middle East."

"What did you do for the CIA? Or can you talk about it?"

"The usual. Not so much like you see in the movies though. Then all you see is the glamorous part—not the hours of boredom."

"You had partners?"

"More than one."

"There were other women, besides Darcie."

I felt him pull back from me.

"Darcie was the first and last partner I had."

He didn't want to talk about her. I could see it. I felt a surge of jealousy. He wasn't hers any longer. He was mine. I reached across the table to take his hand.

"I grew up right here in California; how about you?" he said.

A smooth change of the subject. You are clever My Morgan. "I love San Francisco. I just visited there, and before that New York City. Except for the central coast I prefer big cities."

"So where did you grow up?"

"Chicago. My father is a business man. He trained me to rule beside him, but I chose otherwise."

"You're talking about your husband, aren't you? Your dad objected?"

"He did. My father was ruled by a hunger to conquer. It wasn't enough for me. I loved David, and when I chose him over my father's wishes, he cut me from his life." I sipped from my water. "I don't want to talk about my childhood, or my father, although I think he would like you."

"You think so. I've got a pretty checkered past."

Oh My Morgan, to have your naked skin against mine. When we hold Arahni together, all of the other kills will fade to nothing. I licked my lips, and then smiled as I watched his gaze drop to my mouth."Let's save anymore history for later. How are things going for you in Santa Maria? You notice I have not asked what you spoke to Paddy about."

"That's good. Because it's a job. My client wants major confidentiality."

"What? No pillow talk."

"I'm more of an action guy, than a talker."

I felt heat flare in my core at his words. The waiter came with my water and I drank half of it before placing it on the table. A pianist began to play, Moonlight Serenade. "I love that song. It's not jazz, but..."

"You like jazz?" Morgan interrupted.

"I love it."

"I like the Blues, give me some Billie Holiday and I'm a happy guy."

We spent the time until our steaks came discussing the likenesses of jazz and blues.

*****

I sat back with a satisfied sigh and blotted my lips with the napkin. "Very nice."

"Good steak."

The waiter arrived at our table. "Dessert? We have wonderful caramelized custard with whipped cream."

My Morgan and I exchanged a quick look.

Sounds great, but we'll pass," Morgan said. "Just the check."

In the car I asked again about a cell phone. Instead of answering my question, Morgan pulled me close and kissed me, fierce and desperate. His tongue probed, met my own. When we separated he whispered, "I want you."

"I know. I want you too."

The short drive to the cottage was eons too long.

As we entered my front door Morgan reached for me, but I dodged and moved deeper into the room. "There is soda and juice in the fridge. Help yourself while I get comfortable." I backed into my bedroom while Morgan stared at me in confusion. It's okay My Morgan soon we will be one.

Earlier I'd planned to change into an enticing thing I had with waist-high slits, but staring into my full length mirror I decided on a better plan.

I stepped into the living room, paused at the door, waited as Morgan turned. His face showed the shock I'd intended.

I wore my peep-toe heels and nothing more.

As Morgan stared, a smile slowly worked its way onto his face. "You are beautiful Sherice. Absolutely beautiful."

He moved toward me, lifted me in his arms and carried me into the bedroom. We both went down on the bed in a heap. His mouth came for mine. His passion pressed against my thigh. As his hands explored my body, mine pulled at buttons and zippers.

At last we were both naked. Hot skin slid against skin. Lips and tongues touched while fingers danced, teased aching flesh. I heard moans and gasps, unable to tell whose mouth they came from. Then he entered me, and my breath caught in my throat. Never had I felt this, the connection. Not only physical, but behind my closed eyes our two auras pulsed and twined.

I rode the passion, matching him thrust for thrust. My hands, gripped his shoulders, urged him to even more speed. Morgan pulled me tighter against him. It seemed our bodies were one from navels to knees. He pressed his lips against mine. I felt him tense and then he was spilling into me. I joined him at the pentacle a second later. My cry escaped our joined mouths. Shudders rippled through me...I couldn't stop them. I tore my mouth from his and gasped out his name.

Morgan relaxed on top of me and I welcomed his weight. His heart drummed in time with mine.

"That was...that was..."

I smiled as he searched for words. "Yes, it was."

He lifted himself above me and I snaked my arms around his neck. "Where do you think you're going?"

"I'm too heavy..."

"No. You're just right." I lifted my legs, wrapped them around his waist and pulled him deeper inside.

"Sherice, I'm not a kid anymore..."

I urged his mouth down to mine, teased his lips with my tongue until they parted. He groaned and stirred inside me. I unlocked my legs, pressed my feet against the mattress, lifted my hips and thrust against him.

"Dear God," Morgan whispered against my lips.

"Morgan, you are as young as you feel...and you feel very young to me."

His mouth smothered mine...and there were no more words.

I woke to the sound of the shower. I reached across the bed to find only cold empty space. No, My Morgan. I am not ready to let this end. I kicked the sheet aside, stood. His jacket hung from the back of a chair. Something heavy weighted a pocket. I looked inside. It was a cell phone. Morgan did have one. Why hadn't he told me so when I'd asked? Maybe it had to do with his mysterious client. No matter. I wanted the number, for emergencies only of course.

Glancing toward the bathroom door, I quickly dialed my own phone. Waited, listened as my voice mail kicked in, and then deleted my number from his phone. With a satisfied smile, I padded toward the bathroom.

Inside the door I walked into a curtain of warm mist. I heard Morgan humming off key above the rush of running water. I opened the shower door and stepped inside.

Morgan looked at me in surprise.

"Good Morning. Would you like me to wash your back?" I said and turned to close the shower door.

"Uh...sure. Hey, what's this? You've got a tattoo."

"You didn't notice it last night? Do you like?"

"It's a black widow."

I smiled. "Why, yes it is."

"Are you a black widow?"

"Not hardly. I just like spiders. If I had a pet it would be a spider."

"A black widow?"

I laughed. "I was thinking more of a tarantula."

Morgan shook his head. "No butterflies or roses for my girl. Sherice, you are like no woman I've ever known."

"Is that bad?"

"I don't think so."

I reached around him for the sea sponge, added body shampoo and worked it into a white froth. "Lucky for you I'm into aloe. Can't have you smelling too pretty." I stepped close, made sure my nipples grazed his body as I reached and ran the soaped sponge along his spine. His tensed, turned to face me. My gaze dropped. He was hard and ready. I fondled him with my free hand. Morgan groaned, lifted me and I wrapped my legs around his waist.

The water flowed down our bodies as I matched him thrust for thrust. My fingernails dug into his shoulders. I eased the pressure, watched blood fill the crescents left behind. It mixed with the water and moved downward, a pale pink wash. As the watery blood circled the drain, I climaxed. I arced my body as pleasure raced through each nerve. Oh God. How much better it would be when we washed the blood of our kill from each other. It would happen. It had to happen. I would make it happen.

"Sherice, what is it?" Morgan demanded.

I couldn't speak until the shudders subsided. "I've wounded you," I gasped.

Still holding me, he turned his head and looked at his shoulder. "Good God, girl. You are some wild woman."

"You make me so." Morgan released my hips and I lowered my feet to the shower stall floor. I looked up, laughed into his face. "I don't know if my legs will hold me."

He gripped my waist with his hands. "I've got you."

"Never let me go, Morgan. Never."

He laughed. "I won't."

I'm holding you to that, My Morgan. You are mine...forever.

Chapter Seventeen
Morgan Garrett

On my way out the door to visit Paddy, I passed the hall mirror and caught myself grinning ear-to ear. What a night. I'd never had a woman draw blood during sex, not even Darcie.

After the so-called shower, Sherice had doused the small half-moon circles with peroxide and then coated them with triple antibiotic ointment. Young, she'd called me. Maybe, but young enough to meet her needs? And Sherice did seem a little needy, at least last night. Okay, hell. I was a whole lot needy myself.

I pushed thoughts of Sherice to the background. I had a job to do. I needed a connection in the police department, and Paddy O'Grady was introducing me to the guy I hoped would be it.

Driving into the parking behind the bar I felt my stomach crawl with anticipation and it had nothing to do with talking with Paddy. I wanted a beer. I could almost taste it. Shit. Why was I doing this to myself? I could meet Paddy elsewhere, he'd even offered. I knew why. It plain pissed me off that I'd let booze take control of my life. Lack of control was a weakness and I hated weakness, especially in myself. Macho bullshit, Sherice would call it. I didn't care. The booze wasn't going to win. I got out of my truck and slammed the door.

"Morg me boyo, how's your day?" Paddy set a glass of coke front of me as soon as I settled on the bar stool

"Paddy you don't have to pump soda in me just because I can't drink." My voice came out sharper that I intended and he gave me a hard look.

"What would you have Lad? Coffee? It's fresh made."

"Yeah, coffee."

He dumped the coke into a small sink and then poured me a cup of coffee.

"Did you talk to that cop you know?"

"I did. He's meeting us here in about ten minutes."

"Yeah? He agreed?" That surprised me. My past experiences with local cops had shown me they tended to be closed mouthed and not eager to talk to an outsider.

"Yeah, surprises me too. Wes must have his reasons," Paddy said.

We talked about football as we waited. I thought maybe he would bring up Sherice, but he didn't and so neither did I.

The door opened and a tall, lean, guy wearing tan slacks and a dark brown shirt came in.

"Detective Wesley Smith," Paddy said as way of introduction.

"Call me Wes."

"Sorry no donuts," Paddy said. I could tell by the exchange that it was an ongoing thing between them.

Wes grinned at him. "That's okay. I'm watching my waistline."

"Morgan Garrett," I said. "Can I buy you cup of coffee?"

"I'm not allowed to take drinks from civilians, but if a cup showed up in front of me I'd have to drink it for politeness you know."

Paddy placed coffee in front of Wes before he finished speaking.

Wes looked at me, at Paddy for a moment and then back to me. "Two Irish policemen were sitting at the bar when one says, I'm dying, Pat. Pat, shocked says, what can I do Mike? Mike answers. Pour a bottle of good Irish whiskey over me grave, when I'm gone. Pat places his hand over his heart and

replies, sure and I will, but can I filter it through me kidneys first."

"No Irish jokes. Bar rule." Paddy gave the cop his sternest look.

I laughed.

Wes faced me. "So what can I help you with?"

"I'm looking for a girl." I watched his face to see how he reacted to that.

"Who isn't? 'Course I'm married." Wes smiled.

"Not that kind of girl. A Santa Barbara big shot has lost his daughter and I'm lending him a hand."

Wes remained silent, waiting for me to go on.

"Paddy tells me you just picked up a guy named Flores and that he had a young girl with him."

Wes took a drink of his coffee. "Yeah. What does he have to do with your girl."

"I was told she was living with a guy named Flores."

"What's her name?"

"Theresa Scarsdale."

Wes nodded. "Yeah, it was her. Going by Tisa though."

"Where is she now?"

"We just wanted Flores, so we didn't take her in. But he wouldn't deal unless we offered his Tisa protection. Was damn sure his drug connection would hurt her. We went back, talked to her. Then got a call and had to split. When we got back to her, she'd run on us."

"Any idea where she went?"

He hesitated before answering. "Had a lead, checked it out, but we've hit a dead in."

"Has Flores said anything?"

"Not since we told him we lost her."

"You want to give him to me for an afternoon?"

Wes looked at me for a couple of long seconds before saying, "Man I wish. Say, what is your background? Ex cop?"

"No, I had a government job."

"You mean one of those where if you tell me you have to kill me?

His question hit to close to home. I studied the mirror behind the bar, stalled as I looked for the right answer. The light coming through the small pane in the door reflected off the glasses and reminded me it was still daylight and I had a lot to do. "No, just a pencil pusher." I could see he hadn't for one second bought my lie, but I couldn't help that. "Well, I got a girl to find. You still holding this Flores?"

"Nah, we cut him loose. Keeping eyes on him though. If he leads us to his Tisa, we're picking her up. My take is he cares for the girl and he'll talk to keep her safe."

"How about his address?"

He didn't answer. I saw him working it over in his mind. What would giving me Flores' address get him? What did he want? How could I sweeten the deal?

Detective Wes Smith made his decision. He pulled a notebook from his shirt pocket. Wrote on a page and handed it to me.

I took it, wondering what I'd need to do in the future to earn it. I thought about asking and then said instead, "Thanks for the help. If I find out anything I'll pass it on."

"Yeah, you do that."

Back in my truck I decided to drive over to Flores' and see what was to see. Maybe it'd go down easy and the girl would be there with him.

I pulled the truck to the curb in front of some apartments and cut the motor. At the apartment door, I knocked. No answer. No noise came from inside. I could pick the lock, but I'd seen more than one curtain move as I'd walked past, so it was back to the truck.

Twenty minutes later I still sat. The street had been empty the entire time. Didn't these people ever leave their homes? What kept them trapped inside? It was boring as hell, reminded me of my first year with Darcie as a partner. We'd pulled every shit detail that came in.

I surrendered to a yawn. There hadn't been much sleeping going on last night with Sherice and I had to keep myself from drifting off to dreamland.

I was ready to call it a waste when a pair of teens came from a house across the street from the apartments. We spotted each other at the same time.

They finally gathered up enough courage to start toward me. I grinned down at my legs. Kept my eyes lowered as one of them tapped on my window. He tapped harder. I looked up.

The kid who'd tapped was big, maybe eighteen, with blue tat marks showing above his collar.

"Hey, I dun never see the cop in a peek-up."

"That so?"

"Why you hangin' here? Get movin'."

"Taking a nap," I said.

"You nap elsewheres."

He moved his loose hanging shirt aside and showed me a gun handle sticking from the waistband of his droopy jeans. Stupid way to carry a gun. I hoped he had the safety on…better yet, I hoped he didn't. No sense letting idiots screw up the gene pool even more.

I looked up and down the street. It remained empty. There were probably eyes watching from the curtained windows, but what the hell. Maybe they would enjoy the show.

I slammed the door open. The frame caught the kid across his brow and drove him back out into the street. He didn't go down, but was dazed. His other buddy back-paddled like crazy to a lamp post a few feet away. I climbed from the truck, grabbed the tire iron I'd had resting beside me. "Now, lets you and me have a little talk," I said standing over him. "I'm looking for Flores and his Tisa. Seen them?"

He blinked up at me. "Huh?"

The kid was as bright as a dark moon. "Tomas Flores. He lives right over there. I pointed at the apartment.

"I dun know nuttin."

"Wrong answer." I slammed my foot into his right knee. He screamed.

The guy across the street took off at a run. I only had minutes before he'd be back with reinforcements. That wasn't enough time. I lifted the tire iron. "Get the hell up and into the truck."

"I ain't going nowhere 'ith you."

"I can cave your head in right here and no one will do a damn thing except maybe throw me a party. Not get your ass up, and maybe you'll live to lie about this."

Mister Tough Guy looked around the empty street, then stood, wobbled his way to the right seat of my truck and got in.

I u-turned and took off.

Heading south I saw what I needed...a dark alley. I stopped, put the truck in park. "Now my friend; let's talk."

"I dun talk to yoo. I got rights."

"No, actually right now, you don't. Where's Flores? You tell me and you walk. You don't tell me and we do the other knee."

"I can't walk. You broke my leg."

Reaching across I slapped down on the injured knee. "This is a knee, Einstein."

"God damn, shit." He screamed, fumbled with the truck handle. "You can't do this."

"What happened to your accent?"

"I was born here," he gasped out. "It helps with the gang."

"Flores. Where is he?"

"The cops took him away. Tisa split. That's all I know."

Using my right hand I came down on his knee again. His scream almost blew out my windows. I jumped out of the truck, ran around to the right door, jerked him out and then pushed him to the filthy blacktop. "Okay punk that's all the slack you get. They cut Flores loose. I know he must have been back to his place. Now where'd he go? Is the girl with him? You tell me, or the other knee goes right now. Your choice."

"I...I don't know. Yeah, I seen him, but we didn't talk."

"If we keep this up you'll never walk right again. Which will it be?"

"Tomas was alone. That's all I can tell you."

I turned, walked back to the driver's side.

"Hey, you can't leave me here. I need a doctor," he yelled as I climbed in.

"Yeah, you do." I started the truck and drove away.

Chapter Eighteen
Darcie Devonshire

"English. English. You in there?" Wes' amused words jerked me back from fantasy land where Mayo was doing some mind-boggling things to me.

"What?" I slapped the file in front of me closed.

"Have your sex daydreams on your own time," Wes said and then grinned.

My face heated. "Is there something you wanted?"

"Things are slow. Thought I'd take Janey to lunch."

We were at a dead end and Wes hated waiting. I got it. I didn't like waiting for another door to open either. There was still no word as to when the Metro Club would re-open. We'd checked, new the owner was some guy out of Chicago. The manager, Sam Tyler, was in Italy attending his grandfather's funeral.

"You go back to fantasizing about Mister tall, dark and Italian."

I shot a glower at him. He just laughed as he turned away. It irked me that he had it right. I felt like a greedy kid, too long denied candy, then offered a whole box of chocolates. Slow down, I'd told myself. But I didn't seem to be listening. The telephone rang. "Detective Devonshire."

"Detective Riley Shoels, from Napa police department," a hoarse voice said.

"Yes."

"You'd put it out that you'd liked to be kept informed on any knife homicides."

I sat up straighter in my chair. "You've got one?"

"Last night. A slice across the throat...blood everywhere."

Bloody hell. Ice had moved on to Napa.

"You think it's your guy?" Shoels said.

"Sounds the same. I'd like to see for myself."

"I can fax..."

"No. I'll come there. Tomorrow if it's okay with you."

"You want this guy bad, huh? I want him to. You don't pull shit like this in my town."

Napa was a six hour drive, if I kept things in the vicinity of the speed limit. Wes...I skidded to a halt in mid-thought. No, not Wes. Mayo. A night away in a B&B. I could get Da to pet sit Becky. My hormones went into overdrive at the thought of wine, cheese, chocolate and maybe some whipped cream. We would see whose patience crumbled first. I squirmed in my chair.

"Devonshire, you still there?"

"How about eleven o'clock tomorrow?"

"I'll meet you at the crime scene." He rattled off an address.

"Repeat," I said and then, "I'll be there."

I could feel a thirty-six hour flu bug coming on. I'd have to tell Wes the truth. He wouldn't like it. He'd still probably offer to come with me, but would understand when he heard Mayo was in the mixture. Combining business with a whole lot pleasure. What more could a girl ask for?

*****

The Beamer accelerated by a Cadillac, a Ford Truck and a red Mazda, before I cut back into my lane. I could have taken the blue Camry too before the approaching semi was upon us, but hey....

Mayo looked relaxed as he stared out the passenger-side window, a whole lot different than Wes' white-knuckled response would have been. My good feelings about him intensified. Mayo had jumped at the chance for some time away

in Napa. Mum had been ecstatic when I explained why Becky needed to stay the night. "Don't go making wedding plans yet," I'd warned.

The B&B was in Saint Helena and had a cancellation. We'd be in the Eden Suite, away from the main house. A perfect place. That way no one would hear Mayo scream with pleasure.

Packing had taken me three hours which was stupid, since most likely we wouldn't be wearing many clothes.

I glanced across at the Beamers dashboard clock. It read ten AM, thirty minutes ahead of schedule. I couldn't remember the last time I gotten out of bed and the house before five AM when I wasn't working a case. Knowing how early I'd be up, Becky had been left at Mum and Da's the night before.

Mayo had suggested we spend the night together, but I'd passed. This weekend was going to start out with me getting a full night's sleep, which wouldn't happen if we were in the same room.

The stretch of Highway 101 had flown by as we'd talked about everything and nothing. We both liked 60's rock and roll and had sung along with our favorites, me a little more in tune than him. We'd stopped in Soledad for latte's and a bathroom break and then hit the road again.

"We're ten minutes out from Napa. Feed the address into the GPS for me, please," I said.

He did. Minutes later the GPS' voice kicked in with her first directions.

We were led to a single-story, rambling ranch house and I felt a hollow let down. No way was this an Ice kill. He didn't do private homes.

I pulled up behind a tan sedan, cut the BMW's engine. "Be right back."

"Can't I come in with you...see you work?"

"Won't be working. This isn't my guy."

He shrugged. "Too bad. I bet watching you in action would be a turn on."

"Don't worry. You'll be turned on."

"You first," he said.

I opened the door and got out. My expectation had turned to exasperation at time lost for a homicide that wasn't mine.

The door opened as I reached it. Detective Riley Shoels was a black version of Wes, tall, thin, dressed in tan slacks and white and brown plaid shirt.

"It's not Ice," I said by way of greeting.

His dark eyes narrowed. "Just like that?"

"Ice uses motel rooms." At least most of the time, I thought. "Is there a four poster bed inside?"

"A king-size one, no posts."

I felt a surge of irritation. Didn't he know anything about Ice's S.O.P?

"Well since you're here, you want to take a look?"

No, I didn't...but professional courtesy and all that rot. "Sure."

He led the way down a narrow hallway, past a den, living room and kitchen. The hallway forked and we took the one to the right. It ended at a huge master suite. I didn't spare the brown and gold decor much time.

The king-size frame held only the mattress. Three, maybe six-inch wide, bloodstains, were in its middle. Another stab of irritation came. This wasn't a lot of blood, nothing like the photos and the mattress from the B&B in Santa Maria. "What do you know?"

He reached into his shirt pocket and pulled out a notebook. "Got the call nine in the morning, Wednesday. Maid found the body. The deceased is Mrs. Elizabeth Krycheck. Time of death midnight, give or take an hour on either side." He flipped a page. "A knife used, but no weapon found as of yet. No prints. The only trace from the husband, Cameron."

"What does he say?"

"At his office all night...alone." Detective Shoels grinned.

I raised an eyebrow.

"Says the cleaning guy might have seen him. We're checking it out." He flipped his notebook closed.

"It's not Ice's kill. Not enough blood. I'm betting the knife wasn't the c.o.d. Tox screen?"

"Don't have it yet." He surveyed the room. "Sorry I got you here for nothing. I guess I wanted it to be an out-of-towner."

I shrugged. "No harm done."

Detective Shoels turned toward the bedroom door and I followed.

Back in the car, Mayo gave my face a long look. "So?" he said.

"The husband did it. "

"Just like that?"

"Most of the time it is. My take is he drugged her, then when she couldn't fight back he cut her throat. I'm betting she died from a drug overdose, not the knife wound." I turned the key and the Beamer purred to life. "No more talk of work. We are hereby on vacation for the next..." I glanced at the clock. "...twenty-four hours."

"Come here," Mayo said, leaning toward me. I met him halfway and felt the sizzle down to my toes as we kissed. He sat back, satisfied and smug judging by his expression. "Just want to start the vacation off with a positive note."

I pulled from the curb. Saint Helena seemed an hundred miles away instead of twenty.

*****

Mayo snored beside me. Lust stirred at the sight of his broad expanse of brown back above the pink and white duvet. Damn girl, I thought. You are one greedy bitch. Let the guy sleep; maybe get a little food into him.

Our discarded clothes marred the room's romantic ambiance, but hey then, hadn't it done its job? I stretched. We'd made supreme use of the bed and the floor for that matter. It was nice of them to provide a, Do not disturb, sign.

We had to head back today, so maybe we would try out the breakfast beforehand. My gaze slid over three empty bottles of champagne, two cans of whipped cream and a half-full bag of chocolate kisses. Yep. I made him moan and become extremely impatient. My face heated. But I'd been right there moaning along with him.

The sun streamed through the cracks in the blinds. Today was the second time in six years I'd waken in bed with a man. Maybe Mayo was a keeper. God knows it was time to let

Morgan go. If it hadn't been for the boy and the booze...I shoved the thoughts away. Sometimes shit happens.

I shifted and Mayo's hand stroked my knee.

"Where you going beautiful," he asked. His fingers crept upward and I gasped. To hell with breakfast.

*****

"You all well?" Wes said, as he stopped in front of my desk.

"Fit as a fiddle."

"Must be, judging by that stupid grin I just saw." He admired his fingernails. "Thought maybe you'd call when you got in."

"It was late. Captain okay? How're things here?

"Didn't seem none the wiser. As for me, I'm feeling fine." He smiled. "Jackie slept over at a friend's. Wally's exhausted and satisfied."

With a shake of my head I said, "I can't believe you Yank men name your penis."

Wes roared laughter. "That's good one, English, using yank, men and penis in the same sentence."

I glared at him.

He managed to get himself under control and then said, "Not all of us. I'm sure. Should we take a poll?" Wes turned from me. "Hey Vick..."

I punched Wes in the stomach hard enough to stop his words. "Inquiring minds do not want to know."

Vick shook his head at us as he walked out of the room. Wes watched him. "He'd have a good name for his...maybe Reginald."

I groaned and then noticed Wes held a flier in his hand. "What's up?"

164

"Janey's making me do this and I want someone else to join me in my humiliation."

Wes handed the paper to me. It was the annual, Take A Cop To Lunch, charity drive for SHARE. The thing was, we didn't get taken to lunch, we served the lunch. This year it was at The Fish Shanty in Arroyo Grande. All the money from the meals we served would be donated to SHARE. It happened Wednesday. The shifts were usually two hours.

"Okay, I'm in."

He grinned, pulled his phone from his belt loop. "I'm telling Janey before you change your mind."

My attention shifted back to my desk. Nothing new about Ice. What was going on there? Had he headed back east? Wes hung up his phone.

"We're both doing the mid-day shift, twelve to two. The Fish Shanty is going to be hopping according to Janey. Wear your running shoes."

"Okay." I glanced around the nearly vacant squad room.

"Things are sure quiet around here this morning. You got any appointments?"

"Nothing that can't wait. Why?"

"Thought we'd go make a call on the Metro Club. See if they'd re-opened."

"Nice idea, Partner. Let me grab my coat."

Chapter Nineteen
Sherice Solomon

The Hunger awoke me with its hard, demanding ache. I pressed my fingers against my stomach and willed it to ease. It no longer surprised me how it never completely abated. Sated, it would lay low, sometimes for days and then erupt in a demanding and driving force.

"No," I said. "Not yet. Morgan must be guided slowly. He isn't ready."

You were ready when first we met. Perhaps he is not the one.

"I was born ready, and yes Morgan is the one." My stomach cramped and I drew my knees to my chest and groaned. "It hasn't been that long. Only three days. We will hunt soon."

The knots eased and I stretched my legs. The sun shone brightly, but my world felt cold. I wanted Morgan beside me when I woke. I'd accepted his leaving last night, had clamped my lips against pleading words. What was the mysterious errand that had to be run so early?

I reached for my phone, looked at the number I'd entered for his cell phone, but then scrolled to his home number instead. The phone rang ten times before an answering machine kicked in.

"Garrett. Leave your message."

"Morgan I miss you. Last night...there's so much I want to say. Call me." I hung up the phone, kicked the coverings aside and stood.

The Hunger nipped again. I wouldn't be able to keep it leashed much longer, and the truth was I didn't want to. How could I please both, the Hunger and My Morgan?

Naked, I walked to the chest. My beautiful Arahni was my physical connection to the Hunger. I opened it, lifted the shafra from her wrappings and trailed her sharp edge along my stomach. She felt both hot and cold.

"I'm never totally alone. Not when I have you, my beautiful one."

She did not answer and I knew she was pouting.

"Did you feel as I did last night when we were with our Morgan?"

Not ours. Arahni snapped. *Yours.*

"You had to have felt my pleasure. You are part of me. I've never felt like that, never."

Her answer came...sly." Not even when praised by your father?"

A wave of anger flooded through me. I had never blocked myself from Arahni, but she'd gone too far. I pushed her into the back of my mind and slammed the door. From a seemingly far distance I felt her shock. I placed the shafra back into the Chest. "Yes. I can do so. I've always been able to do so. You will learn who is in control."

I walked back to my tumbled bed and hugged the pillow My Morgan had used close to my heart. I drifted into sleep and into the dream.

A tall woman, wearing a cream colored, flowing linen gown, one golden shoulder bare, stood beside me. Arahni. So this was her response to my blocking her from me. I tried to wake, but couldn't.

Around us was nothing but pure white space. I wore only my Loubotin silver sling backs. Arahni lifted a bowl toward me. Inside of it blood flowed restlessly from side to side. My gaze locked with hers, I dipped my palms into the warm blood, rubbed it across my breasts, down my stomach. Arahni dipped her head toward mine; our lips touched...the jarring ring of the phone jerked me from the dream. I fumbled for my cell phone. "Hello."

"Sherice, I got your message. I've been thinking about you too."

My Morgan. His words made the chill inside me evaporate.

"Then I will see you tonight?"

"Sorry. Can't make it tonight. I've got to meet someone."

"Who?" I heard my jealous tone and wanted the question back.

"Can't tell you anymore. It's just work. I've got to go. I'll call soon."

"Morgan, when...?"My answer was a dial tone. My shoulders trembled. The day had stretched before me, a cavern of aloneness, and now the night would be no better. Tears pricked my eyes.

Stop it. Arahni's command rang in my head. She had broken through my wall. *You are never alone. I am with you always. Remember?*

My gaze went to the chest.

We were one before the man. We will remain one when the man is no more.

"My Morgan will join us."

The man will never be one with me.

"My beautiful one, you will not accept him?"

There was no answer. My knees shook. I wanted Morgan, but I wanted both. Life without Arahni, like before? I caught my reflection in the mirror, could see a woman with a panicked expression. She looked weak. That wasn't me.

The man turns you into one who waits for his convenience to serve. I will be slave to no man. I am a queen!

"I serve no one.

You quake at the thought of a night without his guidance.

I rushed to the chest, flung it open. "Shut up. You don't understand," I shouted at the shafra.

The Hunger knocked me to my knees. On the floor I curled into a ball and shuddered. What would my father say at seeing me in this pathetic mess? His fiery daughter reduced to a whiny, clinging, vine. "No." I sat up. "We will hunt."

The pain in my stomach eased. Arahni's euphoria filled my head. "First we must go to Paso and buy rope."

*****

The girl stood in a wide space at side of the road. She held a sign that read, Homeless and hungry. Please help. God bless. The Hunger jumped in eagerness. "So easy? Karma?"

Yes. Her. I want her.

I drove by, pulled into a parking lot a block away. An internet search had given me two hotels in Paso that had what we required. If either had a room available, then it was ordained. I flipped open my cell phone and dialed.

The first hotel I called had the two rooms. The clerk was chatty. It seemed no one wanted rooms with four poster beds. What with that crazy serial killer in California. Any fool would know that he stuck to big cities. I agreed wholeheartedly and then booked a room for Bradford Smythe. I hung up, called back, listened to his spiel again, and reserved the other room for Cynthia Clark.

My hair was dark for the hunt, in a chin length pageboy, my eyes the warm brown of the Kentucky whisky my father so loved. I wore a pink jogging suit. In the back seat, my suitcase waited, Arahni and the virgin rope inside.

The drive to the hotel was a short one. Suitcase in hand I registered as Cynthia Clark, received my key card and took the elevator to the third floor. Twenty minutes later, salt and pepper haired, Georgia Smythe, picked up the key card for her and her husband, Bradford.

Georgia and Bradford's room was also on the third floor, five doors down from Cynthia's.

I caressed Arahni and placed her in the top drawer of the nightstand. It had been an hour since we'd driven by the girl. "If she waits, then it is her destiny. If not...then we will hunt."

The girl stood in the same spot. I pulled in and stopped beside her. She walked to my window as it lowered. "Would you care to join me for lunch?"

She looked startled. "Say what?"

"I don't give money, but I will buy you lunch."

"Uh...okay."

"Grab your backpack and get in. Is Italian okay with you?"

"Yeah. Sure."

She strolled to her backpack picked it up, walked around the car and got into the passenger seat.

"Seat belt," I said. "What's your name?"

"Amy...Amelia Rose."

"Beautiful. You're named after your grandmother."

"How did you know?"

"It sounds old...like a family name. My name is Cassandra Josephine....my grandmother's name."

I put the car in gear and pulled into the traffic. The Italian restaurant was close by. We were in-between mealtime rushes so had the place to ourselves. It was dim inside with red and white checked tablecloths. In the middle of each table sat an empty Chianti bottle with a candle sticking out of it. Prints of the Italy countryside decorated the walls. The woman who took our orders seemed miffed that we'd interrupted her quiet time. Amy ordered spaghetti and meatballs. I ordered lasagna. We both drank iced tea. Amy had tried for a glass of wine, but couldn't produce I.D.

I waited until she reached for pepper and then reached at the same time. My hand covered hers as I watched her face."You have beautiful eyes," I said.

"Thank you." Red flushed her cheeks.

I released her hand and sat back. "How did you become homeless?"

"I left." She twirled spaghetti onto her fork.

"Parents too strict?"

Amy held my gaze with hers as she took a small bite, chewed, swallowed and then slowly licked her lips. Arahni hummed in my head in reaction. This girl knew the way things were going.

I picked up my glass, sipped tea. "Where are you sleeping tonight?"

She shrugged. "Not sure. Something usually comes up."

"Would you like to share my hotel room? There's only one bed..."

"That sounds great."

The toe of her boot slid along my calf. "Let's get out of here," I said.

*****

The Hunger writhed and I felt Arahni vibrating in expectation, as I put out the, Do Not Disturb sign, closed the door and turned the dead bolt lock. I faced Amy. She stood in the middle of the hotel room, looking around. "Would you like a glass of chardonnay?"

"I'd love one." She came toward me, her cheeks flushed.

"Why don't you take a shower? It will be better that way."

She stopped, pouted. "And put these nasty things back on?"

"No," I said. "I'll find you something of mine...eventually."

Amy smiled. "Okay. Would you like to join me?"

Yes! Yes! Arahni screamed inside my head.

"Maybe later. After. Right now I'll open the wine, bring you a glass in the shower."

"Sounds great." She began to unbutton her blouse, then coyly turned away from me and walked into the bathroom.

I waited until I heard her turn on the shower before I opened the vial, added the GHB to her glass and then filled both to the rim. I gazed at the bed side table as I swirled the wine. In my head Arahni purred while in my stomach the Hunger waited in coiled need. I carried the glass to the bathroom. "Amy, here's your wine."

Her body was a dim outline seen through the translucent shower curtain. Her hand came out from behind it and I placed the glass in it.

"Don't be long," I said.

I heard her laugh. "I won't be. You sure you don't want to join me?"

"Next time." I felt Arahni's displeasure as I walked from the bathroom and closed the door behind me.

You have the man. She is for me.
"Patience."

As Amy completed her shower, I removed my clothes, then walked to my tote bag and pulled out a black pair of stiletto heels.

In front of the window, I sipped wine, and watched the cars flow by below. I heard a soft gasp and turned. Amy stood in the bathroom doorway wrapped in a white towel.

"Cool tat. I've thought of getting one. Black widow. I like it."

"More wine," I asked and crossed to the table where the bottle waited.

"You're beautiful," she said, coming toward me.

When she stopped, only inches from me, I reached and undid the towel. It dropped to the floor. "And you're clean and smell divine." Her small breasts rose and fell with her quick breathing. I noted her pupils had already dilated. It wouldn't be long now. The Hunger quivered inside my stomach. "Let's take the wine to the bed."

Amy walked to the bed and I followed carrying the wine. She stretched out on the brocade comforter with practiced ease. Her head fell back, and her eyes closed. I sat the wine down, walked to the tote and pulled out the length of rope. As I turned toward the bed my cell phone rang. I flipped it open, looked down at the number. It was My Morgan.

No. Arahni screamed.

"Hello," I said.

"Sherice, I'm cutting my meeting short. To see you. Can I come by later?"

My Morgan wanted to be with me. "When?"

"How about ten? I know it'll be late..."

"You'll stay the night?"

"And then we'll have breakfast together," he said. "Maybe even have us another shower, without the bloodshed this time though, okay?"

"Yes Morgan, come tonight, but I'm not making promises about the blood shedding, you do that to me...bring out the animal hunger."

I heard him laugh. "Maybe this time I'll draw first blood."

I'd never had that happen, gave my own blood. What would that be like? A mixture of pleasure and pain. "Get her sooner if you can, Morgan. I'll be waiting."

He hung up.

We will take her. She is mine. Arahni cried.

I turned toward the girl on the bed. I walked to the side table and pulled out the shafra With the blade in my hand, I walked to Lilly. I leaned toward her—and then stopped. No. This is not what I want. My Morgan must be with us.

Arahni shouted her rage, as the Hunger dug its claws deep into my guts. Pain made me moan, my vision grayed at the edges. "I control. You do not," I gasped. "He will be worth it." I battled both of them, Arahni's shrieks and the Hunger's bite. "I'll give you this," I said. With Arahni I made a short, shallow cut along Amy's upper thigh. Blood flowed. I dipped my fingers in it and rubbed the blood on my breasts. The Hunger quieted, but Arahni's anger only grew. "I control," I said again and closed my mind against her.

Oh, My Morgan you must join us...and soon.

Chapter Twenty
Morgan Garrett

I walked into Paddy's and was greeted by the sight of Wes and the barkeep balancing beer bottles on their chins like frat boys at a toga party. As I walked up, Wes lost his bottle and looked sheepish for a moment.

"So what are the children up to here?" I looked at Paddy first and then Wes.

"You had to be there to appreciate the deal," Paddy said setting a cup of coffee on the bar for me. "He should have known better than make a bet with me on bar stunts. I got lots of experience."

"Okay, okay," Wes said as he laid a five spot on the bar. "Just don't ever tell Janey I was betting money on stupid shit like this."

I shook my head as I crawled on a stool. "You said on the phone you had something for me."

"Yeah. We cut Flores loose. He should be leaving the department in about twenty minutes."

"Why'd you let him go?"

Wes took his time answering. I could tell he had something else on his mind so I waited.

"He's not who I want. I want Juan Carlos. I have some info, but I don't have probable cause to touch him. Worse, he's not in our jurisdiction."

I could see how this was going. "How can I help with that little issue?"

"I tell you where he'll be, you bring him here and he's ours. Simple."

"Why can't you give him to the boys-in-blue where he is?"

"The sleaze-bag is mine. He's been the cause of too many deaths in Santa Maria the past six months." Wes looked down into his empty coffee cup and then up and straight into my eyes. "You, on the other hand, don't have any legal restrictions."

I understood. "So when do we do this?"

"You can pick up Juan Carlos tomorrow. Thursday is his regular time to be at the rest stop at the Gaviota tunnel. He drives a big red truck. They tell me he's pretty flashy."

"So you think he'll just smile and climb into my truck?"

Wes grinned. "I figure with your pencil-pushing background you'll figure something out."

I grinned back at him. I knew he hadn't bought that lie. Several possibilities about the drug pusher had all ready come to mind, but first Flores and hopefully the girl.

*****

Flores hustled out of the police department. He didn't look right or left so it made it easy to tail him. All I had to do was lay back and keep him in sight as he hoofed his way south on Broadway. The man's actions were stupid. Whatever had his tidy-whities in a wad had killed his survival instincts.

In the Newlove area he went straight to his old apartment.

Damn. He didn't have her. He was still looking for the girl.

I watched from the street as he went it. Ten minutes later he came back out—still alone. Flores went five units over and pounded on that door. The door only opened a crack, making it impossible for me to determine who opened it.

I heard voices, and then one louder than the other. "Okay. Okay, take the damn car."

Flores turned and left at a run by way of the far stairs. He ducked around the row of garages. I started my truck and drove down the street to the lot behind the garage. I arrived just in time to see him slam the door on an elderly Honda Civic. Well, this would make things more interesting.

Following the old Civic, I kept my distance as he turned left onto Main, heading east. Where are you going fella? Give me a clue.

He drove just like he'd walked. I could have been right on his bumper and he wouldn't have known. He must have found out where Theresa Scarsdale was. Stupid. Stupid. What if you're leading someone right to her, like me?

He drove into the parking lot for some dive called the Metro Club, and continued to the rear. I parked in the front and made my way on foot. Peering around the corner of the building, I was surprised to see him pulling out a key. He opened the rear door and went inside. I looked around before sprinting to follow. At the door I freed my SIG Sauer, eased in, and found myself in a dark hallway. Voices came from down the hall and light spilled out of an open door.

"Tisa, come over here."

If the speaker was Flores, his voice shook.

"She'll come over when I say she come over. Sit down." The order was followed by a loud slapping sound and a woman's shrill scream.

Get your hands off of…." The shout was cut short by the slamming of a human fist hitting flesh. I'd heard the sound enough times to never mistake it.

Shit. I jumped through the door yelling, "Freeze."

The five people in the room did, their gazes fixed on my gun. One was Flores, the other the girl, so the three remaining had to be the threat.

We were in a store room. Wood crates lined one wall, an old couch stood beneath a grimy window. The place smelled of old beer and sweat.

"Down on the floor."I motioned to the three with my gun.

I guess one had a death wish, because he leapt at me. I fired; hit him high up on his left leg. As he hit the floor, the larger of the other two gave it a try. I clipped him behind the ear with my gun and he joined the other idiot on the dirty cement.

"I glared at the last one. "You want to try something?"

"Jesse's bleeding bad." He pointed to the guy I'd shot.

Shit. He was bleeding like a stuck pig. The girl I assumed to be Theresa Scarsdale, was clutching the seat of her wooden chair in complete panic. No help would be coming from that direction. Flores bled from his mouth and a gash on his forehead. I motioned to the guy who still stood. "Then do something about it."

He didn't hesitate, which told me he'd done this before. He pulled the bleeder's belt free, wrapped it around the leg and pulled it tight, maybe too tight since the guy screeched like a little girl.

"Theresa, get up and come over here by me," I said. She sat there, frozen in place. "Theresa, move, now," I repeated louder.

Like a zombie she stood, walked toward me and stopped beside my back. "I'm taking you home to your mother and father."

She remained quiet. I turned toward Flores. "Let's go, unless you've got some more partying to do?"

"What about Jesse?" The skinny one still kneeling said.

I pointed to a wall phone. "Call 911." Somehow I doubted he would.

Outside, I pointed down the building. "The black truck's mine. Get her in it."

So far, so good, but I knew it wouldn't last. At the truck's door, things changed.

"I'm not going anywhere with him," Theresa shouted. She glared at me. "Who the hell are you?"

"Name's Garrett. Your daddy hired me to find you."

"Right. Then what's my father's name?" she demanded.

"Lyndon Scarsdale. He's running for state senator."

"I'm still not going with you."

"Yes, you are." I waved the gun.

She stomped her foot. "I'll be out of there again by tonight."

"That's their problem, but I'm taking you home."

177

Theresa turned her back on me. "I'll be back. You know where," she said to Flores. "I've got the money. We can go to Mexico...."

Flores shook his head. "Juan Carlos, his reach is long."

The girl took a step toward him. "He won't find us, and even if he does, you can..."

"Shit's happened," Flores broke in. "Things change."

"I don't understand. What's happened? What's changed?"

Flores looked straight into Theresa's eyes. "I've got to be free. Can't be tied to no one."

I watched the girl's face grow pale. "We love each other. We're going to..."

"I'm going. You'll slow me down." Flores looked at me. "You're wantin' just her, right?"

"Her daddy said I could just shoot you," I answered. "You stay away and he'll be cool about it."

"No," Theresa cried. She reached a hand toward him. "It's me and you, together."

"Shut-up, girl," Flores snapped. "You never know when to shut your mouth. It's Tomas this and Tomas that." He looked at me. "She one hot number beneath the sheets. Maybe you try her before you give her to daddy." He turned back to the girl. "You blow 'im and he might keep you for awhile."

"You son-of-a bitch," Theresa screamed and then grabbed for my gun.

I twisted, blocked her with my shoulder. "Enough of this soap opera," I snapped. "He used you. Life's a bitch. Now get your ass in the truck."

She glared at Flores. "You'll pay for this. You think Juan Carlos was bad. You just wait." Theresa whipped around and circled the truck. I shared a look with Flores. Pain etched his face. "It's the right thing to do," I said.

His head jerked in a nod, before he turned from me.

I climbed in the truck, started the engine and entered the flow of traffic.

*****

Theresa huddled in the truck as far away from me as she could. She kept her head turned, but once in awhile I heard her sniffle. Love was such a bitch. Flores had made the right call. Maybe a year or two from now the girl would get it.

We were almost to Gaviota before she spoke.

"What am I going to do?"

"Go home and try to get your life back on track I suppose. What do you want to do?"

"Doesn't make any difference. Mom and Lyndon don't give a shit. What they want is all that's important." Out of the corner of my eye I saw her glance at me. "You know I'll run away again."

"Maybe so. But there's no future with a bunch of gang-bangers."

She said nothing more until we reached the house. A man stood on the front steps talking to Scarsdale. He was a slight built Hispanic, neat and well dressed. He turned, faced me for a brief moment, before hurrying to get in a blue sedan.

"Theresa?" Lyndon Scarsdale said, coming toward us. He pulled the girl in for a hug, then pushed her back and looked into her face. "Are you okay? We've been worried sick."

I could tell from his tone Scarsdale meant each word.

Theresa, stupid kid that she was, pulled away from him and stood stiffly. "Where's Mom? Might as well get the joyous home coming totally over with."

I heard a shout and looked up in time to see the front door slammed open. Ramona Scarsdale ran down the steps. She stopped in front of her daughter. Looked her over from head to toe—and then slapped her face.

"Ramona," Scarsdale began.

She turned on him, held up her hand for silence.

Where Theresa had been stoic with Scarsdale's greeting, her mother's slap opened a dam of tears. "I'm sorry, Mami. I'm so sorry. I didn't think you'd care where I was," the girl babbled, tears running down her face.

"You stupid, stupid child," Ramona Scarsdale said. "You are my daughter. I love you. Of course I care, we both care." She opened her arms and Theresa stumbled into them.

That was my clue to get out of there. I turned away, started toward my truck. Scarsdale's voice stopped me.

"Mister Garrett, I'd like to talk to you."

"Okay sir, but I've got several things pending. Could I come by tomorrow?" I had promised Sherice I would make it to her place tonight and I didn't plan on being late. The senator-to-be look startled. I guess he wasn't used to being put on hold.

"Well, I suppose so. I have a meeting in the morning and a rally in the afternoon. Come by about noon. We can have lunch and talk."

"That'll work for me. I'll be here at 11:30."

I continued to the truck, got in. In the rearview mirror I watched mother and daughter, arms wrapped around each other's waists, walk up the stairs. Maybe they would work it out. I started the engine and drove away.

*****

Sherice's cottage looked like something from a fairytale. I hadn't paid much attention to it with my first visit.

Light glowed in the windows. I'd told her ten and it was only eight. I hoped she wouldn't mind.

I got out of the truck, walked to the door and rapped on it. Nothing. I knocked again. Still nothing. Wasn't she home? I felt a surge of disappointment. Where was she? I walked to a window and peered in. Just then Sherice entered the small living room, wrapped in a towel. She must have been in the shower. I stepped back from the window. I didn't want her to take me for a peeping-Tom.

I knocked on the door again.

A couple of seconds passed and then, "Yes?"

"It's Morgan."

"Morgan. You're early." Sherice opened the door. She smelled like lilacs. Her wet hair was a dark-red cap. Her cheeks were flushed from the shower? I felt myself grow hard.

"I'm not ready for company," she said, stepping back.

"Finished early. I guess I should have waited until...."

"No. No. Come in. It won't take me but a minute or two to dress."

"Why?"

"Excuse me?"

I stepped in, closed the door behind me. "You look good right now...except you're wearing too many clothes."

"You think so?" She smiled, and locking my gaze with hers, she shrugged her shoulders. The towel fell to the floor. "Better?"

"Much," I said, reaching for her.

*****

Sherice smiled. "If I was a canary I'd be singing."

We lay together on her bed. "I aim to please, ma'am."

She stretched. "I feel joyfully pleased." Sherice rolled away from me and then stood.

"Where you going?"

"I'm famished. Aren't you?"

I sat up, bunched her pillow beneath my head. "I could eat."

Her gaze moved slowly across me. My God. Did she want to give it another go? I felt myself stir.

"Food first," she murmured. Sherice turned from the bed. "It won't take me long. I'm thinking scrambled eggs with cheese and onions.

I kicked the covers aside. "Let me help."

"No. You stay right where you are, just like you are. I'll bring you a plate." She smiled. "Who knows, I might even feed you, Master. You know, peel me a grape, slave."

I grinned. "Master. Slave. It brings all kinds of thoughts into my head."

"So I can see," she motioned with her hand.

"Not that head," I said. "This one." I touched my temple.

She came to me, leaned, and for one too short minute, pressed her mouth against mine. "I like both of your heads."

I grabbed her hips and tried to pull her down on top of me, but she twisted away with a giggle. "No, we'll get to that, but first I insist we eat. Have to keep up your strength."

"My strength is up." I protested.

She turned her back on me and then swayed from the room.

181

I stretched and smiled at the ceiling. A man could get used to this. Scorching hot sex and then being served food in bed. I heard her moving around in the kitchen. Drawers opened, closed. A faucet came on. I lasted about a minute more. I'd never been good at lying around. Okay. I'd stay out of the kitchen, but the living room hadn't been named forbidden territory.

I stood, thought about putting on my boxers and then shrugged. If Sherice was comfortable in her birthday suit, then so was I. It was time I knew some more about this woman.

In the living room I looked around. Not a dang clue anywhere. She'd told me the cottage came furnished, and except for one ornate looking chest, I'm sure what I could see had already been here.

Sherice had said she and her husband had lived in Iraq. Was the chest from there? I walked to it. It looked more Asian than Middle-Eastern. I ran my fingers across its lid.

"What are you doing?" Sherice's sharp question came from behind me.

I turned. She stood in the doorway, a strange expression on her face. "This is a beauty. You bring it back from Iraq?"

"The only thing that came back from Iraq with me was David's body." Sherice came to stand beside me. "I found this at an estate auction, or maybe I should say it found me." She touched it reverently. "There are keepsakes inside. Maybe someday I'll show you."

"I'd like that. We need to know more about each other."

"Yes, Morgan. I want you to know everything about me."

Sherice had tied a frilly apron around her waist and she'd put on some shiny, red shoes, with high, narrow heels. Where'd she found the shoes? She hadn't been wearing them when she'd

left the bedroom. Did she have shoes stashed all over the place? "Well one thing I know," I drawled the words out. "I sure like the way you dress."

She smiled. "I'm kinda fond of your outfit also." She reached, wrapped her fingers around my jutting hardness. "I

182

told you to stay in bed." She stepped back, gave a little tug and I followed meekly.

We sat, cross-legged, facing each other in the middle of the bed. A platter sat between us. It had been full of scrambled eggs and true to her word, grapes. We hadn't bothered to peel them, but we had taken turns feeding them to each other. It was heavenly torture.

"How's Paddy?" she said.

"If that's your way of asking if I've been back to the bar, then yes I have and he's fine."

"Morgan, is that wise? I know you're strong, but..."

I held up a hand and she stopped in mid-sentence. "It's hard, but I can handle it. Paddy and I needed to do some more talking. He's helping me out with some work."

Sherice combed her fingers through her hair. I liked the way it made her breasts rise and fall. "Is that where you were today?"

I shook my head, but didn't add anything else.

She frowned. "You can't say anything about it?"

"Client prefers it that way."

"Will it always be that way, Morgan? You can't talk about what you're doing?"

I shrugged. "It's whatever the work requires. Not much different than your work, you can't talk about what a patient says in therapy. Can you?"

Her lips tightened for a moment before she answered. "Of course not."

"Hey, I just remembered something. I don't know if you'd be interested." I leaned and grabbed my pants. Inside the back pocket was the flyer Wes had given me. "The Santa Maria police department's having this charity thing where the officers serve food to the public. It's Wednesday afternoon. You have to buy tickets. I thought...."

Sherice took the paper from me. Read it quickly. "You'd like the two of us to go?"

"Thought it might be fun."

"I'd love to." She reached behind her for the phone. "I'll call right now. Who is this Janey Smith?"

The wife of the guy who gave me the flier. He's a cop friend of Paddy's."

Sherice punched in the number. Waited and then. "Janey Smith? I was wondering if there were still tickets available for the police officers luncheon? There is. Terrific. I'd like to get two. Where can we pick them up? Thank you. We're looking forward to it." After giving Janey her name, Sherice hung up the phone. "We can get them at the restaurant on Wednesday."

I scooped up the last of the eggs, chewed, swallowed. "It should be fun."

Sherice rapidly blinked her eyes and alarm bells went off inside me. "Hey, what is it?"

She sniffled. "I'm just so happy. I never thought I'd have this again."

"Yes, it's all damn good. I don't see how it can get much better."

"Oh no, Morgan, It can be better yet," Sherice said softly.

I picked up the platter, laid it beside the bed. "Then show me woman. Show me how it can be better."

My words had an effect I hadn't expected. Sherice sat back. Her gaze shifted toward the living room. Then she looked at me. "Soon, Morgan, soon. For now this will have to do." She reached for me.

*****

The rest stop at Gaviota was quiet. A couple of big rigs and a car pulled away as I drove up. No sign of Juan Carlos or anyone else.

I felt pretty pleased with myself. I'd stayed the night with Sherice and we'd showered and she'd brought me breakfast in bed. It had been hard to pull myself away, but at nine thirty I'd said goodbye with a promise that I'd pick her up at eleven on Wednesday for the police officer event. She didn't ask any

questions about what my day held and that left me feeling positive. Maybe this would work.

My luncheon with Scarsdale had been profitable. He wanted his people checked out, both who worked for him, and those who wanted to. I accepted his offer and we'd shook on it. I'd spent the rest of the afternoon going over a stack of dossiers

Tonight I was doing this for Wes, like we agreed upon, then I would be all Scarsdale's.

I only had a ten minute wait before the first buyer pulled in. A low rider with four young men slumped low, their heads just showing. Next came another low rider with only two punks.

I was parked at the opposite end of the rest area with two eighteen wheelers between me and the action. Great for hiding, but I couldn't see a damn thing past the entrance. There was no choice. I had to get closer.

I moved back through a stand of trees to a position that gave me a view without exposure.

From here I easily saw when the big red F-250 pick-up arrived.

The group of four in the first car climbed out, three of them gathered at the front of the low-rider. One of the punks was on crutches and I laughed softly. The driver walked slowly toward the big truck. The lights came on and nailed him like a deer on the highway. The lights went off and he walked forward again. I watched the exchange of paper bags through the window of the truck. I couldn't determine if our friend, Juan Carlos, was alone or not.

The four in the low-rider sped away and the driver of the second car went through the same procedure, the lights came on and he moved forward. This time Juan Carlos did get out of the truck and the light when the door open showed a second guy in the passenger seat. The crew cab could still hold a couple more in the back seat.

"Holy shit," I murmured. Juan Carlos was in the light from the truck cab for only a moment, but it was long enough for me to see he was the same man I had encountered on Scarsdale's front steps. The big time drug dealer was one of the senator's main people?

Inching closer I stopped at the last tree before the pavement started and then ran at an oblique angle to the back side of the truck. I still didn't know how many were inside. With gun in hand I worked my way forward to the side window. The backseat was empty. In front of me, the passenger door opened.

A bruiser of a man swung out. I aimed at his head. Not the way I wanted to play it, but if he turned....

"I gotta piss, Juan, be right back."

"You need to cut back the Corona, Amigo. Hurry up. I want you here when the next group arrives."

"Yeah, sure." He lumbered forward without looking back. The big guy had to be taken out, but quietly. I didn't want Juan Carlos to panic and drive off.

I backed away, turned and ran to the wooded area. I made my way to the restrooms and flattened against the wall. The guy coughed. I went in. He stood with his back to me. I greeted him alongside the back of his head with the butt of the Sig-Sauer.

He went down with a grunt, tried to get up. I tapped him again. The bastard still tried to rise so I hit him harder, and that time he stayed down.

Now for Juan Carlos.

I walked from the rest room. My target still stood in front of his truck looking down the highway. This was too easy. I came up behind him. "Okay Juan Carlos, stand right there and don't try anything."

He whipped around, they always did.

"Who the hell are you?"

"Your worse bad dream; and you don't know the half of it."

"You can't touch me. You got a badge?"

"I don't need a badge. I have you. Turn around put your hands on the hood."

He glared for a moment before saying. "I have friends. Your ass is dead." He turned and placed his hands on the hood. Patting him down I found a Colt 380 at his back.

"Walk toward my truck. It's back at the rear." I said and pushed the barrel of my gun into his spine for good measure.

He walked.

At my truck I said. "Open the door and hand me that roll of duck tape."

I saw him tense. Shit if he ran I'd have to shoot, not what Wes wanted. Then he reached for the tape. Holding the tape he grinned at me. He's wondering how I'm going to pull it off, tape him up and still hold the gun on him. My answer was a love-tap alongside his head. He fell at my feet, still grinning.

I made quick work of securing his hands, feet and mouth, and then dumped him in the open bed of my truck. I drove across the lot and then parked alongside Juan Carlos's rig. I hated leaving mine behind, but knew Wes would want any evidence in his. I didn't waste any time throwing him in the back. I had to be out of here before his next customer arrived.

I had just started the engine when a highway patrol cruiser came in. Shit. I put the truck in first gear and drove away.

I spent the next five minutes with my gaze more on the rearview mirror than out the windshield, but when no flashing lights chased me down, a deep breath gushed from me. I sure the hell was using up my luck tonight.

Seeing the ridge ahead of me that dropped into the Santa Maria Valley; I called Wes on his cell phone. "Hello there, this is your anonymous friend. I have a package for you and a few surprises. We'll all be in the parking lot at Big Joe's, as we planned."

"Hot damn, you did it."

"You sent me down there and thought I couldn't do it? Oh ye of little faith."

"No I di…well, I'll call my partner and be right there. You going to stick around?"

"I had to drive his truck so you could have all the evidence. You've got to take me back to mine. "

"Shit it will be awhile. You wait in Big Joe's, have a coffee. I have to shake my partner out."

"How are you going to explain him all taped up? You need to get here and get the tape off before you call your partner."

"Tape?"

"Yeah, I had to subdue him a little."

Seated by the window drinking coffee I watched Wes handcuff Juan Carlos just as a SUV parked next to him. A woman got out and walked over to stand beside Wes. There was something familiar with the way she flipped her hair, but I couldn't place it.

She looked down at the suspect and picked a short piece of tape from his pants leg. She shook the tape at Wes and asked something that caused him to shrug his shoulders. Then the parking lot exploded with Police cars.

*****

The driver to the Gaviota rest stop gave me a chance to brief Wes on the connection I had uncovered between Juan Carlos and the potential senator. "Scarsdale may or may not be involved but it's for damn sure Juan is living a double life. I'm meeting the senator tomorrow and maybe I can learn something." I thought of the woman I'd watched through the window, something about her still nagged at me. "Looked like you and your partner were having a disagreement."

Wes shook his head. "It wouldn't be the first time. English is very opinionated, but I'd trust her with my back over anyone else at the station."

"It's the only partner worth having."

Wes glanced at me. "What happened with you at your last job?"

I grimaced. "It was all me. I made some mistakes, a lot of them. We parted ways."

Wes dropped me off by my truck and drove away. Just for shits and giggles I checked out the rest room. The goon was gone. I didn't know if he'd had some help from the police officer or not, and I didn't much care. The last couple of days had been good ones and I found myself humming as I started the truck and drove from the rest area.

*****

I didn't get much sleep, but I made it back to Santa Barbara the next morning in time for my meeting with Scarsdale.

The door opened before I could get my finger off the bell. There stood the senator-to-be, smiling and taking my arm. Not letting go, he led me into the study.

"Ava, bring some coffee, please."

"Yes Mister Scarsdale. It's already made."

"Sit down Morgan, sit down."

Taking in the room, I could see a well decorated study, with one wall covered with books. From the few I noted it was clear the senator-to-be had eclectic reading taste. I saw both Robert B .Parker and Shakespeare on the book shelves. Spencer would like that.

"Morgan, is it okay if I call you Morgan?

"Sure," I said taking a seat in front of the large desk. Scarsdale stood there, idly spinning a floor mounted globe.

The maid entered with the coffee, started to pour, but he waved her out. "Morgan, I have an immediate problem that needs your skills. I have a member of my staff who may be taking money."

"Who was the man at your door when I was here yesterday?" I said.

"It's funny you would ask. He's the man I need you to look into."

Now that was an interesting development. If he wanted me to check on Juan Carlos it wasn't likely he knew about the drug connection. "Is he important to you right now?"

"I picked him for my local campaign because I was told he has some regional influence, however his actions have caused me to suspect something is wrong."

I smiled. "Wrong may be an understatement. Have you ever heard of a drug dealer called Juan Carlos Sebastian?"

"Yes. Charles Gomez, the man I want you to check out, has mentioned him."

I shook my head. Old Juan Carlos was a cool one. "Juan Carlos Sebastian and Charles Gomez are the same person. He was arrested last night and is now in the Santa Maria jail."

"Well I'll be damned."

Chapter Twenty-One
Darcie Devonshire

Waiting for my toast to brown, I thought about last night at Big Joe's Diner. Wes had been strange on the phone. He hadn't wanted to tell me anything. I was just to get my ass there. Driving in I'd seen a crowd of blue uniforms hovering around a big red pick-up. I'd joined them in time to see Wes cuff a slight built Hispanic. A piece of duct tape had been clinging to the guy's pant leg. You didn't have to be a rocket scientist to figure something wasn't adding up.

"Wes, what the hell's going on here?" I demanded.

"English, meet Juan Carlos Sebastian, drug dealer and Flores' supplier."

"Where did you get him?" Before Wes could answer, two more squad cars drove up in full assault mode; lights on and siren blaring.

"Take him," Wes said to one of the officers. "My partner and I'll be right there to book him."

"Sure thing, Detective." They led the man away.

Wes turned to me. "The captain is going to love this one."

"What the hell is going on? Where did you get this guy?"

"I got a tip he'd be here."

"And you didn't call me?" I interrupted. "Not a word? Bloody hell. You're pulling something."

Wes looked like he was going to lie some more and then held up his hands in surrender. "Okay, okay. I traded some information with this guy I met at Paddy's."

"Who's the guy?

"Just a guy, Darcie. Jeez give me a break. We got a good bust here. There's shit in the truck; the guy has bags of money. He was dealing. Ease up will ya?"

The other guys were listening and grinning, so I let it go. "Okay let's go book this creep."

At the station we'd discovered Juan Carlos was really Charles Gomez and that he worked for Lyndon Scarsdale.

My toast popped up, and I mulled it all over again as I smeared it with butter. There was more to this than what he'd told me last night. I had questions for my dear partner and he jolly well had better be giving me some answers.

*****

Wes was in the break room, I wanted some alone time with him so I said. "Drove by the Metro Club. It's open again. Maybe we can get a line on Scarsdale's daughter."

"Why? We've got Juan Carlos?"

"You don't think he can get to her from jail. And we did promise Flores we'd protect her."

"Yeah, guess so, but, we don't have to worry about her anymore. She went home yesterday."

"What? How did that happen?"

"The guy from Paddy's picked her up and took her home. He works for Scarsdale."

"So he works for the, would be Senator and he also put you on to Juan Carlos, AKA, Charles Gomez?"

"English, it was more of a trade and the less you know about the details, the less you'll be involved. Now stop asking me about it."

I could see Wes was completely serious. He was trying to keep me out of something he was afraid might be touchy if revealed. Just what kind of deal had he made with this guy from Paddy's? I knew he wanted those gang-bangers bad, but bad enough to cross the line? Or make a deal with someone who had no qualms about doing what had to be done no matter what? We exchanged a long look. I nodded my head, flipped my hair out of my collar. Okay. We'd play it his way...at least for a while longer. "I still think we should check that club."

Wes stood, grabbed his jacket. "I guess it couldn't hurt."

The Metro Club was closed when we arrived, but it was early yet. Wes went to the rear while I tried to look in the main door.

He came back around the corner. "The doors open back here."

I didn't like the feel of this.

I rounded the corner in time to see Wes open the door wider. "Wait up. Damn, will you use your head for a change."

It was no use he disappeared inside.

I joined Wes in a storeroom that smelled like beer and urine, with vomit undertones. There looked to be fresh bloodstains on the floor.

Wes held a finger to his lips. "There's someone in the bar."

We both drew our guns. I nodded. "You go left."

I broke right and we went through the door together. Tomas Flores stood by the bar. My hip bumped a chair and Flores jerked his head toward the sound.

"What the hell are you doing here?" Wes moved past Flores and searched behind the bar.

I checked the partition that hid the front entrance. "Still waiting for an answer," I said glancing at Flores.

"I work here before they closed. I come to see if they were going to reopen, but, nobody here."

"How did you get in," I asked as I moved toward him.

"The door was open. They still owe me some money. I need my money. I'm going on vacation."

"What they owe you money for," Wes asked. "Drugs?"

"No. For when I worked here."

I stared at him. There were big bags beneath his blood-shot eyes. "You taking your Tisa with you?"

"Tisa went home. It's just me leaving."

"Leaving or running?" I said.

Flores looked away without answering.

192

"We're wasting our time. He don't know anything we can't get out of Gomez," Wes said.

"What's with the bloodstains in the back room."

"Don't know."

"You don't seem to know a bloody lot. Well, you have a nice life, Flores." I turned toward Wes. "Let's get out of here."

Back in the car Wes pulled out is cell phone. "Guess we should report the blood stains. See if any new gang-bangers have showed up in the morgue."

I listened to his one-sided conversation. Nobody dead, but a man had been treated for a gunshot wound to the thigh, seems like he'd accidently shot himself while playing with a gun in the back storeroom of the Metro Club. Yeah, right.

Wes closed his phone.

I placed my hand over his' when he reached to start the engine. "No. We're going to talk."

He looked at me with exasperation. "Drop it, English. Only one of us should be in hot water if the shit hits the fan."

"What have you done?"

"I," Wes stressed the word. "Haven't done anything."

"This guy from Paddy's, who is he?"

"Private help of Scarsdale's." Wes looked away from me. "Less restrictions."

I frowned. "We don't play that way."

"Don't get your knickers in a wad. The guy only gave Gomez a ride into Santa Maria."

"Yeah, all trussed up like a luau pig."

Wes grinned at me. "How do you know that it wasn't the way he wanted it?

"Wes, who-the-hell is the guy?"

"Darcie, it isn't a big deal."

I glared at him.

He held up his hands fine. "The guy's name is..."

My cell phone pealed. I swore before flipping it open. "Devonshire."

"This just came in from that apartment building where the guy got killed a couple of days ago," dispatch said. "The man, Ralph Rienholt, asked for the two of you by name."

"What happened?"

"He said he thinks he killed somebody."

"We're on the way." I flipped my phone shut. "Flores' old place. Sounds bad."

Wes nodded, started the car and gunned the engine.

At the apartment complex, I was out of the car first. What had happened? Who had Ralph Rienholt killed? As I ran toward the stairs I saw a crumpled body lying at the bottom. A male. He wore a brace over one knee, his other leg bent, at a strange angle, was beneath him. Broken for sure. I didn't see any blood pools. There was a huge knot rising on his forehead. He must have banged his head on his trip down the stairway.

"Detective?" A man's voice said

I looked up.

Ralph and Imogene Rienholt were leaning over the stair railing. Imogene looked scared. Ralph too, but he was trying to cover it with bravado. Neither had a gun that I could see.

Wes stopped beside me. We exchanged a look. "What happened," he asked as he knelt and felt for the guy's pulse. "He's alive."

"The hoodlum attacked my Imogene." There was outrage in Ralph's voice. "Tried to steal her pocketbook. Right outside our door. In broad daylight."

"He had a gun," Imogene said in a quivering voice. "Pointed it right in my face."

"A gun?" Wes said. He looked around. "Found it." He pointed behind some green bushes.

Imogene smoothed her white hair. "It went off when I hit him."

I cringed. "You hit him?"

"With my pocket book. Right after I maced him in the face."

"I heard a scream," Ralph said. "Came running out." He smiled. "But it wasn't Imogene. It was him, tumbling down the stairs." He pointed toward the guy still laying comatose on the ground.

"I'll call for an ambulance," Wes said, grinning.

"Are you going to have to take us in?" Imogene said.

Fighting a smile, I shook my head. "It seems a clear case of self-defense."

The guy on the ground moaned.

"What if he tries to sue us?" Ralph demanded.

Out of the corner of my eye I saw a window blind move. "I'll talk to your neighbors. I'm sure there were witnesses."

"Of course," Imogene said. "Margaret would have seen. Nothing gets buy her."

"Which apartment's Margaret's?" I said.

"That one." Imogene pointed to where I'd seen the blind move.

"We start there first then."

Ralph snorted. "Be prepared for some weak tea and a mouth that won't stop."

"Ralph Rienholt," Imogene scolded. "Margaret's very nice. She gets lonely being afraid to go out her place and all."

Wes snapped his cell phone closed. "Ambulance is on the way."

I nodded. "You wait for it. I'm going to talk to the neighbors. I'll start with Margaret."

"See you next year then." I heard Ralph mutter as I turned away.

Chapter Twenty-Two
Sherice Solomon

It was almost time. The morning had crept by minute by slow minute. I had spent most of it deciding on and discarding almost everything in my closet. The shoes had been an easy choice. I knew I wanted to wear my green-python sling-backs, they were my celebratory shoes, and this was a celebration. Morgan was taking me into his world. Once I became an indispensable part of his, I'd lead him into mine.

My reflection in the mirror showed a relaxed smile. I fluffed my hair. It needed a trim. Maybe I'd let it grow. Did Morgan like long hair?

I heard a knock on the door and my heart double thumped in response. My Morgan was here.

At the front door I took a deep breath and then noticed with amusement how my fingers trembled as I curled them around the knob. Would he always make me feel this way? I hoped so.

Morgan stood in the sunlight, my own demi-god. I noticed he had his left hand behind his back. He gave me a sheepish grin and then brought it forward. He held one red rose. Oh dear God. When had a man last given me a flower? I felt heat flare in my core. Unable to speak, I took the flower from him and then pulled him close for a kiss. I'd meant it to be light, but when our mouths touched, light wasn't enough. Holding the rose to the side I pressed against him. His body and mine had to be as one. Morgan's response lay rigid against my lower stomach. I moaned against his lips. His hands dropped to my hips, pulled me tighter against him. With a shudder I lifted my mouth from his, looked into his eyes. "If we don't stop we'll never make it to that restaurant." My voice trembled.

"Not a bad idea," Morgan said, but stepped back further from me. "I did promise Wes, and we've already paid for the tickets. Morgan sounded as if he was talking himself into attending the luncheon and it made me smile.

"Come in for a minute while I grab my jacket."

As I turned from the hall closet, jacket in hand, I heard Morgan say. "That's a beautiful knife."

"What?" He stood in front of the end table where Arahni lay. I'd taken her out earlier to discuss Morgan and our upcoming luncheon. How could I have forgotten to return the shafra to the chest? Again karma? I walked to stand beside Morgan. "My David collected knifes. This was the only one I kept. It was too beautiful not to."

"And deadly," Morgan said. "It's a shafra isn't it? I saw some when I was in Iraq."

I shrugged. "I believe that's what David called it." A desire flowed through me to see Arahni in My Morgan's hands. I picked up the shafra and held it toward him. "David always said it had good balance, whatever that means."

Morgan took Arahni from me. He held it easily in his left hand. "He was right. It does have great balance. You need skill and practice to know how to use one of these."

"Oh, David never did anything with it. He kept it on display in a locked case." I faked a shudder. "I know nothing about knifes." I looked in Morgan's eyes. "You seem to be comfortable holding it."

He laid Arahni on the end table. "Some things you don't unlearn." He turned from me. "Mind if I use the bathroom?"

Morgan walked from me without waiting for my answer.

The man touched me. I felt his essence. Arahni's words full of surprised speculation came into my head.

197

"Yes. You looked as if you belonged in his hand."

I held my breath as I waited for her response.

Perhaps he will do for us.

My breath rushed from me. "He will more than just do."

"What did you say, Sherice?" Morgan's words came from behind me.

I whipped around. "Mentally making a shopping list. I need some orange juice." I glanced at the clock. "We should get going."

Morgan reached for my jacket. "Let me help you with that. We can stop by the store on the way back." I saw him glance at Arahni. "You want to put the shafra away?"

It was too soon for My Morgan to see the keepsakes in the Chest. "I'll do it when I get back. Let's get going. I hate to be late."

*****

We spent the time on the drive to The Fish Shanty talking about NASCAR. I'd become a fan three years ago. Morgan mentioned the Brickyard 500 and how it was his favorite race. I'd argued back that Las Vegas had a superior track for all-over viewing. After his first shocked silence, the debate was on. By the time we .pulled into the parking lot, we'd agreed to disagree and picked a date to attend the November race in Phoenix, Arizona.

I felt like I could float as Morgan parked his pick-up and then came around to my door to help me out. A date in November and this was only August. What else could we be doing together by then? Phoenix was far enough away. We could hunt there and then attend the NASCAR race. I saw in my mind again, Morgan standing in my living room, Arahni resting in his large hands. The Hunger roused at my thoughts, nipped my stomach. I pressed my hand against it.

"Nervous?" Morgan said.

I jerked my head toward him. He nodded toward my hand. "A little. Mostly just hungry."

He laughed. "You won't leave The Fish Shanty hungry. I guarantee that."

Oh, but I will, I thought. And it's a problem that will have to be taken care of, and soon.

Morgan placed his hand beneath my elbow. "Parking lot can be tricky. Those are some hot shoes you're wearing, but they don't look too stable."

"Like them? They're my lucky shoes."

He grinned down at me. "You don't need those shoes today. I can promise you, you're going to get very lucky."

"Oh Morgan, you are such a hound," I said, but I thought of Arahni lying on the end table back at the cottage. Morgan could not see my souvenirs in the chest, but he would think it odd if I did not put the shafra away. I would have to distract him.

We were at the door and he opened it for me. A wave of conversation greeted us. The place was packed. Men stood in the aisles talking, while mothers hushed squirming babies and older children scribbled on coloring pages. Along one wall, neon hued fish swam back and forth in a huge aquarium. Fishing nets, filled with green glass balls hung, from the ceiling.

A harried looking young woman walked to them. "Good afternoon. I'm so happy to see you." And she did sound pleased.

"We have two tickets here for us. Sherice Solomon and Morgan Garrett," I said.

"Yes, they're right here." She held the envelope out to me. I opened it and held the two tickets back out to her.

She picked up two menus. "Right this way, please. It's a little quieter toward the rear."

I followed Morgan as we wove our way toward the back.

The woman stopped in front of a corner table. "Your waiter will be right with you."

I took the seat that faced the window. She handed me a menu and then Morgan one. Outside was a view of the beach and ocean. One lone figure walked a dog along the surf line.

"Morgan, you made it." I looked toward the voice. A tall, thin man, moved toward us. There was a white towel draped across his left arm and an apron tied around his waist.

"Wes," Morgan said. He turned toward me as the man stopped beside the table. "This is Sherice Solomon."

"Glad to meet you. My Janey's around her someplace."
He scanned the area. "I'll bring her by when I have a chance."

"Is this your section?" Morgan said.

"The whole damn place is my section. It's crazy, but it seems to work."

"Oh Waiter Wes, I need another beer." A voice called. "And my kid spilled his soup."

Wes groaned. "That's Hennessey, but I'll get him good. His shift starts in two hours. I'll take care of him and then be back to take your orders."

The man hurried away.

"Wes is a good guy." Morgan opened his menu. "The clam chowder here wins awards every year at the Clam Festival."

"Then I have to have some," I said. "The Captain's Plate looks good."

"That's a lot of food and it's deep-fried."

I looked at Morgan. "So? Do I look like I should be on a diet?"

Red flowed up his neck and across his cheeks. "God no. I just figured you for a salad and white wine gal."

"Hate salad, prefer champagne or beer, and white wine's okay if it's dry." I closed the menu. "Is me having a beer going to be a problem?"

Morgan shook his head. "It's fine. My problem is my problem. Not yours."

"I can have..."

"Have the beer Sherice. If that's what you want."

I heard the impatience in his voice.

Wes appeared again. He whipped out an ordering pad. "What can I get you?" He looked straight at me.

"I'll have a cup of clam chowder, the Captain's Plate and a beer. What's on tap?"

"Firestone Pale Ale."

"Sounds fine."

He looked at Morgan. "I'll have a shrimp salad and a glass of iced tea."

"Got it," Wes said, taking the menus from us. "I'll be right back with your drinks.

"I like salad," Morgan said, as Wes hurried away.

"Did you hear me make a comment?" I picked up the small placard that showed and listed the desserts. "Oh I thought for sure they'd have something chocolate. Funny thing about assumptions, isn't it?"

"Ouch," Morgan said and I looked at him and smiled.

Wes returned with our drinks. He placed them in front of us. "My partner's around here somewhere. I'll stop by when I find her."

"Your partner is a woman?" I said.

"Both on the job and off," Wes said.

I laughed just as the sound of shattering glass came from two tables across.

Wes turned toward it. "Damn, any more damages and we're going to have to pay for them." He rushed away.

I picked up my beer and took a long drink. "How is your iced tea?"

"Perfect."

We talked. Morgan sipped. I drank. The conversation flowed naturally. Morgan had opinions on everything. We didn't always see things the same and I loved it. Our disagreements stimulated me. He never let me off the hook. If I stated something as fact, I had to back it up.

Wes came by, saw our almost empty glasses and came back with refills without even asking.

"Thanks," Morgan said.

"It'll be on your tab." Wes grinned.

"When's the food coming?" Morgan said.

"Soon. We're backed up in the kitchen." Wes hurried away.

I turned to look across the ocean.

Morgan's surprised gasp had me jerking my head around. He had paled to almost the same hue as the white tablecloth. Shock showed in his tense face and frame. "What is it? Are you ill?"

He scrambled to his feet. "My God. It can't be!"

I turned, looked behind me. A woman stood two tables away, talking to a man and small boy. She straightened, faced us with a smile and then went still. The same shock radiated from her. Her smile looked frozen.

"Darcie?" Morgan said. He took a step toward her and stopped.

I saw that his hands trembled.

Darcie. I remembered the nightmare I'd woken him from. My Morgan had called me Darcie.

The woman blinked, shook her head, as if she couldn't believe this was real.

"Darcie Devonshire," Morgan said.

She came to us. "I can't believe it. Morgan Garrett."

They stood facing each other. Emotions rolled off of them. Morgan lifted his arm, reached for her and then let it fall when she did not step forward. The woman stuck out her hand.

Morgan smiled stiffly and then reached to shake it. "What's it been? Six years?"

I knew he lied, Morgan knew just how many years. In my heart I feared he also knew the month, day and minutes also. I noticed he still held the woman's hand. She pulled it from his.

"About that many," the woman said, too casually.

Wes came toward us. Stopped. "Hey Morgan, you've met my partner, Darcie Devonshire. Darcie, this is the guy I mentioned that's a friend of Paddy's."

"He would be," the woman said.

Morgan stiffened and words of defense pressed against my lips. He is not drinking. He only visited with Paddy. I reached to touch his hand. My Morgan turned to me, and for a moment it was as if he did not know who touched him.

"Darcie, this is Sherice Solomon," Wes said.

"Officer," I said with a small nod.

"Actually, it's detective," she replied.

I nodded again without responding.

Morgan seemed to come out of his trance. "Sherice is my doctor. I owe my life to her."

A wave of anger heated me. His doctor? I forced a smile. "Illness brought us together. I never thought I'd be happy to see someone sick."

"I've been lucky, like that," Morgan said. "Having beautiful women around to save my ass." He and the woman shared a long look.

"Surprise," Wes said, "Your food's almost ready."

"Surprise," Morgan echoed. "Darcie's my old CIA partner."

Wes' mouth fell open. "What the hell. That right?" He looked at the woman.

"It is. Small world, huh?"

Wes laughed. "So the partner you were raving about, is the same one I was raving about?"

The woman punched him in the arm. "You were raving about me?"

"More like saying you were a raving lunatic behind the wheel of a car."

The partners exchanged more banter as I watched My Morgan. He couldn't seem to stop looking at the woman's face. He looked hungry, hopeful and sad at the same time. All three expressions left a cold, ball of ice in my stomach. I pressed my hands against it. My movements were noticed by the woman.

"Are you okay? You're looking a little sick," she said.

"Too much beer on an empty stomach" I murmured.

"That happens." The woman darted a look at Morgan.

He frowned, leaned toward me. "Do you want to leave?"

"I think so."

"I'll have them pack your lunch," the woman said. She seemed as anxious to see the back of me as I was to see hers.

"Thanks, Darcie," Morgan said.

They both looked unsure of what to say next.

The woman broke the tableau. "I'll take care of it right now." She turned.

"Darcie," Morgan said. "We'll have to get together. Catch up on things. A lot has happened..." His words trailed away.

"We'll have to do that." She spoke without turning. "I'll give you a call." The woman hurried away.

"Aint that a pisser," Wes said. "You and English knowing each other. The world's getting smaller and smaller.

I felt bile rise into my throat and swallowed. "Fresh air. I need fresh air."

Morgan stood and came to stand beside me. "Can you walk?"

I took his offered hand, let him help me from the seat. The restaurant seemed to dip around me. I swayed and Morgan grabbed my shoulders.

"Sherice!" His arm went around my waist. "Let's get you out of here."

I felt amused gazes on me as Morgan led me toward the door. As he opened it, I heard her voice again.

"Here's your food," the woman said.

I lifted my eyes, stared into her face, let her see the anger I felt. "Thank you."

She thrust the bag toward Morgan. I saw them touch and the woman stepped back as if her fingers burned. She met my eyes again. Smiled stiffly. I swayed into Morgan, this time on purpose.

He jerked his gaze from the woman. "Let's get you home."

Yes. Home. Did you hear that, bitch?

She must have, since I felt her stare, like knives, in the middle of my back as My Morgan led me out the restaurant's door.

Chapter Twenty-Three
Morgan Garrett

Tension rolled from Sherice's body. I knew I must seem as tight to her. God damn. Darcie. I couldn't wrap my mind around it. She looked good. Hadn't aged a bit, but then she hadn't been self-medicating with booze either. We had to talk. I had to tell her alcohol wasn't ruling me any longer. What would she say? I'd felt the coolness flow from her. How could I blame her? The last she'd seen me I'd been determined to drink myself into oblivion. A hand touched my leg, I jumped and glanced toward Sherice. She was staring at me. "What?"

"I asked you a question."

"Sorry, didn't hear you."

"What are you thinking so hard about, Morgan?"

I didn't know how to answer that. Be honest and say Darcie? I didn't think that would go over well.

Sherice smiled. "If it's her, you can tell me. It's only natural. You have a history together, and you haven't seen her in some time."

It all sounded logical coming from Sherice, but I noticed she hadn't once said Darcie's name, just, 'her'. "It was a shock. Not just to see Darcie, but to find out she's Wes' partner."

"Did you love her?"

I kept my eyes straight ahead as I spoke. "Darcie was a great partner. We went through some heavy shit together. I always knew she had my back."

"You didn't part well?"

Good question. I couldn't speak for Darcie. Me, I'd been drunk on my ass and couldn't remember it at all. When I'd halfway sobered up, it had hurt like hell, so I'd grabbed the nearest bottle and dove into oblivion again. "You could say that."

"You'll see her again now." Sherice's words weren't a question, they were a for certain statement.

"Don't know. Maybe." I don't know why I lied.

"You will, you must. You need closure. How can..." she hesitated before adding, "you go forward without addressing the past?"

Right. Darcie was my past, but I needed her to know I'd cleaned up my act. For old times sake. What she thought was important to me. "You're right."

Sherice placed her hand on my thigh. "Of course I am. I'm the doctor."

I glanced at her. "You okay with that...me seeing Darcie?"

"We could talk to her together...group therapy."

Hell no, I thought, almost blurted out the words. I forced out a laugh. "Darcie talking to a shrink? It would never happen. Besides, all I have to tell her is I'm not drinking anymore."

She removed her hand from my thigh. "Morgan, did you think you'd ever be talking to a shrink?"

I heard the hurt beneath Sherice's words and realized I'd stepped in it big time. "Sherice, I didn't mean that the way it sounded. It's just that Darcie's head's always been screwed on straight. She doesn't try to hide from what bothers her."

Silence rolled off of Sherice. I glanced at her. She'd moved as far from me as possible and stared straight ahead. "Sherice...."

"We all have things that haunt. What shapes us is how we deal with them."

Sherice's words were flat, hollow, and empty of emotion. The hairs on the back of my neck rose. I looked at her again. She was smiling at me, but it didn't reach her eyes. "Now can we change the subject?"

"Sure," I replied.

"You don't sound positive. Let me take your mind elsewhere." She moved closer to me, unzipped my pants.

My fingers tightened around the steering wheel. "What the...?"

I felt her hand free me from my shorts and then she lowered her head.

*****

Driving back to Santa Maria after dropping Sherice off at her cottage, there was nothing on my mind but Darcie. Which seemed rather despicable considering what Sherice had just done for me. I'd nixed going inside. Sherice was upset, but she'd only nodded and walked away

Guilt kept me from looking back as I drove away, but I couldn't help it. I had to see Darcie, tell her I wasn't drinking. But how to do it and make her believe me. Maybe Wes could open a door? Seeing her had brought back a flood of memories, all good ones, at least at the beginning, before I shot the kid.

I parked at my apartment, reached for the door handle. My cell phone rang.Not many had this number. "Garrett."

"Morgan, this is Lyndon Scarsdale."

"Hello there, Senator."

He chuckled. "Not until after the election, but it is looking good. I have those two other names. I'd like you to check them out."

Scarsdale gave me a pair of names; both with addresses in Santa Maria, one a former cop with the local police and whoopee, now both were lawyers.

Chapter Twenty-Four
Darcie Devonshire

I frowned into the sink full of dirty coffee cups. From the dining area of The Fish Shanty the roar had lowered in volume, so things must have quieted down.

Well, bloody hell. Morgan Garrett showing up at The Fish Shanty, that was the last thing I expected. I guess it shouldn't have been. Santa Maria wasn't that big of a town. I'd been planning to call him, but I'd been a tad busy. Morgan actually looked sober, but every drunk had an odd good day now and then.

I thought about the woman. No love coming to me from her. If looks could kill…blah…blah…blah… . Sherice something. His doctor? Yes, he'd said Doctor. What does that mean? Hell. I didn't care. Right? Then why are my hands shaking?

Wes came into the kitchen. "So you worked with Morgan? He told me he'd worked for the government. Said he'd been a pencil-pusher, which I knew was a bunch of bull shit, but wow, you and him. That's really something."

"Not such a big deal. Hell, it was a long time ago." I added cups to the dishwasher and pushed the on button.

"He obviously wanted to see you again. You gonna call him?"

"Wes, let it go. It's ancient history."

"History's been known to repeat itself."

With a glare, I turned from him and walked back into the dining area of the restaurant.

*****

On the way home I rolled down all of the windows in my Beamer and tried to blow Morgan out of my mind. I didn't want him there. Damn, I was just moving on, putting him behind me. Mayo was perfect for me. Not a drunk. Dynamite in bed. No history, just the future for us to create.

My vision blurred and I felt my throat tighten. "Bloody hell." I blinked my eyes hard and whipped the car over to the side of the road. "No you don't." I said. "I'm not letting you make me cry." I slapped the steering wheel with my open hand. I'd looked down at how many bodies? Some of them friends, and they didn't make me cry, no drunken bloke was going to either, not any more. "You're out of my life, Morgan. Out. I'm calling Mayo as soon as I get home. He can come over for dinner and we'll take Becky for a walk together."

"You're ducking things, Darcie." Morgan's voice floated through my head. "We don't duck things, unless of course it's bullets."

I closed my eyes tight. "What do you want from me?" I knew the answer to my question. We had to talk. The book of my past had to be closed. I flipped open my cell phone, called Wes."

"What took you so long?" he said.

"Give it to me," I said.

He gave me Morgan's number and I flipped the phone closed without saying more. Before I could change my mind I called him. It rang six times before it went to voice mail. I hung up without saying a word. Let him think about that, I thought, as I pulled back into traffic.

At home I did take Becky for a walk, as I came back in the door the phone rang. My heartbeat went into overdrive. I stood in the doorway and waited for the answering machine to respond.

"Cupcake, it's Da."

I laughed. Of course it was. I'd called Morgan with my cell phone. I hurried to the phone. "Hey Da."

"You sound out of breath."

"Just walked in the door from walking Becky."

"A walk with Becky doesn't wind someone. What's up, Darcie? You're sounding funny."

"It's nothing, Da. You guys enjoy your meal today at The Fish Shanty?"

"Great food as usual."

"Ask her why Mayo wasn't there." I heard Mum call in the background.

"Tell Mum Mayo was working."

"I will. Darcie, what's wrong?"

Oh, hell. Why not. "Had an old friend come in The Fish Shanty today."

Da waited.

"Morgan Garrett," I said.

"That must have been a bit of a bother," Da said.

"It was. Even more so when I found out Wes has been working some with him."

"And you didn't know?"

"I didn't. Isn't that something?" I'd thought I'd kept my voice void of any emotion, but Becky came to me and pressed against my legs, so I must have failed. Da's words confirmed it.

"What now, Cupcake?"

"I'm going to meet with him, do some talking. We've got some things to get past."

"Past is the word there, Cupcake. Morgan Garrett's your past."

"I know, Da, but my past keeps getting in the way of my future." My voice broke and I swallowed.

"You do what needs to be done," Da said. "We're here if you need us."

"I will, Da." I took a deep breath. "How about we get together for some poker?"

"You that anxious to lose more of your hard-earned money?"

I laughed. "Love you, Da. We'll talk soon."

He hung up the phone and I stood a minute staring at it, before I placed it back in its cradle.

Across the room, my cell phone rang. My legs wouldn't move. I knew who it was. I made my feet carry me to the phone. "This is Darcie."

"Caller ID said you'd called," Morgan said.

"I've given it some thought. We should get together."

"Where and when?" Morgan said.

"You choose."

"O'Grady's Pub," Morgan said.

My stomach tightened. Same old Morgan. Of course it would be in a bar. "Tomorrow," I said. "Eleven o'clock."

"I'll be there. Darcie…"

I flipped my cell phone closed on his words and then turned it off for good measure. I'd see him tomorrow, we'd talk, and at last I'd turn that page and end the Morgan Garrett Chapter. It was way past time. I walked to the other phone and punched in Mayo's number.

The next morning the phone rang while I was on my second, much needed cup of coffee. I hadn't slept too well and it wasn't for the right reason. Mayo had been in San Francisco, so I'd spent the night thinking too much. "Hello."

"Why aren't you answering your cell phone?" Wes demanded.

I'd forgotten I hadn't turned it back on. "Good morning to you too."

"You want to go to the hospital with me to talk to that guy that took the tumble at Flores' old place?"

"I'll meet you there," I said, pushing back my chair.

*****

The doctor stood there with the clip board in hand. "He has fractured leg, and a smashed knee. The break will heal but he'll walk with a limp for the rest of his life. Any idea what happened to him? He's being very closed mouth."

"The leg met a staircase to tough for it. We're gonna find out about the knee," Wes said.

I walked past the cop who sat at the door into the room.

"I'm Detective Devonshire, this is Detective Smith." I said to the kid in the bed. "When did you change from drugs to snatching little old ladies purses?"

"I didn't do nuthin. I want a lawyer."

Wes stopped beside me. "Look punk. We got you cold. You may as well be nice, cause you're gonna do time. We might have a say on how much. Now, who knee-capped you?"

He looked sullen and for a moment I thought he'd still lawyer up, but then he said. "Don't know no name. Big ole mean-looking guy. He had a black pick-up, fucked up my knee, took me to an alley and left me the hell there.

"What did he want?" Wes said.

"He wanted to know if I'd seen someone."

I jumped into the conversation "Did you tell him?".

"He done broke my damn knee. Was going for the other one. Hell yes I told him. The skinny Scarsdale bitch ain't worth it."

"By God." Wes laughed as he waved me toward the door.

I walked up to him in the hall.

"It was Morgan, your old boy friend.

"That part of your deal?"

Wes shrugged. "I needed to get the drug dealer back in Santa Maria and Morgan needed to return Theresa Scarsdale to her daddy. It worked."

"How did you get him sober enough to make a deal?"

"What? I've never seen him take a drink."

"You met him at O'Grady's?"

"Yeah, but he was drinking coffee."

My mind did a complete flip over that. Morgan sober? I guess I'd see. "Let's get back to the station."

Chapter Twenty-Five
Sherice Solomon

Behind me I heard the car accelerate. At the door to the cottage I looked back in time to see Morgan drive away. Was I losing him? No it couldn't be.

Inside the cottage, I went to where the shafra still lay on the end table.

You want him?

"I do. Morgan is not like the others."

He is but a man, but if he must be yours, then you know what must be done.

"Yes. I do. Darcie Devonshire must die." I picked up Arahni and carried her toward my bed. "We will plan."

*****

Parked along the street, across from the Santa Maria police station, I did not really have a plan. Watch, learn and one will emerge. I told myself. I tingled inside. I had never hunted a person whose name I knew. My sacrificed had always been random, based on opportunity.

Arahni lay in the tote bag beside me. I had spoken to her a few times, but she remained silent. Darcie-the-bitch, worked days; I had learned that much. Wes, for what I had seen at The Fish Shanty, would not be a factor.

The door of the police station opened and they both came out. I watched her flip her hair over her collar. It was only the second time I had seen the movement, but all ready I hated it. I pictured her hair coated with still wet blood.

She walked to a sporty looking SUV. Wes continued on down the line of cars to a pick-up, got in and drove away.

Darcie sat in her car and talked on a cell phone. I watched her smile.

"Smile bitch." I said aloud. "Your day is coming."

She started the SUV, backed from the parking slot. I followed. It surprised me to see her turn into O'Grady's, even more so when I saw Morgan's truck. She's meeting My Morgan. Was he the reason for her earlier smile? Rage filled me. I turned off the engine, grabbed for the tote bag.

No. Arahni ordered. *You want to confront them, but that would be a mistake.*

"He's mine," I screamed.

He will be, but you must think, not only feel.

I lowered my head to the steering wheel and drew in deep breathes of air.

Leave here. We must plan.

I dug my fingernails into the soft leather of the car seat, imagining it to be Darcie Devonshire's throat. Arahni was right. I did not want to be spotted by either of them, not yet. I put my car in gear and drove away.

214

Chapter Twenty-Six
Morgan Garrett

O'Grady's was empty. Paddy sat at a table eating a sandwich. He looked up as I entered.

"Morg m'boyo, what'll it be?"

"I'm meeting someone Paddy. Have you made any coffee yet?"

"For you lad I'll brew a fresh pot."

"Good man. Quiet in here."

"It'll fill up fast enough."

Throughout our conversation I had one ear aimed toward the door. I heard it open. My heart raced and my stomach felt like it was tied in a knot. I was like a teenager on his first date. I turned on the bar stool. The light fading behind as the door closed, did not disguise Darcie. I knew that figure, that shape, that heavy step, almost a stomp. It all rushed back in an overwhelming wash that stunned me for a moment.

As her image became clear in the dim light her hand went to her hair for that familiar flip. I felt the second she saw me. Her face wasn't clear, but I thought I saw her frown. Why shouldn't she, me in a bar, but I had to make her see that was all a thing of the past.

Darcie came toward me. Stopped and her hand came down to rest on the bar.

"Morgan." Her voice was bland. No emotion.

I wasn't sure I could speak so calmly. "Let's sit there." I pointed at a corner booth.

"What'll you have Miss, I'll bring it over." Paddy looked at her, curious. Was he thinking of Sherice?

"I'll have whatever Morgan is having."

"Okay, coffee it is."

Paddy's comment caused Darcie to look at me with a sharp glance. "Not on my account, I hope?"

I didn't answer. She'd heard all of my lies before. I sat straight and waited for Darcie to speak. She chose to let me squirm. "Darcie, you're looking good. You still run?"

"No small talk, Morgan. Why are you here? What's with the coffee?"

"I've been in rehab. No booze. Johnny got me in a clinic. You remember Johnny Scott?"

"Yeah I remember Johnny, one of your drunken buddies."

"Well, he's not drinking either."

"What do you want Morgan? Why did you come here to Santa Maria?"

"Well it wasn't because of you. If that's what you're thinking. It seems like that would be obvious, with what happened at The Fish Shanty, I didn't even know you were here. I have a job. I'm off the booze. I'm trying to turn my life around. I wasn't chasing you. I met Wes through Paddy. I needed some help finding the Scarsdale girl. Wes turned out to be it."

"You knee cap that kid?"

How could she know about that? "What kid?"

"The one you kidnapped at Flores' place, that kid."

Shit. She did know. "He was a little reluctant to talk to me. I had to convince him."

"I've seen your persuasive ways before," she said.

You were no slouch yourself." I smiled. "Remember that Bulgarian? When you shoved that Glock down his throat he was mighty persuaded." I watched Darcie almost smile before she caught herself

"That was then, this is now. Who was the lady you were with Wednesday?"

Darcie's words were casual, but I caught an edge of jealousy. Maybe things between us weren't so dead and gone.

"I introduced you. That was Sherice, she was my doctor. I think she would like more, but she's not really my type." Now where had that come from? She'd been my type up until I'd spied Darcie.

"She looked pretty smitten with you."

I leaned toward her. "Darcie, I just want us to be friends. Can't we do that?"

"Friends? Morgan, grow up. We went way beyond that. I didn't lose you to another woman. That would have been easier. I lost you to a bottle. I was... I couldn't hang around and watch you go down the loo."

"I'm off the stuff. Really, I am."

"I'll buy that when I see it."

Paddy leaned across the table, made a swipe with his bar towel and sat two cups before us. I had been so involved I had not seen or heard him.

"Fresh and hot, Morg, just as you like it."

"Thanks Paddy. This is Darcie Devonshire. She's a police detective with the Santa Maria department."

"Oh, you're Wes Smith's partner. He's mentioned you. Grew up in Oxfordshire, England, didn't ya?"

"I am and I did."

"Well I won't be holdin, that against ye."

I looked up, grinned at Paddy, but he wasn't smiling.

"Where did you and Morgan meet?"

"We are old friends, from another lifetime," I said.

The door opened.

"Well, enjoy. If you need a refill just holler. Here come my regulars."

I watched Paddy walk away and then turned back to Darcie.

"Have you really quit drinking?" She looked at me with an expression I couldn't read.

"I haven't had a drink since I went into rehab. Can't say I haven't wanted one, but...."

"What happens when you do? Have the cravings?"

217

"I deal with it." It sounded weaker than I wanted, but what could I say that would convince her.

"Words are cheap." She took a drink of her coffee. "You plan to stay in Santa Maria?"

"I'm working for Scarsdale."

Darcie nodded. "You and Wes best pals now?"

"We're getting there."

She pushed her coffee cup toward the middle of the table. "Well, I guess we'll be running in to each other." She slid from the booth and stood.

What could I say to make her stay? Not a damn thing.

She looked into my face for a long moment, and then called toward Paddy. "Thanks for the coffee.

"You're most welcome, Miss."

I sat where I was and watched her walk to the door, and then out of it. I knew it wasn't going to be easy, most things with Darcie weren't. She hadn't disappointed me.

Our past lives zoomed in fast forward through my head. Damn we'd been good together. So what's the point Garrett? Your drinking sure as hell wiped that out.

I crawled out of the booth and walked toward the bar. Before I got there Wes walked in, blinking. "Hey just the guy I wanted to see," I said and watched as his eyes adjusted and recognition came to him.

"Morgan, what's shaking?'"

"Grab a stool. What'll you have?" Paddy said.

"Coffee?"

"You bet. You want more, Morg?"

"Nah, I'm good." I turned to face Wes as Paddy placed the coffee in front of him. "Do you know a lawyer by the name of Robert Grindle? He was on the job a few years back."

"Sure, I believe I do. Used to be in Criminal."

"He wants to work for Scarsdale. I'm doing some background on him."

"The guy's married, but frequently forgets that. Darcie could tell you more than I can. He's some kind of friend of the family."

"Good idea. I'll give her a call."

Wes frowned. "Why don't I ask her? If she knows anything I'll call you."

I looked into his face. "Darcie told you about us, huh? Then you know that sooner or later we have to sort it all out. We talked some today. You just missed her, but there's plenty more shit to work through. I'm not going to hurt her."

"You've already did that Pal. More than she needs."

"That's a two-way street," I said. "What about I talk to her at the station? What's the best time?"

"I don't feel good about giving out information…"

"I'll tell her I used the Tibetan Pinch on you."

"What the hell's that?"

I smiled. "Ask Darcie."

His cell phone rang. He glanced at it, grimaced, and then flipped it open. "Hey, English."

I didn't even pretend not to listen. Judging from his response she asked him if he wanted something from Starbucks and he said no. Wes closed his phone. "Tell me more about this Scarsdale. Do I want to vote for him?"

I told him the little I knew.

He stood. "I'm taking my wife to lunch. It's her birthday." He hesitated and added. "Go easy on Darcie. I think she's going through some heavy stuff."

I nodded.

Wes looked like he wanted to say more, but instead he shook his head and walked toward the door.

With Wes leaving I moved to the corner booth away from some of the noise to make the call. The bar had filled up with the lunch crowd and I thought about taking off too, but I wanted one of Paddy's corned beef sandwiches. I realized Wes had gotten away without telling me when would be a good time to see Darcie at the police station. I guess I'd have to call her and ask.

The phone rang four times before Darcie's recorded voice answered and told me to leave a message.

Chapter Twenty-Seven
Darcie Devonshire

Inside my Beamer I let the shakes begin. My vision blurred. "Damn you, Morgan. Damn you. Why show up now? And sober." I leaned my head against the steering wheel. "I don't love you anymore. You hear me? It's over. History."

I sat up, brushed tears from my cheeks, counted to ten and then phoned Mayo. I really wanted to see him, but he was still in San Francisco until tomorrow. His voice mail answered. A thought hit me as I ended the call. I didn't even know what Mayo did for a living. What did I really know about him? Frowning, I started the car.

Halfway to the station I pulled into a Starbucks instead. Would Wes like a cappuccino? I speed-dialed him.

"Smith here."

"I'm at Starbucks. Heading to the office, you want anything?"

There was a moment of silence and then. "Thanks, but I already have a cup of coffee in front of me."

Through the phone I heard Paddy O'Grady's voice call to someone in the background. Wes was at the pub. One guess who he was talking too. I felt a surge of betrayal. My head knew I wasn't being fair, but my heart didn't give a rat's ass. "Oh. Okay, I'll see you at the office."

"English, I'm taking the rest of the afternoon off. It's Janey's birthday. I've already cleared it with the captain.

"Wish her happy birthday from me," I said. "See you in the morning." I flipped the phone closed. My stomach seized and the coffee didn't seem a good idea any longer. A day off, huh? That sounded pretty good. God knows I had plenty more sick days saved up. My yard needed mowing and the flower beds hadn't been weeded in a while. Becky would love a trip to the beach. I reached for my phone again to call the captain. I'd be sure to let him know that it was okay to send any major calls my way.

*****

In the backyard I stared at my manicured lawn and weed-free flower beds. I'd forgotten that last week, at Mum's insistence, I'd hired a yard guy. He'd started this morning.

Becky stood beside me her tail whipping side-to-side. She was obviously delighted I was home early. I patted her head. "Looks like it's me and you, baby. Wanta go?"

She barked and danced in a circle around me, which in basset hound language meant, "Hell, yes."

In minutes we were at the end of Pier Avenue in Oceano. I exited the Beamer, shaded my eyes with my hand and scanned the beach. It didn't look bad. We wouldn't have to dodge too many cars to get in a good walk.

Becky and I strolled to where the sand turned damp from the played out waves. The ocean stretched before us, a flat sheen of blue-green, until it met a line of gray fog that hovered on the horizon. Overhead, gulls squabbled with each other.

We turned towards Pismo Beach. If we'd gone to Avila, I would have let Becky off her leash, but here there were too many cars.

She made the most of her six feet of length, running in front of me, then turning and jogging back. I kept my gaze on the played-out waves and a search for sand dollars. I glanced at a piece of driftwood. It was cool, but it didn't interest me, that had been Morgan's thing. I stopped, stared across the water. There he was in my head again. I frowned at my feet and then shrugged. In my head was okay, bound to happen. we'd shared some scary times with the Company, but I didn't want the man in my heart any longer.

221

Becky barked a warning and I looked her way. "It's kelp, you silly hound." She didn't stop until I walked by her and gave the gray-green strand a kick. Then she threw me a sheepish look and bounded ahead again. A gust of wind made me shiver. "Come on let's pick up the pace.

*****

At my back patio door, I wiped sand from Becky's feet. "How about some dinner?" Inside the kitchen I checked the cupboards. I had some canned salmon, so decided on fish burgers. I'd just finished crushing the crackers with a ketchup bottle, when I noticed the red light blinking on my answering machine. I left the crackers in a white pile and walked to the phone.

Morgan's voice said. "Uh…Darc. I need to talk to you. Your office would be fine. I tried to pry the information from Wes. No go. I even threatened his manhood with the Tibetan Pinch. You remember that, right?" There was a second of silence and then he went on. "Well, I guess you're still not there. I hope you're not just letting me yack into some damn machine. You know how I hate that. Darcie, we need to talk more. You have my number." I heard his soft laughter. "You always have haven't you? Good bye, Darcie Devonshire."

A wave of panic had me reaching for the phone. Good bye? He sounded so final. The salmon burgers forgotten I ran to my phone, flipped it open and then stared at his number under received calls. Wait. What was I doing? So it was over between us? That's what I wanted. Right? My knees started to shake and sank down onto the sofa. Dear God, what did I want?

I played his words over in my head, smiled at Tibetan Pinch, my version of Spock's pinch on Star Trek, but much less effective. Invented when I'd been doing tequila shoots one night at a bar, trying to keep pace with Morgan. Some big sloppy guy had been hanging all over me. Morgan had known better than to interfere. My Tibetan Pinch had just pissed off the moon-faced Lothario. A different response had been called for, so I'd swept his feet out from beneath him. After the guy was on the floor, we'd been, not so politely, asked to leave. A hell of a hangover

222

greeted me the next morning, three weeks later I walked out of Morgan's life.

But if he's kicked the booze? No. I wasn't going through all of that again. I punched the speed dial number for Mayo. He answered on the second ring. "Hello, beautiful."

"You're home. How do you feel about salmon burgers," I asked.

"Love them."

"Can you be here in twenty minutes?"

"I'll be there in fifteen."

Chapter Twenty-Eight
Sherice Solomon

I paced the front room of the cottage. My gaze kept drifting to the phone. My fingers ached to call My Morgan. What had he and the bitch talked about? Where they still together, maybe in his bed? Did he touch her? Make love to her in the shower?

"No." My stomach rolled at the thought. He is mine, Darcie Devonshire. We'll see how long he mourns when you are dead. My anger fed the Hunger and I felt it surge inside me.

We must hunt. It has been too long. Arahni screamed the words inside my head.

She lay on the sofa. I crossed to her, caressed the edge of the blade. "We need a plan, but nothing can link her to us. A different car. I will wear my frump outfit and that awful brown wig. She must not notice us."

The hunt will be a true hunt. We will stalk; then we will kill.

Inside my heart I felt her excitement.

The cottage walls seemed to creep closer around me. I needed to be free to breathe. I picked up Arahni. "Let's go for a ride."

*****

I parked down the street from the bitch's house. The Internet's reverse directory had provided me with her address. My heart had pounded as I neared. If My Morgan's truck was in the driveway, I didn't know if I would be been able to control myself. It wasn't, but I watched another man arrive. Tall and handsome. I felt relief and then anger at the bitch's betrayal. "Oh, My Morgan, you are so much better than her."

Arahni and I sat and watched for some time, but the man did not come out. It was time to move on. I did not want to be noticed. Who is the man? I jotted down his license plate number as I inched past. Isaiah would get me his name.

I drove aimlessly through neighborhoods, watching dogs and children play in yards. Would Morgan and I have a child? Could there be three to do the hunt?

A road went down a hill into a valley. I entered the small town of Guadalupe, stopped at a Mexican restaurant and bought a taco and a burrito. I knew there had to be a beach access nearby so I asked the man. He gave me directions to Guadalupe Dunes

The narrow road went up a hill, on the other side I could see sand had drifted across the pavement. I stayed in its center, but still the Mustang slipped.

The parking lot held no other cars. I placed Arahni in my tote bag, and with it over my shoulder and the food in my other hand, I exited the Mustang. Signs protecting the Snowy Plover guided my way. On the beach I turned left and walked until I felt the urge to stop. Arahni and I had the sand to ourselves.

Now we would plan.

My fingers caressed Arahni through the tote bag. A quick death, or humiliation first? Darcie's immediate demise appealed to me, her sightless eyes staring up, and a flow of red pumping from her. Yet, she struck me as prideful. To strike there first, make her feel helpless and stupid. I would love for her to feel pain in her heart, the same pain knifing mine. Then My Morgan would see how weak she was, how she was not worthy of him.

I bit into the taco, chewed as I stared across the waves. Did the bitch, like all of the others, think Ice was a man? Of course she did. Well, let her keep looking for one. It made things simpler for Arahni and myself. I swallowed. Laughed.

"Hey there, son. What yah doing out here all by yourself? It'll be dark soon.

I jerked my head toward the speaker. Engrossed in my thoughts, I hadn't heard him approach. He was average in every way. Much like my Miss Mouse disguise. In a crowd your eyes would skim over him.

"You a runaway?" He motioned toward my tote bag.

The fool thinks I'm a boy. I guess with my loose jeans, over-sized sweatshirt and dark watch-cap I looked the part. I didn't correct him, just nodded my head.

The man settled beside me, so close his thigh touched mine. "Gonna get cold tonight. Where you sleeping?"

The truth was the night would be a mild one. I looked down at my hands, smiled. He stalked me. I knew the predator game. I lifted my shoulders in a shrug.

"I could put you up for the night." He placed his hand on my thigh. "Son, you make me feel good, and I'll do the same for you."

My amusement fled. His touch made my skin crawl. Pedophiles. How sick could you get? Without replying, I scrambled to my feet as Arahni screamed her own disgust inside my head.

He jumped up to stand beside me; clamped his fingers around my arm. "Where the hell you going?"

"Get your damn hand off of me," I said, twisting away.

My clearly female voice startled him. He stepped back. It was all I needed. I pushed him hard in the middle of his chest and he fell. I heard the dull crack as his head struck a rock. He lay there stunned. I could walk away, but it wasn't enough, not nearly enough. At my feet was another rock. I scooped it up, jumped toward him. "You sick, sick, bastard," I said as I smashed it into his face. Again and again I pounded, while inside me the Hunger roared in ecstasy. When I could not lift the rock again, I stopped, looked into what remained of his face. Not many of his features could be recognized. "You won't abuse any more little boys."

I turned, walked to the edge of the lapping water and threw the rock into the surf.

Next to the man's body, Arahni waited in the tote bag. No words came from her, but I felt her waves of displeasure. I stubbornly refused to defend myself, it was what it was.

Tote bag in hand, I turned back toward the parking lot. As I passed the man, I took a minute to kick sand into his wide-open mouth.

In the Mustang, Arahni remained quiet no longer.

The crude death demeans us.

Her icy tone of voice made me cringe. "His breathing of air offended me," I said.

You must learn control. If...

"I am in control. When haven't I used the discipline of the hunt?"

You let Morgan play with your mind. He is not good for us.

I removed Arahni from the tote bag, caressed her with my fingers. "I need My Morgan. Without him I might as well walk into those waves."

I am no longer enough? Surprise and hurt made Arahni's voice sharp.

"You are not."

There was no response.

"Arahni?" Panic twisted inside me. "I want both of you. Why can't I have both? I deserve both." Still only silence. I picked up the shafra. "I will not live without you also." I held the blade's tip at my heart. Inside me the Hunger leapt in excitement. Was this what it wanted? It's ultimate desire, to be fed with my own death? I pressed Arahni's tip against my breast, felt her bite, saw red flow from my skin. Slow was not the way. Could I end it now? Leave My Morgan to the bitch? Who would care for Arahni? Would she take a new love? Speak to them? Would they hunt?

We will live, Arahni said.

Tears filled my eyes, ran down my cheeks as I laid the shafra beside me. "I will practice more control. I will never cheapen our hunt again." Her satisfaction warmed my chilled skin.

Now we plan.

Chapter Twenty-Nine
Morgan Garrett

Wes was true to his word. The folder on Robert Grindle had arrived this morning; skimpy, but I hadn't expected much. A note from Wes said they only had this because a judge had ordered an investigation of the man when he had been considered for a judgeship. I frowned. Grindle was still a lawyer. What had been the problem?

So far the information was all ordinary, bordering on boring. Where he was born, grew up, went to school. The year he married, when his first, and only, kid arrived. The guy didn't so much as have an unpaid library fine. Squeaky clean. Warning bells went off inside my head. No one was that clean.

I'd shuffled the papers together, opened the envelope to stuff them inside when I saw the corner of a photo sticking out of a side pocket.

There wasn't one, but three pictures. The first showed a middle aged man wearing a dark-blue suit. A red and lighter-blue tie rested against a white shirt. He had dark hair, just starting to gray. It was a little on the long side. He wore black rimmed glasses. I turned the photo over. Robert Grindle,12-10-09 was written on the back. Well that helped. At least I knew what the guy looked like.

The next photo showed Grindle in a restaurant, he leaned toward a good-looking redhead. I flipped it over. There was nothing on the back. Wife or girlfriend? I'd have to find out.

The last photograph made me frown. Grindle again, but this time he was with Darcie's mom and dad. He stood between them with his arms around their shoulders. Her parents hadn't changed a bit. Darcie had inherited her dad's smile and her mom's gorgeous eyes. I turned the photo over. Nothing. Wes had said Grindle knew the Devonshires. Just how well?

My clock read nine AM. Darcie would be in the office? I could call. I pushed my chair back and stood. Nope. I needed to see her face when I asked her my questions. Faces told a lot, even when lips lied.

Inside the police station I sidled up to the long counter and said to the sergeant, "My name is Garrett, I'd like to see Detective Devonshire."

He looked me over and then picked up his phone and punched in a number. After a brief conversation he said, "Down the hall. She'll meet you."

Darcie waited for me. Balanced on the balls of her feet she looked ready for anything, typical Darcie.

"This way." She turned to the left.

I followed as she led me into a space that looked to be an interrogation room. Two chairs on each side of a square table.

"Morgan." Nothing else.

"Darcie." Two could play the game.

She broke first. "Why did you come back to Santa Maria?"

I'd already told her once. Did she think the story would be different this time around? Was this some sort of damn test? What the hell, if telling it one more time made her believe me. "I hit bottom Darcie. This was one place where I'd been happy. No dead kid, no bullets flying. I didn't know you were here. I thought you were still with the Company.

"When Paddy alibied me and I was released, I got drunk, ran my truck into a tree." I looked away from her. "I couldn't remember a damn thing. That was it. I just wanted to get well. Johnny helped me do that. Dr. Solomon showed me the way."

Darcie snorted. "Looks to me like she is still trying to show you the way."

The look on Darcie's face branded the snort and sarcastic words a lie. She seemed sad, or maybe I just wanted her to be.

She looked into my face a long moment before saying. "Were you going to get in touch with Da and Mum?"

"No, at least not right away. Darcie, I haven't had a drink since I got out of the clinic. I'm trying to kick it. I make no promises. I did that in the past, but I am trying. One day at a time, that's working with the booze, do you think it could work with us? One day at a...."

The door opened and Wes stuck his head in. "English, phone call, line two. Hey Morgan, what's up?"

"I've got to take this." She looked like she welcomed the excuse not to answer my question. "Wes, how about you giving Morgan a tour?"

"Sure thing."

I followed Wes down the hall to the coffee pot. Not speaking he poured us both a cup and pointed at the sugar and some kind of powdered creamer.

"Thanks, but I take it black."

"You're a little pale. I figure you needed it. You and Darcie…" He shook his head. "You want to share?"

"Why not? We were close once. I fucked it up bad. Now I'm trying to make it right, but she is a tough nut to crack. We can't go back, but I would like to make friends."

He patted my shoulder. "Hang in there. We all need friends."

We walked into the office the two of them shared. Darcie was there. As we entered she hung up the phone and then stared at the wall. It didn't look like she'd received welcomed news.

"Everything okay?" Wes said.

She turned to face us. "Come on in Morgan, this is our place."

I looked around at the bulletin boards laden with notices of everything from parties to wanted posters. A lot of the info was about the serial killer Ice. I'd seen reports about him on the national news. He'd struck in San Francisco, but not in the Santa Maria area as far as I knew. Why was Darcie so into him? I

230

walked to her desk, looked down and spotted a picture of a shafra. "Interesting pixs. Are you starting a collection?" I leaned over to get a better look.

She flipped the photo over. "It's one of a few clues we have to Ice."

"You expecting him to make a visit here?"

Wes and Darcie exchanged a quick look.

I nodded. "You think he's already been here. I didn't read anything in the paper."

"Nothing more to say," Darcie said.

"Ice using a shafra?"

She gave me a warning look. "Drop it Morgan."

I put some pieces together. "That guy in the alley, the one I stumbled on. His throat had been cut." I tried to remember. Had there been two cuts, one shallow one deep? I knew how a shafra worked.

Darcie's lips tightened. She flicked her hair free from the back of her collar and began to drum her fingers on the desk as she said, "Ice kills in beds."

I knew all her tell signs and backed off. "What do you know about a lawyer named Robert Grindle?"

Darcie looked surprised by my question. "He's a friend of Da's. Why are you looking at him?"

"He wants to work for Scarsdale. I'm just doing some background checking."

"You want to talk to Da?" Darcie seemed open and receptive now that we weren't talking about Ice.

"Yeah, that might help, but I can't see your dad being happy to see me."

"He knows you're in the area," she said.

I frowned. What had she told her parents? At one time her father had been calling me son. "Darcie could we maybe have dinner, talk a little? Catch up on each other's lives."

I watched the cloud move onto her face and then felt relief as I saw it fade away. Maybe there was a ray of hope?

"Sure. Why not? We'll double date. You bring your doctor friend. I'd like you to meet Mayo."

Mayo. Who the hell was Mayo? I felt a stab of jealousy. Was that they way it was going to be? Friends only? It seemed to be the answer as far as Darcie was concerned. I knew without a mirror that the cloud had settled upon my face. Hell, what I had expected? She'd open her arms and we'd go back to the way things were before I'd shot the kid? A double date? Darcie's message was clear. Past was the past. I could do worse than have Sherice in my future, but I sure the hell was going to check out this Mayo, God what a stupid name. He'd damned well better be good enough for her. "Sounds good. Let me check with Sherice and we'll set a date."

I heard a soft snort. Darcie and I both glanced at Wes who'd suddenly seemed to find the office bulletin board to be all consuming.

Chapter Thirty
Darcie Devonshire

The papers on my desk blurred. Bloody hell, what had I done? Agreed to a double date with Morgan and his doctor friend? Talk about torture. What was I trying to prove? I had to get out of it. I willed the phone to ring. Where was a good, all consuming crime, when you needed one?

Wes came into the office. "We lucked out," he said by way of greeting. "We'd be the whole day sifting through the sand."

"What are you talking about?"

"Couple of joggers found a body on Guadalupe beach."

My ears perked up. Maybe they would need some help. "Who is it?"

"No ID. The face too bashed in to tell. His prints weren't in the system."

"Dental?"

"If they can find some of his teeth that weren't shattered."

I winced. "Sounds personal; that much rage."

Wes shrugged. "So you and Morgan are double-dating? That should be interesting."

It was my turn to shrug. "He seems to be planning on staying in the area. We need to be civilized about everything."

"Oh. Of course." Wes moved to his desk, settled behind it. "When is this date going to happen?"

"I have to check with Mayo."

"I guess our overload of cases is making that a problem."

I shot him a hard look. "I can't call Mayo until he's home from work."

"What does tall, dark and Italian do anyway?"

I was happy I knew the answer. I just discovered for myself yesterday what Mayo did as an occupation. "He's owns a company in San Francisco that makes pasta sauce. It's been in his family for years."

"Impressive."

"Devonshire. Smith." The captain's voice coming from the doorway of our office made us both jump.

I jerked my head toward him. He looked liked he'd aged ten years since this morning. What the hell had happened? .

"Ice has struck again."

*****

I leaned against the hotel room's door. Newer place, I thought numbly. I hadn't checked this hotel out yet. Maybe if I had I could have warned…. Why was he here? Why wasn't he home with his wife? My hands began to shake and my legs felt like they'd turned into over-cooked spaghetti. How could I tell Da? I'd never had to tell someone from my immediate family.

From in front of the blood-drenched bed, Wes glanced back. Alarm filled his face and he rushed to me. "English, what is it?" He grabbed me by my shoulders, guided me to a chair.

"I know him." I managed to say. "Robert Grindle."

"The same Grindle Morgan was asking about?"

I felt my head jerk in a nod

"You sit this one out. I'll take care of it," Wes ordered.

I gulped in air, dug my fingernails into the chair arms. "No. The worse is over. It was the shock." I pushed myself to my feet, walked to the bed. Grindle lay in a pool of blood. His hands and feet were bound to the four posts of the bed. The two slices across his throat were evident, one deeper, one shallow. I swallowed.

"Coroner's here," Wes said.

I turned toward the doorway. County Sheriff Jeff Macon stood there.

"Darcie. Wes," he said and walked past us. He stood, looking down at Robert Grindle's body. "So Ice has made it to Santa Maria?"

"And it's the last bloody place he'll kill," I said. "We're going to catch this asshole." I turned. "Wes, who called it in?"

"Hotel maid. She's waiting at the front desk."

"Let's go talk to her."

The woman sat with her head buried in her hands. A uniformed officer stood next to her holding a bottle of water. Both looked as white as the bleached walls surrounding them. I didn't recognize the young officer. He must have been new to the force. His name tag read Carl Clark.

"Officer Clark," I said. "You were first on the scene?"

His head bobbed in a short nod. I saw him swallow. "Close by," he murmured.

The hotel maid looked up. Her eyes were still wide and red from crying. Her name tag read Abigail Prentiss. "I called out housekeeping. He didn't answer. I used my key…" her voice trailed away. A shudder moved through her. "So much blood."

"Were you on last night when Mister Grindle checked in?" Wes asked, his pen poised over his notebook.

"I came on this morning, but if that's a Mister Grindle, then this isn't his room. This room's registered to a Charles Lang."

I frowned. A fake name could have been used. I didn't know if Robert Grindle played around or not, but it was beginning to look that way.

"The night clerk's been called," Officer Clark said. "He's on the way."

My cell phone vibrated. I pulled it out, looked at the number. It was Mayo. I put it back in my pocket. "Wes, I'll take the night clerk."

He nodded. As I walked toward the registration desk, my cell phone vibrated again. It was Morgan. "Hello."

"I've talked to Sherice. How about tonight for that date?"

"I'll have to get back to you. We've had a murder."

There was a moment of silence, then. "We'll talk later, Darcie."

And just like that, I felt like I'd been thrown a lifeline. Morgan and I would talk later, like a hundred times before. My partner had my back, he'd put my feet beneath me again. Taking a deep breath I pushed the door open and walked into a sea of shouted questions. Microphones were thrust into my face. I held up my hands in surrender. "One question at a time please."

Chapter Thirty-One
Sherice Solomon

My gaze returned to the chest. From inside I felt Arahni's hum of contentment and in my stomach the Hunger slumbered. I walked to the chest and ran my fingers along its top. The hunt last night had been needed to appease Arahni, to remove the taint of the beach slaughter.

I opened the chest, reached beneath the shafra and removed the blood-splattered hand towel. One dried-brown spot resembled a heart. I held the towel against mine, remembered and smiled.

*****

All was prepared. After researching nearby hotels on the Internet, there were few with four poster beds, I'd found one, called and made the reservations for two rooms. One as Isabelle Kramer, the other as Charles Lang's executive assistant. They hadn't batted an eye when I'd arrived to pick up his key, saying Mister Lang's flight had been delayed.

I did wander why they did not warm me about the notorious serial killer Ice, after all I did request a room with a four-poster bed, but not a word was said. They were more concerned that I knew that check out time was at 12:00 noon.

Our late evening drive had been fruitless. I had stopped at three night spots, but all had been on the quiet side. I was beginning to think our preparation was all for nothing, that we would have to hunt again tomorrow, a thought that made the Hunger growl in denial. Arahni suggested we stop for a drink, re-plan, and I'd pulled in to the parking lot of the Metro Club.

In a dim corner I turned off the car. The ease from which I climbed from the rented Ford Escape branded my little, senior-lady appearance a lie. I smoothed my polyester tunic and slacks with my hands, and placing my tote bag on my shoulder, shuffled toward the Metro Club's door.

Inside I paused, scanning the room. There were enough bodies for me to blend in. "Who?" I said to Arahni.

That one calls to me.

She led my eyes to a man who sat alone toward the end of the bar. He wore, jeans, and a tan golf shirt, just like the one My Morgan wore yesterday. I frowned. The man also had the same dark hair as Morgan. I felt Arahni's pleased amusement as the realization flowed through my mind. "We will talk of this later," I promised.

Next to the man, I made much of my climb onto the stool and the placing of my bag on the bar in front of me. I bumped his shoulder and felt him back from me. The bartender glanced my way and then went back to talking with some under-age tart. I gave him a few more minutes and then loudly cleared my throat. When he still ignored me, I went into a loud coughing fit and clutched at my chest.

"Damn-it, Raul. Another one dies in here and they'll close us for sure."

The words came from behind me and I turned. A cocktail waitress stood there, Doreen her name tag read.

"What do you want, honey?"

"A champagne cocktail," I said.

She laughed. "For that you should go to the Santa Maria Inn. How about a nice Chardonnay in a clean glass?"

I glanced at the prey next to me. "What are you drinking?"

"Seven and seven," he answered.

"I'll have that."

Doreen glared at the bartender. "You got that?"

He shrugged and picked up a glass from behind the bar.

Doreen gave me another smile and then shimmied away.

Raul placed the drink in front of me.

"You sure you want that?" The man next to me said.

"Sonny, I was doing tequila shots while you were still in diapers."

He grinned. "I'm Robert Grindle."

"Twyla Burbank," I said. "You a local?"

"The past twenty years."

"I'm only over night. I snuck away from my keepers."

Alarm flared in his face. "You did what?"

"They tucked me in at eight God-damn o'clock. Can you believe that, and then headed off to same Indian casino." I winked at him. "Didn't stay as you can see."

His alarm changed to amusement. "Well good for you. I can see my mom doing the same."

I took a long drink from my glass while from the bag on the bar Arahni disapproved of my course language. "You come here much? Not exactly the Four Seasons." The place was a dingy-dive. I spotted a drug deal going down in the far corner and a young prostitute headed toward the door, her arm hooked through that of a man easily as old as what I pretended to be.

Robert Grindle shrugged. "I drop in when I don't want to be recognized. If I am they keep it to themselves. The same way I do for them."

I leaned toward him. "You some kind of celebrity?"

He laughed. "I work for some who are high profile."

I emptied my glass. "Well, times awaiting." I slid from stool, made much of creaking knees, and grabbed by bag. "Nice meeting you, Robert Grindle."

He smiled and I hobbled away.

In the car, I pulled the wig from my head, added a long platinum-blonde one in its place. I shimmied out of the tunic and slacks. Beneath them I wore an almost painted-on, leopard print bodysuit. The one thing I didn't need to change were my gold, stiletto, sling backs. I should have worn loafers, but I couldn't force myself to do it.

With one eye on the Metro Club's door I applied red lipstick, sprayed musk perfume and then settled back to wait. It wasn't long. Our prey came out the door, walked to silver

BMW. The car started, backed from the parking slot. I followed. Before he turned onto the street, I gunned the motor,

swept around him and then side-swiped a dumpster. I turned off the car, kicked open the door and scrambled out.

Grindle looked as if he was going to drive by, so I slapped the side of his car and screamed. "Look what the hell you made me do."

He stopped, rolled down his driver's side window. "Me?" He pointed at my car. "How's that my fault?"

I thrust my shoulders back, letting my breasts almost pop from my low-cut top. His gaze dropped to where I'd intended. "Okay, so it was my fault. How about a ride to my hotel? I'll make it worth your time."

"Your car's drivable."

"Really. You think so? I'd still like that ride. How about you?"

It took him about a nano-second to decide. "Sure. Hop in."

At the hotel, I'd slipped him my key. "Give me a minute and then come on in. It's room 319."

"How will you get in?"

"I always get two keys."

I leaned toward him, gave the bulge in his pants a pat, and then threw in an exaggerated sway of my hips as I walked from him, just in case he was having second thoughts.

Inside the hotel's front door, I ducked into the bathroom, pulled a long black, silk sheathe from the tote bag and slipped it over the leopard body suit, blotted lipstick from my mouth and gathered all of the blonde hair into a loose ponytail. I came out of the bathroom and minced my way toward the elevators. From the front desk the night clerk called. "Good evening. May I help you?

I waved my room key and kept on walking."

In Charles Lang's room I only had time to strip the clothes from my body and slide into a red kimono before I heard the soft knock.

"Come on in."

He did. Looked around. "Nice place. You don't see many rooms with four-poster beds."

"Want a drink? I only have fixings for a seven and seven though."

"That works great."

"Would you mind opening the doors out to the balcony. It's stuffy in here."

He walked to the sliding doors. "Sure, no problem."

I smiled down at the drinks I mixed.

The rest had had been easy. Afterward, I'd showered, dressed, slipped from the room and walked two doors down. Inside the other room, I'd fell into the bed and slept like a baby.

Arahni and the Hunger had gloried in the kill, radiated pleasure as I'd painted myself with Robert Grindle's blood. I'd fantasized that it was Morgan's hands moving over my body, leaving behind their bloody trail.

I stretched out on the sofa, Arahni against my breasts. "Last night My Morgan's hands upon me had been a fantasy, but soon it will be real. We will make it so, won't we my beauty?" In my mind Arahni continued her contented humming.

Chapter Thirty-Two
Morgan Garrett

On the ride back to my apartment I played the conversation with Darcie back in my head seeking for something I might have missed. No matter which way I looked, it always came out the same. She'd made it clear friendship was all I could hope for. Well, that was better than hate. At home the first thing I did was call Sherice. "Hey."

"Morgan, I was just thinking about you."

"How about having dinner with some old friends?"

"Who? What old friends?"

"Uh…Darcie and her boyfriend."

"Darcie?" Softly, and then with a happy lilt, "Sure why not."

We talked some more, but I found myself searching for something to say that didn't include Darcie's name. I finally made an excuse about things to do and we punched off.

Now I needed to get a time for the date. I called Darcie. Two minutes later I closed the phone. A murder, she'd said. Who had been killed? I turned on the TV and there she was answering reporter's questions about some homicide.

My cell phone rang. I'd left it in the kitchen. "Yeah, Garrett."

"Morgan. Lyndon Scarsdale, we've got some trouble."

"What's up?"

"I just got a call from Robert Grindle's wife. The Santa Maria police called to tell her he was dead. Find out what happened."

"Dead? I completed my investigation. Didn't find anything big. You think this is tied in with your candidacy?"

"I don't know, but...."

"I'll get on it. See what I can uncover. First thing to do is to talk Mrs. Grindle."

"She was real hot to know what had happened, but didn't seem overly broken up."

Now that was an interesting little tidbit. "What's her number?" I scribbled it on a bill notice. "I'll call back in a hour."

"One other thing," Scarsdale said. "That political rally I mentioned the other day, the one that is tomorrow on the beach. I want you here."

"Won't you have security?"

"Yes, but I'd feel better if you were here."

"Mister Scarsdale, is there something you haven't told me?"

"I'm sure it's nothing, just a crackpot..."

"What happened?"

"Someone isn't happy with my position on curtailing drug trafficking."

"What time tomorrow?"

"2:00 PM."

"I'll be there." I hung up the phone.

My mind went back to Darcie. Was Grindle the homicide she was working? It would explain her tense tone. I walked back to the television, but the weather guy was on now. I called Darcie again. This time she didn't answer, so I left a message. "Darcie, meet me at the Starbucks in the Penny's shopping center at four."

It was 1:30 now. That gave me two and a half hours to see what I could dig up on Grindle's death. First thing was to make that call to the Mrs. I punched in the number. It rang ten times before an accented voice answered.

"Grindle residence."

"Mrs. Grindle, please."

"Mrs. Grindle is not available. I will take a message."

"This is Morgan Garrett, a friend of Lyndon Scarsdale. He asked me to get in touch with her."

"One moment please."

A minute later another voice came on the line.

"Mister Garrett, you found out something?"

"Not yet, but I'd like to drop by and talk to you about your husband."

Oh? Okay you can come now if you want."

*****

Edith Grindle turned out to be a nice looking woman accepting her age and not being pretentious about it. The Grindle's home was a large ranch set well back on a manicured lawn. The inside matched the exterior, hardwood floors and throw rugs with just the proper number of porcelain gadgets in perfect order. When I was a kid I had an Aunt with a house like this. It scared hell out of me. I was always afraid I would break something.

Her greeting told me a lot.

"Mr. Garrett, you find the whore he was with and you'll have your killer."

"Did he say where he was going?"

She smiled coldly. "He never did. Robert was always meeting a client—the kind you pay $50.00 to for a blow job. Try the Metro club. I followed him one time to there." She shook her head. "Poor Robert, he had no sense where cheap women were concerned."

We talked for a few more minutes but it was clear she did not know any more than she had all ready told me. There didn't seem to be any connection to Scarsdale, unless he liked purchased company also? I couldn't see that, but stranger things had happened. My next stop was the Metro club.

*****

It's funny how dumps like the Metro Club always look worse in broad daylight. The front door was propped open for air, but I doubted it was working. At the bar a guy in his

244

undershirt played bartender while schmoozing with two girls in tight jeans and even tighter tube tops.

"Wha cha have?"

"Answers. Were you working last night?" I placed a twenty dollar bill on the bar.

"I was." The words came from behind me and I turned. A tall blonde stood in the doorway that led into the back. .

"Did you see this guy?" I held up a picture of Grindle.

She moved toward me."Yeah, he's a regular. He was talking to an old broad. It was weird. She seemed way out of her element. Really slumming it. Those shoes she wore could have paid a month's mortgage on my place."

"Did he leave with her?"

She laughed. "God no. Young and younger are, or was, his turn ons. No she left earlier. You a cop?"

"Did he leave with anyone?"

"Nope. All by himself. Right around midnight, I was getting ready to take my smoke break." She leaned toward me. "If you are a cop you're the cutest one I've seen lately. That creep from vice, Henderson, sucks buttermilk."

Our friendly bar keep finally spoke up. "Doreen, zip it."

"Anything else you remember."

"Nothing but those shoes, gold stiletto sling backs. Sure as I'm not a virgin, they were Manolo Blahnik's. Damn, I'd have to take fifty guys in the back to afford even one of them.

"Shut up you mouthy bitch, this'll be last time I tell you…" The bartender's words trailed away, but his glare finished the threat.

I could see his point. Wasn't good to have just anybody know there was entertaining-for-cash going on in the back room.

"Thanks for information." I didn't bother giving them my name…hell, I didn't want .either of them to have it.

I sat in the car and mulled over what was said. It wasn't much. Fancy shoes on a grandmother type. I'd have to ask Sherice about them. I'd written the name down, Manolo Blahnik's. It didn't mean a damn thing to me, but Sherice had a thing for expensive shoes.

I frowned. Grindle didn't leave with the elderly lady. He'd left by himself. I needed to plan my next move, but nothing came to me. I glanced at my watch. 3:45. Time to hotfoot it to Starbucks. I hoped Darcie would show.

She was there waiting for me. I saw her in corner. She stared out the window and sipped from a coffee cup. I moved to the counter ordered my cappuccino, and then walked to her."Waiting long?"

"About ten minutes."

"The homicide, was it Robert Grindle?

"That information hasn't been released," she answered stiffly.

"Scarsdale called me. They'd already notified Mrs. Grindle. She called him."

"Wes is talking to Edith now."

"You're not?" That surprised the hell out of me.

"Edith and I rub each other the wrong way. She doesn't approve of lady cops." Darcie sipped from her cup, looked at me over the rim. "She give you anything?"

"Grindle liked to pay for it. His favorite scoring spot seems to the Metro Club."

The girl behind the counter motioned toward me and I fetched my coffee drink.

"The Metro Club huh?" Darcie said as I sat across from her again.

"He was there last night. I talked to a cocktail waitress. He left the place alone around midnight."

"Well sometime between there and 1:00 today he got himself killed."

"Was it Ice?"

"Sorry, I can't tell you that Morgan."

I grinned. "Well you didn't say it wasn't." I looked closer at Darcie's face. Saw the tenseness around her eyes and mouth. "You doing okay with this? You told your dad?"

"I did. He's pretty shook up. Told me to find the bastard who did it."

I chanced reaching across to touch her hand. "You will Darcie. That's how you're made."

She let my hand cover hers for a moment and then gently pulled it away. "Let's talk about that date. Tonight works for Mayo too."

"Sounds good. Where did you have in mind?"

"Steamers in Pismo Beach. How about 7:00?"

"Fine."

Darcie slid her chair book and stood. "I've got to get going. I told Da I'd drop by."

"You want me to go with you?"

She smiled. "Now that would be interesting. No, but thanks for the offer. I'll see you tonight."

I watched her walk out the door and then reached for my coffee. Friends, I told myself, just friends.

Chapter Thirty-Three
Darcie Devonshire

I smoothed the emerald green dress down over my hips, frowned and turned again toward the closet. I took two steps and then stopped. "No Devonshire, you're bloody well not changing again." Five times I'd almost called the whole thing off. I had a damn good excuse. I'd been up to my eyebrows in the Grindle case all afternoon, and still knew little. Luckily, ten minutes into the impromptu news conference the captain had arrived and I'd dumped it all in his lap. I hadn't felt like making nice.

I'd went back inside in time to see the night clerk arrive, he'd confirmed the room was signed out to a Mister Charles Lang.

I frowned at the window. Then where was the missing Lang? The night clerk couldn't remember what Lang had looked like. I showed him a photo of Grindel's body, asked if that was Lang?

"I don't think so. I don't remember seeing that guy," he said. "But Lang's secretary picked up the key card. She said Mister Lang would be arriving late."

"What did she look like? Did you get her name?"

"Average. Brown hair, tortoise shell glasses, dark business suit."

"A name?" I said.

The desk clerk had shrugged. "Don't remember."

I rubbed the back of my neck. How had Robert Grindle ended up dead in that room? Was Charles Lang, Ice? I'd went back to the station and did a check on the name, Charles Lang, there were fifty of them in the United States. Not one of them lived in California though, but that didn't mean anything. So far I'd found nothing that showed where a Charles Lang had flown or taken Amtrak or a bus to anywhere in California either, but I'd had to call it quits before getting through the entire list and head home to get ready for the big double date.

I walked to the bathroom and jerked a comb through my hair. "There has to be something. No one's that good."

I picked up a bottle of perfume, dotted it on my wrists. "Think about something else." My mind imminently went to Starbucks and Morgan and that wasn't much better. Our talk had been hard on both of us. I'd seen in his eyes how he wanted to hold me, like he'd always did before, and yes, I'd wanted to lay my head against his chest, listen to his heart beat, but too much had happened. We couldn't go back.

I'd went right to Da after that. He had been grim and I knew he seethed with questions, but he listened to what I could give him, nodded stiffly and asked me to keep him in the loop.

In the front of the house, Becky barked and I glanced at the clock. 6:45. Mayo, right on time.

I opened the door and as usual Mayo's looks took my breath away. Tonight he wore white. Silk shirt, the first two button undone, and close fitting slacks.

His teeth flashed in a smile. "You look beautiful. I haven't seen you in green before."

"Thanks. Let me put Becky in the bedroom." I already had a small bite of treat ready for her. Becky went with her usual token grumble, but then settled right down for a nap. "I won't be long, baby." I planned to make this a short and sweet meal. No dessert and coffee, unless Mayo and I had it right here in my kitchen.

I grabbed my shawl as I passed and wrapped it around my shoulders.

Mayo had the top up on his MGB. He held the door open as I settled into the seat. He strapped himself in the driver's side and then glanced at me. "Rough day?"

"Very. I don't want to talk work. Okay?"

He nodded. "Tell me about this Morgan Garrett." Mayo turned the MGB and headed down my driveway.

"Not much to tell. We were partners in the CIA. Six years ago we both went our separate ways. Luck brought him to Santa Maria. More luck threw him together with Wes." I glossed over our reunion at The Fish Shanty.

"And Wes did not know that you and he were ex-partners?"

"I'd never mentioned Morgan by name."

Mayo accelerated onto Highway 101. "Tell me about this Morgan's lady friend."

I frowned at the side window. "I don't know much about her. Her name is Sherice Solomon. She's a shrink."

"Attractive?"

I felt a little nip from the old green-eyed monster and didn't welcome it one little bit. "I guess so. If you like the waif type." I turned to face him. "How are things going with that new pasta sauce? Did you discover the right cheese to add?"

Mayo took the hint and neither Morgan or Sherice's names were mentioned for the remainder of the trip.

At Steamers we found a parking spot close the door and made it inside with three minutes to spare. I'd thought I'd have a few moments to catch my breath, but Morgan and Sherice were waiting for us.

"Morgan, Miss Solomon this is Mayo Gerardi. Mayo, Morgan Garrett and Sherice Solomon."

"Doctor Sherice Solomon," she corrected with a chilly smile.

My nod was just as cool.

Morgan looked good, all in black to Mayo's white. I wondered if that meant anything. Sherice wore a bronze-colored dress that shimmered as she moved. It had a cowl neckline, demure, until she turned. The back did not exist, the fabric started again just above her butt. I watched Morgan's hand resting against her pale flesh and my stomach knotted. Oh, this was going to be bloody fun.

I glanced at Mayo, who was looking at everything except Sherice's naked back. Nice try, I thought, but it did make me feel better. He reached to take my hand and I smiled up at him.

"I asked for a booth by a window," Morgan said, over his shoulder to us.

"Sounds great."

Mayo and I followed them.

Mayo slid into the booth seat across from Sherice. That left me facing Morgan. The hostess handed up menus and then waltzed back toward the front.

"Beautiful dress. I love that color of green," Sherice said.

"Darcie always did look good in green," Morgan said before I could respond.

The waiter arrived. Introduced himself, rattled off the night's specials, took our order for a bottle of Zinfandel, and then speed-walked away.

"What are you having, Darcie," Mayo asked.

"I'll be you're having the sea bass, right?" Morgan said.

That had been my first choice, but an imp inside of me said, "I'm thinking king crab legs."

Mayo grinned at me. "My choice too."

The wine arrived. It was poured, sampled, and orders given. Mayo leaned toward Sherice. "You are a doctor of psychiatry?"

I listened to them talk and sipped my wine. I felt Morgan's gaze upon me and sipped more wine. The waiter brought our salads, I started to sip more wine and saw my glass was empty. With a strange look in my direction, Mayo refilled my glass. I felt my cheeks heat, so I sipped more wine. I did note that Morgan drank only water. Maybe he was for real. The conversation slid to a halt. Silence stretched.

Sherice looked into my eyes. "How many years were you and Morgan partners?"

"Six," I said, reaching for my wine.

"You were with him when the boy was killed?"

I heard Morgan's sharp intake of breath. Bitch, I thought. "I was."

"You are in his nightmares."

I sat back in the booth. "Excuse me."

"Sherice," Morgan said. "I thought you didn't talk about what was said in session?"

"The nightmare I witnessed was outside of session." Sherice took a sip of her wine.

I saw Morgan look at me. "It wasn't like that. I told her just how it went down."

Sherice shrugged, reached to take his hand. "It's all good. I've helped Morgan cast out his demons."

Damn. She's not talking about booze, she bloody well means me. I wanted to reach across the table and slap her simpering face. How the hell had she gotten her hooks into Morgan? The booze must have fried half of his brain cells. I curled my fingers around my wine glass' stem.

"Mayo, what's your line of work?" Morgan said.

"I own a food company. We make pasta sauce."

"It's been his family for years," I added. "Mayo drives a MGB and has an Indian motorcycle."

"Motorcycle?" Sherice shuddered. "They're so dangerous. You'd never catch me on one of them."

Morgan and I shared a look. Glancing away from him, toward Sherice, I saw her eyes narrow.

Our dinners arrived.

I kept my eyes down, worked on my crab legs and let the conversation flow over my head, but my ears kept searching for Morgan's voice. This wasn't good. I couldn't still love him. I couldn't. He was a drunk who shattered my heart. He was also the man who held me to his chest as bullets whizzed above our heads, and still another time made love to me as waves whispered into our moon-drenched window.

Mayo's voice broke into my thoughts. "Darcie? Darcie?"

I looked toward him. "Yes?"

"I asked how your crab was?"

"It's great. Yours?"

"I said mine was fine."

"The sea bass is terrific," Morgan said. "You should have tried it."

"I think I know what I want," I said, sharper than I had intended. Morgan and Mayo looked shocked. The bitch smiled.

I pulled my napkin from my lap, placed it on the table next to me. "I need to make a call. I'll be right back."

Mayo slid from the booth, stepped back to let me pass. "Would you like dessert?"

I forced a smile. "No. Let's have it later."

He grinned at me and then nodded.

Outside in the cool air, I leaned my hot cheek against the side of the building. Mayo was so perfect for me. Handsome, great in bed, damn, he owned his own company, but bloody hell, I didn't love him. I liked him. I could pretend, but he deserved so much more. Bloody-damn-Morgan, still owned my heart. How could that be after everything that had happened between us?

I'd told him we couldn't be anything but friends, insisted even and from the way he looked at Sherice, he believed me. What now? I say I changed my mind?

I turned and stared across the water.

Morgan looked happy. I hadn't seen him happy since he'd shot that boy in Iraq. Wouldn't I be a painful memory for him? He was battling the alcohol. I couldn't be responsible for his retreat back into that hell. He had Sherice now. It was easy to see she loved him, maybe too much.

I frowned. Now I was just being catty. I was glad for him—I was With Morgan I'd known what real love was. I didn't feel that for Mayo and I knew I couldn't settle for anything less, and Mayo shouldn't either.

I felt tears threaten and blinked my eyes. I had to tell him tonight. It was the right thing to do. I grimaced at the stars. Not the dessert I'm sure he had in mind.

I straightened. Walked back to the booth. "Sorry guys, but Wes says we've got a lead on the Grindle murder. I've got to go to the station."

No one questioned my lie. Morgan insisted on getting the check. Mayo argued. Morgan won. Quick good-bye's were said and Mayo and I were out the door in short time.

Mayo stopped the car in my driveway. "Sorry you have to go into the station."

"I lied. Why don't you come in?"

There must have been something in my voice, because he hesitated before he switched off the engine. "Okay."

In the kitchen I avoided Mayo's gaze as I asked. "Coffee."

"Aren't you going to free the princess from her prison?"

I did hear Becky stirring. She would be wondering why I hadn't let her from the bedroom. "She can wait for a minute. There's something I have to say."

"Darcie, I'm not liking the vibes I'm getting here."

I took a deep breath. "Mayo, you're a great guy. Funny, charming, sexy as hell…"

"Stop right there. I can see the way this is going and I'm not accepting the ride."

He tried to take my hands and I stepped back. "I have to do this…"

"No, you don't." He turned from me. "I'll call you tomorrow."

"Mayo, I can't fall in love with you."

He went still. "Can't or won't?"

"Can't."

"Is it Morgan?"

I looked away. "That road's closed."

"You still want to travel it." His words were a statement.

I met his eyes. "I still love him."

"And Sherice?"

I didn't have an answer to that. I shrugged. "I can't do this to you. I care too much…."

"If he hadn't come back into your life…?

"Maybe? I don't know, but he has."

"He has someone else now." He turned toward the sink. "I can wait until you see…"

"No. I didn't want to tell you, but, Morgan and I talked, today at Starbucks." That part was the truth. "We're going to give it another try." The lies came easy to me. "He's not drinking now. That's what broke us up. It was never that we didn't love each other. We'd all ready made plans for dinner, so decided to keep them. He's telling Sherice tonight also."

Mayo didn't turn, but I watched his back stiffen. "I see."

A soft whine came from my bedroom.

"You should see to Becky." He turned toward the doorway.

"Mayo ...?"

He stopped, but didn't turn to face me. "Don't ask can we still be friends? Don't insult us both."

"I'm sorry."

He walked out of the kitchen. A moment later the front door closed. I heard the MGB start, rev, and he drove out of my life.

Dizziness washed over me and I realized I was holding my breath. I released it a loud whoosh. My God. What had I done? Morgan was lost to me and I'd pushed Mayo away

I turned and walked to my bedroom. Becky looked up at me with confused brown eyes. I dropped to the rug beside her. She climbed into my lap, all 50 pounds of her. I wrapped my arms around her, buried my face in her fur and let the tears fall.

Chapter Thirty-Four
Sherice Solomon

Morgan remained quiet as he drove me toward my cottage. I'd tried twice to engage him in conversation, but his one word responses had filled me with apprehension. I feared I knew what occupied his thoughts. I glanced at him. He looked sad. Why can't you see? Darcie Devonshire is no good for you. She will be a constant reminder of the boy you killed. She will force you back into the hole I lifted you from. No. I will not let that happen to you, My Morgan. If you cannot resist the step backward into hell, then I will remove the temptation.

Morgan stopped the car. We had arrived. I noticed he did not turn off the motor. "Wonderful food," I said.

"Steamer's is always great."

"Would you like to come in?" I watched his face for my answer. Oh My Morgan, you give everything away.

"Why not," he at last said.

A flame of anger licked the cold inside my stomach. I would not be a substitute for much longer. "You know what? I'd like a rain check. I feel a headache coming on."

Morgan looked surprised, and then relieved. "Hate those headaches. Hope they don't become a habit." He leaned toward me, brushed his lips against mine. "I'll call you."

Nodding, not trusting my voice, I exited the car. He managed to wait until I made it to the door and went inside, before he roared away.

Did he go to her?

I walked to an end table, picked up the lamp and threw it against the wall. It made a satisfying crash, but it wasn't enough. I looked around for something else to destroy and settled for ripping the drapes from the windows. It did nothing to quench my rage. I knew only one thing would. I stood with eyes closed; willing my breathing and heart beat to slow. Control. I would have control. I moved to the chest and removed Arahni. She was quiet, brooding, clearly unhappy with my actions. "The bitch Devonshire has to die."

Still Arahni did not respond.

"With her dead Morgan will be again ours."

Not ours, yours.

I ignored her words. "With her it will be slower. You're first bite will be shallow." I saw it in my mind, the slow, flow of blood, trailing down her neck. Inside of me the Hunger awoke, nipped, while in my head Arahni sighed.

Why must you have the man?

"He is mine! No one takes what is mine!"

If it must be, then when?

I smiled, reached to pick her up. "Darcie has made me hurt, so first we will make her hurt.

Yes. I see it in your heart. It is a good plan.

"We will do it tomorrow at the Grapevine Bed and Breakfast."

Where we killed Jake Holt?

"A further slap in her face."

Arahni began to hum.

Behind me the telephone rang. Maybe it was My Morgan. He realized it was me he wanted. I leapt upon it. "Yes."

"Doctor Solomon?"

It took a couple of heart beats for me to recognize Walter Granger's voice. I coughed loudly before I went on. "Oh, Mister Granger. How are things getting along without me at Pacific Winds?" I coughed again.

"You sound terrible, and you are very much missed."

"This horrible flu. It keeps me in my bed, except when I heat more chicken soup."

"I can come by. Would you like that? I have a wonderful bedside manner."

I shuddered at the thought. "Oh no. I'll be fine. I can't let you see me like this, all mussed. I haven't showered…"

"I'd very much like to help you with that."

I realized I still held Arahni and that I was making slashing movements with my hand. Could I?

No. Arahni snapped. *You are not thinking. The man…*

"Has nothing to do with it."

"What? Excuse me," Walter Granger said.

"Sorry, I was talking to my cat."

"I didn't know you had a cat."

Well, why would you little man? There is much you don't know about me. "I adopted her a few days ago. She's a ginger striped tabby. It's been wonderful to have her to stroke."

I heard him moan at my words and he cleared his throat before he went on. "Well then, I'll call tomorrow to see how you are."

"That's so kind. Goodnight, Mister Granger." I hung up the phone.

*****

So the man I'd seen at the bitch's place had been Mayo Gerardi. I clicked the button to move to the next screen on my computer monitor. Who would think there could be so many Mayo Gerardi's in California, but there was only one who owned Gerardi's Gourmet Pasta Sauces, and there he was. I clicked on the link, went to the website and clicked on contact information. It listed his email. It took me another twenty minutes to locate his Santa Maria address.

I moved to the chest, picked up Arahni. "Feel like a ride?"

Mayo Gerardi lived in the Elkmeadow housing development in south Santa Maria. Beyond the expanse of manicured, green law, sprawled a stucco, ranch house. I wondered if it had belonged to his parents. I knew from my Internet search they'd died two years ago.

I parked three houses up, placed an open map in my lap and watched his house in my rearview mirror. Ten minutes later he came from the house and stumbled down the driveway to pick up a newspaper. He looked hung over, or maybe still drunk. He hadn't struck me as a drinker? He'd only had two glasses of wine at dinner. Last night he'd seemed to be walking on a cloud of love. So what had happened? I feared I knew. "So, bitch. You've destroyed another man and they call me a serial killer."

I gave him five minutes and then punched in his cell phone number. It rang ten times before he answered.

"Hello," he snapped.

"Mayo," I said in a faint voice."

"Who is this? I have no wish to purchase anything. How did you get my private number?"

"It's Sherice..." I let my voice trail away. "Morgan...he...Darcie..." I faked a sob.

There was a long moment of silence. "I see."

"You too?" I said.

"Last night."

"Oh," I whispered. "They must have planned it that way."

"It would seem so."

"I'm sorry I bothered you. I thought you'd...."

"Sherice, you are not bothering me. It's been a long, rough night."

"I know what you mean." I caressed Arahni with my fingers. I waited. The next move must be his.

"Perhaps we can get together and talk," Mayo said, and I smiled.

"I'd love that. It hurts so damn much. How can they do this to us?"

"Tonight at the Starlight. Let's say nine. Do you know it?"

"I'll find it." I flipped my cell phone shut, reached to pick up Arahni. "Our journey to the end has begun. Soon Morgan will be ours."

On the return trip to Morro Bay I stopped at Von's supermarket and bought a bottle of Zinfandel. At my cottage I called the Grapevine Bed and Breakfast.

"Why yes, the Cabernet Room is available for tomorrow. Would you like it for the weekend?" the woman said.

I would, and it now belonged to Angelica de' Muerte. I smiled, placed the length of rope and the GHB in my tote bag. The name had come to me as I'd chosen between a cantaloupe and a papaya.

In my bedroom I created a new me. Angelica de' Muerte…angel of death. What did Angelica look like? My hands moved over my hairpieces. I chose a dark wig of flowing waves. My eyes. What color of eyes went with such hair and name? Dark, almost black. "My skin. It must be dusky and my lips, as red as blood." I laughed at my words.

What outfit would best suit Angelica? I wanted the woman to be noticed. She had to capture our prey's attention, draw him into the web to be devoured by the black widow.

I walked naked to the chest, opened it and removed Arahni. "What will Angelica wear?" I said, standing in front of the open closet door. "Shall she be demure? Sexy? Shy? Aggressive?" I trailed Arahni along the rack of clothing. "Do you see anything that strikes your fancy?"

There. Arahni said. *We will dress so.*

She had chosen red leather pants and a matching halter-top. So sexy and aggressive it would be.

I slid into the leather pants and top, looked into the mirror. Angelica de' Muerte would be most men's wet dream.

Smiling I chose black, stiletto heels from the closest, fastened the straps around my ankles. The huntress was ready to stalk. In my stomach the Hunger growled its agreement. The outfit was a bit much for checking into a B&B so I grabbed a black silk tunic from my closest and slipped it over the red leather halter top. Much better.

The clock read 1:00. Late enough to leave for the Grapevine Bed and Breakfast. Arahni and I hummed together as I placed her in the tote bag next to the length of rope.

*****

The Grapevine Bed and Breakfast looked different in the bright sunlight, inviting. I'd always liked blue and white houses. That's what My Morgan and I will have. Maybe in Santa Barbara. With a view of the ocean. I could picture the two of us lounging on the picturesque swing, discussing our hunt from the night before.

I parked the rental car at the curb and got out. The front door opened before I could ring the doorbell. A tall, thin man, stood there. Behind black-framed glasses, his watery blue eyes crawled over me. "Hello there. I'm Scott Stevens, your Innkeeper. Let me help you with your bag."

I recognized the voice. I'd not seen his face, but he was the man who'd spoken to Jake Holt and me. I'd only said a few words to him, but would he recognize my voice. I lowered my voice an octave. "Angelica de' Meurte. I'm in the Cabernet Room." I let him take the suitcase from me.

"Beautiful name for a beautiful woman. This all of it?"

"Just a weekend stay," I said.

"You meeting your husband?"

"It's just me."

"A pretty lady like you? Every man you know blind?"

"What a nice thing to say, Mister Stevens." I smiled into his face.

He stepped back. "After you. The rooms up the stairs on the left. Second door to the right."

We stepped into a foyer. In the bright light, it was like I was seeing it for the first time. A dark wood hat rack was on my left. The walls were painted a pale green. Someone had stenciled a border of spring flowers and vines across the top. Light oak hardwood covered the floor, super charming.

I felt his gaze on my ass as we climbed the stairs and then walked down the hallway.

I opened the door. The room was branded in my memory, all burgundy and gold. My gaze went to the large four-poster bed of dark wood that gleamed from fresh polish. "It's perfect."

He moved by me. "Thank you. I aim to please."

"Are you the only Innkeeper?"

"My sister-in-law helps out, does the baking and cleans the rooms. I had to let the maid go, caught her stealing sheets."

I sighed. "You just can't trust anybody these days. What's the world coming to?"

He placed my suitcase on the bed. "Anything else I can do for you?"

Not on your life, I thought, but shook my head. "I'm going to take a long bath and settle in."

A flush rose into his face. "Maybe I should stick around and wash your back?"

His offer made me want to puke, but I giggled. "Not this time."

"Well then, we have wine-tasting at five."

"Thank you." I waited for a heartbeat and softly added. "Scott."

He swaggered to the door, went out and closed behind him

I hurried to it and turned the lock. Back at the bed I removed Arahni from my tote bag. "What a disgusting ass."

Holding her in front of me I turned in a slow circle. "Remember?" I felt her pleasure. I picked up one of the lace trimmed, pillows, moved it to the dressing table, and lay Arahni upon it. It was four-o'clock I had seven hours to kill until our rendezvous with Mayo. "Arahni, tell me more about your life as a Greek queen."

*****

Shadowed, intimate corners were the largest part of the Starlight Lounge's décor. The rest was gold and black. Plants in ornate pots, screened tables and provided intimate corners.

I stood to the side, hidden by one with spiky leaves, and breathed in stale air from a cloud of cloying perfumes and aftershave. If Mayo had arrived on time to meet me, he would have been here two hours. I spied him at a corner table. I smiled at the tower of empty shot glasses in front of him.

I sauntered to the bar, squirmed up onto a seat. In the wall of glass behind the racks of bottles, I could see avid gazes upon me. Mayo's was one of them. "Vodka martini," I ordered from the bartender. I met Mayo's gaze in the mirror and winked. It took him a moment to comprehend, and then he smiled. The bartender placed my drink in front of me. "I'd like to buy that gentleman a drink." I turned and pointed to Mayo.

"I'll send one over."

I slid from the barstool. "I'll take it."

He shrugged and turned away. It only took a minute for him to hand me a shot glass. "Tequila," he said. "A warning. He recently got dumped, and then some other broad stood him up."

"Oh. Poor guy. I'll make it all better."

"I just bet you will." I heard him murmur as I wiggled my way toward Mayo, a drink in each hand.

He scrambled to his feet and then swayed and caught his balance.

"May I join you? I hate to drink alone." Without waiting for his reply, I placed the drinks on the table and settled into the chair across from him. "It seems like a woman alone in a bar brings out all of the circling sharks."

"I can understand if she looks like you." He dropped into his chair.

"What a nice think to say." I held out my hand. "Anjelica."

His warm hand enveloped mine. "Mayo."

I smiled. "You're Italian."

"And you're beautiful."

Inside me the Hunger squirmed with eagerness.

*****

The Starlight Lounge's lights dimmed and then brightened. "Last call," Mayo said.

I pouted. "How can that be? We've only been talking a few minutes."

He laughed. "More like a few hours."

I pushed back my chair, stood. I placed my hand on his arm. "I so enjoyed meeting you."

His eyes told me, he wanted to ask the question.

I held his gaze with mine, waited.

"Would you like to come back to my place?" he said.

"I don't go to men's places that I meet in bars," I said, and watched disappointment cloud his face. "Why don't you come back to mine?"

He looked surprised and then smiled. "I'd love to."

*****

The Grapevine Bed and Breakfast's foyer was as empty as I'd counted on. I held my finger to my lips, indicating silence. Mayo and I hurried up the stairs. At the door to the room I felt a moment of panic. Had I put the shafra away? I couldn't let Mayo see it. Not until all was ready.

I am away. You placed me in the nightstand beside the bed.

Are you sure?

I am sure. I do not make mistakes.

Like you have been doing. She did not say the words, but I heard them screamed inside my head anyway.

I opened the door.

In the room I let Mayo pull me close. His lips were warm, his body signaling his eagerness for action. Firm hands rested on my hips, pulled me closer against him still. He kissed my neck, murmured soft words. I leaned back from him. "Would you like a glass of wine?"

"Bathroom?" he said.

I pointed.

Mayo weaved toward it. I watched until the door closed behind him and then opened the small drawer and pulled out the GHB. I stared at the vial. Perhaps I did not need to kill him. Mayo could have Darcie. I would have Morgan. We could all be friends…

Save the fantasies for bedtime reading. Arahni's cutting voice came into my head. *The man wants the other women. Remember how eager he was to leave you alone. He will lust for her as long as she lives.*

Yes, Darcie had to die, to save Morgan, but did Mayo? He was but another of her victims.

His death will bring her to her knees. She will weep, feel the knife of pain, as you did at the man's betrayal.

264

My Morgan had betrayed me, but it was the bitch's fault. She'd clouded his mind. I felt rage rise again within me.

Do what must be done. It will bring us much pleasure.

I felt the Hunger writhe in eager agreement.

It is to be.

I poured the drug into the glass of wine, swirled it around. Holding it in my right hand, I turned and waited for Mayo.

Naked, he walked from the bathroom. He was a magnificent sight, already at full mast. I held the glass toward him, watched unsmiling as he drank it down in three gulps.

"I can't wait to see all of you," he said.

"Lie on the bed."

He stretched out, his hands beneath his head. I began to hum softly as I untied the red halter top. I held it against my breasts for a moment, and then tossed it aside. Mayo moaned, started to rise. "No. Stay right there."

He lifted his hands. "At least let me touch you."

I moved to the side of the bed. Mayo ran his fingertips across my stomach, up to trace along the underside of my breasts.

"You are beautiful."

"Unzip my pants." I turned my back to him.

I felt his fingers trembling as he worked the zipper down. I stepped away, turned to face him and then shimmied as I peeled the red leather pants down my body. Naked, except for the gold stilettos, I remained just out of his reach.

"Good God, Angelica…Angel, you're killing me."

Inside of me the Hunger roared while in my head Arahni laughed and then whispered. *Not yet. Not yet we have not.*

Mayo's hands fell back onto the quilt and then his eyes closed.

"Mayo? Mayo," I said. I walked to him, lifted his eye lid. He was unconscious. I moved to the dresser drawer, opened it and drew out the rope.

*****

I heard a moan and turned toward the bed where Mayo lay bound with tape across his mouth. The Hunger twisted inside my stomach, demanded action. I ignored it. I would not be rushed. Arahni held at my side, I walked to him, stared down. He tried to move, frowned, jerked his bound arms. His confused eyes begged for answers.

"I am Ice," was my response.

I saw within his gaze the second my words registered. He whipped his head from side-to-side in denial.

"I know. Darcie thinks Ice is a man. How stupid is that?" I pulled the wig from my head. "I want you to know who I am."

His eyes widened.

"You have Darcie to thank for this. If she had only stayed away from My Morgan. Because of her, he betrayed me, caused me pain. Now she will feel pain."

I slowly lifted the shafra. "I'll make you a promise. I won't allow myself to feel pleasure at your death."

A hoarse scream gurgled from him and he jerked against his restraints.

"Good bye, Mayo." I grabbed his hair, held his head still and then swiped Arahni across his throat.

Warm blood spurted into my face, coated my hair. I watched the life pump from him, felt the Hunger lap with greed, but I did not feel joy, only more anger at what the bitch had forced me to do. "Darcie Devonshire, you will pay for this. Mayo did not need to die."

I pulled the black marker from my tote bag and walked to the mirror. I wanted there to be no doubt as to why this kill had happened. In bold letters I left her my message, Detective Devonshire, you do not touch what is mine.

My shower was quick. I had brought nothing with me but the rope. With the Arahni back in the tote bag, I moved to the door, opened it. The hall was empty, the house quiet. I switched off the light and closed the bedroom door behind me. Outside I walked to the porch swing, settled into it. I breathed in the chill morning air, trying to cool the burning rage inside of me. It didn't help. The only thing that would, would be Darcie Devonshire's lifeless body sprawled in front of me.

Chapter Thirty-Five
Morgan Garrett

I unwrapped the newspaper and glanced at the headlines. They were all about Grindel's murder, but told very little details. Darcie hadn't said much either, but the dicey way she was behaving had me wondering if Ice hadn't been the one who'd killed Grindel.

I looked over at the clock. It was about time for me to leave for Santa Barbara and Scarsdale's rally. I'd rather stay home and work on the Grindle case, but he was the boss.

For some reason I kept thinking about the old lady's shoes. I read the words I'd scribbled down on my tablet, and hoped I'd gotten the spelling somewhat right. Manolo Blahniks. It meant nothing to me. I could ask Darcie about them. I laughed. As if she would know anything about high-end shoes. Darcie had regular and dress athletic shoes.

Okay what had I learned? The old broad had spiffy shoes. Did that mean anything? Maybe disguise? Shoes are the hardest thing to cover up. Darcie and I once found a guy in Tangiers because he dressed as a bum, but wore Gucci loafers. Sherice had a thing for shoes. Shit. I hadn't called her yet. I'd meant to do so earlier. I pulled out my cell phone. It rang six times before she answered.

"Hello."

"Hey?"

"Morgan. I was beginning to wonder if you were going to call."

"Sorry, this morning's been crazy. I didn't tell you the other night, but one of my bosses' people got killed, Robert Grindle. It's Darcie's case so that's all I can say about it. Look, I called about some shoes called sling backs. Mano something."

"Manolo Blahniks?"

"Yeah."

"Where in the world did you hear about them? Morgan, are you doing some early Christmas shopping for me? If so think reptile…maybe Iguana."

"Are those shoes expensive?" I said.

"Well, everything is relative. I love them and think they are well worth the money, but the average working girl may find them pricey."

"How about an older person?"

"Depends. They are spike heels. How about the next time we get together I model a pair for you, just like I did last time."

"Sounds intriguing. I don't know if I'll be able to get by today. I have to head into Santa Barbara. It's a work thing."

"Oh don't worry about me, Morgan. My days going to be packed also."

"Walter Granger keeping you busy?"

"Who?"

"You know, Pacific Winds. Who did they give to you as a patient after me?"

There was a long pause before Sherice went on. "Yes, a patient. Well it's Alyssa Crane. Mister Granger thought talking with another woman would be easier accepted by her. Up until now she's refused therapy."

"Whoa, I bet she's got some stories."

"She has, but I won't be hearing many more of them."

"Why not?"

"Miss Crane is checking out tomorrow. Heading back to San Jose."

"That surprises me. I thought she looked mighty comfortable at Pacific Winds."

"She and her ex-husband are getting back together."

That was another shocker. I could have sworn Alyssa had told me her husband had been killed in a car crash. That's why she'd started drinking and abusing prescription meds. I guess I must have heard wrong. "So it's work for you today?"

"Very much so. I've already started my research."

"Well, like I said. It's Santa Barbara this afternoon, but if I..."

"Everything is fine, Morgan. If my research provides me what I need, then I won't have time for you today anyway, and tonight, well, I need some me space. You understand. We'll have years to spend with each other."

I didn't know how to respond to that so I simply said. "I'll call you later and then we need to talk."

"Of course. Good bye."

She hung up and I flipped my cell phone closed. Years together? I frowned. What should I do about Sherice? I liked her. She wasn't Darcie, but Darcie wasn't mine anymore, she'd made that clear. What I offered Sherice, was it enough? I had to come clean. If Sherice still wanted what I could give, then, I shook my head enough of this shit. I'd concentrate on what I could control.

I called the police station. After another chat with the desk sergeant, Darcie came on the line.

"Morgan, not a good time. We've said all...."

"This is business Darcie."

"What business?"

"About Grindle."

"My case." I heard the prickle in her voice.

"Hey ease up. I just remembered something more that you might like to know."

"Sorry. Didn't sleep much last night."

What had kept her awake all night? The Italian stud. My fingers tightened around the phone. "The cocktail waitress at the Metro Club said the old woman Grindle talked to was wearing some hot shoe called a sling back. Gold ones. Manolo Blahniks. She was really impressed."

"She should be. Those babies are bloody expensive."

Her answer floored me. Darcie into shoes? What else had changed?

"What was the waitresses' name?" she said.
"Doreen, she works from four to closing."

"Thanks Morgan, we'll check it out."
She hung up.
"Damn." That woman made me want a drink.
I had less than two hours to get to Scarsdale's political rally. I had to get a move on.

*****

My GPS took me right to the beachside park in Santa Barbara with no problems, but parking was a joke. I ended up curbside on Cabrillo with a good walk back to the rally location.
The crowd was still gathering as I walked up to the temporary stand erected to spoil the beachside ambiance. I started around the stand, looking for Scarsdale.
Someone called to me. "Are you Garrett?"
"Yeah, Garrett." He was a small rabbit-like, little guy.
"I'm Jerry Waldren, the senator's assistant. The senator is waiting for you back this way."
The senator? Well that may be optimistic, or maybe thinking positive.
A small tent had been erected in the rear of the stand. There seem to be an argument in progress as to whether Scarsdale should go on stage in shirtsleeves or with his coat on. Politics.
"Morgan, hey what do you think; should I go out with my coat on and take it off as we go along, or just go out in shirt sleeves?"
"Depends on whether you are hot I guess, or cold. Not really my field."
"I'll wear the coat, Jerry."
"Yes sir," the rabbit said.
"Now Morgan, what I need from you. I want you to just keep an eye on things. You know what to look for. I'm really not expecting any trouble."
Yeah, right, that's why he keeps looking over my shoulder. Maybe I should put a stop to this road show right now."

"Just mingle and listen. We'll talk later. Okay Jerry; let's do this."

Mingle? I'd heard recognizance called some weird things, but mingling. Well what the hell? With that profound thought I went out to mingle.

The mob along the rail that separated the throng from the speakers seemed excited, but not unduly loud. A group of what looked to be gang-bangers had gathered at one side of the rail. That could be trouble brewing. Could they be Juan Carlos' thugs, maybe looking for a little payback? But then, they wouldn't think Scarsdale was behind their boss being locked up. Still those punks were not famous for their interest in politics. I spotted three Slavic-looking guys in dark suits. Russians. I'd bet my left foot on it. And suits? A little warm out here for suits. No one else in the crowd wore one. My old brown corduroy jacket sure as hell didn't qualify as a suit.

Suddenly the people around me started backing away from the rail. I looked to see why and spotted the gangbangers scuffling. What the hell?

I started toward them, and then stopped. Distraction? Ages old move and still effective. I glanced back over my shoulder toward Scarsdale and directly in my line of vision I saw one of the dark suits pull out a pistol with a silencer.

"Out of the way," I yelled, pushing my way through the mob of confused people.

I hurdled the rail and landed on top of the gunman, grabbed for the Glock. We hit the ground and I felt the gun buck in my hand.

I grabbed him by the hair, slammed his face into the ground and then rabbit punched him two quick chops in the neck. I heard a woman scream, loud and piercing. Shit. Had someone been hit?

Hands grabbed my shoulders. I rolled to the side. It was a second Slavic-looking dude. I swung the Glock by its silencer, caught him on the jaw. He went down, blood splattering. I whirled in time to see the third man shove a spectator aside as he fled.

271

"Out of the way," I screamed as I sprinted after the man. Up ahead I saw him jerk the door of dark sedan open and scramble in. The car raced away.

Shit, shit, shit. At least I'd gotten two of them.

A couple of guys, who appeared to be rent-a-cops, stood over the two I'd taken down.

"Are the police coming?" I said.

"Yes, Sir." The private cop didn't sound to stable. "Uh, you kicked the shit out of both of 'em."

"Yeah, I did. Let's get them in the tent. You got cuffs?" The tall guy held out his set.

"Don't give them to me. Put 'em on them. Damn."

Everyone around me had a shocked look, all except an attractive woman standing in front of Scarsdale. She held a Glock in a two-handed FBI grip.

"One git away?" She eased up on her spread foot stance and lowered her weapon more.

"Yeah. They had a car. Dark sedan. I couldn't get the plate number."

Scarsdale came over and took my arm with a shaky hand. "Morgan, this is Gail Crane. She's with the FBI up in Santa Maria. Gail, meet my head of security, Morgan Garrett." Scarsdale spoke in a voice barely under control.

"Hell if I had known the FBI was on the job I would have stayed out of the way." I spoke in a rush, adrenal still flowing through my veins.

"Not on the job," Gail Crane said. "I was here to support Lyndon." She turned toward him. "I warned you this could go bad. You don't give a press conference, call out the largest Mexican cartel and not expect retaliation."

"Well the police are here now," Scarsdale said and gestured toward the swat team pouring into the park.

I looked around. Not a gang-banger in site."Sir," I said to Scarsdale. "I think we have more to talk about. I didn't hire on to take on a Mexican cartel."

He tried to grin at me. "I didn't know you did either. Can you? Will you?"

I thought for a second and then answered. "Why the hell not.

Chapter Thirty-Six
Darcie Devonshire

Wes and I parked in front of the Metro Club. We'd been here way too much lately. Inside, the dive looked vacant.

"Maybe the guy's getting some perks in the backroom," Wes said.

I pounded on the bar. A man came from the back with a case of something on his shoulder.

"Be right with you." He put the box down.

"Doreen here," I asked.

He gave Wes and I the once over. "You cops?"

We both badged him.

"Doreen's mouth's made her plenty popular last couple of days." He hesitated for a moment and then laughed.

"What's so funny?" Wes said.

"You know…Doreen's mouth."

I lifted an eyebrow and he turned away to rip the carton open. "She's on her break."

"When is she back?" I said.

"Just left. Maybe an hour."

"You know where she takes her break?" Wes said.

"Sure don't, officer. You got a card? I'll have her give you a call."

I glanced at Wes. "Thank you for your time."

Wes followed me from the club. I looked up and down the street. There were a few eating places within walking distance, but somehow I didn't think Doreen was the walking type.

"Next move?" Wes said.

"We could grab some food, come back and wait?"

He looked as excited about the idea as I was. " Okay. It's your turn to choose lunch, but please no sushi."

My stomach didn't feel like it would accept anything, but passing out wouldn't help. "How about a corned beef and rye at O'Grady's?"

"You're not afraid we'll run into Morgan?"

I looked hard at him. "So what?"

He held up his hands. "Fine. Fine." Wes' cell phone went off. "Smith." I watched his face drain of color. "When? Is she all right? I'll be right there."

"Wes, what is it?"

He threw me a terrified look. "Janey's been in a car crash...."

"Oh my God. Is she...?"

"At Marion Medical....I've got to...."

"We've got to. Get your arse in the car."

*****

I watched Wes pace. They hadn't let him see Janey yet. She was in x-ray. The doctor said she was conscious though. Janey's mom said a car had run a red light, plowed into the passenger side.

Wes stopped in front of me. "She was on her way to the school. PTA. She could have had Jackie..."

I touched his hand. "She didn't."

*****

The doctor came toward us. "Mister Smith, you can see your wife now."

Wes hurried away with him.

I crushed my Styrofoam coffee cup with my hand. Bloody hell, life just wasn't fair. My cell phone rang. It was the captain.

"How is she?"

"I don't know."

"You take the rest of the day off."

"Captain, the Grindle case…"

"You be there with Smith. That's an order."

"Yes, Sir," I said, but the captain had already hug up.

I paced. Drank more coffee. Visited the gift shop. I was browsing the cards when I saw Wes. I hurried to him.

"She's in a lot of pain. Broke her leg, some ribs and has a concussion. They've given her something and she's a little looped." He raked his fingers through his hair. "Jackie's with her grandma. I'm staying here."

It was a stretch for me, but I wrapped an arm around his shoulders. His body shook. "You want something?"

He shook his head. "I'm going back to be with Janey."

"I'll be right here." He started to protest and I cut him off. "Got the rest of the day off. Captain's orders."

"Don't hang around here. I know how you love hospitals, English. Go home. I'll call you later."

I hesitated. I did hate hospitals. "You'll call if you need anything, and I mean anything?"

Wes took a deep breath. "I will, and thanks partner." He turned and walked back down the hallway.

*****

In the car I called Morgan. He and Wes were friends. He'd want to know I assured myself. It has nothing to do with me.

His voice mail answered. "Garrett, leave a message."

"Morgan, it's Darcie. Wes' wife was in a car accident. She's gonna be okay, but I thought you'd like to know." I hung up.

I thought about calling Mayo. I hoped we'd be able to be friends. What had I said to Morgan, grow up, when he'd said the same words to me.

I started the Beamer and headed home. Becky would be delighted to see me. We could do some sunning in the back yard, catch up on recorded television shows. Hell, I could take a long bubble bath.

*****

I glanced at the clock again, whoopee, a whole ten minutes had passed. I'd been home over three hours. Why hadn't Wes called? I pushed Becky off my lap, walked to the fridge again, opened it and looked inside. Still nothing grabbed my fancy.

My cell phone rang. It was Wes. "Hey partner. How's Janey?"

"She's going to be fine. They're letting me stay the night with her."

"That's good to know. Did Morgan call you?"

"No. Why would he?"

"I left him a message." Where was Morgan? I mentally shrugged. He didn't answer to me. "Well, tell Janey I said hi."

"Sure thing. I'll check in with you tomorrow."

I heard other voices.

"They've brought us our dinner."

"Good night, Wes." I ended the call.

Becky gave me a disgusted look when I settled back on the sofa beside her, still empty handed. I tried to focus on the television show. Ten minutes later I gave up when I realized my attention was all on my cell phone. Morgan's not going to call you anyway. He'd call Wes. It was only 8:30, but I decided to head to bed. I'd get up early, get into the office and go over my files on Ice. As I flipped off the living room light my phone rang. Heart pounding I pounced on it. It was Mayo. I held it in my hand and let it ring. A few seconds later it rang again. I had a voice message. I called, listened. Mayo was drunk.

"Darshie, we can't give up, jus cuz you have feelin's for a man from your past."

I didn't listen to any more. I hung up. It rang again. Mayo. I waited until it stopped, then turned my cell phone off and placed it softly on the end table.

*****

With my second cup of coffee of the morning in one hand, and Becky's treat in the other I headed toward the bedroom. "Come on and there better not be any complaints about excessive barking."

She looked up at me with innocent brown eyes.

"Yeah, right," I murmured.

I released a sigh of relief when I saw the captain wasn't in his office. He hadn't said anything about me not coming in today. I had my argument all prepared just in case, but was glad I didn't need it.

At my desk I pulled out my files on Ice. Went over them slowly. What was I missing? In the middle of my third time through, my desk phone rang. "Detective Devonshire."

"Darcie, it's Hennessey."

His voice sounded odd and my radar went on alert. "What's up?"

"The Captain called us out. It's another murder. Looks like Ice again."

I pushed my chair back and stood. Two in two days. Talk about escalating. We'd pushed Ice's buttons, but how? "Where?"

"At the Grapevine Bed and Breakfast."

That floored me. What was that place? Murder central. As far as I knew Ice had never used the same place twice.

"Darcie, you need to get over here and see this."

"What is it Hennessey?" I felt a cold shiver along my neck.

"Just get your ass over here."

"I'm on the way."

*****

Helen Thatcher answered the door. "Detective."

Her eyes and her voice were cool. I couldn't blame her. Styles, Hennessey's partner, stood just beyond her. Styles was a two-year rookie. He looked a little green. Understandable, judging by Ice's pervious kill-scenes.

"Detective Devonshire," he said. "This is what we know. When Mrs. Thatcher walked by the Cabernet room this morning, she noticed the door was partially opened. When she knocked it opened more and she saw…and called it in."

"What time?"

"9:00 AM. The room's registered to an Angelica de' Muerte."

I flinched. Angel of death. A woman? Did Ice have a partner? "Was she alone?"

"Scott helped her with her bags. She was quite alone," Helen Thatcher said.

"Is your brother-in-law here? I'd like to speak with him."

"I called him and Viola. Scott's calling our lawyer." There was a definite chill in her voice. "They all should be here any minute."

As if on cue I heard a door somewhere in the back slam shut.

"This better be damn good." A male voice said loudly

"Scott. Viola. In here." Mrs. Thatcher called.

The Stevens' joined us. Scott and Viola looked overjoyed at seeing me.

"What the hell is this?" Scott Stevens demanded. "Our lawyer's out of town. Do I need to contact a different one?"

"Hello Scott," I said. "It seems there's been another murder in the Cabernet Room."

"Oh my God. Someone killed Angelica?"

"No. The victim's a man," Styles said.

"She picked up some guy?" Scott said. "That's a surprise. She didn't seem the type."

"Describe Miss de' Muerte," I said.

"She was hot."

I scowled. "Could you be more precise?"

"About five feet four. Long dark hair, a body that wouldn't quit. Dark eyes, that's about it."

"Are you sure she was a she?" I said.

Scott Stevens glared at me. "What do you mean?"

"Could it have been a man dressed like a woman?"

"Hell, no. I know a woman when I see one."

I frowned. "When was the last time she was seen?"

"She checked in around four. I showed her to her room." He looked at Helen.

"I never saw here at all," Helen Thatcher said. "I locked up around ten and went to bed."

"All of the guests have a key to the front door, as well as their rooms," Scott Stevens added.

"No one heard anything odd last night?" I said. They all three shook their heads. "Okay. Thank you."

"Darcie, that you?" I heard Hennessey call down the stairs.

"In the flesh," I said.

"You'd better come up here and see this."

I walked to the stairs, and started up.

I stepped inside the Cabernet room. Hennessey stood with his back to the four poster bed watching for me. He's a mountain of a man, so made it hard to see beyond him. "What was so hellfire important for me to see?"

"Take a look at the mirror."

I read the large, black words, read them again. Detective Devonshire, you do not touch what is mine. What the bloody hell? I hadn't moved the first body in this room. Stevens had, but Ice didn't seem to know that. "I see what you mean." Was all I could get out.

"It's gotten personal between you and Ice."

I swallowed. "It looks like it."

Hennessey and I exchanged a long look, and then he stepped away from the bed.

At first all that registered was the blood. I ran my gaze along the length of body. Halfway up a frigid foreboding gripped me. A voice in my head started screaming, "Stop. Don't look any farther." The in control, larger cop portion of my brain ignored the voice. When my gaze made it to the victims face, that same brain refused to comprehend what my eyes were telling it. No it wasn't Mayo. It couldn't be. How could it be? I blinked, took a step closer. "Oh God. Oh God," I moaned. My knees buckled and I went to the floor.

"Devonshire. What is it?" Hennessey's panicked voice seemed to come from far away.

I couldn't turn my head away from the bloody mess bound on the bed. Mayo's dead eyes stared into mine. It had been bad with Grindle, but this...I felt brittle. If I moved I'd crack into a thousand parts. Hands gripped my shoulders.

"You know him? Christ...you do." Hennessey tried to pull me to my feet.

"No," I screamed. I reached toward Mayo's face.

Hennessey grabbed my hand. "You can't do that, Darcie. Ah shit...but you can't, this is a crime scene. Styles." I heard him yell. "Get your ass up here."

I couldn't look away from Mayo's eyes. I felt my stomach heave. I turned my head to the side and vomited.

"She's sitting in the blood," Styles' voice said.

"Help me get her out of here," Hennessey ordered.

I felt hands grab my shoulders.

"Come on, Darcie. Shit if I'd known...."

Hennessey sounded like he wanted to cry. The thought drew a laugh from me, that immediately turned into a gut-wrenching sob.

"God-damn-it to hell," Hennessey snapped. "Where's Wes when you need him?"

"Janey...accident," I choked out.

"Get up. You just can't sit there in his...."

I looked at the floor. I sat in a puddle that was as red as the carpet it flowed across. "Oh God. Oh God." I surged to my feet. The room seemed to sway around me, my stomach dipped and heaved. "Bathroom," I gasped out.

Hands pulled me forward, led me to a toilet. I kneeled and vomited into it.

"Jesus, Darcie. I didn't know."

"Of course you didn't." I grabbed a mound of toilet paper and wiped my mouth.

"Get Wes Smith." Hennessey yelled.

"No, he's with Janey." Inside my head I was stepping away, letting my years with the CIA take charge. I heard Morgan's voice in my head. Get it done, Devonshire. Fall apart later.

I levered myself to my feet. "His name's Mayo Gerardi. He and I were," I paused for a second, "Friends."

Styles came to the bathroom door. "I left a message for Smith."

"That's good." I felt wrapped in yards and yards of stoicism. I liked it. Maybe I'd just stay this way. You didn't feel…you didn't hurt. "I'm getting out of your crime scene. Sorry about that slip in there, trying to touch the body."

"No biggie." Hennessey stared at me like he was afraid I'd lose it again in a heartbeat. "Why don't you wait downstairs?"

"Yeah, I'll do that." I walked into the bedroom, looked at the words on the mirror and then walked from the room.

In the hallway I could see some cross-stitched, plaques. Each was one word. It took a minute for them to register. Peace. Joy. Love. "When did I ever feel peace, joy, love?" I murmured. A scene flashed through my mind. Morgan and I at a pub in Cayucos, holding hands across a table. Dancing dolphins in a picture behind him. "The dancing dolphins."

"Detective?" Styles said from beside me

"I'm fine. I'm going back to the station."

I moved by Styles, down the stairs, past three blurred faces, and out the front door.

Chapter Thirty-Seven
Sherice Solomon

From across the street I watched the bitch come out from the bed and breakfast. She stumbled at reaching the street and I smiled. I lifted the binoculars to my eyes and focused on her face. She looked stunned as she opened the door to her car and more fell than climbed in. "Shame, shame, officer. You shouldn't be driving like that. Someone should let them know. I guess it will have to be me." I watched her drive away and then reached for my cell phone. Jane Q Public, reporting that one of Santa Maria's finest was driving erratically. I carefully gave them the bitch's license number.

The street had filled with cars, but no one paid attention to mine. An ambulance arrived.

I should leave. It was stupid to sit here. But I owed it to Mayo.

I watched them bring his body out. "She's begun to pay, Mayo, but not enough. Don't worry though. She will." I started my car and drove away. It was time to put the final plan into motion.

Chapter Thirty-Eight
Morgan Garrett

I called Darcie's cell phone again, and again got her voice mail. Swearing I tried Wes' and got the same thing. "Where the hell is everybody?"

My briefing with Scarsdale and lasted until after two AM, and he'd put me up for the night. I hadn't checked my messages until eight this morning and had found out then about Janey's accident.

I flipped the phone closed and glared ahead of me at the line of unmoving cars. Anxiety twisted inside my stomach. My head said there wasn't any cause, Wes' Janey was okay, Darcie had said so, but my gut wasn't listening.

The line of traffic started to inch forward and I put my truck in gear.

I'd just passed the Santa Maria town limits sign, when my cell phone at last rang. It was Wes. Swearing loudly, I pulled to the side of the road.

"You heard from Darcie?" Was Wes' greeting. His voice sounded anxious.

"No. Been trying to reach her. All I get is here damn voicemail."

"Shit."

"What's happened, Wes?"

"Ice killed again, it was Mayo."

"God Almighty!"

"It gets worse. Ice left a message for Darcie on the damn mirror. Said that Mayo was a warning for her not to touch what was his."

Not touch what was his? What the hell did that mean?

Wes went on. "Hennessey didn't know she and Mayo...."

My stomach clenched. Shit. Shit. Shit. "He called her to the scene."

"It was bad."

"Where is she now?"

"I don't know. Can't find her. She hasn't called anybody. She said she was going back to the station. No show. She didn't call her folks. I went by her house...."

"Where are you?"

"At the B and B. I'm heading back to the station. I don't know what else to do."

I slammed my hand against the steering wheel.

I heard muffled voices and then Wes said. "Styles said Darcie mumbled something about dancing dolphins. Mean anything to you?"

Dancing dolphins? It took me a minute. "I think I know where she went."

"Where?" Wes said.

"Let me check it out. I'll call when I get there."

"Damn it, Morgan. Tell me. She's my partner. I ..."

"Yeah. I love her too. I think she was talking about a pub in Cayucos. Don't know the name, but I'll know it when I see it. Let me get to her first. I'll call. I promise."

"You'd damn well better."

I hung up my phone. Ah shit, Darcie. You can't out run pain. Go to ground, girl. I'll help you through it.

*****

In Cayucos, I stopped in front of a man-sized, carved mermaid. I hadn't remembered I remembered it until I stood in front of it. Darcie had named her Merry. It was the eyes, she'd said, they looked merry.

I stepped inside, stood for a moment to let my eyes adjust. The décor was nautical, with drooping fish nets full of glass floats, and white life preservers. The tables were large, empty spools that once would have cable wrapped around them. At one of them Darcie sat with her back to me. Her focus was on a painting of dolphins. I remembered the first time we'd seen them. Darcie had said they were dancing in happiness.

I walked to her, settled down on the chair next to her.

She glanced at me.

"Hey there," I said.

She had a full shot glass in front of her. Holding my gaze with hers, she picked up the glass and drank the golden liquid down in one, not so smooth, movement and then placed the glass back on the table, "Join me," she said, and it wasn't a question. More like an order.

I licked my lips. Darcie needed me to have a drink with her. Just one couldn't hurt. No. I wasn't getting back on that bandwagon. I shook my head. "Don't do the booze anymore, remember?"

"You want to. I can see it." Darcie laughed. "Barkeep, another and make it a double."

He looked at me, I shook my head, pointed at myself, indicating I'd take it from here.

"Sorry Miss. Boss' orders. You're cut off."

"He bloody hell isn't my boss."

"Not talking about him.

"Let me take you home, Darcie," I said.

She surged to her feet, swayed. "Fine. This isn't the only blood bar in town. I can't quit drinking, not yet."

"What do you mean you can't?"

She gripped the back of the chair, stared across the pub. "I can still see his eyes."

I didn't have to ask whose. "The booze won't help. I ought to know."

She flopped back into the chair. "You have one drink with me, and I'll leave with you."

"Darcie…"

"Hell, how many times did I drink with you when I didn't want to. You owe me." She glared into my face.

"Fine. I'll drink with you." I turned to the bartender. "Two black coffees."

Darcie hiccupped a laugh. "You gettin' forgetful in your advanced age? Not black. Cream and sugar. You take it black though, and too bloody damn strong."

The man brought the coffees.

Darcie stirred in cream and sugar, sloshing coffee over the side of the cup. "You know you can't stop a person if they want to drink."

"Mayo wouldn't…"

"Shut the fuck up! Don't say it. You didn't know him well enough to know…" She laughed again. "Hell, I didn't know well enough. Not really. But I killed him anyway."

"You didn't kill him, Ice did."

"Because of me. You know about the mirror?"

I nodded.

"He's dressing in drag, you know."

She'd lost me. "Who?"

"I don't see him with a partner. So that 'as to be it."

"You're talking about Ice."

She nodded. "That old lady at the Metro Club, that was him. He likes playing with them. Dressing like a woman. Makes crazy sense. You men let your little head make too many decisions for you."

I frowned. "That lady wore three inch stiletto heels. No guy can walk in those."

"Shit." Darcie waved her hand. "You ever been to a drag show? Those guys look more like women than some women." She pushed her coffee aside. "I can't drink that."

"Okay, but a deals a deal. I had a drink with you. Now let's get out of here."

"When I find Ice. I'm going to…"

I didn't hear the rest of her sentence. I leaned toward her. "What did you say?"

"I'm going to kill him."

"Don't think so."

"Why the hell not? You can help me. It wouldn't be the first time…"

"You're a cop now. Cops don't play that way."

"Maybe for right at that moment I won't be a cop." She pushed her chair back, stood, swayed. I grabbed her by the shoulders. "I think I'm drunk. How am I going to get my car home?"

"We'll worry about that tomorrow."

"Oh. Good." She looked into my face for a moment and then crumpled. I picked her up and carried her from the pub.

We were halfway to Santa Maria, before she roused at all. "Where are you taking me?"

"My place."

"No. Home," she mumbled. "Becky can't be by herself all night."

I wasn't sure who Becky was, but I agreed. "Okay, your place. What's the address."

She mumbled more words at me and then went out again. Shit. It was time to call Wes, like I'd promised. "I found her," I said by way of greeting.

"About damn time. How is she?"

"Drunk on her ass. She wants me to take her home, but I don't know where home is. I'm sure she's got some ID somewhere on her…"

Wes gave me the address.

"Who's Becky?" I said.

Wes laughed. "Darcie's basset hound."

A basset hound? Darcie had finally gotten her basset hound. "Thanks Wes. I'll call you in the morning." I hung up the phone and gave the truck a little more gas.

*****

I propped Darcie against the wall of her house. In side her jacket pocket I found found her keys and a Glock all tangled together. A drunk with heavy artillery, what a combination. I could hear her basset hound inside raising hell. I hope she wouldn't bite when she saw me carrying Darcie in.

There was no irate basset hound ready to attack when I opened the door, but I could still hear her. It was coming from down the hall. The closer I got to what I hoped was the master bedroom, the louder and more frantic the barking became.

Shit. The dog was in there. "Becky. Becky," I called, "it's okay."

The barking grew louder, this time mixed with low growls. To hell with that. I backtracked to another door, opened it. Clearly a guest room, but it had a made-up bed. I put Darcie on it, removed her shoes, debated and discarded the idea of undressing her. She wouldn't like that and I'd have enough to deal with in the morning.

The basset hound had not let up her barking. I didn't know what to do to calm her. The doorbell rang. Fucking great. Had the neighbors turned me in?

I walked to the door, opened it. Wes stood there. He looked toward the master bedroom and grinned. "Knew Becky would give you a hard time. Let me see to her."

I followed as far as the living room.

"Hey, Becky." I heard Wes say. The barking stopped. Instead I heard soft whines. "Yeah, your mom's just fine."

Nails clicked on hardwood. A moment passed and then a brown and black head poked around the corner of the living room door. Brown eyes locked with mine.

"Becky, this is Morgan."

"Glad to meet you, Becky," I said.

"She's a little protective," Wes said.

"Nothing wrong with that." I looked closer at Wes. Dark circles ringed his eyes The guy was in need of some hours of sleep. "How's Janey?"

"She's going to be fine."

The basset hound turned and padded away from us.

"You get on home, Wes. Everything will be okay now."

"I see it is. Give me a call in the morning."

"I'll do that."

I locked the door behind Wes and then walked to the bedroom.

Becky lay on the floor, not too far from the door. It was clear from the look in her eyes and the low rumble in her chest I was still on probation.

"Okay girl, I get it. I'll be on the couch if you need me." The basset looked at me and then hopped up onto a low coffee table at the end of the bed, and from there upward to snuggle next to Darcie.

Becky's brown-eyed gaze was still on me when I shut the bedroom door.

Chapter Thirty-Nine
Darcie Devonshire

A cold nose nuzzled my cheek. I turned my head, and a bass drum began pounding in my skull. I groaned, heard a soft whine. I cracked an eye open, winced, and pressed it closed again. A soft head worked its way beneath my hand. "Hey girl," I murmured. God, the inside of my mouth tasted vile.

Taking a deep breath, I opened my eyes. I wasn't in my bedroom. It took a minute to recognize the guest room. How…? My bladder screamed a need for relief. I kicked the quilt aside and could see I still wore yesterday's clothes. What the bloody hell?

I sat up, dug my fingernails into the mattress as I waited for the room to stop wobbling. Something tried to surface in my mind. In an almost panic I pushed it away. I stood and on shaking legs made it to the bathroom. On the toilet it was a toss up which end would empty from me first. I swallowed the nausea.

Back in the bedroom I perched on the edge of the bed, petted Becky's head. Part of me hoped for the flu, but I was ducking, what I had was one hell of a hangover. But why?

The question did it.

Memories drowned me.

With a sob I curled into a fetal position.

Mayo.

Ice.

I buried my face in my pillow and cried. Becky pressed against me. I felt her trembling. Suddenly rage replaced tears. "God damn you!"

The smell of coffee registered. I wasn't alone. I remembered going into the pub in Cayucos. How had I gotten home? "Who's our company, baby?" I stood. Waited for the room to steady and then walked toward the kitchen.

I knew Morgan's back instantly. He stood in front of the range, stirring something. The sight of the full coffee pot drew me like a magnet. I poured coffee, added cream and sugar. I felt his gaze upon me as I walked slowly to a kitchen chair and lowered myself into it.

"Becky needs to go out," I said.

Morgan walked to the sliding glass doors that led into the back yard, opened them.

Becky looked from me, to the open door, then toward Morgan. "It's okay baby."

She walked to the patio doors, and with a look at Morgan, walked out of it.

I faced him. "Tell me."

"I found you. I brought you home."

"How?"

He didn't even pretend not to know what I asked.

"Styles said you mentioned dancing dolphins. I remembered." Morgan placed dry toast in front of me. My stomach protested, but I picked up a piece and nibbled on a corner. He sat across from me with a plate of scrambled eggs and my stomach protested louder.

"Do you have to eat that right now?"

"Yeah, I do. I hate cold eggs."

I drank more coffee, nibbled toast, my eyes away from his plate. Becky came back in, settled at my feet. "This is Becky."

Morgan nodded. "We met last night."

"Some watch dog you are," I muttered.

"Actually, she's a damn good watch dog. She still be barking if Wes hadn't come over."

"Wes was here?" I felt tears threaten and blinked my eyes.

"He knew Becky would be throwing a fit, and I'm sure he wanted to see for himself that you were okay."

I pushed the coffee away. "Thanks for getting me home. I'm going to take a shower and go into work."

"You sure…"

I cut him off. "Very sure."

Morgan stood, carried his plate and cup to the sink. "It wasn't your fault, Darcie."

I shrugged, instantly regretting the move. "Maybe. Maybe not, but I'm going to find the bastard."

"You still want me to help you kill him?" Morgan's grin did not reach his eyes.

I dimly remembered my words. "No," I said.

"No, you don't want to kill him, or no you'd rather do it yourself?"

I frowned. "Not in the bloody mood for jokes, Morgan."

He picked up my coffee cup and remaining piece of toast. "We'll talk tonight after I get back from Santa Barbara."

I shook my head.

"Then we'll talk over breakfast."

"No, Morgan. I don't have time for…"

"Darcie, stop. You're not burying yourself in work. It won't help."

I glared into his face. "All else stops until I find him."

"I can help."

"I don't want your help." I snapped the words out. "You've helped enough."

"What the hell does that mean?"

"I didn't take Mayo's call. He left a message. I knew he was drinking." I dug my fingernails into the palms of my hands. "If I'd just answered the damn phone. If I hadn't been mooning over you. Why the bloody hell didn't you just stay away from me, from Santa Barbara, hell way from the whole damn state of California."

"You're blaming me? That's crazy."

"I'm not. I'm blaming me. But when I look at you…"

Morgan pushed away from the sink. His cheeks were flushed with anger. He opened his mouth to speak, then closed it and stalked toward the kitchen door.

"Where are you going? Running back to your pretty little shrink? Big bad Darcie making you want to drink again?"

He whipped around. "You know I wonder why I even stopped. Life was a hell of a lot rosier seen from the bottom of a bottle."

I closed my eyes took a deep breath. "Ah, Morgan, stop. I didn't mean it. Come on. You're not going to start drinking again."

"What the hell do you care?"

I snapped my eyes open in time in time to see him stormed from the kitchen. I heard the front door slam behind him.

It wasn't until I heard his truck roar away that it hit me. I couldn't go into work...the Beamer was still in Cayucos. Bloody hell.

*****

I hadn't been home long from picking up the Beamer when the phone rang.

"Darcie Devonshire?"

"Yes."

"It's Doctor Sherice Solomon."

What could she want with me? Had I been right. Had Morgan went from me to her? The thought made my heart stutter.

"Why couldn't you leave him alone? I knew this would happen when you walked back into his life. Wasn't killing one man enough? You should have the black widow tattoo, not me."

"You bitch...."

"It's Morgan, Darcie. He keeps saying the kid won't let him be."

He had gone to her. "Where are you?"

"The Valley Inn. Room 340. He's on the balcony, threatening to jump and I can't get through to him. He only wants you." I heard the bitterness in her voice.

"Is he drunk?"

"Yes, thanks to you."

"I'm on the way."

I punched in Wes' number. "Sherice Solomon called, said Morgan's in trouble. I'm going to the Valley Inn, room 340, to check it out."

"What kind of trouble? I can be right there."

"The bottle kind of trouble. I'll call if I need you."

Chapter Forty
Sherice Solomon

I paced the floor, smiled. It had all been so easy. The bitch was quick to believe My Morgan would drink again, want to kill himself over her. What an arrogant fool.

I walked to the four lengths of rope coiled next to the bed. I'd already measured and cut them.

How long would it take the bitch to get here? Twenty minutes at the most. I picked up the small revolver from the bedside table. I hadn't shot a gun in a long time, but it had to be like riding a bicycle, no doubt it would all come back to me.

Someone pounded on the motel room door. Holding the gun I moved to it, looked through the peephole. "Darcie."

I unlocked the door. She rushed in and then went very still at the sight of my naked body and the gun.

"Close it," I said.

"What is this?"

"The door, Darcie. I don't wish to shoot you, but I will."

She closed the door and then stepped further into the room. I saw her look linger on my feet. "Nice shoes. I've always wanted a pair of gold stilettos. Don't they hurt your feet after awhile?"

"Sometimes a little pain is required, even makes things more enjoyable."

I saw her sweep a quick look over the room. "Morgan isn't here. Is he?"

I smiled. "This is to be between us."

"It was you at the Metro Club wasn't it? You were the old lady. Are you Ice's partner?"

"I don't have a partner, not yet. Move to the bed."

What of me? Arahni said.

"Now is not the time."

"What?"

I waved the gun. "I said move to the bed."

"Are you going to kill me? Because of Morgan? That's insane. There's nothing between us. That was over a long time ago. Call him. He'll tell you what I told him. It's friends now. That's all we can be. You can never go back. The only thing I care about is finding Ice. The bloody bastard killed Mayo last…"

I laughed. "Don't you understand? Don't you get it? Look at the bed. Four posts. I am Ice."

"Ice is a man."

"No. I am Ice." I smiled. "Darcie, don't feel bad. That's what they all thought. What makes you better than them?"

Her fingers curled into a fist. "You're crazy."

I laughed. "Did you enjoy my gift to you? The one left on the bed at the Grapevine Bed and Breakfast." I watched her face. Saw when she accepted. "Mayo's death is your fault. If you'd stayed away from My Morgan…"

"What did Mayo have to do with Morgan?" she said.

"My Morgan betrays me in his heart because of you. You caused me pain. Now move to the bed." She stood where she was. "Do as I say, Darcie and you may live to leave this room."

She laughed. "If you are Ice, how is that going to happen?"

"True, but perhaps you will find away to save yourself. Now move."

Darcie walked to the bed, perched on its edge.

"You look thirsty. Drink the water," I said, pointing at the glass bottle on the nightstand.

"I'm fine, thank you."

I moved to her, held the barrel of the gun against her forehead. "Drink."

Her eyes glared into mine, but she picked up the bottle of water and drank it down.

"It will take a few minutes for the drug to work," I said. "So we will chat. Would you like to know how I killed them?"

We killed them.

"Yes. Yes, we."

"Who are you talking too?"

"You of course. I will tell you how easily they walked into my web."

"I don't want to know."

"Of course you do. It was quite simple. There isn't time to tell you about all of them, so who shall it be, yes, Robert Grindle."

"You crazy bitch." Her words were slurred.

"Maybe, but they all made it so simple. A show of leg, some cleavage."

"Why? Why kill them?"

"Why? Because we like it. You've killed. I know you have. The same as My Morgan. Did it not make you feel more alive?"

She shook her head. "Whose we?"

"What?"

"You said we like it."

"Arahni."

"Who...Arahni?"

"I am Arahni and she is I."

Darcie's head lowered and she slumped to her side.

Ten minutes later I had her tied to the posts and her mouth taped. I splashed water in her face. Her eyes opened and she glared at me. I held the shafra in my hand and lifted it so she could see it clearly.

Inside me the Hunger leapt in victorious need. "Arahni and I will so enjoy this, Darcie Devonshire."

Someone pounded on the motel room door. "Sherice. Darcie. Open up." It was My Morgan.

Chapter Forty-One
Morgan Garrett

The traffic on South Broadway was bad, I should have turned over to the 101 sooner, but I still had plenty of time to get to Santa Barbara for my meeting. I'd almost called Scarsdale and rescheduled, but had decided against it.

I hated leaving Darcie, but when she was like that you couldn't reason with her. Maybe Wes could help. Between the two of us we ought to be able to knock some sense into her head. There was no time like the present. I pulled to the curb, punched in his number and was surprised when he answered the phone almost before it rang.

"Hey Wes, how abou…?"

"Morgan? Where are you?" Wes broke in before I could finish my question.

"I'm on my way to Santa Barbara. Meeting with Scarsdale."

"You don't sound drunk or suicidal to me."

"What the hell are you talking about?"

"Darcie just called to tell me you were in trouble and she was on the way to the Valley Inn to meet with you and Sherice."

"Sherice? Why Sherice?"

"She called Darcie…"

"Something is way wrong here." The Valley Inn was in Pismo Beach. I pulled back into traffic, ignored the blaring horns. "Did she say what room?" I made a u-turn at the first red light and headed toward 101 North.

"340. I'll meet you there."

What the hell was going on?

*****

I pulled under the portico, jumped out of the pick-up, and tossed my keys to the valet who trotted toward me. "Police emergency," I said, running toward the elevator. Luck was with me. It was on the first floor. I punched number three. My heart pounded. Something was so wrong about this.

I didn't wait for the doors to open all the way before I ran through them. The rising elevator seemed to be taking all day. "Come on. Come on. At last the door opened on the third floor. A sign on the wall said 340 was to the right.

At the door I twisted the doorknob. It was locked. I pounded it. "Darcie. Sherice." I yelled. "Open up." I'd kick the damned door open if I had to.

I heard the latch click and the door opened a crack. I could see the safety chain still in place.

"Morgan, My Morgan. It is so right that you are here now."

I couldn't see beyond Sherice but I heard a muffled moan that I hoped like hell was the TV. "Sherice, what's going on? Let me in."

"Of course, My Morgan."

The door closed and I heard the chain clatter. It opened.

Sherice stood there naked. In one hand she held a gun and in other the shafra I'd seen in her cottage.

"Come in, My Morgan. It is time."

Inside the room I could see Darcie was on a bed. It was a four poster one. Her hands and feet were tied to each of the four posts.

I turned toward Sherice, and in a blink it all came together. The high end shoes, the shafra, Mayo's death. Sherice had been in San Francisco when Ice had killed there and in New York City. God, she'd told me herself. How could I have missed all this? I had to play for time, keep her talking. Wes was on the way. "You're Ice."

"We are Ice."

"We?"

She waved the shafra. "Queen Arahni and myself, the two are one, soon three will be one."

"Who's Queen Arahni?"

"She is the soul of the shafra. It is Arahni who showed me how to control the Hunger and get much pleasure at the same time."

I felt my stomach turn. "Pleasure?"

"Oh yes, My Morgan, when the blood flows, when you coat your body with its heat, there is nothing like it. Remember in the shower, when I put my marks upon you, the pleasure we felt. It's a hundredfold beyond that."

I glanced toward Darcie. She hadn't made a sound. Was she conscious? Talking. I had to keep her talking. Come on, Wes. "What's this hunger you must control?"

"It lives inside me, like it does with my father. He feeds his by his ruthless, seeking of power. He taught me his methods, but it was never enough. I felt its bite continually, until Arahni showed me how to make it purr."

"Why Darcie? Why me?"

"I wish a partner. You know how it is with a partner. Someone to share all with."

"You've got your Arahni. Isn't she…"

Sherice sighed. "I adore my queen. But she can't be physically beside me. She can't touch me, I can't touch her, make love to her."

Come on Wes, Come on. All I need is a distraction. "Why me? There has to be a hundred guys who could join you."

"Destiny brought us together. When first I saw you, I felt it, and then you ordered me from your room, sounding much like my father. I knew you were the one. You would not let me dominate you, not be weak like my David."

Dominate? She wanted someone to tell her what to do. "Yeah, I remember the shower. How could I not. It was fantastic. You're telling me it can be a hundred times better."

Sherice smiled. "Each time we hunt it grows better. We will glory in our pleasure. Do what we want. Live where we want. Take what we want." She waved the gun toward Darcie.

"They are all so stupid. Looking only for a man. Arahni assured me it would be so."

Her words made my skin crawl, but I forced myself to smile. "How will we live? It seems we'll have to move around a lot."

"I am rich My Morgan. Very rich."

"It all sounds good, but some things are going to have to change." I made my voice hard and unyielding. It had the desired effect. I saw Sherice draw in a deep breath.

"Yes, My Morgan, what do you desire?"

"We're not killing Darcie. Put down the gun and the knife."

"It is not a knife." She held the shafra out toward me. "This is Arahni. Say her name."

"What?"

"Say her name. Speak to her. She has been slow to accept you.

"Arahni," I said. "Glad to meet you. Now listen to me, the both of you. We're leaving. I want a true first hunt. Not some trussed up pig." I watched the quick rise and fall of Sherice's breasts.

She moaned softly; cast a quick glance at Darcie. Then she frowned. "Arahni says no. You have no right to order us...not yet. First you must prove yourself, slice away your holds to this life." Sherice pointed the shafra at me. "You must kill Darcie. This kill is yours alone. The others we will do together. Arahni is correct, and I did promise Mayo the bitch would die."

I stood frozen. Through all of this, the gun Sherice held pointed at Darcie's head had not wavered. I had to get between them.

"I haven't killed in a long time. I don't know..."

"You remember, My Morgan. I know you do."

When I still couldn't move, Sherice's eyes narrowed

"Am I again wrong? Are you like my David? You have betrayed me?"

"I haven't been with another woman since we got together," I said in a rush.

"Not with another woman, with weakness. I thought My David was strong. I abandoned my father for him, but he grew weak, could not make a simple decision without me. He could never be our partner. He had to die."

"You killed your husband?"

"My David's death was not a true hunt. Arahni saw to David. I was too sloppy, he did not die easy, but still it was pleasurable."

I swallowed. "I want some of that pleasure."

Sherice smiled. "And you will have it, but first." She held the shafra toward me. "Take Arahni. I ache to see her again in your hand."

I reached for the knife. "You can put the gun down…"

"No, Arahni says I must keep it where it is until you prove yourself to her. See it is not me My Morgan. It is Arahni you must win over."

I took the shafra. It felt frigid and somehow evil in my hands. I moved to the bed. Sherice stepped back, but not much. She still aimed the gun at Darcie's head.

I bent over Darcie. The complete trust I saw in her eyes hardened my resolve. We were going to live, both of us. I lifted the shafra, out of the corner of my eye I saw Sherice bend closer and the gun lowered, it was all I needed.

I pivoted, swung for Sherice's throat—and missed. Instead the knife cut a deep gouge along her breast bone. Blood gushed. She screamed, pointed the gun at me and fired. Searing pain erupted inside my left thigh. My leg went from under me and I went down.

"What have you done? What have you done? You've ruined everything," Sherice screamed. "The police will be coming. How could I be so wrong? Yes, Arahni, I hear you. We must flee, but not before they die, both of them."

The door crashed inward. Sherice turned, fired at the figure rushing in. Wes dropped to the floor.

A scream came from behind the tape on Darcie's mouth. Her body arced upward into Sherice's arm and the gun flew from her hand. On the floor, I still gripped the shafra. With my one good leg, I swept both of Sherice's from beneath her. She

fell toward me. I brought the shafra up, cutting into her
stomach, and upward still into the diaphragm.

Sherice lay atop of me. The blood gushed from her
stomach, across my chest.

"Feel the blood, My Morgan. Feel it's heat."

I couldn't get her off of me fast enough. The shafra went
with her, still embedded in her stomach. Sherice reached for me,
a pleading look in her eyes. "Morgan, My Morgan."

I heard a loud moan and turned to see Wes struggling up
from the floor.

A hand touch my arm and I looked again at Sherice.
"We could hav…" Blood flowed from her mouth. Her hand
dropped and she was silent.

From a distance I heard the wail of a siren.

I crawled to Darcie and removed the tape.

"Morgan."

Her lips continued to move, but I couldn't seem to hear
her. The room tilted toward a black hole and I was rushing
toward it. With a last look at Darcie's anguished face, I fell in.

Chapter Forty-Two
Darcie Devonshire

The hospital was cold. Hospitals are always cold. That's one of the reasons I hated them. I ran to the nurses' station. Flashed my badge. "The two guys brought in from The Valley Inn? Where are they?"

"To the left, second room." As I was running away she called. "They're both stable." Bursting in the door I found Janey, crutches, cast and all holding Wes' hand. He was sitting up with his usual silly grin.

"Morgan? Where is he?"

Janey pointed at the curtain drawn around the next bed just as I heard Morgan groan. "I'm over here and I don't have any water."

I pulled the curtain back. Morgan was bandaged, immobilized, and looking miserable. I thought he looked wonderful.

"Should you be up and about?" he said. You had a…"

I leaned toward him, "Shut the bloody hell up and kiss me."

"Your wish is my command."

His lips were warm and firm, just like I'd remembered and dreamed about for so many years. When he moaned I lifted my mouth from his. "Does it hurt?"

"Not at all. Hell Darcie, that's not why I was moaning." Smiling I straightened, reached for the curtain. "Excuse us but my man needs some TLD." I said as I slid it closed.

304

"English, what the hell's TLD?" Wes said

Sticking my head back through the curtain I answered. "That's some tender loving Darcie."

ABOUT THE AUTHORS

Barbara M. Hodges lives on the central coast of California with her husband Jeff, two basset hounds, Hamlet and Heidi, as well as a sassy ginger striped feline, Wallace. Barbara is a big NASCAR fan as well as a decorative painter.

Website:http://barbaramhodoges.com

Blog http://barbhodges.blogspot.com/

Facebook http://www.facebook.com/barbara.m.hodges

Randolph Tower is the writer of adventure and action thrillers and is retired from the United States Air Force. With more than 20,000 hours of flying time he is a lover of all things aviation. Mr. Tower lives on the central coast of California and enjoys the many golfing opportunities in that area.

Website: http://sites.google.com/site/randolphtower

Blog: http://randolphtoweronwritong.blogspot.com

www.ingramcontent.com/pod-product-compliance
Lightning Source LLC
Chambersburg PA
CBHW060405260626
47160CB00006B/2437